To solve the meaning and place of love
in her own life, she must reconsider the
lives of her grandmother, her mother, her sister
—and even the great-aunt who had run away
into love and disaster. She must ponder the
choices of the friends of her own generation
—and, most of all, she must search herself.

THE ODD WOMAN

"A fine book . . . a collaboration of the mind and the
heart . . . a novel of experience which can enlarge our
lives."

—Kirkus Reviews

"Brilliant . . . witty . . . moving . . . you wonder what
happens to the heroine next and you are interested
enough to wish the author would carry on this story for
a few more years."

—The Literary Lantern

"Marvelous . . . exciting and affirmative . . . It is a
privilege to watch the unfolding of (Godwin's) impressive talent."

—Minneapolis Tribune

Other Novels By
Gail Godwin

Glass People
The Perfectionists
Violet Clay

Published By
WARNER BOOKS

THE ODD WOMAN

GAIL GODWIN

WARNER BOOKS

A Warner Communications Company

WARNER BOOKS EDITION

ISBN: 0-446-91215-8

This Warner Books Edition is published by arrangement with
Alfred A. Knopf, Inc., 201 East 50th Street, New York, N.Y.

Warner Books, Inc., 75 Rockefeller Plaza, New York, N.Y. 10019

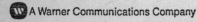 A Warner Communications Company

First Printing: January, 1980

10 9 8 7 6 5 4 3 2 1

to Robert Starer

In knowing ourselves to be unique in our personal combination—that is, ultimately limited— we possess also the capacity for becoming conscious of the infinite. But only then!

—C. G. JUNG

THE ODD WOMAN

I

On a mid-January morning in the early nineteen-seventies, at 2 A.M., Central Standard Time, Jane Clifford lay awake in a Midwestern university town, thinking about insomnia: traditions of insomnia, all the people she knew who had it, the poets and artists and saints who had left written testimonies of their sleeplessness. Donne had looked upon his "continual waking" in this life as a rehearsal for the life to come, where one would always want to be awake. But Jane did not share his certainty of the afterlife; she wanted to understand this life, however. What she wanted was a metaphor of her own. Once she had truly named her insomnia, she felt sure she could befriend it. It might even go away, having been noticed for itself at last, like a neglected child. Her profession was words and she believed in them deeply. The articulation, interpretation, appreciation, and preservation of good words. She believed in their power. If you truly named something, you had that degree of control over it. Words could incite, soothe, destroy, exorcise, redeem. Putting a nebulous "something" into precise words often made it so —or not so. The right word or the wrong word could change a person's life, the course of the world. If you called things by their name, you had more control of your life, and she liked to be in control.

She was not, however, in control of this recent insomnia, in spite of a growing arsenal of remedies: hot milk and rum; a cathartic rerun of the day's events, filtering out the impurities to apply against future mistakes, salvaging

9

and savoring the victories, if any; a book she had to read or wanted to read; and if all else failed, an erotic fantasy.

Her mother, Kitty, a veteran insomniac of many years, read spiritual guides. She had a large collection of them in different languages, spanning the centuries from Boethius to Thomas Merton, and she kept them stacked, according to a private rotating system, on the tray table next to her side of the bed which she shared—after almost twenty-five years of marriage—with Jane's stepfather, Ray. Ray was a contractor. Twenty-five years ago, he had been a student in Kitty's Romantic Poetry class. Now he put on a hard hat and worked outdoors with his men, and usually fell asleep by nine. He apologized to Kitty for not reading more, but the fresh air made him sleepy, he said. His all-time favorite book was *The Fountainhead*. When it was reissued in a special anniversary edition, Kitty gave it to him and he kept it by the bed, intending to reread it one of these nights. Kitty's reading in bed did not disturb him at all. He fell securely asleep by her side, snoring deeply, while she sat propped up on foam-rubber pillows and razed the advice, admonitions, and turmoils of Theresa, Richard Rolle of Hampole, Thomas à Kempis, and her favorite "Unknown" of *The Cloud of Unknowing*. For her run-of-the-mill insomnia, she read in English, or her college French or Spanish. When the malady grew more challenging, dimming toward a true Dark Night, she chose to fight it honorably in the more difficult languages. She resurrected her Latin or went into the tongue of her father's Prussian forebears. And recently—as if she anticipated further demands on her night strengths—she had been teaching herself Italian with a dual-language edition of *La Vita Nuova*.

And Jane's grandmother Edith, who had possessed from childhood the shameful fluency of sleep as soon as her head touched the down pillows scented with lavender, surprised everyone by suddenly becoming a firm insomniac in her eightieth year. She asked Ray to buy her an AM-FM radio, the kind that could get police calls, and now, after a lifetime of avoiding all thoughts of violence and antisocial behavior, Edith Dewar Barnstorff turned off the lights in her little apartment every night and tuned in to crime.

Jane was sure her lover, Gabriel Weeks, was still awake at this hour. He was no insomniac, however; he simply needed less sleep than ordinary people. Three or four hours would do for him, he said. It was three now in Kitty's and Edith's time zone, in the South, but Gabriel was keeping Jane company in her own. It was 2 A.M. at his house, too. She felt grateful to him for being so close. He was in the next state over. If she were to get in her car now and start driving, she could be in front of his house in less than four hours. It comforted her to know this, although she also knew she would never do it. She had never seen the house, but knew it intimately in her mind, just as she knew certain great houses in literature. She had made him describe it to her over the almost two years of their affair: a room here, a corner there, what was stored in the basement (summer screens, car carrier rack, garden hose), where things were in the kitchen, what pictures he had in his attic study and how they were framed (a Samuel Palmer landscape; one of Rossetti's Beatrices, posed for by Jane Morris; and a detail of Brueghel's Tower of Babel as a Roman Colosseum—all reproductions, matted and pressed between non-glare glass), and even what books and magazines he kept on his desk up there, where he sat reading till three or four every morning. He was a professor of Art History, specializing in the Pre-Raphaelites. He had a wife, Ann, to whom he had been married for as long as Jane's mother had been married to Ray. They had no children.

Ann Weeks. Sometimes Jane believed that if she added up all the thoughts she had ever had about Gabriel and all the thoughts she had had about Ann, his wife would win. Jane did not even know what she looked like. Once, when Gabriel had been showering in a motel, Jane had gone through his wallet. No photograph. She had dreamed more times than she could count of meetings with Ann Weeks. In most of these dreams, the two of them were friends. Jane had a favorite daydream in which Gabriel would have to go away to an Art History convention and she would drive to his town and contrive to meet his wife. In the local A. & P., perhaps. She would accidentally bump her cart against Ann's and say, "Excuse me, but I'm looking for a certain brand of olive oil and they don't seem to have it. I'm new in town." And the two of them would discuss inferior and superior brands of olive oil, and maybe Ann would invite her to the house for coffee. But how could she bump carts with the woman if she didn't know what she looked like?

"Well, why the fuck don't you *ask?*" Jane's confidante, Gerda Mulvaney, would say in their long-distance telephone calls. "Ask him to describe her. Ask him to bring a picture. Ask him if he loves her and still sleeps with her and why they don't have any children and if and when he plans to leave her for you and all the things you ask *me,* for Christ's sake. I've never even met the man. The whole thing sounds very vague, if you ask me."

"We don't talk about—his marriage. He's never brought it up, except, of course, to tell me he was married. He never even mentions her name. I had to find it from his checkbook. They have a joint account. I hate to be the one to bring it up. It would seem small-minded, especially as he told me right from the beginning. I accepted him, knowing."

"Oh, small-minded," scoffed Gerda, who was impatient with Jane's obsession with decorum. "I don't understand how two people can go two years without discussing anything. How many times have you actually seen him in two years, Jane?"

"Well, it's not easy for him to get away. But when we do get together, it's always intense. It's always for several days. We do discuss things. We talk about what we're doing at the moment; sometimes he teaches me interesting things about paintings. We talk about ideas, mostly. I don't want to lower things, drag them down. When I'm with him, I'm happier than when I'm with anyone else, and I'd rather have that than nothing. I'm afraid you get the worst of it, Gerda, in these late night calls when I'm here alone feeling sorry for myself and thinking about them in their house together." She knew exactly the number of times she had seen him. It had been twelve, at that

12

particular time. Twelve times in two years. Not counting the first time she saw him and went away and slowly dreamed him as a lover, and, at last, wrote him a letter praising certain remarks he had made in a lecture on the Pre-Raphaelites. But she didn't want Gerda to start in on the twelve times.

"Does he ever ask *you* things, about your past? Did you tell him about your engagement to James, for instance?" asked Gerda.

"No, it never came up. Gabriel doesn't go in much for pasts. He stays in the present. More than anybody I know. It's one of the things I admire most about him, and yet it torments me."

"Well, suit yourself, then. Go on tormenting yourself. Only don't expect me to be the *I Ching*."

And so, one month ago, when Jane and Gabriel got together for the thirteenth time, she decided to ask him, tentatively, not getting small-minded or too specific, how large a place she filled in his life. They met in her hotel room at the Modern Language Association in late December, in New York. In the same hotel where she had first heard him speak, two years ago. Ann Weeks's father was having eye surgery in Montclair, New Jersey, and Gabriel came to New York for two days on the morning bus, stayed with Jane all day, then went back in the evening to Montclair.

"I don't want to make you uncomfortable," she said, lying beside him in one of the two single beds, "but there is something that troubles me. It's about your—wife, and me. Is it that you need different things from each of us, or what?"

He had looked extremely uncomfortable. "The two of you are completely different," he said. "I'll admit, it troubles *me* at times. I think I could be more to each of you if it were not for the other. It makes me feel sad, I don't deny that. Why should I live in *The Captain's Paradise?* That's a movie you're too young to remember. I'm not sure I 'need' anybody. I am married, but I live very much alone. I think you would understand if . . . you had been married for as long as I have. Why don't I choose one of you? Better men than myself choose every day.

I've thought of that, too. I suppose if either of you ever demands it, I will have to. But it would be in some ways like deciding to give up apples for oranges, or the other way round."

"I don't think I could care deeply for two people at the same time," she had said, trying not to break down and cry.

He nodded gravely. "It's true, some people seem to be more monogamous than others. But, of course, you're not married. You haven't lived for a long time in a marriage. A long marriage is a different species of relationship altogether."

"Well, I don't expect I'll experience that species of relationship. I'm already too old to have a long marriage to look back on."

He had laughed. "Jane, you're going to live through your nineties. Beyond, maybe. You are indestructible. That's what I like about you."

"That would make it about 2030. If I live till 2030, and you become free one day, I suppose you might marry me."

"That might well happen," he said. And they got up and dressed and went for a five-thirty supper, so he could catch his bus back to Montclair, where he and Ann were visiting her father. And Jane had been left back at her hotel room, to sit beneath a lamp and ponder the rumpled sheets of the bed they had shared, and think about this question of faithfulness.

Faithfulness between a man and a woman. *Oh, love, let us be true to one another. . . .* Faithfulness to the one you loved. Could two people remain faithful to each other, willingly, passionately faithful, throughout decades, until death did them part? George Eliot and George Henry Lewes did it. *Lions* did it; she had read about it. What was the "truth" about faithfulness? Did it change with the times, did it depend on the mores of the decade, or the individual case, or what? Did any eternal constant lie beneath the variables in the thousands of case studies and stories and novels which dealt with fidelities and infidelities between men and women? Or was the only "eternal constant" to be found in humorous quotation

14

marks, like "eternal triangle"? Or like the title of a recent article in a magazine for swinging women, which she often bought at the grocery store and read in secret with her supper, rating her sex-appeal quotient, chances of marriage, degree of "chutzpah," etc. The article was called "So You're in Love with a Married Man and You Think Your Case Is *Different!*"

Were women by nature more faithful than men? "Why didn't you marry again?" she had asked Edith. "Oh! It was out of the question," her grandmother replied. "Hans once told me that if I married after he died, he would sit on the foot of our bed and laugh." Edith's standards of faithfulness applied right to the end of her own widowhood. Jane's mother's case haunted her even more. Ever since college, Kitty had loved a man and he had loved her. But a jealous god was plotting their chapters. She missed a promised phone call and thought he didn't love her and married someone else, because war was breathing down everybody's neck. Her lover enlisted and got engaged the week her husband's ship sank. They were to meet the night *his* ship sailed, but she was out pushing her daughter Jane in her stroller, missed his telegram, and the other woman got there first and got a daughter of her own. They snatched wartime meetings, on his leaves. Both believed in marital fidelity, so they only wept into each other's arms and kissed. He was married, with a child, but considered divorce. But when he came home from the war, his wife got pregnant again. Meanwhile Kitty, a pretty young widow wearing Navy wings pinned to her suit, taught Romantic Poetry to a classful of ex-G.I.'s, and Ray Sparks wrote at the end of his exam book: "I have met my Belle Dame sans Merci."

But the thwarted lovers continued to keep in touch. As far back as Jane could remember, Kitty kept her purse full of dimes and quarters. She was always running into pay phones, when they were out together, rushing into drugstores, screeching the car to a stop beside the bus station, saying, "I'll just be a minute, I can catch him between classes now. . . ." He was a professor of English at Tulane. A Southern gentleman. She called him at his office, knew the number by heart, once gave it by mistake when somebody asked her for her own number. He sent her his class schedules every semester. She would not allow him to call her, because Ray always got to the phone first in their house. She had another daughter, Emily. A son, Jack. Another son when she thought she was too old to conceive anymore: Ronnie. She asked the professor at Tulane to be godfather to Jack, and he accepted. Ray met him at the baptism, knowing nothing except he was an old friend of Kitty's family. "He's a nice man, but a little prissy," said Ray.

And then one day the jealous god grew bored with sustaining this melodrama. One day Kitty put her dimes and quarters into a pay phone and heard the professor say that his wife had filed for divorce the same day she got her Ph.D. "We've been at each other's throats for years," he said, "but I didn't feel I could say anything till now." His daughters were both in college. He had done his duty. Would Kitty—could she still care for him? He understood her situation. Her children still needed her. They would be very careful and hurt no one. Hadn't they waited long enough? Kitty's daughter Emily was now a freshman at Tulane, so the whole thing could be managed discreetly. Kitty would take the train to New Orleans and, under the excuse of visiting Emily, they would consummate this long and faithful passion at last.

On a weekday morning in early spring, Ray Sparks drove his Belle Dame to the train depot. It was 6 A.M., the birds were singing, the sun was rising over the Blue Ridge Mountains. Ray parked in front of the depot: the same depot where Hans Barnstorff, a young immigrant, had been working as night dispatcher when he met the elegant Edith Dewar; the same depot where Edith's headstrong sister Cleva boarded the northbound train in November of 1905, to run off with the villain in a traveling melodrama and never be seen alive again. And now this depot became the setting for one more turning point in the family's history.

Ray kissed his wife goodbye. He said she had never looked so pretty. Then he suddenly laughed. "What the hell am I doing?" he cried. "What the hell am I thinking about? Why have I worked myself half to death to have this business of my own, so I don't have to take orders from anybody, if I can't take off when I please and drive my wife down to New Orleans to see our daughter?" He went into the depot and used the pay phone to call his foreman, stopped at the five-and-ten and bought himself a shirt and tie and change of underwear, and off they went together.

"Oh, God!" Jane had screamed when Kitty told her this story. "Why did you let him? What did you say? What did you do?"

"I thanked him," said Kitty. "Then, after we'd been driving awhile, I looked out the window and cried a little. He didn't see. It's so much simpler now. I was so sick of always having to clutter up my purse with all that heavy loose change."

Ever since Jane's tepid confrontation with Gabriel last month, she could see her mother's choice as a sensible one: to close off the uncertain option, however joyous, to throw out the heavy loose change, and stay home at nights where you belonged, building your own interior castle. Now Kitty's night thoughts could huddle safely inside her, warming her against old age and death. They did not have to spread their wings and use up all their metabolism soaring up and out into cold nights, across state lines, to perch shivering outside storm windows of imagined houses and wait and watch to see what time lovers went to bed with their wives.

Once, just after she had talked to Gabriel on his office phone, she had called his home. It was midafternoon. A woman's breathless voice answered after several rings, "Hello?" The voice sounded young: it tilted up on the "o." Then, when no one replied, it grew querulous. "Hello. Who is this?" Jane had hung up, shaking. She hated herself.

(" . . . deciding to give up apples for oranges, or the other way round.") Which was she? The apple or the orange? Ah, but he had said "or the other way round." He was a careful scholar. He knew how to cover himself.

Twenty past two, said the little clock. Above the old-fashioned time face was a night-blue background, a little Ptolemaic sky of planets, moon and stars. Inside the flat gold full moon was inscribed in Gothic lettering, *"Tempus Fugit."* It did indeed. The clock had been a thirtieth-birthday present from a couple she'd known in graduate school. Once they had been the happiest couple she knew. They were now divorced. For the past two years, this quaint timepiece had ticked out the stately measures of the love affair of Jane Clifford and Gabriel Weeks. It accompanied them on trysts. They set it, in hotel rooms, to get up in time to visit art museums. Gabriel called it affectionately "old T.F." It was almost like their child.

Jane got out of bed, fetched a stack of term papers from the other room, and climbed back between the covers with an exasperated sigh. She turned up the small multi-intensity lamp, from "NIGHT" to "WORK." It had four intensities: "NIGHT," a sepulchral amber color; "TELEVISION"; "READ"; and "WORK." Some executive on Panasonic's advertising payroll had probably lain awake nights, thinking, Now what four things do Americans do most after dark that they need light for? Lovemaking had most certainly crossed his mind; he had probably smiled to himself, pleased that it *had* crossed his mind. Maybe that's what NIGHT was for.

She picked up the top term paper. It was typed faultlessly, on an IBM, with the even margins and Snopaked-over errors that bespoke the University Typing Service. It was sheathed in a brand-new red plastic cover.

The Marriage of Heaven and Hell: A Radical Poem
BY
PORTIA PRENTISS

She knew only too well what moral problems awaited her in the grading of this paper. The assignment had been: "Come to terms with the meaning of *visionary, the visionary experience,* through the assessment of that quality as shown in any of the works, or portions of the work, we have read in class." She scanned the paper quickly. It was under the assigned length. It did not mention the word "visionary" a single time. The word had been replaced, mysteriously, by "radical." It seemed to be a collage of quotations from Blake, not just the *Marriage,* either, which did not add up. Except, every other paragraph or so, the sentence that came like a refrain: "This is a radical statement."

Portia Prentiss, the one student who called her "Dr. Clifford," was the first member of her family ever to finish high school. She came from a Chicago ghetto. Her father was a postman. Her mother, she had explained to Jane in her husky, deadpan voice, had got lint in her eyes from the textile mill where she formerly worked and was now blind. Portia's only brother, while still in high school, had taken part in an armed robbery and been shot down dead. Her younger sister had died of blood poisoning while a girl friend was giving her an abortion. Portia had told Jane all this in their initial conference. As she related these details in a darkly resigned voice, dark as her skin, Jane slowly pulled Kleenexes apart beneath her desk. She wondered if Portia told this story to all her new teachers, then immediately felt disgusted with her own cynicism. "So my dad kind of thinks I'm it, if you see what I mean," the girl had concluded. Jane saw. She knew she could not ever give this student an F, this last hope.

She slid the red plastic folder to the bottom of the pile. Its problems were too much for her now. Perhaps they would always be too much. Even more than those presented by the contents of the manila folder Howard Cecil had handed her this afternoon with his sweet smile.

An hour before school closed officially for semester break, Howard had come to her office, as usual without an appointment. He knocked but didn't wait for her to say come in, and walked in on her while she was rereading Gabriel's latest letter, researching it for clues that their December talk had sunk in, that he was making up his mind between apples and oranges at last.

"Hi, Jane," said Howard. "Mind if I come in?"

He and one other student, an ex-Army officer who had lost three of his fingers in Vietnam, called her Jane. The rest, except for Portia, called her "Miss Clifford," or "you."

"No, come in, Howard." Folding Gabriel's letter and tucking it back into its plain white envelope.

19

He slumped agreeably into the chair on the other side of her desk. On his knee he laid a manila folder with some papers inside. She hoped it was his term paper; everybody else had turned theirs in. But what could he have written about? He would not even buy the books for the course. He had been the first student in her entire teaching experience to come to her before signing up and demand to know why he should take her course. How would his life be changed if he read her booklist? (He had been attracted by the course title: Visionary Literature.) What did Jane think "visionary" meant? Had she herself ever had a visionary experience? What did she personally feel about the subject? Howard spoke in terms of "feeling" always. He was suspicious of the rational process, deplored definitions, was wary and a little scornful of succinctness. The past held no place of honor for him. Yet he never missed a class. Jane suspected him, in her low moments, of coming on purpose to heckle her. Often, as she said something in class which she thought was particularly insightful, she would look up and find Howard smiling his gentle smile of disbelief. Once, after the class had spent an hour on Blake's elusive little poem about the angel and the maiden queen, and the class had divided solidly down the middle in interpreting the mysterious crux which goes

> And I wept both day and night
> And hid from him my heart's delight.
>
> So he took his wings and fled . . .

Howard had condescended to raise his hand and break the tie. "I don't know," he began. "I mean, I haven't really read the poem too carefully, but it seems to me that all these Freudian and Metaphysical interpretations are beside the point. It's simple, really. The poem means just what it says. When we try to lay our bad trip of 'personality' on the angels—well, like, they just aren't having any. They don't understand what it is to be hung up with personality."

"How are your exams going, Howard?"

"Oh, I only had Political Science. I'm only taking that and T'ai Chi. Oh, and your class, of course. There are no exams, no papers in T'ai Chi."

He lapsed back into an easy silence, watching her. It made her nervous. It did not bother him. He was twenty-four, older than her other students, even the Army officer. Howard had avoided the draft, he had told her in a conference, by wearing braces on top of his perfect teeth. He had spent a year in a Zen monastery in California.

Once, last fall, she had been walking home from the liquor store and Howard had roared down on her and offered her a lift on the most frightening machine she had ever seen. It resembled a big silver grasshopper, and Howard sat astride it at an angle which made his legs uncannily long. Her pride made her accept and she climbed on behind him, put her bottle of Scotch in its brown bag between his back and her breasts, and away they went. It was mad. She was sure they would both be killed or horribly mutilated in a crash. Did he take the curves at ninety-degree angles to show her that in some things he was the teacher? She clung to him and closed her eyes tight and smelled his damp, sweaty shirt. Afterward, she had made a point of thanking him with the formality of a Jane Austen heroine climbing decorously from a carriage. He beamed at her and raised two fingers in a peace sign. That night she had dreamed Howard and she were lying naked together and he was teaching her other things as well.

Jane put on her glasses.

"Look," said Howard pleasantly, "do you mind if we talk serious for a minute?"

"I think we should talk seriously," she said. There was a thumbprint in the middle of the left lens. She decided to keep them on anyway.

"I want to know why you picked these particular authors for a visionary course. Why do you feel they are visionary?"

"The course is over now, Howard. I'm hoping you'll tell me why you—feel—they are. In your term paper." She looked hopefully toward his folder.

"Yeah, well, I want to talk to you about that, only not right now. But, look," smiling his characteristic apologetic

21

yet forgiving smile, "now that it's all over, won't you tell me what you wouldn't at the beginning? Why you dig Blake and Dante and Donne. I mean, I appreciate what Blake did: he wasn't afraid to go against the establishment of his time; he knocked that soldier down and got arrested for it. . . . Did you ever get that record I told you about, that Ginsberg record of Blake's songs?"

"I'm sorry, I never did."

"That's too bad. It's wild. What I'm getting at, Jane, is why does everything worthwhile have to be two hundred years old? Why this worship of what's old and established? You probably wouldn't put Blake on your book list if he was alive today, like Ginsberg. You said yourself that even Blake's friends thought he was nuts; only his wife thought he was a genius, and"—he paused meaningfully—"Mrs. Blake couldn't read. What turns you on about these old guys? Is it because you are impressed with their credentials, or are you seeing something I can't see? Your eyes light up like you see all these answers we can't share—except for Shelly Rossinger, of course— when you quote them. And if it's there in the poetry I should be able to see it, too, according to your theories."

"I'm not quite sure what you mean by my 'theories,'" said Jane. She was thinking, Is this the first generation to question the entire past or does every teacher go through this? "Seeing the things you're talking about is a skill. It has to be learned, just as in every other discipline. You wouldn't expect to walk into an operating room on the first day of medical school and take out a person's appendix. In the discipline of literature, you have to train yourself to use words. You have to learn what they mean, how they have been used before, and how they might profitably be used again. You have to learn to name things, and then they are there when you need them."

"But you see, I don't think certain things can be named. Things in art and poetry, I mean. Sure, medicine, I agree, you have to know what a scalpel is and how it has been used before and how it should be used again before you start cutting open a live human being, but what I'm questioning is your theory of poetry, your standards

22

of poetry. I think a poem just *is*. I get what I have to get out of it and you get what you have to get out of it. There are no rules. There is no way of saying that is a 'good' poem, and this is a 'bad' poem. A work of art is personal. The person who made it gets one thing out of it and you get another. And I get another, and Shelly Rossinger gets another. Each person does his own thing."

"Look," said Jane, "the study of literature is based on the best that has been known and thought—and felt—in the world." (Sorry, Matthew Arnold, but this is an emergency.) "Now, of course we're all different, we all react differently, to our experiences. Of course we all have to"—she made a sour face, which amused Howard, as she shrank into his idiom—"do our own thing. But there are universal emotions, too. Things we all experience, which tug at all of us, however different we are. Youth, being young and happy and exuberant . . . and death . . . and being in love . . . grief. . . . You're a student of Eastern Philosophy; you'll accept that, won't you?"

"Oh, yes."

"Well, literature is the collection of the best expressions of these universal emotions and thoughts. By 'best,' we mean the ones which have a special, extra power to tug at us. The ones which have endured because of a richness of language, an amazing distillation of many, many connected things, arranged in such a way that we see connections we hadn't seen before."

"I have this feeling you're just repeating things some teacher repeated to you," said Howard. "What I want to know is how *you* feel. What have Blake and Dante and Donne done for you personally?"

"They've helped me," Jane said lamely. "They've helped me understand things."

"How have they helped you? Understand what things?"

"Oh, God, Howard! The experiences and words of others *can* help you. Even if they have been dead hundreds of years. That's what education is. Learning from the words and experiences of others, other human beings who wanted answers just as badly as you do now. They were once just as alive as you are—even Dante, who's

23

been dead a *lot* of hundred years. Dante may have been more alive than either of us! He may have been operating on more cylinders."

"I'm sorry. I keep making you angry," said Howard. "That's a shame. I think really you and I are very much alike. But, like, what happens is every time we try to communicate, language gets in the way."

"I'm very sorry, too, Howard. Can you think of some way we can carry on this conversation without language?"

"Well, I've thought about it. That day on my motorbike we experienced the same thing. For instance, there was this fabulous full moon the other night. I think if you and I had been standing outside in the dark, looking at that moon, we would have felt the same thing."

Jane suddenly had an image of Ray Sparks, twenty-five years ago, saying to his teacher Kitty Clifford in a conference, "For instance, there was this fabulous full moon . . ."

"Howard," she said softly, "I'm not so sure. You would experience, God knows, some sort of Zen moon, and I —what would I see? Oh, maybe

> The moving moon went up the sky,
> And nowhere did abide;
> Softly she was going up,
> And a star or two beside."

She became moved as she recited the words. I am glad I lived in a time when students were still forced to memorize, she thought. Howard sat curled in his chair. He gazed at her raptly, with the look of a convert.

"Coleridge," she said, in case he was interested.

"I'm sorry, I don't know it," said Howard, getting to his feet. "Jane, do you mind if I ask you a personal question?"

"What, Howard?"

"Don't you want to be *happy?*"

And he handed her the manila folder. "You aren't going to like this, probably," he had said, "but it represents the visionary, in me, at a point in my life. I wrote them last summer when I camped alone for two weeks on an

24

island in Michigan. What I'm hoping is you'll be able to see your way clear to accepting these as my term paper. To me, a conventional term paper is just an empty form."

After he had gone, Jane looked through the folder. A dozen poems written out by hand, in colored inks, on some sort of rice paper. The first one was a haiku about red ants.

Then there was Sheldon Rossinger. When you said "angel" to Sheldon, all the memorable angels of recorded civilization shimmered in his alert, dark eyes. He had once impressed her by telling her what all the names of the major angels meant in Hebrew. "But, after all, we invented them," he said. She had skimmed his term paper as soon as he had turned it in (early) and given him an A. In her head, that was. Because she did not understand all of it and felt she ought to go to the library and look up some elementary Einstein and some principles of Newton. Sheldon was a double major, English and Physics. This paper, entitled "The Visionary Arrow Flies Backwards," took that image from Canto II of the *Paradiso,* meshed it neatly with relativity, and managed, as Sheldon always did, to come out with a conclusion which sounded to Jane like a sure guarantee of grace. With his papers she always felt that if she could truly grasp all the *science,* which he wove so subtly into the literature, she would be saved. Did she favor him because he reassured her that everything would turn out all right when, at last, you had looked up all the words you didn't know, because he found for her new clues of optimism in his second major? She often thought of him as the teacher and herself as the eternal student posing as teacher. Some part of her persisted in believing that if only she kept on reading the right books, doing research on the things she did not understand, the mystery of her life would come clear.

Her mother, Kitty, who still taught Medieval History at the former convent school at home, would have no problems with these term papers. Kitty had a superb talent for airbrushing the messy complexities from her life.

"The little Negro girl gets an F. She did not follow directions. I know she has not had the usual advantages and

25

I'll tell her she may do it over, but even if she writes an A paper second time round—which she'd be incapable of—I can't give her more than a C, because it would be unfair to the others who only had one chance.

"Howard the Hippie gets an F. He certainly did not follow directions! An island in Michigan! That may have been his Paradiso, but if he wants to get along with me he'd better look into Dante's. Rice paper! Red ants! I'll tell him he can do it over. I can't give the privilege to the Negro girl and then not to Howard. That would be prejudice in reverse.

"Sheldon: A-minus. His paper is, of course, way above the others. His people stress mental achievement. He is so articulate, and I like his manners. He always calls for an appointment and always asks if he may sit down before he goes and plops into the nearest chair. But I will not accept pencil, even from a genius—therefore the minus. It will keep him from arrogance. It will come out an A on his transcript, anyway."

One day in class, Howard had been groping for words. "What I want is to—like—clean out my mind of preconceptions. I want to empty my mind of all the—stuff that's been laid on me. I want to just exist, if you know what I mean."

"Why not have a lobotomy?" asked Sheldon pleasantly, cutting his dark eyes at Jane.

It was easy to like Sheldon. He did not question the past: he was too ambitious for his own future. Was it *too* easy, was it out of date, to have a Sheldon Rossinger as your teacher's pet? As the world spun faster, maddeningly, toward the year 2000, shaking off cumbersome old courtesies, abolishing language requirements (in the hope of universal telepathy?), exchanging archaic enchantments for newer, more "relevant" derangements, wasn't it a cowardly retreat for her to expect clear answers, articulable standards, concisely formulated duties for herself and others, firm shapes? Wasn't the challenge—always in human progress—with the unformed rather than the solidly formed, the set, the congealed? But she was not a reformer. Damage distressed her too much. She liked to work with the materials of excellence, undamaged, ready to be worked into something marvelous. She would possibly always be shredding Kleenexes to bits under desks when confronted with ignorance, waste, hopelessness, misdirected energies, damaged human goods, human potential unnecessarily bled away.

And beyond the problem of her frustrated expectations of others was the ever-present problem of her unclear, undefined, unresolved self. Sometimes, lately, she wondered if the concept of the "self" was a myth which had died with the nineteenth century. It sometimes seemed so. Even in novels now, people were not so easily marked off, here and here and here, their seams so easily visible. Characters were not so wholly good or bad, heroes or villains, anymore. They were no longer so beautifully whole as they were a century ago, no longer undefiled, true, pure "characters." They were fragmented, shapeshifting. They tended to lose themselves in the current landscape, fall through the floorboards of their scenes, forget what part they were supposed to be playing. Was there, then—had there ever been—such a thing as a basic personality, or was that only a bygone literary convention? Could there exist a true, pure "character" who was nobody but himself—subject, of course, to the usual accidents of existence—but capable of subordinating his (her) terrain as he progressed through time and space, cutting a swath of chapters that would be meaningful in retrospect? Or had Howard Cecil intuitively grasped it somehow: was "personality" just one more bad trip humans laid on themselves, the angels having no part of it, covering their animal nakedness in the clothing of language and then mistaking these clever noises they had learned to make about themselves and others for their "personalities"? She had recently read an article by a psychiatrist who believed this to be so.

On bad days, when things had been particularly blurry, when the shape of her own life bled more than usual at the edges, she played a game with herself, a game that was possibly as archaic as trying to locate Einstein's universe with a Ptolemaic chart. "If Jane Austen were putting me in a novel, how would she define me? In that first succinct sentence where I 'come on,' how would she pre-

27

sent me?" Or: "If George Eliot were making me a heroine in one of her books—though I doubt my character would meet her standards for a heroine—what would she say in that long, involved, philosophic passage where she justifies who and what I am and how I got that way?"

But the game remained a game, and Jane knew it. Jane Austen dealt with people who lived in the same village all their lives; she dealt with marriages and the making of marriages. She would be confused by all the airports where Jane did so much commuting from scene to scene. She would be horrified at the hotel rooms in which Jane consummated her union with a man already united to someone else. No, Jane would have a better chance in an Eliot novel. She might even marry a nice man at the end and lead a useful life helping him. There would be no ecstasy, however. Though Marian Evans had found success in her profession and ecstasy with her married lover, she had forbade her characters to do so. No ecstasy for Jane, then. And no crashing, dramatic dénouement.

Jane's family was full of women with crashing, dramatic turning points in their lives. Her great-aunt Cleva, Edith's sister, had run away from teachers' college with the villain in a melodrama passing through town. Edith woke next morning in their shared room at the college and found a note on her pillow: *"Have gone to New York with an actor in the play. Don't try and trace me. It's for the best. Your loving sister Cleva."* Edith wept, but she understood. She knew her sister hated the college. Neither of them was suited to be teachers. They had managed to get as far as they had by splitting up the work, each girl doing what she was best at for both of them. When Cleva ran off, she took Math and Latin and English with her, and so Edith dropped out, too, and married Hans Barnstorff, who had been pressing her for months. Cleva returned ten months later, in a coffin. Her death remained a mystery. Hans had gone to New York on the night train and returned with the coffin and the infant girl, after Edith had received a note from Cleva, scrawled in pencil on the back of a torn theatre program: *"Sister I am in grave trouble please can somebody come the villain has left me,"* and an address. Edith had often

28

brandished Cleva's last communication before Jane, even when she was a small girl. It was never too early, said Edith, to begin warning a girl of the price to be paid for certain kinds of folly. She pointed to the cast of characters, where the Villain was listed as Hugo Von Vorst. The very villain who had done her sister in. There was a small ad in the corner of the program, which Jane learned to read, in successive attempts. *"Louis Hirshowitz, Watchmaker and Jeweler,"* it said, *"Money Loaned at Low Rates. 'He who knows most, Gives most for wasted time.'"* The program was from a town called Wilkes-Barre. The play, which was the play Cleva and Edith had seen together, was called *The Fatal Wedding.*

Jane's grandmother Edith had managed to faint away dramatically at the feet of the man she would marry.

At a fireworks celebration on the Fourth of July, the explosions had terrified her, the common crowds had disgusted her; she was coming down with typhoid and didn't know it. "Life is a disease," she moaned, and fell forthwith in a slender heap of white lawn at the feet of a young German immigrant named Hans Barnstorff, who adored her on sight. When she woke from the fever, on her daddy's farm, all her hair fallen out, there was Hans, who still saw the most beautiful woman in the world. "Let me protect you from it," he said. It took Cleva's running away and months of pleading before she said yes.

You had your choice: a disastrous ending with a Villain; a satisfactory ending with a Good Man. The message was simple, according to Edith. And Jane, a born student, fingered the torn page from an old melodrama, learned to sound out Mr. Hirshowitz's message about wasted time, and thought on these things.

Jane's mother, Kitty, not taken in by the ominous program, had eloped twice. Both times with "questionable" men of her own choice, if nobody else's. And Jane's young half-sister Emily had spotted the man she wanted when she was twelve, and married him with the approval of family and Church, at age fifteen.

While Jane, at thirty-two, continued to lie in a double bed alone. She ransacked novels for answers to life, she wheedled confidences out of friends, investigated and ruminated over the women she had sprung from, searched for models in persons who had made good use of their lives, admirable women who, even if not dramatic, might guide her through their examples. So much remained unclear.

For a start: where on earth would she be next year?

Would Gabriel get a Guggenheim? If he did, they would spend next winter in London together. She could follow him around to the Tate and the Victoria and Albert, take trains with him to Oxford, Liverpool, and Birmingham, Cambridge and Manchester, amuse herself while he took his tireless notes on paintings. Would they share the same flat? She hadn't dared ask him yet. What would be the danger in it? Ann would be four thousand miles away. She would not have to know she was sending letters to the same address where Jane received hers. But why wasn't Ann going? "Won't—she want to go with you to England," she had asked Gabriel. "No," he said. "She doesn't like the climate." What kind of marriage was it, then, where a mere climate could separate you for nine months? He had not volunteered more information, and, true to the decorum of their stately affair, she had not wanted to push.

He would not hear until March or April. She was saving half her salary.

What if he didn't get it? What would she do then? Her present job had been a two-year appointment, and in June the two years were up. Sonia Marks, her colleague, had spoken recently of the terrible budget problems in the department, of the possibility of having to retrench, of there being no positions open in the department for the next seven years. "But everyone likes you," she said. "And the department needs women, and there's always a slim hope that someone will take a leave of absence and you could stay on for another year." Musical chairs, thought Jane. When the music stops, will I have a place to sit down?

Did she want to "sit down" here? The university library was one of the best in the country, but the town itself was like a disturbing dream. Set in the midst of dead-flat prairie, its plain streets and houses huddled together as if trying to cheer one another up. Driving her car down these short, straight blocks, most of which had a "STOP" or "YIELD" at the corners, she could never gain any momentum. She had to keep hitting her brakes, there were so many dogs and cats and small children. It was a safe town to bring up children in, everybody said. It was, for this day and age, a comparatively safe town altogether, with its nineteen-thirties street lamps and cycling lanes. Because of its flatness, it was a center for handicapped students. Jane had been disturbed at first by the wheelchair ramps everywhere: in buildings, at bus stops, on either side of the steps leading to the Student Union. The ramps added to her feeling of being limited, of being suppressed: safe but suppressed. One could always get out, of course. Highway 74 was five blocks from her own front door, and there was an airport with direct flights to New York and Chicago. But the airport had no radar equipment, and no plane would land without a 300-foot visibility. Every time Jane planned to fly somewhere to meet Gabriel, she worried for days beforehand about visibility. She listened to weather reports. She called the airport the night before and in the early morning. Every faculty member had his own horror story about the airport, how his crucial connection to somewhere had been missed, how you sometimes never knew your plane was going to pass you by till you heard it rev up and roar away toward Chicago, up there above the clouds, leaving you stranded. As those wheelchair students must feel, bracing their arm muscles for the long ascent, while fellow students took the stairs two at a time.

If he did not get the Guggenheim, her staying here would be best for the affair. He could continue to pay visits to this very bedroom, driving between his house and hers within four hours, on the pretext of coming to use the university's excellent library. But hadn't she come further than that: arranging her existence to accommodate a man?

She remembered Kitty's famous card file for the pulp

stories she wrote so successfully and sold during the war years. The file was divided into three sections: looks, wardrobes, and occupations. Kitty indulged her imagination in the looks and wardrobes because she was so limited by her market in the occupations. Editors liked heroines of pulp stories to have unusual combinations of conventional beauty, so Kitty racked her poetry anthologies and stole "floating hair" from Coleridge, which she then colored with the recognizable tints of amber, jet, or —the current favorite—wheat. She gave her girls tiger eyes, sphinx or odalisque eyes, eyes clear as an honest blue brook, or sometimes clouded as a summer storm. Their skins she made milky, golden, peachy, dusky (but not *too* dusky in 1942), and their expressions were secret, hopeful, valiant, or, once, "full of beauty born of murmuring sound" (nicked from Wordsworth's Lucy). For the wardrobes, she went through the fashion magazines at the drugstore, jotting notes quickly on a piece of paper folded against her purse (she could not afford to buy them): "Green chiffon dress, wafting against her legs like a sea breeze . . . rose linen sheath, which matched her cheeks . . ."

But the occupations got her down. She was always running out of suitable occupations for her heroines. As a small child, Jane had lain awake at night and listened to Kitty discuss her next story with Edith. "I'm going to make my new heroine a . . . a Red Cross worker. Do you think that would be all right?" As long as Edith murmured, "Oh, that would be nice," Kitty knew she was safely within the bounds of her market's approval. You had to be so careful about what they did, she said. Her girls were stuck behind desks and counters in banks, behind typewriters (in offices only), or they were models (with impeccable morals) or—rarely, very rarely— aspiring actresses who were always rescued just this side of the wings by a man who had a full-time part in mind for them.

One day Jane, who was four or five at the time, asked Kitty, "Why don't you write a story about a woman who teaches school at the college and writes love stories on the weekend and has a little girl like me?"

"It wouldn't sell, that's why," replied Kitty.

"Oh, I think it would be very interesting to read," said Jane.

"It would be interesting to people like you and me," Kitty said, "but I can assure you, *Love Short Stories* wouldn't buy it. My girls have to have respectable, slightly glamorous jobs, but nothing too important. There must be nothing too permanent or heavy in their lives, because they have to throw it all out the window when the man comes along."

Jane tried to imagine herself in England, with Gabriel. He would have a job, a purpose. She would have—Gabriel. On loan, for nine months. How long would it take before she started hating herself? Well, perhaps she could dream up a project of her own. Convince herself it was important. Only, how important could she make it seem when nobody was paying her any money for it? She knew her own history well enough to give money its proper due. Her best efforts, for so many years, had been those which could free her from having to be beholden to someone like Ray Sparks, who would jingle money in his pocket and ask her what time they could expect her back.

She picked up the book she had to reread in order to teach it when the new semester opened. It was George Gissing's *The Odd Women.* Jane and Sonia Marks were offering two sections of Women in Literature because of the sudden wide demand for women's courses. The chairman had asked Sonia to do them both, repeating the same course at two different hours, but Sonia had suggested that her friend Jane do the British section and she would do the American. Sonia had all she needed from the department: respect, tenure, and its most publicized scholar as a new husband. She could afford to pass on her surplus to a friend. Jane welcomed the change. She had had enough Romantics and Visionaries just now. It would do her good to come out of the sky and focus for a while on the needs of her sex. She had chosen Gissing for an opener because of his unrelenting pessimism. It was one of the few nineteenth-century novels she could think of in which every main female character who was allowed to live through the last page had to do so alone. The book's ending depressed her utterly, and she was eager to fling it into a classroom of young women (and men?) who still believed they would get everything and see how they would deal with Gissing's assurance that they certainly would not.

There was a noise outside her bedroom window. It sounded like something, or somebody, slumping against the side of the house. Jane rented part of a duplex, on one floor. Her bedroom was at street level, less than fifteen feet from the sidewalk. She froze, holding the unopened book.

Although this city boasted of its low crime rate, its best known unsolved crime was the continued exploits of "the Enema Bandit." For nearly two years, this person had prowled the softly lit streets near campus, a stocking pulled over his face, carrying his pistol and his enema bag. His victims were always women. He abided by a certain self-imposed decorum. He never broke into a dwelling. He walked into unlocked houses or apartments, or accosted his victims on the street and led them quietly home for treatment. He had been known on two occasions to desist gallantly. Once when an older woman, who had just lost her husband, broke down and cried, and told him of her sorrow; and once when a young girl, whose roommate was getting the enema, begged him not to because she had her period.

On last evening's newscast, the state attorney general's humorless countenance appeared briefly to announce that police continued in their progress toward unmasking the degenerate. "We have several suspects but cannot reveal more at this time. We have reason to believe he is in the area at present, and urge all single women not to go out alone after dark, and to lock all doors and windows. . . ."

Had she refastened the back screen door after taking out the garbage? Of course, the inside door was locked, but he might break the glass pane.

But he never broke in.

There was always a first time. People's obsessions grew on them; they burgeoned out of control until those in thrall took more and wilder chances to satisfy their cravings. . . .

She lay rigid, all problems but this forgotten. Could he see her, bathed in the light of her reading lamp; could he see her through that chink she had just noticed, where the shade did not quite meet the window frame?

Why hadn't she put up curtains? She had been going to, but kept postponing it, kept telling herself, "Oh, well, it's only a temporary apartment. I won't be here next year if he gets the Guggenheim. We'll go to England, so why waste money on curtains here?"

It would be her own fault, her own lack of self-respect, should the Enema Bandit now be peering at her through that chink, thinking, that woman alone in bed . . . at almost three in the morning . . . Why can't she sleep? Perhaps she needs a good enema. I'll break my rule for once and smash in her back-door windowpane.

And she could hear it, the quick shattering of glass, the hand reaching in to turn the lock, the soft footsteps, the stealthy approach through the kitchen until he would be visible in the doorway of her bedroom. . . .

She reasoned with him, in her best nineteenth-century English, to make him feel ashamed. "You have intruded on my privacy in a most unforgivable way. I am sorry for you, of course, but this I cannot tolerate. Do you realize your problem? I'll tell you, if you will first put down that absurd equipment and that ridiculous pistol. You were born too late. You would have been perfect at the court of Louis XIV, or during the Roman Empire. Think of it! All those people overeating. You would have had a real vocation. A real vocation is what we are all in search of. Something that is so close to us it fits our psyche like a snug sock . . . that meshes so thoroughly with our nature it keeps us from intruding our needs on other people— which is what you are doing, don't you see? Though I get the point of what you are doing, *symbolically*. . . ."

But if she saw that smashed-in stocking face, she would be speechless. She would probably faint. She was an inveterate fainter, like her grandmother Edith.

"Please listen to me. I can't sleep, but it has nothing to

do with my bowels. It comes straight from my soul. You can't help me; you can't alleviate it with that little bag. I'll tell you what I'll do. You can have my cash and my American Express card. I promise not to report it stolen for one week. But try and be a gentleman. I have five thousand in savings and I need four of it to pay my half for a stolen residency in England with my married lover if he gets a Guggenheim. Don't spend over a thousand. A thousand a week doesn't seem to me ungenerous. Perhaps *you* ought to apply for a Guggenheim."

She waited, unable to move, unable even to look out of the sides of her aching eyes at "old T.F.," which ticked placidly toward the new hour. Afraid as she was, something in her began to let go. Her mind loosened. Almost as if the spirit of the intruder had slipped through the walls and was applying his remedy to her insomnia. Her language loosened as her tense consciousness dissolved. George Gissing's *The Odd Women* dropped softly to the floor beside the bed.

"Look here, you cute prick, let's take off that crazy stocking and cover up with this nice warm eiderdown. I don't need your remedy, but I've got another in mind. . . ."

What time had she fallen asleep? What time? Was it before three, after three? How long after? It became important to her afterward to remember exactly where her thoughts had been at 3 A.M. Central Standard Time, 4 A.M. Eastern. It became important to convince herself that she had been thinking something proper, something respectable, as T.F.'s tiny pointed minute hand crossed the hour. She could not bear to think that Edith's passing spirit, deciding to look in on her granddaughter for a brief farewell, had caught her rollicking in her last-ditch remedy: an erotic fantasy with the Enema Bandit.

II

At 7 a.m. the telephone began ringing. She stumbled, still three-quarters asleep, to answer it.

"Jane?" Kitty's voice, very faint.

"What's wrong? Can you talk louder? Do we have a bad connection?"

It was not a bad connection. Kitty was crying. "Edith died this morning."

Jane had expected this phone call for years. Even Edith had prepared her for it, rather relishing the prediction: "One day, I'll be gone. You and your mother won't have me anymore. I can't live forever, you know." Yet now that it finally came, she was shocked, somehow outraged. She felt she should have had some notice, some intimation of her own grandmother's passing from the world.

"But how? She wasn't ill? What *time?*"

"Well, she's been at Pinewood, that nice private hospital. Her back was hurting her again and the doctor put her in for observation."

"But why didn't anyone tell me she was in the hospital?" asked Jane, knowing Kitty's answer before it came.

"We didn't want to worry you. After all, we didn't think it was anything. . . . It *wasn't* anything like—you know." Kitty lowered her voice ominously. She never spoke the word "cancer." "It seems she just took one more breath and stopped. You'd better drink a little brandy, Jane."

"I don't have any. I only have rum. Look, what happened? She wasn't alone, was she? Was she alone?"

"No, the nurse was with her. It seems apparently . . ." Here Kitty stopped and cried a bit, then pulled herself together and resumed: "It seems she couldn't sleep last night. So she rang for the nurse and asked for a sleeping pill. Then, early this morning, she rang for the same nurse again and said she still couldn't sleep. It was too soon to give her another pill, so the nurse sat by her bed and rubbed her hands, because they were cold, and talked to her a little. Then Edith said, 'You might as well prop up my pillows. I'm not going to sleep anymore, I can feel it,' and . . ." More weeping.

"Go on," said Jane, beginning to tremble. "God! I couldn't sleep myself last night, early this morning. I could have telephoned Edith and talked to her! Oh, why . . . But what happened?"

"Well, nothing exactly. The nurse said she propped up the pillows and sat down again for a moment on the radiator and Edith gave a little gasp, as if something had startled her, and that was all. The nurse said she didn't think she even knew what was happening. Are you all right?"

"I'm fine. But what time was it, Kitty?"

"Well, it was early this morning—around four, I think."

"That would have been three my time," said Jane. "She really said that? She really said, 'I'm not going to sleep anymore, I can feel it'?"

"Something like that. Yes, that was it."

Kitty and her "around"s, her "something like that"s. Jane's own baby book recorded birth (in Kitty's hard-to-read scrawl) as "around 6:30 P.M." Couldn't she have made it her business to find out for sure, the exact moment? How odd, the way people felt better when they could fix the events of their lives down to the moment. And down to the second was even better, according to the astrologers. She knew some fathers stood, masked and gowned, in delivery rooms, stopwatch in hand.

"I wish we knew exactly what time," said Jane, rather angrily.

"It was four," Kitty assured her, but Jane recognized the "glossing over" note in her mother's voice. Kitty sometimes prevaricated to keep peace. Then she added, "Well, she had her wish. She did it with dignity."

"Yes, that pleases me, too," replied Jane. "Where is she now—I mean—"

"At John Plemmons's. He came right out and took over beautifully. That's their job. The nurse asked us who we wanted when she called, and by the time Ray and I got to the hospital, John was already there. Ray went into the room—I couldn't—and put all her things in a suitcase, all her cleansing creams and stuff, and got her coat. How are you? Are you all right?"

"It hasn't hit yet. Not really."

"Well, when it does, just take a drop of brandy. No, you don't have any. Well, I suppose rum will do as well. The funeral is Saturday, to give you time to get here."

"I don't think I can make the morning plane. I'm not packed. I'll get the evening plane to Chicago and spend the night there and fly down first thing tomorrow morning."

"Good, darling. Call us back when you know your flight time, so we can meet you."

"Oh, Lord," said Jane. "All her things."

"We'll do them together. We'll make it easier for each other."

"She did it with dignity," repeated Jane, not wanting her mother to hang up. "She finally made the train."

"Yes." Kitty began weeping again softly. The shared allusion to Edith's recurring dream, in which she kept missing a train that Hans was on, cut two ways for Kitty. "I think I am going to go down to the Health Club as soon as it opens and swim my mile. After I make the calls. I need to relax. I don't think she'd mind, do you?"

Ray picked up another phone. "You two can talk for nothing when Jane gets here," he said.

"We're just getting off," said Kitty apologetically, and, within seconds, Jane was alone in the kitchen of her apartment, her eyes filling up with tears of hate for her stepfather.

Unable to confront all the implications of this new fact, that the consciousness of Edith Dewar Barnstorff was no longer available to her in this world, however

39

much or little Jane had chosen to take advantage of it these past few busy years, she quickly dialed another number, that of her best friend, Gerda, in Chicago.

"What . . . hello?" Gerda's voice, bogged down with sleep.

"I'm sorry, it's me. It's important or I wouldn't have done it. Wake up. Edith's died, and that son of a bitch made Kitty get off the phone because it was costing money. I can't bear to be alone."

"Oh, God. You poor thing. Look, I *understand*. I know how close you were to her. Let me get a cigarette, okay? Hold on."

She does know how I feel, thought Jane in a rush of gratitude that made her forget she and Gerda had for some time now been growing apart. She's never met them, possibly never will, but she knows their stories. She's even taken what she needs from these stories to describe her own inner life. Kitty's train story, for instance, the train Kitty never caught, had become for Gerda a metaphor for how she often found some part of herself defeating another part. "I'm driving myself to the train again," she'd say, "to make sure I don't catch it."

Jane had known Gerda twelve years. Gerda was her oldest friend. Rather, Gerda was the only person from Jane's past, outside of her family, who had "lasted" more than a decade. The idea of lasting relationships was strong in her and it was thus that she found herself in the odd position of clinging to this friendship increasingly as the years mounted up, even though the two women's affinities continued to decline. Jane and Gerda had been undergraduates at their state university in the South. They had met in their last year. In background, attitudes, and habits, they were almost polar opposites. But they had started with two things in common: their very quick, curious minds, ravenous for the sort of details of the soul most people either did not or could not discuss; minds which reveled more than anything in endless detailed probes into the dark corners. And their physical appearance: they had met as a result of being repeatedly mistaken for each other.

Their abiding addiction to the "endless probes" kept

them close through the years. But their physical resemblance decreased, then faded altogether, as their life preoccupations diverged. Jane ventured briefly into the outside world after college, went to Europe, got engaged and unengaged from a nice Englishman, and hurried back into graduate school with relief, where, ever since, she had lived more in the nineteenth century than in her own. Gerda flung herself wholeheartedly into each successive ripple of the *Zeitgeist* until she had squeezed her own wave out of it. She rode the forefront of movements and dressed vividly in their costumes. She took up people and lovers and causes with a zealous, greedy intensity, seeing her personal salvation in each one. Yes, this was right, this was *it,* at last; this was really for her! And the next time Jane talked to her, "it" was over; she had gone on to something else. In the spring of their graduation year, Jane had listened to her coldly plot her marriage to Judge Mulvaney's brilliant, crippled son. Five months later she was in Washington, a good-looking divorcée (with the Mulvaney name) come to the New Camelot where, for the first time in years, government shimmered with charisma. Gerda got a GS-6 position in the Department of Economics and, chicly bouffant and couturish in the Jacqueline Kennedy style, shimmered with charisma and danced till morning with diplomats from Brazil. When Camelot collapsed, she cashed in her retirement fund and went to Sweden with a film maker, riding on the back of his motorcycle down to Torremolinos, where some action was that he wanted to film. She marched on Washington, martyred herself for one semester teaching in a black high school, and completed her twenties by boarding the Greyhound bus for Chicago, with only a backpack and the jeans she was wearing (the chic having long since been boxed up and sent to Goodwill), to be in time for the Chicago riots. She met a painter there and liked him and moved into his rent-controlled basement flat on West Irving Park Road and became his muse and drudge and smoked dope with him after supper. When he was sentenced to jail for possession, she agreed to keep his flat for him till he got out again. She had a disastrous affair with a young radical who made wild, imag-

41

inative love to her in the painter's bed, then flung himself down on his knees and asked God to forgive him for sinning with this woman. Then she met a graduate student from the University of Chicago named Phil. She loved him, she cooked sophisticated meals for him, she rented an IBM Selectric and typed his multi-lingual term papers for Comp Lit. He put down his fork one evening after her salmon soufflé and confided in her: he had met this wonderful girl in one of the classes he instructed. He was thinking of marrying her. But she was so young! And her father owned one of the famous department-store chains in the Midwest. He did not sacrifice his integrity, did he, if he contemplated such a step. After all, contemplating was not actually doing it. Gerda attempted gamely to "help Phil contemplate" for several months. He became engaged to the girl, but he still wanted to see Gerda a few nights a week. The last time Jane had stayed with Gerda, stopping off on her way back from last month's MLA, Gerda had affected a new cheerful, slovenly plumpness to go with her pigtails and jeans. "You look like a little girl!" exclaimed Jane, amazed at her friend's continued ability to re-create herself. "Look at me! You make me feel like a dowdy old spinster."

"That's because I've given up love," said Gerda, her face shining between the new pert, shaggy pigtails. And she told Jane of her newest project. She was editor of a feminist newspaper, with headquarters in the painter's flat. She had several women working for her.

Now Gerda came back to the telephone. She said, "Your poor mother, too. Your psyches were terribly bound up with Edith. You know that."

"Yes. But I wanted to go on talking to Kitty when she called just now and he actually broke in and said, 'You two can talk for nothing when she gets here.' And you know Kitty. She hung up at once."

Gerda said in a low, caressing tone, resurrecting her lost Southern drawl for the occasion, "That ignorant piece of trash." And Jane's heart thrilled, in spite of itself. Gerda was from origins that were sometimes called "trash." Ten years ago, during her Washington career, she always replied casually that her family was "in tobacco"

42

when asked about her background. Now, however, times had changed. Gerda volunteered the information. "I'm from lower-class origins, actually," she would say. "My mother and father are what the snobs down South call 'poor white trash.' They pull tobacco in the summer and go on welfare in the winter."

"Oh, Gerda, I feel so strange. Edith's death is the end of something for me. And it leaves a great big gap and I don't know what I'm going to fill it with. Do you know what I mean?"

"Sure I know. She was a symbol to you, and to people like you the death of a symbol can be pretty disrupting. To Kitty, too, I imagine. It'll be hard for her, too. Though didn't you say she's into religion now?"

"Yes." Jane had heard, just beneath the surface of her friend's words, the rumblings of Gerda's favorite sermon: how "some people" escaped into symbols and myths, and others, the more courageous, went out and faced facts. Over the years, Jane had become so used to this sermon that it had incorporated itself into her own consciousness. Often she'd be going about her life, doing what she thought she must do, and there would be the cynical accompaniment of Gerda's voice, criticizing.

But she needed this friendship to sustain her now; this morning she felt the need to hold on to as much of the past as possible, and so she by-passed the subject which was at the core of their differences. It had led again and again to ill will between them.

"It's good to talk to you, Gerda. When I say 'Do you know what I mean?' and you say you do, I know you really do."

"Sure I do. I know what she meant to you," said Gerda. "I'm real sorry, though you knew she had to die sometime. Our two *minds* are still sisters, even though a lot else has changed."

"The two scholarship girls," recalled Jane, in a feeble attempt to repave their much-rutted dozen years with nostalgia. *Edith just a symbol?* But no, she would not challenge Gerda today. *Gerda* was an important symbol to her just now, she thought wryly.

"Yeah. Worth two hundred and eighty dollars each in

those days, after taxes." replied Gerda. "I can't say I'm doing all that much better now, per month. Why don't you stop off in Chicago on your way back from the funeral?"

"I don't know if I'll have time. I've got all these term papers to grade over the break, and I have to read the first book for the new course."

"That's right. It's your semester break! God, isn't she something? Waiting for your semester break to die."

"She always tried to do the appropriate thing. She hated a fuss. Look, can't you come down here for a few days, after I get back? I really do need to have one of our old probes. There's so much I don't understand just now. I need that . . . stimulus you always bring."

Gerda laughed. "I can't possibly. This is the first year I've had people working for me and I have to fill out all these income-tax forms for them. It's scary; I was just thinking about it last night: me, an employer. Although we do run *Feme Sole* by group decision."

"Yes," said Jane, knowing she had lost Gerda to her latest life, with these women who stayed till all hours in Gerda's basement, smoking and drinking coffee, and talking and typing, going over their lifetimes with men, rethinking everything according to this new cause. She was a little jealous of Gerda's new-found companions and their solidarity. She would like to be sitting with them, her hair in pigtails again. It would be like starting all over again as a tomboy. Only Jane had never been a good tomboy. She was afraid of heights and couldn't climb trees, and Edith would always come looking for her when she played baseball in the park.

When Gerda had given up "lovers" and "love," she had done it in a ritual, in the painter's bedroom filled with her latest interest at that time: books on astrology and witchcraft. She had sat down in a chalk circle on the floor, and said certain words backward and burned a black candle at exactly midnight, after having mailed a special-delivery letter to Phil, the Comp Lit man who wanted to have his cake and eat it, too. This letter, unlike the dozens of others she had written to him, pleading with him on the IBM Selectric for pages and pages (single-spaced) to see her side of it, offering lengthy analyses and psychoanalyses of both their personalities, her tone veering wildly between monumental arrogance and debasing self-pity—this letter had been simple and to the point: "FUCK OFF." Signed, "GERDA."

After this ritual, she changed. From somewhere, fresh bravado and new energies came pouring in. She had long told Jane she had "always wanted to write, but couldn't seem to do anything about it," and now she clarified her desire even further: she didn't just want to write. She wanted to be a voice and a voice people would listen to. With her refound "nerve" from the old Gerda days, she made an appointment to see the publisher of a men's magazine. She dressed herself up in the costume of a twenties vamp and walked into his office and said: "Look, somebody is going to start a feminist newspaper in this town and it's going to catch on and make somebody a lot of money, even if it's tasteless and hysterical, because that's what's coming, that's what's in. Why not get there first, with somebody who's got taste and energy—and experience. Most of these feminists are losers with a cause. They don't know men. They've never had enough men, and now they're saying they don't want any. To create a really first-rate propaganda organ, you have to have been there, in enemy camp. You have to know your enemy inside out, all his weaknesses, all his strengths, all his little habits. And I am that woman. Every mote of my bloodstream vibrates with my knowledge of the enemy. I can tell you what total bastards men can be, and I can tell the world. Not hysterically, but in cool, correct syntax, and in rich, exciting prose. I also have a degree in economics, I've worked for the government, and I understand money. Write me a check to cover the expenses of the first issue. I'm going to call it *Feme Sole*. The words derived from the Old French 'woman alone.' In legal terms, as you no doubt know, it means an unmarried woman, divorcée, or widow." And she had presented him with an itemized estimate of what the first issue would cost: labor, printing, advertising, and distribution. She had left his office with the check—and printer's proofs of an old Egyptian tale which he had decided at the last minute not to run. "It's not right for my market," he said. The tale was an archetype of certain sexual injustices perpetrated on women down through the ages. Gerda had written a stunning footnote on it, and it appeared with a clever illustration, done by a fifteen-year-old black girl, in the first issue of *Feme Sole*. Every copy was sold and the publisher took Gerda to dinner. They celebrated with oysters and champagne and Gerda did not wear jeans and pigtails. "I wore my Southern accent, too," she had told Jane. "Why are all men so fascinated by Southern accents, do you think?" But she was sure of herself again, flagrantly so. All her energies went into "my new organ," as she loved to call her successful little paper. Jane followed Gerda's latest turn with interest, wondering what its example might contribute to her own, less colorful life. She was not sure she wanted to sacrifice one god to another, or one sex to another. She wanted, if possible, both sexes and all the gods working for her.

She said now, "Listen, Gerda. When you burned that black candle against Phil, remember how you said you gave up love. What exactly has that come to mean for you?"

"Simply that I no longer ask or expect to be fulfilled or emotionally completed by a member of the opposite sex. Notice I said 'emotionally.' I will take other things from them. I mean. I take the publisher's check every month for my paper. A personal check. It amuses him, the whole thing. He can't afford to let our secret get out. His auditor thinks it's for a high-priced woman. And I let Lenny, that nice queer I told you I met, cook for me and we go to the flicks together. And when Frank's in town with his rock group, I go to his concert and then we come back here and ball."

"But is that enough?" pressed Jane.

"It's all anybody gets. Jane, face it: we are all just basically neurotic creatures trying to get through our days and nights. When we begin telling ourselves we can be anything more than that to each other, we're kidding ourselves."

"But the way you're dividing it up. That's what worries me. Don't you think there's a unit a man and a woman can make? A unit that requires a man and a woman? A communion that insists on two othernesses? Don't you envision a form of getting through the days and nights together, each experiencing more because able to do it through the mind and body of the other, as well?"

"Have you ever experienced such a communion?"

"No, but something tells me it exists, even though I haven't had it for myself."

"That's because you are a romantic," said Gerda.

"You say it as if it's a handicap."

"I'm sorry, but I think it is." Gerda paused and Jane could hear her smoking and thinking. Gerda would have liked to carry it further but remembered her role as sympathetic friend. "I'm real sorry about Edith," she said, therefore, "and I want you to remember I'll be thinking about you down there. Say hello to the dear old home state."

"I will."

Jane called the airport and made a reservation for the Chicago evening flight to continue South first thing in the morning. She forgot to ask about expected visibility. Why? Because she was "only" going to the funeral of a person who had loved her from infancy, rather than flying off to keep a secret appointment with a man who liked apples *and* oranges? She must ask Sonia Marks, her wise colleague: "Tell me, Sonia, has it been your experience that women find it easier to demean themselves, devalue their dearest friends, rather than be disloyal or cause inconvenience to a man?" But would it be proper to have Sonia come to lunch now? Oh, was everything becoming a moral decision?

Last night when she put out the garbage, she found a soft brown cat with yellow eyes crying on her back porch. She stroked him, wanted to feed him, keep him. But she remembered the man who lived in the little concrete-block house behind. He kept bird-feeders. A modern-day hermit if there ever was one, he worked in the library's Special Collections and kept to himself. She had watched him often from her window, frail, nervously alert, refilling those feeders. At night, after the rest of the

47

street was long asleep, she heard him playing Mozart. Was one cat's hunger worth upsetting the balance of power in the back yard? Was one meal's worth of gratified purrs worth the careful relationship that the man had built up with his birds?

Jane had not fed the cat.

Suddenly it wearied her, this shortage of precedents from which one constructed a worthy life. She longed for more of the underpinnings other people seemed to have. What would an ordinary person do, a *nice* ordinary human being, if he had invited a friend and colleague to lunch and in the interim his grandmother had died?

What would Edith have done? Canceled the lunch, of course. Her decision would be based simply on what "tradition" expected of her. It would be written out in some etiquette book, copyrighted about 1890.

And Kitty? Canceled the lunch, of course. When in doubt, Kitty made a rule of choosing renunciation.

You were expected to be heartbroken at such times.

Jane remembered a scene from an English novel. A woman was having a tea party in 1916. Suddenly her butler brought her a message. She opened it, closed it, tucked it away in her pocket, and poured everybody more tea. When all her guests left, she went up to her room and went to pieces over her son's death in battle.

But the party was already in progress when the message came.

Then there was the behavior of Swift. At 6 P.M. his beloved Stella died. He received the news at eight. But it was Sunday, his night for receiving company. Only at 11 P.M., when the last guest had left, did he go upstairs to his room and begin writing his famous eulogy to his beloved. He also stayed home from the funeral, complaining he was too sick to go. While it was in progress, he sat up in bed and continued working on the eulogy.

Jane knew her grief was there inside, perfecting itself. But she feared to loose it prematurely. Not here, alone in this apartment, with her flight twelve hours away and only a bottle of rum between them.

She made herself a pot of coffee and wrote a neat shopping list while drinking it.

Apples
Curry powder
One pint whipping cream
Spring onions, if any
2 bottles white wine
Lettuce
Green peppers
Cheese

She would simply not mention Edith's death when Sonia came.

Another story immediately began to surface murkily into memory. Several stories. All to do with the malevolent intentions of delayed announcements, suppressions of certain persons' deaths. That terrible Hardy story in *Life's Little Ironies* where—

Suddenly Edith's voice, every intonation and inflection intact, said, "Don't you think you read too much?"

Jane laughed aloud in the kitchen. Tears filled her eyes. "You're right; I do."

Then she had an insight—the beginning of one, rather —about stories. Stories were all right, as long as you read them as what they were: single visions, one person's way of interpreting something. You could learn from stories, be warned by stories. But stories, by their very nature, were Procrustean. Even the longest of them had to end somewhere. If a living human being tried to squeeze himself into a particular story, he might find vital parts of himself lopped off. Even worse, he might find himself unable to get out again.

There were many "mistress" stories, for instance. There were sinister mistresses, villainesses, home-breakers, with whom the reader understood he was not to sympathize on the very first page. There were the Patient Griselda mistresses, like Dreiser's Jennie Gerhardt. Or like the mistress about whom Michael Caine remarked in the movie *X Y & Zee* "My tailor asked me, 'If your wife and your mistress were drowning, which one would you save?' And I said, 'My wife, because my mistress would understand.'"

There were many kinds of mistresses, but they were all single visions, limited characterizations. The word "mistress" itself was a story.

As was "career woman," or "spinster," or "professor of English," or "intellectual," or "Romantic." I am all of these, thought Jane, but all of them are only parts of me. Her lover had called her indestructible. She had a glimmer of what he meant. You remained indestructible by eluding for dear life the hundreds and thousands of already written, already completed stories. You climbed out of them before they rose too high. You reminded yourself that you were more than they were, that you had to write yourself as you went along, that your story could not and should not possibly be completed until *you* were: i.e., dead. Even then, no matter how good it was, others might learn from it, be strengthened or even transformed by it, but it could never, never be a perfect fit for anyone else again.

So, on the morning of Edith's death, Jane was granted a moment of passionate, giddy hope. *She* was not dead yet. Nothing was finished. nothing at all. As far as she could see, she had not written herself into any premature endings. False middles, perhaps, but there was time, she felt, still time, still hope to do, be anything, as long as every experience, every incident, pleasant and unpleasant, trivial and annoying, could be used in some way toward the spiritual financing of her quest.

"In the really great novels," she often told her students, "every character, every incident, every tree that is mentioned specifically can be seen by the careful reader as belonging in an organic way to the landscape of that book. Every little thing in the book enhances and enriches the total effect of the work."

If my life were a book, I would like it to make sense to the careful reader, she thought. However sadly or happily "I" ended, the reader would say, "Yes, this existence felt its acts as irrevocably necessary."

"But life's not like that," she could hear Howard saying. "Life's not *linear*. It ebbs and flows. It's, like, Yang and Yin. It's contradictions, the Unnamable, the Inexplicable. People don't plot anymore; they just flow."

And she would probably quote him George Eliot, who wrote in a letter to a friend when she was twenty: "I have adopted as my motto,—*Certum pete finem*—Seek a sure end."

And Howard would reply, "I don't know it. But look, don't you want to be happy?"

III

A HALF-HOUR before Sonia Marks was due to arrive, all details of the lunch had been taken care of. The chicory-and-mushroom salad was tucked inside the refrigerator beneath a sheet of plastic wrap, the curry soup had been blended and was simmering over a low gas flame, the black bread was cut and arranged attractively (with another sheet of plastic wrap guarding its freshness) on the breadboard between the two places set with bright Danish mats and napkins, and the butter and cheese had been taken out to soften to room temperature. The first bottle of wine, a dependable Soave Bolla, had been uncorked, for quick serving, and then put back in the refrigerator to chill. Jane walked to and fro in the rooms of her duplex, trying to see the rooms as Sonia might see them, trying to read the person who lived in them. Frequently she slipped into the bathroom and checked herself in the medicine-chest mirror. She was nervous because Sonia Marks meant something to her: Jane looked on her as a winner.

When she had arrived at the university, a year and a half ago, she heard almost immediately about this woman whose dissertation had been published by the Oxford Press; whose seminars had such a large preregistration that the chairman had asked her, as a favor, to repeat the topic a second, and a third, time; who, at the age of thirty-five, had nineteen publications to her credit, and five listed in the MLA International Bibliography for the same year she had married another woman's husband of twenty years! She also had "two darling children," the department's friendly gossips informed Jane. "She sounds like a paragon," said Jane, physically weak with the gnawings of envy, but wanting to know more about this person who seemed to have captured with such ease all the things that she herself wanted. "Ah," said the gossips, "but she's hard; she's very hard. When she stops to talk to you in the hall, her eyes are already going ahead to the next achievement. And at parties you can see her fidgeting and rolling her eyes at her new husband the moment the conversation gets the least bit boring. She has very little charity for the ordinary run of mankind, does Sonia Marks."

Jane watched for the right opportunity to meet Sonia. She saw her, or course, at all the English Department receptions and meetings, during the early part of the year. But she could never get the courage to go up and introduce herself; she was too afraid of causing this remarkable woman to "fidget and roll her eyes at her new husband." She met the husband, however; he came up and introduced himself. Jane knew his biography from the gossips as well. A Guggenheim, stream of publications exceeding his new wife's, his cast-off wife (who had money of her own) and three children gone back to the East. Jane stood holding her paper mug of coffee and a cookie in one hand (wishing she hadn't taken the cookie; it was awkward) and chatting with this man, Max Covington, who was married to the paragon Sonia Marks. ("She's always gone under her maiden name," said the gossips. "Even when she was married to that bright young historian; he was the reason they came here. The university waived their nepotism policy for her, to get *him*.") Max Covington asked her if she knew——— and ———and ———at her old university. "Ah, he directed my thesis." she was relieved to be able to say of the third. "A fine scholar," he said. "He writes something when he has something final to say. He isn't like some of us, who clutter up the world of print every time they have a new enthusiasm." Jane had looked into the mild face of this man, wondering if he was putting down her old professor or himself. "Enthusiasms are important," she had ventured at last, wondering what his old wife had been like: he looked so boyish; he dressed young, like a student. "Sometimes they generate something quite wonderful in other scholars. I think it's showing good will to offer one's professional colleagues the first seed of an interesting idea. Then somebody else might take it up and polish it and rewrite it a hundred times and *make* it final. But the seed gave the first push."

Later, she saw Max Covington talking to his wife in a corner. They were looking toward her. She left the reception, slipping through clusters of people. She wasn't ready yet.

She found a note in her department mailbox. At first she couldn't decipher the scrawl. Her first thought was that it was a hate note from one of her hippie students. She had inaugurated her own courses with fierceness, to cover up her feelings of inadequacy. But the scrawl was from Sonia, asking her if she would be interested in having lunch at the Union.

To Jane's amazement, the lunch went splendidly. What was all this about fidgeting and roving eyes? Sonia's attention never once wavered from their table, and Jane was disarmed by her colleague's openness, her reckless way of exposing her private life. Before the lunch was over, Jane's curiosity had been satisfied concerning all the little details of the "marriage merry-go-round year" which even the gossips had left dark. "Max's wife had a lover first," said Sonia. She had a way of blushing to the roots of her hair as she gave away these things, as if the intellect Jane had heard so much about were admonishing her impetuous revelations. "So, of course, that made it easier. Of course, her lover had moved away by the time she confided it, during a fight with Max; but that made him less guilty about confessing his love for me. Then she staged a scene, one of these scenes women stage when they really want to threaten but not act out the threat; she said she and the children could not possibly sleep under the same roof with him another night if he was carrying on with a married woman in his own department; so he said she didn't have to, and moved out to a hotel that very night. I know the gossips say he moved in

54

with me, because Jacob was still away; he was on a research leave that semester—that famous semester!—though of course I later found out he was living with Vicky, the girl he's now married to."

"The gossip about you is fascinating," Jane put in, deciding she could afford to be a little reckless herself, under the tutelage of this marvelously open companion. "It makes you sound like some sort of superwoman. I was so impressed I was afraid of meeting you. I was afraid my conversation would bore you. I heard your seminars are so popular that the chairman begs you to do reruns. I wish I could come to one. I was getting up the courage to write you a note, asking you if I could. I am terribly uncertain about my own teaching. I always seem to do all right once I'm in there, but I have this fear—I always have had—of losing them, all of them. Once, when I had just begun teaching, as a teaching assistant, I remember a boy suddenly got up and walked out. A few days later I received a slip from the registrar informing me he'd dropped the course. I guess, deep down, I expect them all to get up and walk out one day. I've dreamed about it, even."

"Nobody's going to walk out," said Sonia. "I've heard you're very good, very enthusiastic. One of my students is in your British novel course, and he said he comes just to hear what you're going to say next. And he's not a fool, this student."

"I do try to teach from the standpoint of what *interests* me," Jane said, her heart glowing absurdly from the news that someone who was not a fool came to class just to hear what she was going to say next; "enthusiastic," applied to her, did not interest her much; and yet, if Sonia used the word the way her husband did, it was a tribute to her, she supposed.

"Good teaching is one-fourth preparation and three-fourths theatre," Sonia said. "It's in the very physical structure of the classroom, and I'm referring to the old-fashioned structure, not this 'we're all in a circle together' junk that the half-assed, ill-prepared, uncharismatic teachers adore so much. In the conventional classroom, what do you have: students in the 'audience,' teacher 'up front.' I make it my business to utilize that separation, and it hasn't seemed to be so unpopular around here." Then she really did blush, having attributed charisma to herself, as well as reminding them both of the well-known fact that she was the most popular teacher with the students as well as the most hated, or envied, by her fellow faculty members. But Jane liked the security her arrogant frankness implied, and felt it to be a compliment to herself that Sonia could deliver these unpopular statements with such relish to her. It meant that she considered her, if not her equal in achievement, her equal in intention.

She visited Sonia's seminar, and it *was* theatre: instructive theatre. Sonia walked "onstage" at precisely the dot of the hour. Her first words, uttered in a rather girlish, offhand way, were the words Jane had not heard since convent school: "All right, let's settle down in here. We've got a lot to get done today." To a graduate seminar! And, like obedient children, they did settle down. Barefoot toes were removed from the backs of chairs and slipped respectfully back into sandals or loafers; texts were opened, and in a way that indicated they had been looked at before; ball-point pens were clicked and poised expectantly above notebooks. "I will talk first today," said Sonia, settling herself into a chair and briskly opening a large looseleaf notebook, "because I had a lot of ideas when I was rereading my old friend Hawthorne last night, and I want you to have them hot from the presses. *Now, then . . .*" And she had not looked up, but Jane saw her go red to the roots again, and knew it was because she was suddenly conscious of being onstage for a colleague. The first hour passed as though it were fifteen minutes, and when Sonia slapped shut the big notebook and said, "Take a five-minute break, and then come back and *you* talk awhile," Jane looked round the room and realized she was not the only one who was disappointed that the curtain had fallen on Act One. During the break, several students hovered round Sonia's desk, waiting their turn to talk with her. Jane looked down and discovered she had used up every inch on both sides of the two sheets of paper she had brought with her. But perhaps that most telling proof of Sonia's success as a teacher was that, immediately after the second hour of the seminar, Jane went to the bookstore and bought the "Tales and Sketches" they had been discussing. Hawthorne no longer seemed "regional" or "denominational" or merely a successful allegorist to her. He seemed of immediate importance to her own life, and this was due, in large part, to Sonia's method of presenting him. How did she do it? Jane went over her notes and tried to reconstruct that engrossing hour. But it was like reading an abridged version of a play after the star has gone home.

She wrote Sonia a note, trying to thank her without flattering her for the experience; and received a rather curt note back, thanking Jane for "all the nice things you said, but I really have a tenth-rate imagination. What I said during the first hour was not drawn from *it* at all. I read literature as a means of moving out of my own subjectivity, and use my mind to get into the minds of others, and this makes the world a bigger place for me. This is what I try to show students: that literature is a way out of their own minds, and a consequent expansion unlike anything in the world." Jane burned with remorse as she read this note. What exactly had her own note implied that Sonia misunderstood? She remembered using the word "imagination," but surely it was in Sonia's sense: a method of getting into the minds of others; whereas this cold reply made it sound as if Jane were accusing her of regaling her students with her own fantasies, not Hawthorne's. Had she implied such a thing in her note, which she had written quickly, assuming it would be received in the spirit of that charmingly frank lunch? She stopped by the library, on her way home after classes, and looked up "imagination" in the Oxford English Dictionary, already writing in her mind an explanatory answer to Sonia. She ate supper alone full of snippets and definitions of imagination, and how she could rephrase them to fit what she had meant. What had she meant? She went to bed and dreamed Sonia was having lunch with a new teacher at the Union, explaining how Jane and all the other teachers in the department were "half-assed, ill-prepared" and, what is more, in Jane

Clifford's case, tried to dissect true charisma. She awoke hearing Sonia's ringing laugh. "She actually tried to steal some of mine!" Sonia cried.

Why, oh, why had she written such a note? What business had she trying to analyze and define Sonia's success with her students? Perhaps she was trying to steal Sonia's success. After all, she was successful in so many things Jane wanted to win at, too.

But when she arrived at school, there was another note in her box. "Dear Jane. Here is a story: 'A woman sends another woman (a friend) a note, in answer to the friend's very nice note. She's not in the habit of writing notes. Her articles are redrafted sometimes as often as fifty times, even her letters go through three or four drafts. But her friend's note was spontaneous and candid, and it called for the same sort of answer, so she tried to express in her own note, exactly as she would talk to this friend, certain things important to her, very accurately. The next day, in another frame of mind, away from her children (who are down with flu), she thinks over what she wrote and in her memory it's partial, pompous, and even a bit insulting. So she writes another note, redoing the first. The next day, in another frame of mind *again* . . . etc.!' Anyway, what I am saying is I really appreciated your note; it made me start thinking about certain things that interested me, and even gave me an idea for an article. For which I thank you again. I hope you weren't put off by my pomposity. Have a good week. Sonia."

Jane would have written a warm epistle in reply if she hadn't had to rush to a class. As it was, she had only time to scrawl "not put off at all. And I love your 'etc.'s," and put it in Sonia's box. She could not remember ever having been so relieved at a cleared-up misunderstanding. Sonia had actually used the word "friend" four times in her note. Jane decided her terrible previous evening had been worth it, to find out that not only could this intelligent woman be so open about her private life but, unlike so many intellectuals and scholars with "reputations" to uphold, she could so easily, disarmingly, revise herself.

They met for lunch every other week, at least, continuing their dialogue; and sometimes, on Monday nights, Sonia would invite Jane to have supper with her and the children while Max played squash with a graduate student. The notes between them became a habit when either one of them had an idea; they also served as addenda or revisions of their last meeting.

. . . Tomorrow in class I'm doing a pop woman's fiction book published in the 1860's, and the thought of the soap opera is much on my mind. *Jane Eyre* is great soap opera! Too many women's lives conform to its pattern. Do you think the soap opera follows life or do we pattern our lives with their innumerable crises and catastrophes and shifting casts of characters after this model? Have a good week. Sonia.

Dear Sonia: Today when we were talking about Hawthorne again, you said that for him the woman represented all the qualities which the man has self-destructively despised in himself and thus projected onto, or "stored" in the woman for safekeeping. You said that (according to Hawthorne) the man needs union with her to *re*store into himself the sundered parts which would make him a whole human being. *Now* I can't get out of my mind the possibility that over the centuries we may have abandoned certain human qualities, too: "left them to the men," so to speak, as we leave the garbage and the storm windows to men. I wonder what are these qualities we have given up? Have you any ideas?

Since the first note, which had caused the misunderstanding, Jane kept carbons of her notes to Sonia. She had all their notes in a little folder and sometimes she took out the folder and read through their entire correspondence. She came to feel more comfortable with the notes than with their meetings. In spite of the ease of that first lunch, a nervousness had developed in their personal contacts. The first parts of their lunches and suppers and visits to each other were clumsy and distracted. Their first moments of conversation—when Sonia came to Jane's and fidgeted with whatever books and magazines were on the coffee table, or when Jane went to Sonia's and ruffled the children's hair and talked more to them, ducking her head toward the floor, than to Sonia —could be a scene in an afternoon soap opera on TV, where a woman drops by to see another woman. Jane had tried to analyze this nervousness; she supposed Sonia had, too. She believed it, in part, to be that they lived such different routines, Sonia taken up with her many activities and roles of motherhood, wifehood, star teacher, and herself taken up in dealing with the many selves that make solitary living such a crowded occupation. But she also believed the nervousness to be some primal, instinctual reaction from their very flesh. As if the flesh shrank at the first quiverings of these meetings, which drew so heavily on its energies, and so sent forth its own warning, in the form of erratic little inattentions and unfocusings, trying to short-circuit the two women back into their fleshly, historical species, which used its energies to survive, not to probe and soar.

So, when Jane's doorbell rang on the dot of noon, she went to answer it with misgivings, and she knew that the person on the other side of the door was fighting an unreasonable urge to run down the steps and flee across the frozen lawn before it was too late and the door was opened. Well, it can't be helped, she thought. This is the price we pay for evolving: the deadly drain on our energies, and what security we have stored up for ourselves, when we dare to open our mind and let another examine its contents and afterward go away again, leaving us to pick up the spillings, as an only child regathers his toys after his playmate has left.

Jane opened the door to Sonia.

"Hi, am I late?" said Sonia, who was never early or never late for anything.

"No, right on time."

"Oh, good. I had to get a different baby-sitter today. The girl we have living with us has gone to Chicago with her boyfriend for semester break. My, something smells good. I hope you haven't gone to a lot of trouble."

"No trouble at all. Would you like anything to drink

first, to get warm?" Then Jane realized she had only chilled white wine to offer. She laughed and explained.

"Chilled white wine would be lovely," said Sonia. "Only, I have to save some of my wits for later, because I want to grade all my papers tonight. Jacob is taking the kids for semester break and Max and I will have some time to ourselves, which we badly need."

"Sit down. I'll bring the wine in here." Jane waved Sonia toward the sofa.

She heard her sigh as she went out of the room. She heard the experimental rustlings of Sonia turning over the pages of various books and magazines. When Jane came back, Sonia had garrisoned herself into a far corner of the sofa, kicked off her clogs, tucked her feet under her, and was looking through *The Odd Women*.

"Any good? You're using it for the spring course, aren't you?"

"It's a tough little book. Inelegant, maybe but I like it. It will work well in the course. What I like about Gissing is that he lets his characters think. They come to horrible ends, most of them, but they keep track of themselves so beautifully along the way. And he writes women well. He doesn't keep the sexual-ironic distance of many male writers when writing about female characters."

"Or female writers writing about male characters," added Sonia. "We must be fair, mustn't we? Ellen Glasgow makes her men seem such fools. Now *there*'s a challenge. *Barren Ground*. I'm doing it last. It's the book which tests the mettle of the sincerest militant. Most women can identify with heroines who learn to live without marriage; but not so many want to live without love of any kind."

"How true!" And the two women looked at each other for the first time. Thank God for Gissing and Glasgow, thought Jane, pouring them each a full glass of cold white wine.

"What will you do over the break?" asked Sonia.

On an impulse, Jane decided to sacrifice her planned reticence over Edith for the further success of this lunch. Edith would not mind. In fact, if she were able to know, she would probably prefer having her death discussed.

She had discussed it herself so often, as if she were planning for it, like a future vacation.

"Actually, I have to go South. My grandmother died early this morning. I'm leaving on the evening plane."

"Oh, I'm sorry! Was she very old? Has she been sick for a long time?"

Jane could see Edith through Sonia's eyes: a "grandmother."

"No. I think parts of her were wearing out. Her back gave her trouble. But when the doctor x-rayed it, he said the spine was simply disintegrating and there was nothing he could do. He said, 'What do you expect, at your age,' and she changed doctors. The new doctor, it seems, put her into a small private hospital to see if rest would improve it. She died there—quite painlessly, my mother said. Almost like taking the next breath."

"How old was she?"

"Well, I figured it up once. She was eighty-six. But she would have been furious if I ever let on that I knew."

"Was she one of those traditional Southern belles?" asked Sonia.

"Oh, Lord, yes," said Jane, beginning to get animated over the prospect of what Gerda would call "mythmaking about your family." "Edith—we all called her Edith— was the perfect Southern lady. She was elegant, snobbish, beautiful to the very end. Her skin—and I'm not exaggerating—when I saw her this past Christmas was smoother than mine. She took exquisite care of herself. She was a woman who was always in style. I'll tell you a strange story. It just came to me. When I went home this Christmas, Kitty—that's my mother—and I went to take Edith to the new doctor, for her back. When we arrived at her apartment, she was sitting very straight in her armchair. She had put up her hair by herself, though we came early especially so we could help her with it. She had her make-up on, her diamond earrings screwed through her ears, her silk blouse, her little diamond brooch, her slip, her stockings, her shoes, and all of her rings. Her face had odd little spots of color in each cheek though she is normally very pale. She prides herself —I mean prided herself—on this pallor.

"Now she looked as though she were blushing for shame. As if something had embarrassed her greatly. She looked at us both rather coldly, as if she had forgotten exactly who we were—these two women who had walked into her apartment. Then she said, rather haughtily, 'I don't think I'll be able to go to that doctor. I haven't the strength to put on my skirt, you see. Kitty, will you please call and cancel the appointment?'

"While Kitty was on the phone, talking to the receptionist, Edith motioned me closer. 'Do you know what happened this morning, Jane? I saw the awfulest thing while I was sitting in front of that mirror getting ready.' I could see her reflection and mine in her triple mirror. It's one of those old-fashioned things with drawers on each side. The three of us have watched ourselves grow older in these funny mirrors. Those mirrors are the only ones I know that show you how you used to look, how you look now, and how you're going to look.

"I asked Edith what she had seen. I had no idea what she would reply, she looked so strange. I have never seen her look so . . . chastened. 'Well,' she said very softly, leaning toward me, 'I saw this . . . I saw this *tired little old lady,* that's what I saw.' And I've just realized this, Sonia, talking to you: Edith had made up her mind that morning she was going to die. She had died to herself, to her image of herself. It was now only a matter of finding an excuse to justify her death to us."

"Ah," said Sonia significantly. She drank more wine. "Yes."

Jane was gratified. She knew she had found an audience who appreciated the shape of this story, grasped its symbols and implications.

"I've only been to one funeral," began Sonia. "Jacob, my first husband, and I were in Sweden. We had had a fight and I went for a walk by myself in the country. I came to this pretty little white church and went in. Some service was in progress. It was a funeral. I decided to stay. It was very simple and dignified—in Swedish; I understood the cadence if not the words. When they carried out the coffin, the widow, who was about the age I am now, looked straight at me. It was incredible! At that moment, I understood that I, too, had lost my husband. Our love was dead. That woman had made me see it in one glance. I began crying. Then she smiled, kindly. It was as if we had both buried our husbands that day."

"Oh, my God," cried Jane. The two friends looked into their wineglasses, thinking. Then Jane suggested they go into the kitchen and have lunch.

"Excellent soup," said Sonia. She had a way of puckering her mouth, sweet and childlike, as she pronounced her words. Jane liked her sharp, pointy face: like a determined elf's. "Did you make it? How?"

"An apple, and onion, a can of consommé, and a spoonful of curry. Throw it into the blender and slowly add a half-cup of cream."

"Delicious."

"I think I may have put too much paprika in. It tastes a little bitter, doesn't it?"

"I don't taste any bitterness. Do you have any sisters or brothers?"

"Two half-brothers and a half-sister. Much younger. The boys are thirteen and sixteen and Emily is nineteen. She's in law school. She got married at fifteen."

"You're kidding."

"No. She's a unique person, all right. I don't think she likes me very much. I think she thinks I have too many problems when life, according to her, has been so simple. I am sure she feels herself, secretly, to be the older sister. I have never known her to be a real child." That's quite enough, thought Jane. No more family myths. We'll have a few moments of awkward silence and soup-slurping and then attempt a mental flight somewhere, as planned.

But Sonia said, "How do you mean? Tell me about her. I'm fascinated."

"Well, to begin with, she decided she wanted this boy who is now her husband when she was twelve years old. He was eighteen at the time. A very shy, isolated boy, the son of one of my mother's best friends, a woman who had died very suddenly and tragically. Kitty often had John—that's the boy—and his father to dinner. Emily decided she wanted to marry John one day, and went to work."

"Oh, I want to hear this. How did she go to work? What do you mean by that: *going to work?*" Sonia's dark eyes snapped with lively interest and Jane knew she was spellbound.

Yes, that is the story we still love most, she thought. How some woman went to work and got her man. Even "emancipated women" like Sonia love to hear the old, old story one more time.

So Jane launched into the story of how Emily Sparks, age twelve, had looked across the roast beef and potatoes at this shy young man and begun her campaign to annex him to her life. Jane described the fierce Ping-Pong matches in the basement after dinner. "She would rip her best dresses to pieces under the arms to win her point." And the elaborate table settings, the candlelight, the poring over *The Joy of Cooking* to get it right. "Even at twelve, Emily was an excellent cook, the best in the family, much better than Kitty, because she could organize things and she never got ruffled and she chopped all her onions and things ahead of time—that kind of thing. Emily would say, 'Kitty, can we have John and his daddy to dinner on Saturday?' and Kitty would say, 'Oh, no, Emily, we just had them and I don't feel like cooking a great big feast.' 'I'll do everything—if you ask them,' Emily would say, and Kitty, who loathes cooking, fell for the bribe every time.

"The next thing in Emily's favor was that John was lazy. He was *not* organized. She slowly began taking over his life. She typed his term papers. When she got older, she wrote them. I should mention that Emily is brilliant, perhaps a genius. She skipped three grades; that's how she was ready for college at fifteen. So, at fifteen, she had been offered scholarships to seven colleges. By this time, of course, John had his B.A. and was living at home with his father, sleeping till noon, reading Dickens—one novel at a time from his father's set of classics—playing tennis, and on rare occasions riding his own horse, which he kept stabled in the country and sometimes saw as seldom as twice a year. He seemed to be ready to do anything Emily wanted, as long as she took care of the practical arrangements. You must wonder why my sister would want such a passive person; I have wondered myself. But for some reason or reasons he makes her happy and vice versa. I have watched them be together for hours, doing nothing much, drinking Cokes and smoking and reading the funny papers. He is brilliant, too, in an offhand sort of way. He can do anything in math or physics, run computers, build things with his hands, fix any kind of machine that has broken down. I think Emily and John have found in each other the childhood they never had. Well, Emily decided on Tulane, and then she sat down and went through the New Orleans telephone directory and wrote innumerable letters, which John agreeably signed, and he got a job designing refrigerators in that city, and off they went. The first semester, Emily lived in a dormitory because Kitty wanted her to have a *taste* of college life, she said, and then at Christmas they came home and had a big wedding and went back to the apartment Emily had found and rented for them."

"I love this story," said Sonia. "May I pour myself some more wine? Here, let me pour you some, too."

"And then, when Emily graduated and decided she wanted to go to law school in her own state—as she intends to practice there—she finished completing all her own forms and once again got out the telephone directory, and now John has a job programming computers. It's a good job for John because it doesn't start till one, so he can continue to sleep till noon.

"I've been to visit them once—they have a house now; they bought a small house near the campus. While it's not a life I could lead for one minute, I can't help but admire the accommodation they have made to each other. Emily seems always terribly busy, abstracted, with all her studies, and then she's in all sorts of political activities which she drags John along to if he wants to come or leaves him home if not. Their house is a mess and yet it's organized. John has arranged all her books in one room, in alphabetical order, and all his in another, in alphabetical order, and their records, according to the type of music and then also in alphabetical order, and even Emily's spices in the kitchen in alphabetical order. But there are cigarette burns all over the sheets and the ashtrays are always overflowing—both of them smoke like fiends; they have to go to the dentist every two or three months to get the stains scraped off their teeth, and God knows what their lungs look like—and when Kitty was down there, she discovered some strange sticky, syrupy substance on either side of their bed. It turned out to be the leakage from Coke bottles. Apparently, they lie in bed and smoke and read comics and drink Cokes all the time. The funny thing, when I was staying with them, I got the feeling 'Here are two children playing house,' except that's not the way real children would do it. Real children would ape the 'responsible routines' they have observed in grownups. Emily and John have no routine. They don't seem to have any guilt, somehow, about when they should be doing what and what they should be doing next in their lives. Even Emily's law school—she never gets upset about it. Once I asked her, 'What would you do if you flunked out; don't you have a horror of flunking out?' You know what she said? 'Oh, Calamity Jane'—she has a trunkload of 'Jane epithets' for me: 'Plain Jane,' 'Calamity Jane,' 'Pain'—'you worry too much. If I flunk out, I'll do something else. I'll have a little baby, maybe, and John will teach it how to make model airplanes.' John, by the way, makes the loveliest model airplanes. He gave me one for my thirtieth birthday, a Flying Tiger. You know what he said? 'Here, Jane, have yourself a ball.' Sonia what is it? We weren't like them. But how are they different? They *are* different. I study my students, their attitudes, even the way they walk along the halls— more dreamy, somehow—but I can't put my finger on it."

"I know what you mean," said Sonia. "Well, for one thing, they are pretty much *in love* with themselves. We hated ourselves."

"Yes, that's certainly true."

Jane opened a second bottle of wine and poured each a generous amount. Sonia did not protest. She seemed to have forgotten her decision to save a few wits in order to grade papers. Perhaps that had been ladies' lunch talk; perhaps Sonia Marks could grade papers after swigging many glasses of wine as triumphantly as she did everything else.

"Jane, what's it like to live alone? Do you know I never have? I married Jacob right out of college. I went from my roommate to Jacob. The only time I came anywhere close to it was when Jacob went away on that research semester and Max and I hadn't gotten together openly yet. And I had the children then, so it doesn't fully count."

"What is it like?" Jane wanted to give Sonia as much of the truth as she could, because for a long time she had felt miserly in the confidences department with this friend. Sonia did not know about Gabriel, and thus remained in the dark concerning a whole side of Jane. Jane had kept back Gabriel, despite frequent urges to confess all and ask Sonia's advice about how one won a man away from his old wife. But the circumstances in her case were so different. And she did not want to give up a certain advantage in this relationship (Sonia had so many advantages!); the advantage of appearing to be a person content in her solitude, who functioned alone out of fastidious choice.

"Some of the time I like it," she said. "There is an intensity about it which can work toward your clarifying things more quickly. Though this same intensity can often turn itself inside out and work to haunt you. Everything takes on more weight, even little things, when there is no one, no outside thing, to diffuse your attention from yourself. Another thing that happens is that time functions differently. I mean the minutes tick by, but sometimes one minute can take a whole hour. Or the other way round. Same with chronology. When you are alone, you are all over your life: a child one minute, an old woman the next. I often forget my age when I'm alone. There is no one in present time with you to reassure you that you are in the year 1971 or 1972 and not in 1948 or 1986. All your ages sort of enter your head and swim round and round like little fish. Only, sometimes a dark fish surfaces and pervades everything. Another thing is, I think living alone spoils you. It makes it harder to get together with someone, if you ever do. Living alone makes you your own only child. There is nobody else to please, nobody's schedule or temper to consult but your own. Your only lonely self's. I say self, but that is another aspect of living alone: the self splits into many. Say, for instance, I'm in a bad mood and would like to pick a fight, only I don't have parents or a sister or a husband to pick a fight with. So I find some part of myself to have my fight with. I single it out and focus on it and make it miserable. I divide myself into tormentor and victim. One torments, the other cries out in pain, and the whole thing hurts. I I suppose if one divided oneself and didn't manage to keep track of the whole thing, madness would result. Then there are the scary times. I don't have them often, thank God. These awful states of dangerous awareness, as if someone had slit a gash in that thin web of sanity that holds in my wholeness, and I start to believe that this web is the only thing that makes me *me*. Inside the web is a sort of liquid state, which contains all the things in everybody, all the things in the world, not 'mine' anymore than anybody else's. And I am terrified that this liquid will start running out of me and seek its natural source, some kind of Source Sea which contains elements of everybody, all kinds of habits and attitudes and characteristics of future people. If this should happen, I know I will cease to be. What was 'I' will be a crumpled empty skin, a web vacated. Like—well, for instance, afterbirth, if you want to look at it positively, with Hindu detachment; like a corpse, if you are in the mood to mourn the loss of your self." Jane took some more wine. Her "web" at this minute was quivering with opposing sensations. Self-satisfaction, because she could see she had impressed the other woman, had described a state to her that she had not been privileged to experience, living with so many people; and fear, as if the impersonal tides pushed against the web with vengeance, murmuring, *"Just you wait till she leaves and you're alone again with us. We'll fix you for giving away what should never be put into words."*

"That is very strange," said Sonia. "I can't quite get hold of it. I don't think I have ever felt anything quite like it, no. It's like another plane of living altogether." She puckered up her face, looking like a contemplative imp, if there was such a thing. Behind her forehead, things seemed to move very quickly; Jane felt them move, could almost see waves and eddies of thought, knocking against one another, now and then stilled by a great shadow of the incomprehensible. "Perhaps I would have had it after Jacob left, if I hadn't had Ruthie and Michael. Oh, sometimes at night, after they were asleep, I would be lying in bed reading or correcting papers and I would suddenly remember the old life, when Jacob would be lying next to me, also reading, or we would be talking, and he would say, "Sonia, baby, how about a salami sandwich?' God, how I sometimes hated him for that, because you know who had to go and make it. When he was next to me, all those years, there was always a little part of my brain separate from whatever I was doing or reading, waiting, sort of hoping in a masochistic way, to hear those words which would send me downstairs in the cold, into the dark kitchen to make that damn salami sandwich. But after he was gone, you know what happened? I still waited for the voice, and I still heard it: *Sonia, baby, how about a salami sandwich?*' And I got in the habit of going down in the dark and making them for myself. Now I'm mad about salami sandwiches; I have been ever since that funny period which is as near as I ever came to being truly alone. Max makes them for me now. I love him for that. I had told him this little story, you see; and one night, not too long after we had been married, we were both correcting papers in bed, and suddenly he laughed to himself and put on his bathrobe and socks and went downstairs and came back with two plates with salami sandwiches, and potato chips and pickles on the side. Oh!" And Sonia was suddenly somewhere else; she gave her famous blush, to the roots of her hair. "I remember how much I loved him at that moment. Afterwards . . . well! We didn't get all the potato chips out of the bed for months. In fact, I still think I feel one scraping against me occasionally." She laughed to herself and looked quite touching, very vulnerable, and Jane saw for a second the woman Max Covington saw late at night, a woman who would be unrecognizable to the gossips who saw Sonia Marks rolling impatient eyes toward the next achievement, or controlling her students like a Russian dictator.

Then she suddenly changed expression and was back

with Jane. "It's odd to me that you never married," she said. "How ever did you manage to avoid it? You can't tell me you haven't had some close calls."

"I was engaged once, when I was in England. After I finished undergraduate school, Edith gave me a trip abroad. I got engaged to a nice boy, just out of Oxford, who was apprenticed to a solicitor's firm in London. I used to spend weekends with him and his parents in the country. It fell through, and I really think we were both relieved. We had a huge celebration at the Old Bell in Hurley the night we decided to break it off. He spent more on the meal than he had ever spent on any previous occasion. And we laughed more that evening than we had ever laughed during the entire time we had known each other. Then, in graduate school, there was several—I don't want to call them lovers, because there wasn't much love. It was as if each was using the other to resolve some separate loneliness. But I actually think we increased each other's loneliness. And this is the sad thing: each of us knew the other was not *really* what was wanted. It was all so sad that after a while I gave up that sort of thing. It was like going to bed with one's own dissatisfaction, and who could blame whom if it wasn't satisfying?"

"You gave up that sort of thing," repeated Sonia, looking at the wine in her glass, and Jane knew Sonia was dying to ask if this "giving up" had lasted into the present moment. Now was the time to tell about Gabriel, maybe just a little bit today, maybe just the simple words "There is someone I love now. . . ." She was on the verge, just on the edge of saying it when Sonia continued: "I've been trying to think of a man you *would* find satisfying."

"Oh, there's no one around *here*," said Jane, feeling her mouth turn down at the corners, all on its own. She was slightly drunk. *Now,* she thought, *now.* Now is the time to add, "But there *is* someone. . . ."

"Oh, I didn't mean in real life," Sonia surprised and dismayed her by replying. "I meant in literature. I considered Knightley seriously, but I think you need a little more pzazz. Heathcliff has pzazz, but I don't think you'd fall for someone that unstable. Then there's Rochester, but there's also his wife in the attic, and I'd wish you better than that. I gave up for the time being. I couldn't come up with anyone."

Jane felt bereft.

Sonia had to rush off at two to relieve the baby-sitter. Jane stood behind the curtain and watched her friend pull her knitted cap down over her head, tucking in all her hair, and pedal off quickly down the street. From behind, in her jeans and clogs, she looked like a little Dutch boy. Jane could tell by the sudden forward shift of her body as she bent low over her handlebars and pedaled first ruminatively, then, gathering speed, with increased purpose, that she was actually changing shape as she moved from one house to another: she was leaving behind the Sonia who was "friend and colleague of Jane Clifford" and taking on the Sonia who was "mother of Ruthie and Michael."

Jane went slowly back into the kitchen. She threw out the empty wine bottles. She put on her rubber gloves and washed all the dishes. She decided what could be left for a week in the refrigerator, and what would rot, and threw out the latter. She moved efficiently about the kitchen, slightly drunk, yet willing her mechanical self to sponge surfaces, wrap unused portions of food, empty garbage, straighten objects.

Soon there was not a single trace left of Sonia Marks or the lunch they had shared.

She sat down at the clean table and stroked a silver salt-shaker absently. Many thoughts passed through her head at high velocity, clashing and rebounding against one another, often turning into the next thought before the previous one was even finished. She picked up, examined, and put down again various fragments from the lunch, how it had succeeded, how it could have gone differently, how it had failed from what it might have been.

Suddenly the kitchen became ominous. The web she had described to Sonia was straining, pulling at itself softly from the tides within. The little time-fishes swam madly, then began to kill or swallow one another, change shape and grow into less friendly deep-sea creatures. *Who am I?* she thought. *And why am I here, staring at*

a silver salt-shaker under fluorescent light? Who sees me?
Who knows me? Sonia sat there, she reminded herself.
There, at the end of the table, the table made out of a
door; she puckered her face like an imp in thought; her
voice is high, like a young girl's. I can still hear the pitch
of it. Gabriel has also sat in that empty chair, stirring a
whole pint of milk into his Familia, exactly as he would
do at home, in his own kitchen. And I have sat here
watching him, hardly daring to breathe, overcome with
my good luck at being allowed to experience such do-
mestic boredom.

By now, Sonia had reached home. She was with her
children, perhaps being irritated by their demands, perhaps thinking: Oh, and there is Jane over there, who can
do exactly what she pleases. But Sonia was seeing them
and being seen by them at this moment. There was an
interchange of real physical presences.

At this moment, Gabriel was in his office. She had his
schedules. She had made him describe his office to her.
The radiator with the peeling yellow paint. The pictures
he had hung to cheer the old walls up, and to hide stains.
"Dante's Dream," by Rossetti, hung above his desk, and
to his right—"Really for the students who come for conferences; I can't see it"—the Paradise panel of "The
Garden of Earthly Delights." In his desk drawers he
kept hundreds of postcards, collected from museums he
had visited. He always included a postcard with his letter,
and the picture on the card (it seemed to her) made an
oblique comment on the current state of their relationship. Gabriel used paintings and pictures, or words of
other people, to tell her what he could not seem to say.
After their "apples and oranges" dialogue, he had sent
a postcard of a terrible sixteenth-century engraving of an
emblem, "Time Cutting the Wings of Cupid," and a clip-
ping from the *New York Review of Books* of a poem
by Richard Wilbur, which began: "If you would have my
heart love on, Grant me such years as suit the lover, And
teach my twilight to recover (If it but could) the flush
of dawn."

Gabriel's school was still in session. His semester break
did not start till the weekend. At this minute he was hav-

ing office hours. Some student was sitting to the left of his desk, perhaps looking at "The Garden of Earthly Delights," or attending to the movements of his large hands and his placid face, which almost never showed anxiety or tension, as he droned on in his self-absorbed way about the simple wonders of some painting, leading this student into the moment with him, into the moment of appreciation. All else was out of his head. Gabriel devoted himself to each moment in which he lived. She was out of his head. In this moment, he could not see her. But he was being seen, Gabriel Weeks, Professor of Art History. He was a visible, audible, physical reality to another human being.

At this moment, no one saw Jane. No one in the living world could testify exactly how she sat, a silver saltshaker cradled like a small animal in her palm.

Even if Sonia and Gabriel and Gerda and Kitty, and perhaps other friends as well, were all remembering her at *precisely this moment,* she could only be a memory to them, an image summoned by their own imaginations, aided by the past.

She was no more to them at this moment, could be no more, than her grandmother Edith was to her at this moment: a memory.

That's what it was to be dead.

IV

Outside the tiny airport, the temperature was dropping by the minute. The stars in the black sky which ran parallel to the flat wasteland were as clear as the closer searchlights and beacons.

We'll fly tonight, thought Jane, carrying her suitcases through the swinging doors into the overheated room. An Air Force sergeant walked away from the ticket counter, shaking his cropped head and waving his hands in the air.

"The thing hasn't even left Chicago yet!" he announced to the other passengers, a bitter triumph in his voice.

Jane saw a familiar figure ahead of her in line: a tall, pretty woman with curly jet-black hair, pale skin, and a black maxicoat.

"Marsha?"

The woman turned. She looked worried, unsure of herself, then her face lit up. "Jane! What are you doing here?"

"I'm flying to Chicago tonight."

"Oh, good! So am I. I'm going to meet somebody in New York tomorrow and I got so scared the morning plane wouldn't leave—this morning it was fogged in— so I decided to go a day early to make sure nothing would happen. Where are you staying in Chicago? If you're staying in a motel, perhaps we could share a room and save money."

"Of course we can. We can stay at one of those places near O'Hare."

"Oh, good. I don't know anything at all about it."

"Well, I do," said Jane. "Leave it to me."

"Wonderful," sighed the other, looking at Jane with real trust. The anxiety which had marred her perfect features relaxed and she was serene and beautiful again. "Thank you." She always spoke in a breathless, deferential voice—the exact opposite, Jane now reflected, of Sonia Marks's voice—and she often ended her sentences with "Thank you."

Marsha Pedersen, graduate student. Two years younger than Jane. Divorced with two sons, eight and eleven.

("I can't make up my mind whether to specialize in the Romantics or the Victorians," Marsha had told Jane at their first conference. Jane was Marsha's "adviser." "Well," began Jane, "is yours a Romantic or a Victorian soul? The visions are quite different, you know." "I can't decide," wailed Marsha. "I think I probably tend to be more Romantic, but I admire the Victorians so much." "Take your time," said Jane. "It's a decision you'll have to live with." "Yes, I will," said Marsha. "Thank you." They had had several conferences since but not about literature. "You seem so strong," Marsha would say. "You are a strong woman. You don't need men. I want you to tell me how to become strong like you. I am so afraid of being alone, of getting old alone. I'm afraid my sons are going to turn queer without a father. Advise me. What do you think I should do?" "Well, right now," said Jane, "I think if I were you, I would finish my degree. To do that, you ought to decide on your specialty, because you can't apply for qualification till you do. It's not all that difficult. Think of it like one of those 'Test Yourself for Grooming,' and so on. Make a list of the major names you connect with each period and then ask yourself: 'Do I want my life to read like a stanza from Byron or a stanza from Matthew Arnold; or like a chapter from *Wuthering Heights* or a chapter from *Middlemarch?*' Do this and come back to see me next week." Marsha had thought this was a wonderful idea. She thanked Jane, but she had not come back the next week.)

76

She must have something else on her mind, thought Jane now, suspecting it might have to do with the "somebody" in New York.

"Is our plane going to be late, then?" asked Jane, nodding toward the Air Force sergeant, who was ranting to a small group of companion travelers.

"Oh, no," Marsha said, laughing. "That's another flight. Ours is on time, thank goodness. I ought to know. I've already checked three times. I am so nervous, you have no idea. What luck, to be able to travel with you!"

Beside Marsha was an enormous suitcase which looked roomy enough to hold a month's wardrobe. "Aren't you going to check that heavy suitcase, Marsha?"

"Well, no. I'm afraid to risk it. They're always losing luggage and my new dress for a very important dinner party is in there."

"Oh."

Their flight was called and a few passengers milled through the door into the clear, freezing night. There was only one gate. The Air Force sergeant remained behind, hat balanced on his knee, glowering at the deserters.

Their plane was a small Fairchild, in which the passengers sat beneath the wings. "Let's sit near the back," said Marsha. "It's safer." Jane always preferred the front. The ride was smoother. But she gave in to Marsha, feeling the stronger tonight.

As they took off, Marsha looked so alarmed that Jane found herself parodying some Spanish women she remembered on a flight once, making frantic signs of the cross. Marsha laughed, delighted. "I feel better already," she said, and began relating the details of her hectic day, how she had run around town recruiting three days' worth of baby-sitters for her sons, promising all sorts of outrageous favors in return ("practically mortgaging my whole spring semester!"), buying vitamin C for a potential cold she felt coming on, buying a dress for this important dinner, getting home and wondering if the back was too low to be decent, taking it back and exchanging it, getting all the way home only to discover a bump on her face, rushing to the drugstore for something to dry it up before tomorrow. . . .

"Good lord, what are you going to?"

The Fairchild cruised low, between stars and the lights of scattered towns. Jane was able to look past Marsha at both, since she had given Marsha the window seat, as Marsha related how she had met the famous poet——— at the MLA last month, and "we both fell for each other rather hard. Tomorrow there is a dinner for seventy-five couples in his honor and he wanted me to be there. My name will even be printed on the little guest list that comes with the menu, he said. He told me some of the people on the list: just about everybody famous. I said, 'But I'll be the only nobody there,' and he was very sweet. He said, 'Then nobody's enough for me.' But look! My face is breaking out: can you see this awful bump? No? I guess it's too dark. Tell me, Jane, how should I behave in front of all those famous people? As you can guess, this person means a lot to me."

"But how often have you seen him, Marsha? The MLA was only last month. Not quite a month ago, even."

"Oh, every weekend. We've managed to meet in some city or other every weekend. I'm going crazy getting people to keep the boys! I've taken advantage of my friends something awful, but this is no casual affair. He does a lot of readings. Last week I flew to Minnesota to meet him."

"Is he married?"

"He's getting a divorce. But he's been married lots of times. I told him one more time wouldn't hurt him, and he agreed."

"Well! In that case, I think you might as well practice being the next Mrs.——— at this dinner. I've always found it's best to be courteous and quiet and not try to be witty or anything. When a nervous person tries to be witty, the results can sometimes backfire and you end up being insulting. Just look beautiful and serene, which you do anyway, and if you get nervous tell yourself this is a rehearsal of some kind of a movie you're going to be in. You want to get the part perfect."

"What a good idea! That's exactly what I'll do. Thank you. Where are you going? Anywhere interesting?"

"Not exactly. My grandmother died this morning. I'm going to her funeral."

"Oh, my goodness. I'm sorry. Here I've been boring you with all this trivia."

"No, it's not. My grandmother would have enjoyed listening to it herself."

The plane parked some distance from a lower-level gate, making it necessary for the passengers to walk across the tarmac. Jane and Marsha tucked their faces into their upturned coat collars and hurried through the freezing night. It was too cold to speak. Jane felt exhausted and depressed. She did not think she could bear up if this gentle companion, who gave off an air of not being able to do a thing for herself, were not hurrying along beside her, depending on her to take care of them both for this night. Having to make decisions for them both made Jane stronger. And she understood how, perhaps, in certain marriages, one partner could actually derive strength from the weakness of the other. She knew—Gabriel had alluded to it tactfully several times—that Ann was the "weaker" one. She depended on him for everything. And this perhaps had given him the rocklike durability Jane so admired. But what if he should suddenly find himself married to a woman who could take care of herself? Would he find himself freed, able to use his strength for other projects? Or would he crumple?

They had walked halfway down the corridor to the main lobby when Marsha gave a little cry of distress. "I've left my make-up kit on the seat of the plane!"

Jane sat down on one of the benches along the wall, guarding the enormous suitcase which Marsha would not check, and watched her companion flee down the passageway. In her long coat and laced-up boots, she looked like a Gothic heroine in distress.

There was not much human traffic at this time of night. Jane saw the pilot of their plane and the stewardess coming slowly along the corridor. His uniform was rumpled and he was carrying a flight bag. Something in the way he gripped it, as if he had set the muscles of his hands and fingers in place and commanded them to stay there so he could propel his body like an automaton toward some bed (whether shared by a tired wife, this stewardess, or perhaps no one at all), exemplified his state of exhaustion. Jane had several times used airline pilots as heroes for her erotic fantasies—their anonymous, in-transit qualities suited them for such roles—but this man: there was not much left of him for anybody, even anybody's fantasy. The stewardess had taken off her smile for the night, but she swung along beside him gamely, like a comrade sharing the final half-mile of a killing routine march. She spoke to him quietly, without much energy or enthusiasm, as they walked in step along the floor littered with cigarette butts and pieces of paper, beneath the too white, glaring lights, and Jane liked her for this, for trying to keep alive this small reminder of human interchange, when there was so little comfort in their surroundings, so very little of the human about them.

And yet they had been *flying* together! But they were so exhausted, so bogged down in the routine details of "the flight," that the word, with its attendant miracle, had been stripped for them of any ecstasy.

Marsha returned with her make-up kit, and the two women continued on through the lobby and down the escalator to retrieve Jane's checked bag. Then they went to a row of courtesy telephones and Jane selected a motel while Marsha, seeming weary now, sat down on her big suitcase and looked trusting.

They went outside to wait for the courtesy car. Every other motel seemed to send their car first. A drunk tried to pick them up. "I'd be happy to take you young ladies *anywhere* you wish to go."

Marsha laughed and shrugged, embarrassed.

"Bug off," said Jane to the man. Then felt angry: at the man, at Marsha, at herself, at all the forces that conspired to make her suddenly take up this "male" role. For God's sake, it was as if she were defending Marsha. It was late and cold and dark. She wanted to be defended herself.

The courtesy car arrived at last. It needed a wash. The driver was a very old, fat man wearing a Tyrolean costume. He looked half asleep or drunk. Inside, the car was filthy. The motor kept stalling on the driver whenever he stopped at intersections. Marsha and Jane exchanged exasperated looks the third time this happened—just as he was pulling out into a dangerous thoroughfare—and fastened their seat belts. Jane's did not work. So she sat, a fist clenched on each side, rocking and lurching through the remainder of the ride.

When they checked in at the motel desk, they were told they would each have to pay $15.50 for the room they would share. "That doesn't seem like such a great saving," Jane said to Marsha as the same man in the Tyrolean hat wheeled their luggage onto the elevator, up a floor, and then down a long corridor that smelled musty. There was a party going on in one of the rooms. Two men in cheap business suits, wearing smile buttons on the lapels, poked their heads out of an open doorway from which music blared. "I know. It does seem like a lot," said Marsha apologetically, as if it were all her fault. Jane suddenly longed to be alone at any price. She was on the verge of suggesting it to Marsha, pleading depression, eccentricity, insanity. She would gladly pay another $15.50 for the privilege of being left alone with her own demons.

"You girls like to come to a party?"

"No, thank you," said Jane. She saw Marsha look back at the men over her shoulder and give a regretful smile and shrug. She could have slapped her.

The man in the Tyrolean hat could not get their door unlocked. He twisted the key this way, that way, shook the knob angrily.

The women stood politely, pretending not to notice his agitation. Jane, feeling more unwillingly like a "husband" by the minute, was just ready to snatch the key from him when, somehow, the door swung open of its own accord.

Once inside, he began fumbling with the heating system. He could not seem to make that work either.

81

"Oh, it's all right. We'll figure it out," said Jane. She gave him a dollar while Marsha was still rummaging in her purse, protesting.

The two women were left alone together.

"What a relief!" said Marsha. But she didn't really feel it.

"Yes," said Jane, who didn't either. If I were the poet————, we would bridge this moment with an embrace, she thought. Likewise, if Marsha were Gabriel . . . Suddenly Jane had a vision of an updated pulp magazine: love stories in which the heroine always met her man at the MLA—everybody seemed to be doing it these days. If Kitty were writing a story about Marsha and a story about me for this new pulp, after she finished describing Marsha's looks and my looks, put in a word about our occupations (she would probably airbrush us both into "schoolteachers," since Marsha teaches freshman Rhetoric), how would she depict the way our stories differ? *Do they differ in any significant way?* wondered Jane darkly. Or is the only difference in surface biographical statistics: Marsha has two children. I have none; Marsha's lover is getting a divorce and might conceivably marry her; I have a piece of paper that states I have fulfilled all requirements for a doctorate; Marsha has a very similar piece of paper stating she has fulfilled all requirements for a master's.

She wished she could pat herself on the back and say, "But, of course, my story is on a higher plane altogether." But she could not think, using all the powers of her tired mind, wherein the qualitative difference might lie that would make "Jane Clifford's Story" a nobler one than "Marsha Pedersen's Story." And, if the noble element was made a factor, wasn't it noble for the mother of two growing boys to fly around the country to get them a father? Whereas, thought Jane, I only have myself to consider.

She sat down on the bed nearest the window. The room was cold. Marsha laid the big suitcase flat on the floor and started unpacking at once.

"I don't want this dress to get crushed. Do you like it?" She held the long silken thing against her body, a pattern of bright summery flowers, the modest neckline and long sleeves edged in black grosgrain ribbon which brought out Marsha's black curls.

"It's lovely, Marsha. Do you know, it reminds me of . . . Do you remember those pretty women in the advertisements for Springmaid sheets? They were country maids; I think one of them even had long black curls, like your curls. She looked exactly as I have always imagined Tess of the d'Urbervilles, ever since. Do you do that? Take some picture you have seen and stick it on to a character as you read? Or apply some house you've been in, maybe only once in your life, to a house in literature—sort of apply it as you would a decal, and then it's there forever? I have a picture of a vicarage, for example, taken from my one visit to this little English vicarage in a village near Oxford, and now whenever I'm reading a story or a novel with a vicarage, I seem to pull out my mental decal labeled "vicarage" and slap it onto whatever vicarage the author may have had in mind. In fact, he may have had his own decal."

"How interesting," said Marsha. "I don't know whether I do that when I read or not. I'll have to check, next time. But what you said about the Springmaid ad convinces me I did exactly right, taking that other dress back this afternoon and exchanging it for this one, even though it was more money. The other dress was more classic and sophisticated. It was black and cut very low in the back. But . . . then I tried it on again at home and said no, it was too low. He said I was the most maidenly woman he had ever met and that dress was just not maidenly."

"Ah," said Jane. What does Gabriel think I am, she wondered suddenly. Would I recognize myself if I were shown a picture of me as seen through Gabriel's vision? Does Gabriel have a mental decal, labeled "the most ———woman I have ever met," which he slips onto me whenever he thinks about me or sees me?

"Do you think this black coat will go all right?" asked Marsha. "I mean it's long, but it's only cloth. The wives and—friends of the other people at the dinner will probably all have fur."

"That's all right. What *maiden* wears a fur coat, that's the point. Take my word for it, Marsha, you'll be the freshest thing there."

"If this damned bump will just dry up."

Jane put her own, smaller suitcase on a chair and opened it. She didn't need to take anything out. There was nothing she had to keep from creasing. She was "only going home," where there was always an iron and where a crease or two didn't matter anyway. Oh, hell. She hadn't packed a nightgown. Ray kept a drawer full of clean woolen nightshirts he ordered out of the Ward's catalogue, which everyone in the family had taken to wearing, and Jane, though she hated Ray, liked to sleep in those soft, sweet-smelling shirts when she came home.

But she couldn't sleep naked tonight in this room with Marsha Pedersen. She must wear something.

And immediately her fingers touched the heavy yellow silk of the dressing gown she had almost decided not to bring, then had, for sentimental reasons. It had been Edith's last gift to her—at Christmas, less than a month ago. "I don't want you to run around in your cold apartment and get a chill," said Edith, who had always consulted daily temperatures for whatever place Jane was living in or visiting. She thought that if the Midwest had below-zero temperatures, Jane's apartment would also. But "It's lovely, Edith," Jane had said, thinking how, sooner or later, Gabriel would see it, this beautifully tailored robe of tawny-colored silk.

The thought that Edith continued to provide her with proprieties—she would not have to appear naked in front of Marsha now—even after her death hit Jane with its poignancy. It hit her even harder because she was very tired.

She turned away. She did not want to show these tears to Marsha.

"Do you want to use the bathroom first?" asked Marsha politely.

"Not just now. You go ahead."

"Oh, thank you."

While Marsha splashed in the bathroom, clinking

bottles and jars, Jane hurried out of her clothes and into the luxurious dressing gown. She took "old T.F." out of the suitcase and set him for seven. Then she climbed into bed with *The Odd Women,* thinking she would read away the night if it would not disturb Marsha.

But the bed was cold. The room was cold. That damn man in the Tyrolean hat had not turned on their heat. Jane got out of bed and fumbled around with the thermostat. She heard a whirring noise start up, but could not feel heat coming from anywhere. Marsha emerged from the bathroom in a navy-blue gown with red-and-white trimming. Her face was shining, except for a very large spot which she had covered with a dry white salve.

"It's so cold in here," she said, daintily rubbing her arms.

"Yes, I know. Let's see if there are any extra blankets." Jane went through the drawers. There was none. "I guess we'll just have to use our coats." Jane got her coat and spread it on top of the covers and climbed in bed.

"What a good idea," said Marsha. She fetched her black maxi-coat, spread it carefully across her bed, and climbed in, giving Jane an admiring smile. "Oh, dear. How will we ever wake up?"

"I've set my clock," said Jane.

"Oh, wonderful," said Marsha. "Thank you." She wriggled around in her bed for several minutes, curled herself into position, and fell asleep almost instantly.

Jane turned on her bedside lamp, made herself small under the coat, which was not a maxi-coat, and tried to read. But somehow she did not want to waste this book when she was less than lucid. She sniffed it and caressed its cover. Published in 1893—Edith had been seven years old in 1893—and just reissued last year in a Norton paperback. She had seen the book at the MLA book fair and ordered an examination copy. That was one of the best things about being an academic: the free books. She admired the glossy black-and-orange cover. A handsome woman in full-length traveling dress, holding her plumed hat in one hand, stood erectly, turned three-quarters away from the readers. She looked elegant, arrogant, independent. Which one of the women was she?

Alice and Virginia Madden, suddenly left adrift by the death of their improvident father, must take grinding and humiliating "genteel" work. Pretty, vulnerable, and terrified of sharing their fate, their younger sister Monica accepts a proposal of marriage from a man who gives her financial security but drives her to reckless action by his insane jealousy.

Interwoven with their fortunes are Mary Barfoot and Rhoda Nunn, who are dedicating their lives to training young women for independent and useful lives, for emotional as well as economic freedom. Feminine and spirited, they are seeking not to overthrow men but to free both sexes from everything that distorts or depletes their humanity—including, if necessary, marriage.

Jane put down the book. She gave a brief look at Marsha's dark curls as she turned out the light. ". . . training young women for independent and useful lives": that could describe her role, her usefulness, to Marsha. But tomorrow Marsha would be in New York with her poet, and hopefully minus her bump.

Edith's husband, Hans, had died thirty years ago. He was a railroad man. Kitty had told Jane that he was the last good man in the world, and that Edith had fallen truly in love with him after he died. For years, Edith had dreamed a particular dream after his death. In this dream she was standing out in a freezing winter night in a flat prairie landscape, trying to flag down a train. She knew Hans was aboard this train. As it came nearer, she stood as close to the tracks as she dared and waved her hand and cried out. But the train always hurtled by.

Jane did not sleep until almost 5 A.M. Just before waking, she dreamed that she was trying to make the train herself. Only first it was necessary to empty Edith's purse and put in all her own things, her money, her comb, her identification. The train was coming. Edith lay sick in a little waiting shed near the tracks. Jane would have to run like fury to make that train. "Come back!" wailed Edith pitifully. "I'm sick!"

"I can't!" cried Jane. "Not if I'm going to make the train."

She woke, freezing, before Tempus Fugit went off. She packed and took a long, hot bath. Marsha seemed no longer in the next room. Jane was already gone from this place, this freezing overnight waiting room between existences. Marsha was a person she had left behind in the other existence.

She had a two-and-a-half-hour layover in the Nashville airport. Vile place, she hated it. Big posters of country-music stars, giant bottles of bourbon whiskey in glass cases, a "Ladies" shop which sold black underwear trimmed with lace and sequins.

At last, it was forty-five minutes before her plane left. She went to the waiting area, the last lone gate on the south concourse. She sat down, took off her coat, and began to read *The Odd Women*. Some time passed. She looked up and met the glance of a gray-haired man, dressed in tweeds. He, too, was reading a book. His was hardcover; she could not see its title. It looked old. She was impressed. She hoped he would sit next to her on the flight. He seemed to communicate that he would try. There was an appealing mixture of strength and kindness in the brief look he gave her before returning to his book. Where had she seen such a look before? Another man was also eying her, neither kindly nor discreetly: a young man with orange hair and a pockmarked face and a scarlet corduroy jacket.

Aboard the plane, she turned her face to the window and hoped the good man would get there first. But it was scarlet jacket who sat down beside her. "Mind if I sit here?" he asked confidently.

"Of course not," said Jane coldly. She opened her book and pretended to be engrossed.

The minute they were in the air, he unbuckled his seat belt and got down to business. "Do you work in Nashville?"

Jane closed the book. She signaled the stewardess and ordered a Bloody Mary. He seemed impressed. "No," she said, "I do not work in Nashville."

"Where *do* you work, then?" He thought they were going to play a game.

"Why don't you guess?" she said. "What do you imagine that I do? Can you picture my life? What did you imagine I was when you first saw me, back in that waiting room?"

He was startled; he looked slightly distasteful of this dialogue. It was not what he had expected, registered his face, so openly. This dame was slightly crazy, saying these things, holding a book on her lap called *The Odd Women*; now what kind of a book was that? But he would show he could play along.

"Well, the first thing I noticed about you was that you looked lonely. And the next thing was, I—well then I saw you weren't wearing a ring. So I figured you must be going off for the weekend to, you know, meet somebody."

Jane sighed and looked at this creature for a long time. Then she decided to strike. "As a matter of fact, I am going to a funeral," she said. "Someone close to me has died. Someone in my family."

"I'm sorry," he said. He turned his face away and looked up and down the aisle. He shifted about for several minutes. Then, "Excuse me," he said, and got up and went to the magazine rack and took down a *Sports Illustrated* and, as if it were the most natural thing in the world, returned to another seat. Jane finished her Bloody Mary and ordered another, thinking that her victory had been a cheap one.

As the plane made its approach for landing in the mountains where Edith had been born, married, and would soon be buried, the stewardess asked if there was a doctor on board. She rushed to the back of the plane. Jane's gray-haired man in tweeds got up and followed her. Together they propped up a very old man. The other stewardess held an oxygen mask to his face. Jane got her glasses out of her purse so she could see better. She watched, near tears, how tenderly the man in tweeds supported the old man by his shoulders. Was he a doctor? Or just a good, strong man who knew how to take care of people. In an instant, Jane imagined a lifetime with this man, who had been denied her by the careless act of an ass in a scarlet jacket from Nashville. She saw how he would lift her up tenderly when she was sick, tired, or unhappy.

The plane landed. Now, to her dismay, she noticed that the old man had slumped out of view. The good man was still bending over the seat with one of the stewardesses. The other stewardess had detached herself and now stood at the front exit, smiling and thanking each disembarking passenger.

As Jane collected her things, she stooped to peer through the plane window at her family. There they stood in a row, blondes in descending order (Edith missing from the top of the line, tall Edith; and where was Emily today?), except for Ray, who was dark. They had stood so for years of her landings, these people, waiting for her to come back to them, expecting her to come back, never doubting she had any choice but to fall back from the sky into their nets of family and region and social standing and—most compelling weave of all—their image of her, Jane, their Jane. My family, she thought, studying them curiously through the little window. For this moment she saw them objectively, just four people standing in a row waiting for an airplane. Good heavens, she thought, who are they, what do they mean to me, what can I possibly do for them or they for me? That woman, that blond woman—anyone can see she is what they call a "lady," and thinks of herself as a lady, with her straight-held shoulders and expensive suit with the little silk scarf tucked in the neck, and the black kid gloves covering all of the wrists. That woman and I will have at least one confidential talk, which in itself won't be very confidential at all, yet we'll both go away from it and make it over into some heightened communication. Then we'll write letters about it, idealizing it until we are desperate to get together for the next talk, which, when it comes, will be a disappointment till we do it over in our memories. When did this discrepancy between our real talks and our expectations and memories of them begin? We were once confidantes, close friends. Weren't we? Is that I have "grown away" from her, as other daughters do, or is it she who has given me the slip, into that mystical, religious realm of hers?

And there are Jack and Ronnie. My "brothers"—or "half-brothers" when I am angry with them or wanting to think of myself as the only child again. How little I know of these boys: one born the year I made my escape from Ray through the first of a long series of scholarships and fellowships; the other born two and a half years later, when I felt independent enough to come home again to visit, bringing the new baby toys, to show I had money of my own. Yes, I did my share to spoil Ronnie. Yet I know him no better than I know Jack.

And there, Ladies and Gentlemen, is the villain in my life. If every woman has a villain in her life, then Ray Sparks is surely mine. He looks, I know, like a perfectly ordinary man, the kind of American man who is often held up as "the backbone of our nation." To a stranger, his very appearance must seem reassuring: this lean, sunburned man in his plaid wool McGregor shirt and mudsplattered work shoes, his short-clipped nails, his swarthy right hand caressing, quite unconsciously, the wallet he wears clipped to his belt. Did you know that banks loan thousands of dollars to this man, on his signature alone, this man in his late forties, with his grizzled brown crew cut, standing with the blond, well-dressed lady and her two blond boys in their navy-blue blazers with the crest of an expensive private school sewn on the pockets? If someone told this man, "Do you know, there is a young woman, says she is your stepdaughter; this young woman schoolteacher who teaches college somewhere in the Midwest. Says she still has nightmares about you, where you're beating her up, or locking her in rooms, or taking all her money and clothes so she can't get away. Says she sometimes wakes up shaking and screaming like a little child, and she's going on thirty-three years old"—if someone were to tell Ray Sparks such a thing, he would look extremely shocked. "Why, I only did my best," he'd say. "It's not easy, taking on a stepdaughter nine years old who's been spoiled to death by a grandmother who never knew what it was to work a day in her life. I am a simple man, an ordinary citizen of this country, trying to make my own living and support my family. I never tried to hold anyone back. Me? I believe in free enterprise and tending to your own business and standing on your own two feet. The values this country was founded on. I am very sorry to hear she thinks I am a villain. I only tried to do my best, and with a child like her it wasn't easy." Far from a villain, he has so often felt a victim. His father was brutally killed by two Negroes, who robbed his cash register and got away with it all, the murder and everything. When the blacks marched on Washington, Ray Sparks canceled his subscription to *Newsweek* in a letter which denounced slanted reporting. (He received, and kept, a lovely reply, from a woman named Evelyn Robinson, telling him *Newsweek* was trying to do the best it could and begging him to reconsider.)

This is all in the past, thought Jane. She shouldered her bag, tucked her book under her arm, and descended the plane's metal stairs. I am not going to be pulled back this time. I will be compassionate to them, but I will not betray myself to make things easier for them. I will not show my emotions. I will not show favoritism to Ronnie over Jack, and I'll give Jack some of my time if he wants to talk. I will not have the slightest disagreement with Ray no matter how he provokes me. I will be a person they all respect, and perhaps even like, but I will not give them a single weakness they can fasten on and thus retain me as theirs, their same old Jane. And I will try, really try, to resurrect the bygone flavor of those talks with Kitty. Even if they were fictions, I will revive them into reality with my detached, yet expanding sympathies. It will please her. I also will not cry at the funeral, nor at any time. Anybody can blubber. Ray will probably weep loudly at the funeral, as he did at John's mother's, embarrassing everybody.

She walked across the tarmac. Kitty came forward and hugged her. "Darling," she said. She smelled of Nuit de Noël. one of her winter perfumes. When she opened her mouth, Jane saw that a front tooth had been capped. Its shade was slightly different from the next tooth. "I'm so glad you're here," said Kitty. Her voice sounded a little like someone parodying a Southern accent.

Over her mother's shoulder, Jane greeted the boys and nodded at Ray, who shot up a hand casually. "Jack, you have grown so tall," said Jane. Jack gave a shy smile, trying to keep his mouth shut, and turned away. Ronnie stood his ground, waiting for his due. Jane bent and kissed him: "Mmm! You darling!" When she kissed her baby brother, she saw Jack's shoulder blades wince as he stood with his back to all of them, studying the airfield. I should have kissed him, she realized, too late. Then she thought simultaneously of Edith, lying in a funeral home, and of the fact that she would never lay eyes on that nice man in tweeds again, the man who might have been everything, and her face pulled apart and she burst into vulgar tears.

"Darling. Let's go on to the car," said Kitty, taking her gloved hand in her own.

"I'm sorry, I was up all night grading papers," she lied. "And then I think some old man on the plane died."

"No wonder, then," said Kitty. "Along with everything else."

"Dad, can we stay and watch them bring the dead man off?" asked Ronnie. Ray did not answer, but indicated that he would be willing to stay. He looked a little embarrassed by Jane's public outburst. Other passengers were looking, as well.

Jane allowed herself to be led docilely, hand in hand with her mother, into the terminal. Jack, taller than either of the women, followed respectfully behind, more fascinated by his sister's tears than by any prospective corpse emerging from the plane.

"I'll get your bag," he said. "Is it still that same old black one with the zipper?"

"The same old black one with the zipper," repeated Jane. She watched him go off, walking tentatively on the balls of his feet, as if still unaccustomed to his new inches. "I'm so damn sorry about my little display," she said to Kitty.

"That's all right," replied the other. "You're still our same little Jane."

"Where's Emily?"

"She's having her last exam. They'll drive in this evening."

V

KITTY and her two daughters, her totally unlike daughters by different fathers, were together at last, in "Emily's room." It was after supper, the day of Jane's arrival. Ray was in his basement office, making out the weekly payroll for his construction workers. Kitty's sons and Emily's husband, John, were in the basement TV room, watching the Friday night programs and playing desultory games of Ping-Pong during the commercials. All the men in the family were downstairs.

Ray had completed this house in the summer of '68, and Emily had left for college two months later. By Christmas she was married. So there was very little of her personality in this room which was officially hers. What girlhood this strange child could claim had been left behind in other bedrooms of other houses built by Ray, who had a habit of selling his own home right out from under his family. He was the true enterprising American. He never resisted a good offer. Jane, on her visits since home had been in this house, had probably spent as many nights in "Emily's room" as Emily had in the two months before she left for college. Now Emily and John slept in the pine-paneled guest room.

This was a new-smelling, spacious room. All Ray's rooms were so: empty of histories; hard to fill up with the interesting eccentricities of longer ownership, accumulated habits, and traditions; hard to fill up with furniture. The floors were of shining light wood, new wood, not a warped board or a stain or an imperfection of the kind a child might spend pre-sleep moments turning into a clown's face or a menacing animal. The walls were spray-painted evenly in an eggshell tint. There was never anything old or settled or the slightest bit dark or quaint in Ray's houses. He was often asked by friends of Kitty's to assess some old house they wanted to buy and "restore." How he ridiculed them! Buy some ramshackle old barn, which was built before the days of plumbing, whose floors slanted and sagged, whose walls—eleven inches thick or not—bulged with goiters from years of rot and mildew. Who gave a damn about the "secret room" beneath the eaves, where somebody or other had hidden the family silver from the plundering Yankees? He could build them all the secret rooms they wanted in a new house, with straight floors of new wood and up-to-date plumbing. Kitty's friends usually bought the old house, anyway, and then Ray's phone was always ringing, and not without a certain "I told you so" in his voice did he sigh and agree to send the men he could spare to repair a circular staircase (which had given way, nearly fatally, while being descended by a guest), or to replace a three-story column, eaten from the inside by termites. How he loathed rot and age and decay. The minute the walls of his own home started to settle, he spray-painted the telltale cracks and sold the thing to the first good bidder and built a new house for his family. Kitty had learned to joke about it. "My husband knows how I detest housecleaning. When my house gets dirty, he builds me another one."

The furniture of Emily's room had been bought in a single afternoon, on a visit to a furniture store. "Isn't this lovely? This is just the kind of thing I would have given anything to have," said Kitty, fingering the light yellow maple furniture of a delicate Chinese design. The wood smelled new. Jane had been along on that trip, home for a summer visit. "It's not all that *cheap*," said Kitty, looking at a tag on one of the twin beds, "but I'd rather get something you really like and pay a little more for it. You can have your friends to spend the night. And the little dressing table that turns into a desk! And this delicate, lovely chest of drawers, so thin and tall; and I love

95

the way they've painted those little panels on the drawers white. Don't you love it, Emily? Shall we buy it for your room?" "It's okay, I guess," said Emily, inscrutable Emily. "But do you *like* it?" asked Kitty. "I *like* it!" shouted Emily, showing the beginnings of one of her formidable tempers, and Kitty had said at once, "Oh, good. I'm so glad. I'll see if we can't have it delivered tomorrow, so you can have as much use as possible before you go away to college."

Jane had once tried to use the little yellow dressing table as a desk, but found its surface too small. The whole piece of furniture had wobbled on its dainty legs, in spite of Ray's even floors. She did not think Emily had ever sat down at this desk to study or think. When could she have? Those last two months, she had been down in her daddy's office, at his man-sized desk, typing John's letters of job application on the office-sized Remington. Girls to spend the night in those little twin beds? When she already had her plans made for a double bed with a husband in it? But she had let Kitty buy the silly yellow furniture, all the same. Emily kept her mouth shut, or exploded in quick effective bursts of temper: she did not explain, or analyze and agonize, or protest. Strange child. Jane was fascinated by her half-sister. Sometimes she envied her; sometimes she thought some important human quality had been left out of her.

Emily's desk—dressing table was at the moment propped open; the underside of the lid was a mirror. Jane, from where she lay in one of the twin beds, saw a reflection of eggshell-colored wall. There was something grudging, even morose about the mirror. Kitty had often commented on it; Jane noticed it. Emily did not seem to care. It was as if, feeling itself cheated of the proper attentions that teen-age girls usually render their mirrors, it now made a point of refusing to reflect anything interesting. Nobody who looked into this mirror could see the mystery of herself. It gave you back a clean, flat square—yourself in the middle, your most mundane self that could be caught by the 25¢ photo machine uptown in Woolworth's. The magical dimension was lacking. You could not glimpse, as you could in Edith's well-beloved, often-consulted triple mirror, the mysterious rustlings of your life in front and behind.

The remarkable things in this room were the curtains and bedspreads. Kitty had made every stitch of them herself, spending months on them, months into the winter that Emily abandoned her room forever, took John as a husband, and returned with him to sleep in the guest room. They were of an expensive beige linen, very heavy, lined with pale silk of the same color, which Kitty had had to order. They were a world in themselves, and anyone who looked closely at these curtains or bedspreads understood that the person who had so lovingly crafted them had entered into that world while doing so. For they were embroidered with hundreds of little people. Chinese people: families, babies, lovers, old men and women, solitaries, flower-smellers; sitting on rocks, or in gardens drinking tea (even the cups were different) or balancing water buckets on their kimonoed shoulders, or chasing butterflies, or mounting steps to a pagoda, or meditating under a stylized Chinese tree. If you really scrutinized the little population, living out its multiple lives on the beige landscape, you would come across other figures penciled in, like ghosts, which Kitty had forgotten to fill in with her colored threads. You could get very philosophical looking at these curtains and spreads. Jane very much coveted them; she felt Emily did not really appreciate them. "You never spent so much time on anything for *me*," she once complained to her mother. "You had me all to yourself for nine years," said Kitty. "Emily has always had to share me. Don't begrudge her these spreads and curtains. And don't think she doesn't appreciate them. She has her own way of showing things, and not showing things."

Jane supposed it was true. At least, it was *one* truth, and the one Kitty had chosen. The way Kitty saw it, she had been "owned" by Jane (*and* Edith) during her young widowhood. Motherhood had taken Kitty too soon, before she was ready. She was a young mother, then a young widow; then life seemed over before it had begun. "You've *been* married," Edith would tell her when the three of them lived together during the war years, when Kitty went out and worked "like a father" for Jane, and Edith stayed home and minded Jane "like a mother."

But she had been ready for motherhood when Emily was born. She and Ray planned Emily, planned and failed twice before this healthy baby girl tumbled, via Dr. Read's natural-childbirth method, into the world. Kitty had remained awake through the birth. Ray had jealously watched the delivery, every movement of the doctor's hands, every contraction of his wife; he stood, trembling, masked and gowned, holding his stopwatch. Emily knew the exact second she was born. After the birth, Kitty suddenly understood the pattern of the universe. She begged the nurse for a pencil and paper, but was denied it, and the vision faded. But she had seen it for a moment, she told them all later. Emily's birth had opened the eternal keyhold for Kitty—for a brief moment.

Jane had been thirteen when Emily was born. The baby upset her, and she spent more and more time with Edith, sleeping and studying at Edith's. She got in the habit of staying with Edith in her apartment during the week; her mental life was there. On the weekends, she would go over to Kitty's, especially when she started to have dates. She knew Kitty would let her stay out later. On these weekends, she would play with the baby Emily. She came to like her, as long as she did not have to smell her in her worst moments or hear her cry when she was trying to memorize her Latin. Sometimes Jane danced Emily round in her arms while listening to music: Al Martino's "Here in My Heart"; Nat King Cole's "Somewhere Along the Way." Jane and Emily were alone together in the bedroom, Kitty and Ray's bedroom, when Emily opened her arms and stumbled toward Jane: her first step. And Jane liked her little teeth, so fresh and wet with baby spit. What amazing teeth! They were hard and white and grew straight down, with plenty of space between. To this day Emily had incredible teeth, strong and thick, with no cavities. They looked capable of tearing through a telephone book.

When Emily was five, Jane went off to college. On a subsequent visit home, little Emily had curled up in her lap and said, "Oh, Mother, I'm so glad Aunt Jane is home." *"Aunt* Jane? But, darling," said Kitty to the child, "Jane is your sister. Jane is my little girl too." The child had slid from Jane's lap and run weeping from the room.

Now the three of them sat in "Emily's room" discussing aspects of Edith's funeral: the mother and her two daughters. The baby was a married woman, and "Aunt Jane" the single daughter in the single bed.

Jane was propped on foam-rubber pillows. She had taken a hot bath with some of Kitty's aromatic bath salts, and was wearing one of Ray's famous stock of night-shirts. This was an old one, which had been laundered many times, and every so often, as the women talked, Jane would lift the long frayed sleeve to her nose and sniff. She felt agreeably tired, as one is supposed to feel after travel; the familiar "coming home" apathy had descended pleasantly upon her during the bath; she had lost all intellectual desire. She seemed to herself the younger daughter, the one with whom everything is still tentative, still in process. Since her last visit, another landmark had been added to this room. From somewhere, Kitty had dug out the little mobile of multicolored cardboard fish that Jane had once brought Emily as a present, and now it hung from the center of the light fixture on the ceiling. The fish swam slowly round and round in the air, propelled by the gentle tides from the heat register. A certain dark fish bobbed a bit more than the others. Jane remembered her conversation with Sonia Marks about living alone. Why had Kitty hung the fish? Was it one more accumulation toward the shrine she seemed to be making to Emily's foreshortened girlhood (Kitty loved the teen years best in Jane, when she could advise her how to get and keep boys; she had possibly been disappointed that Emily refused from the beginning to play the dating game); or had she hung Jane's old gift high in the center of the room so its moving figures might remind both sisters that they had some shared past, if not much? "I wish my two girls loved each other more," Kitty often said in the presence of both, who would then, of course, answer, "But we do. Don't worry so much about it." Each knowing perfectly well that the only thing they really had in common, which would bring them together for years to come, was their attraction for their mother. Each sister was mistrustful of the other's differences, slightly anxious that Kitty might love the other more.

Even now, each in her own style kept a possessive eye on Kitty. She was there on borrowed time, till Ray came upstairs and took her away. Yes, thought Jane, very much interested in the many invisible configurations of the triangle in this room, in a strange way Kitty has managed to evade both Emily and me, evade all her children; and she has managed to evade Ray, too; in a sense, she has "jilted" Ray for God, for the higher things of the spirit that he cannot ever amass enough money to purchase for her. To whom does Kitty belong? To whom has she ever belonged? "Never let a man be sure of you," Kitty had instructed Jane early in her relations with the opposite sex. "Always let there be a little doubt in his mind; it keeps them coming back." Kitty was the belle of the family, the archetypal belle. Nobody was sure of Kitty. She had made elusiveness, soft gentle evasiveness—of persons and of facts which threatened to come too close—her style. Jane wondered if she flirted with God, too, kept a little doubt in His mind. Jane had bungled Kitty's instructions badly in her very first romance. At fourteen, she had loved a boy. When he began to return her interest, she hinted that there was someone else, as well. There wasn't. He had dropped her for another girl, a steadier girl who did not play such tricks with his heart. "Oh, well," Kitty had consoled her. "If he's going to be so *serious*. I don't understand all this seriousness. You and your classmates go to a dance with one date and spend the whole evening dancing with the same date. I used to feel the dance was a flop if I didn't have a different partner for every dance."

Kitty sat on the edge of Jane's bed, her back very straight. She had better posture than either of her daughters. She wore a floor-length orange silk kimono with a gold dragon guarding her back, and her bare legs were crossed at the knee. She wore white beaded Indian moccasins, which Ray bought for her every summer, as well as several pairs for himself, when they went to Cherokee. Her pale gold hair, which she tinted but denied doing, was loosening in its day-old bun from her most recent shower. Her face, which was naturally pink, was flushed with heat. Ray kept his houses too hot for her taste; he could never get warm enough, but she took frequent showers, sprayed cologne on herself, and insisted that perspiration was what kept her skin so young. From her face and body came the pampered aroma of a variety of excellent products: Dorothy Gray's hormone cream, the same lady's dry-skin lotion for hands and body, Joy bath powder (a present from Jane several Christmases ago), and—probably emanating from the kimono itself—just a suggestion of Tabac Blond, Kitty's latest preference in perfume. Jane could never find Tabac Blond in stores in the Midwest, even the best store in Kitty's town did not carry it, and only Emily could bring it—as only Emily had brought to her mother that one and only unrecorded peek through the eternal keyhole. They sold Tabac Blond in a drugstore in Emily's college town, and she bought it for her mother in two-ounce bottles. From time to time, Kitty surveyed her daughters, the light blue eyes grazing the heads of both, and she had just said, in a vague, soft, satisfied drawl: "How nice having both my little girls home, even if it is for a sad occasion." Her eyes seemed to get lighter, thought Jane: was too much straining at the keyhole burning the former earthly blue—the color of gentians—into the almost colorless celestial of high skies?

Was Kitty happy? Jane tried to remember the last time she had seen her mother lose her temper, shriek, and weep. She did it regularly when Jane was a little girl, in her early widowed days, when she was trying to be a writer of romances and a "father" to Jane, when there was too much on her—no wonder she shrieked, usually at Edith: "You're killing me! You've got to leave me alone! I've got to have some life of my own! You spoil everything for me, everything!" After she married Ray, she still shrieked, wept, but in a different key. There was something in those married rages that expected to be

101

comforted; a bright little spark behind the floods of tears that flickered in and out of Kitty's red, streaming eyes, that announced covertly, femininely, *I am going to win.*

When had Kitty stopped being so emotional? Was it when she began reading Saint John of the Cross and Thomas á Kempis and going to church every morning? The "new" Kitty was so serene, so distant. She read devotional guides and science fiction into the night, she prepared her course in Medieval History for the girls' school, she swam a mile every morning (back and forth across the Health Club pool, seventy-five times, quite leisurely, alternating strokes, losing herself in the other element—whereas Jane or Emily would do three laps and quit from boredom or exertion), and she prayed: she stopped off at Saint Mark's, freshly exercised, smelling faintly of chlorine and Tabac Blond, and hurried eagerly toward a front pew, making a graceful curtsy and an elegantly Roman sign of the cross, and resumed her secret dialogue with God. What did they talk about? Did Kitty ask for things? Or had she gone past that; did she only ask to accept everything? Was she becoming a mystic? Or was her increasing spiritual fervor one of the results (rewards?) of menopause?

Emily was still dressed. She sat on the other twin bed, facing Jane and Kitty, chain-smoking. If she did not start holding her shoulders up, she would have a dowager's hump before she reached thirty ("What the hell do I care if I have a dowager's hump or not?") Of the three women, she was the least likely to be called feminine. Yet there was a female power in her, something much older and stronger than any cultivated practices of the subtle and delicate art of Being a Woman. Jane could imagine Emily as President or Queen in some matriarchal society, where women did all the organizing and governing. Look how she had organized John. Married at fifteen. Law school at eighteen. She also planned to have some babies. One morning, Jane could just see her, probably the morning she had been notified she had passed the bar: Emily would toss her little white heart-shaped compact of birth-control pills into the garbage can, shake John awake, get her baby, and allow him to go back to sleep till noon. Emily was the person in this family whose thoughts Jane had most difficulty imagining. Look at her now, this big girl, hulking over her Pall Mall, nostrils flaring with smoke. She wore her skirts as close to the top of her thighs as John would tolerate—after all, he did have some rights: she saw to that—and her legs fascinated Jane in the same way her teeth did: they were super-strong super-human, capable of feats they would never be called to. Emily's legs could kick her across the Channel, walk her stolidly across the country. But she seldom swam, and then only to follow her mother to the Health Club. She deplored walking. John drove them everywhere. She had not bothered to learn to drive. Her eyes were her best feature. Almond-shaped and blond, they narrowed at you—like a cat's at certain times—the only sign that perhaps you had set the mind behind to work, to smolder, to ponder something. Most of the time they remained open, deceptively bland, yellow. Emily's hair was no longer blond. "Why not put a little rinse on it," Kitty would say. "Lighten it back to where it matches your eyes again. Everyone thought you had such a stunning combination of hair and eyes." "No," said Emily, narrowing her eyes, and that was that.

Jane hoarded three memories—clues, she believed, to her half-sister's personality. The first was of Emily at seven, the second of Emily at twelve, the third of Emily at fourteen.

When Emily was seven, Jane was home on a visit. The family lived in a smaller house then; Ray had not yet become successful. So Jane had taken Emily's little room and Emily had doubled up with her brothers. In the morning she would return to her own room to dress for school. Jane, pretending to be asleep, watched her little sister dress. But it was no ordinary event for the child and soon Jane became dismayed. Emily plodded back and forth from closet to mirror, a little girl seven years old, trying and discarding outfits. She grew more agitated as she continued rejecting skirts and blouses and sweater combinations, after having gazed stolidly at herself in each combination. Nothing seemed to satisfy her, and her unhappiness communicated itself painfully to Jane, who spied from beneath an arm thrown across her forehead. What was going on here? What did Emily see as she gazed—that heavy, impervious little face—at her child's reflection in the mirror? She was only going to school, to a girls' school, the same convent school Jane had gone to. She was only a little girl. Jane had searched through her own memories and remembered. Of course! How cruel little girls could be! And second grade was not too early to start comparing clothes and looks. It was already clear to everyone in the family that Emily was not going to be a beauty. And she was not going to be a belle. Some group of little girls was making Emily miserable. She had a notion to "wake up" and comfort Emily, tell her this, recall her own experiences at that school, joke and tell her how Kim Seagram, that nasty rich child who couldn't read, had once said to her, Jane, *My*, you must enjoy that skirt. You wear it every day." But Emily had worked it out for herself. Jane had watched with awe. At last Emily found a combination that satisfied her: the dullest, to Jane's taste. A brown skirt and a gray sweater. She stood in front of the mirror, wearing these clothes, and then picked up a little rabbit's foot from her dresser and, cocking her head to one side, stroked the rabbit's foot rhythmically against her round cheek, all the time watching herself, unsmiling, in the mirror. Then she uttered a strange sound, a sort of triumphant angry "hmpff!" and picked up her book bag and went out.

This ritual was repeated each morning.

The second memory, clue: Emily now twelve. Jane home on a visit, once more sleeping in Emily's room. A different room, a different house. But Ray still not rich, still not able to build a house big enough for all his family *and* Jane. Kitty had given Emily a diary, plum-colored leather with a gold lock. Lying in Emily's bed one morning, Jane had plucked this diary from Emily's bedside shelf, tried the lock—fully expecting it to be locked—and opened it. There was a single entry, on the first page, and no more. "I am twelve years and I have no secrets worth writing in this diary," it said. "I am now almost 5'9". I will never have a boyfriend. I hate the girls in my class.

I will never flick my fingers helplessly in the air and cry, 'Oh, *you!*' and act like an ass." Ashamed of herself, Jane confessed to Kitty what she had done. Kitty had looked equally ashamed and confessed that she had also read it. "I have been so worried about her," she said. "She never has little friends home to spend the night; she's become so sullen." Jane said, "I wonder why she didn't lock it? It's almost as if she *wanted*—" "I know," said Kitty. "I thought of that, too. But what I'm wondering is if she was bewailing her situation or boasting about it. I know she's tall for her age, but she doesn't seem to mind. But I can't be sure." Jane said, " 'I will never have a boyfriend' sounds bewailing to me." "I'm not altogether sure of that," answered Kitty. "One thing about my children, they have been taught perfect grammer. Emily is perfectly well aware of the difference between 'will' and 'shall.' In fact, that's why I'm worried all the more. Has she determined that she will never have a boyfriend . . . I mean that she shall never?" "I hardly think so," Jane had consoled Kitty.

Emily had never had a boyfriend. Managing to elude the dating game altogether, having never flicked her fingers helplessly in the air and cried 'Oh, *you,*' she had simply metamorphosed from child to bride, disappearing after dinner to the Ping-Pong room with the son of her mother's late friend, and emerging, three years and how many Ping-Pong matches later, with a husband.

Third memory, third clue. Emily fourteen. A perfect summer's day, a Sunday. The family together on the lawn of another new house that Ray built: the best house, the best lawn yet. Ray was coming up in the world. They were all playing croquet. Jane home on a visit, in graduate school now. John, who stayed at Emily's house these days more than he stayed at his own, had brought over his father's English croquet set, and they had dusted the heavy, beautifully colored mallets and balls and set up the wickets. John "refreshed" everyone's memory about the rules. Ray had never played before, and John, who, as a daily visitor to the Sparks household, had already witnessed the father's frightening eruptions of temper, had been very careful not to show in any way that he suspected Ray's childhood world had not included all the leisurely games of his own.

Everyone except Edith, the grandmother, and Ronnie, the younger son, who had recently broken his arm when he fell off his new bicycle, was playing croquet. Edith presided coolly from a lawn chair set up for her beneath a tree. Ronnie followed both teams around, correcting plays and calling everyone stupid. Jane, usually bored by organized games, was enjoying the *idea* of the one in progress. It seemed proper, it was elegant. For once, this family was behaving like a civilized, traditional family, all their uncomfortable oddnesses and asymmetries assimilated into this softly moving, structured game. She participated, but did not particularly care which side won or lost. The women were playing the men: Kitty and Emily and Jane against Ray and John and Jack, the older son. But in spirit Jane was with Edith, under the tree, cool in summer linen and pleased in the reassurance that some things still survived, such as family games on well-kept lawns, with nobody shouting too loudly or knocking anybody down.

Then Ray had become unfashionably involved in the game, as he became involved in his competitive ventures in construction, in the stock market. As his team spirit rose ("Let's show these ladies a thing or two!"), so did his voice, with its twanging mountain dipthongs. Jane's blue ball and Emily's yellow one lay cheek to cheek: the two sisters close, for once. Ray, with a Rebel yell, sent his orange ball thwacking into them, sending Jane's hopelessly far away. Emily's yellow ball shuddered, but remained where it was. Ray strutted over to survey his triumph-in-progress. His face deeply lined and browned from year-round exposure, was as nakedly greedy for winning as a boy's. He bent low and scrutinized the situation. His ball against Emily's, and at a rather tricky angle, near the wicket. If he hit his ball the least bit wrong, he would carry his daughter through the wicket with him. Deftly, looking up at John, who had explained the mallet's-length privilege so recently, Ray separated the balls. His mallet was down and up—quicker than the eye, it seemed.

"Hey, Dad, that's some mallet's length!" mocked Ronnie, with his arm in a sling. "At least two."

"Son, when I need your advice on how to play this game, I'll let you know."

"He's right. That was more than a mallet's length" came Emily's voice, very sternly. "Put it back like it was —right there—and measure again." She stood with her arms crossed, mallet swinging loosely from one clenched hand, as though she might be preparing to knock her father, who still knelt, scoldingly on the head. She wore a pink-and-white striped cotton dress, her church dress. Kitty had not insisted upon her changing it, because she knew Emily would just change back into her jeans.

"I can tell a mallet's length as well as anybody else, I guess," said Ray, looking up with a challenge at Emily from where he knelt. There was a note of wheedling in his voice. He looked up rather guiltily at his big daughter, standing so critically over him.

"Put it back," ordered Emily, curling her mouth into an odd little smile. It was clear that she was enjoying this power over her father.

Ray stood up. He was a wiry, powerfully built man. He and Emily were exactly the same height: five feet ten. All wheedling faded out of him when their gazes locked at eye level. "Emily," he said slowly, in the beginnings of a tone Jane recognized all too well from her adolescent memories, "There is nothing to put back."

"Oh, *really*," said John. He turned his face toward the woods, away from the lawn. He leaned on his croquet mallet and looked purposely away. Every angle in his languid, detached posture proclaimed: It would be beneath *my* family ever to have such a scene in front of an outsider.

"Oh, yes, there is and you know there is! So *put it back!*" Emily shouted. She thrust her face into her father's. Jane, in spite of herself, flinched violently; her face burned. There was a return of the sudden muffled blankness in her right ear.

"Oh, come on, you-all. Let's get on with the game," she said nervously. "What does a mallet's length or more matter? What does it matter?"

Emily turned and gave Jane a look of moral scorn. "It does matter, Jane. It matters very much. I refuse to play until he puts my ball back exactly where it was and measures again."

"It was exactly a mallet's length," spoke up Jack for his father, trying to catch Ray's eye. Jack was uncertain of himself, wanted so much to please, to be securely on somebody's team.

"Oh, *please*, everybody," came Edith's plaintive voice, the voice of respectability, from the shade. "Just when everything was so lovely."

"Isn't it the truth," murmured Kitty, who had been standing quite silently, in a sort of suspension, as if she, by obliterating herself, might also obliterate this unpleasantness erupting on the family lawn. She, too, had her memories of Ray's tempers.

"No, no, no!" shrieked Emily. "Not until he puts my goddamn *ball* back!"

Ray's taut brown arm flashed through the sunlit air. A sharp clean *crack*, and Emily in candy-striped cotton toppled to the grass. Ray had hit her like an equal, like a man.

"Oh, *really!*" cried John. He flung down his mallet and stalked off to his father's Lincoln, parked in the circular drive. He got in, a flash of white trousers and Italian sandals, slammed the door, and turned on the motor. He gunned the powerful engine.

"Oh, now look," moaned Edith from the shade. "John is leaving. Oh, what a shame! Ohhh. Jane. I'm afraid you'd better run into the house and bring me my purse with my smelling salts."

"He's not going anywhere," said Emily, picking herself off the grass. "He's just racing his motor."

Which seemed to be so. John sat in the Lincoln with the windows closed, air conditioning on, gunning the motor, glaring through the windshield murderously at nothing.

Jane, glad to be off on Edith's errand, started toward

the new house. As she walked away, she heard Kitty ask Ray sadly, "Why did you have to go and do that? Why did you have to spoil it?"

"I don't like her filthy language, that's why. I'm sick and tired of all these snobs, who have never known what it is to make an honest living, telling me how I spoil everything!"

"I didn't say . . . Oh, dear . . . I just meant . . ." Kitty began, backing away from the facts, anything to calm Ray.

As Jane entered the house, she heard the great rumble of Ray's truck being backed out of the garage below. It was Sunday, the stock exchange was closed. He needed some reinforcement. He would go and see his mother in town. Mrs. Sparks, who "took in sewing," whose husband had run a tavern during Prohibition in this town. He had been held up by Negroes for the $9.22 in his cash register, knocked over the head by one of them with a lead pipe, and never regained consciousness. For almost two years he lay unconscious in the hospital before he died. The family savings, what little there had been, were wiped out. No wonder Ray hated Negroes and hospitals . . . and people who raced the motors of their father's Lincolns, or sat in the cool of shade trees when turbulence erupted in the sun, calling out, "Oh, *please!* Just when everything was so lovely!"

As Jane returned with Edith's smelling salts, Emily swept out of her room wearing her jeans and hiking shoes. The left side of her cheek, beneath the eye, was beginning to darken and swell. She said to Jane, "None of you are any damn good."

Out on the lawn, the two young boys had started another game of croquet, Ronnie improvising the rules for his "handicap." They played self-consciously, with the chastened glee of siblings who have been spared.

"Emily, please. Ray didn't mean it," said Kitty, who was standing beside Edith. The color had gone out of her handsome face and she looked haggard.

"Like hell he didn't mean it, that bastard," said Emily. With several giant steps, she crossed the lawn and began ascending the deep slope into the woods.

"Where are you going?" cried Edith.

"None of your business, you old witch."

"Ohhh," moaned Edith. "Jane, quick, did you bring my salts?"

"Please, Emily, don't go off in the woods again," called Kitty to the big girl crashing angrily out of sight. "John, John!"

John was getting out of the Lincoln uncertainly. So he had been watching the progress of things out of the side of his eye.

"John, please go after Emily," said Kitty. "When Ray is here, he always goes after her, but he's gone into town at the moment. I'm afraid she'll get bitten by a copperhead, or something."

John looked up the slope at his retreating giantess. There was awe and hesitation in his long-lashed dark eyes. He looked down at his slender pale feet in their Italian sandals.

"Oh, dear, you don't have any shoes," said Kitty, understanding at once. "What size do you take? Maybe you can fit into Ray's. Come on, I'll go with you and show you where they are. I really don't want Emily to run off again."

"Once she got all the way to the Blue Ridge Parkway," put in Ronnie. Both boys had ceased their game for this greater entertainment.

John and Kitty went toward the house. Jane sat down in the grass beside Edith, who had her little green bottle out and was wafting it back and forth beneath her nostrils, her eyes closed. A whiff of old-fashioned self-indulgence floated agreeably past Jane's nostrils. "I really can't take this sort of thing," said Edith. "With my high blood pressure. Oh, what a shame, what a shame."

"Well, at least he didn't burst her eardrum," said Jane. "He's getting older. He's losing his touch."

"I regretted for years that I didn't take him to court for that," said Edith. "But how could I? My own daughter was married to him. She would have been so disgraced. Oh, it killed me. Bursting a child's eardrum in anger."

"I wasn't exactly a child. I was old enough to vote,"

admitted Jane. They were both silent, remembering the crisis: Jane, home on a visit from college, filled with fervor about civil rights from a popular Political Science professor. She and Ray had fought viciously. His arguments, summoned more frequently, had threatened to win. As a last resort, she had called him ignorant. *Whap, Whap.* "Cracked right down the middle, like a leaf," the ear doctor had said. In the end, Jane had won. Ray was scared of his own furies. The ear had healed perfectly. He never hit her again.

Edith continued to take deep, languorous whiffs from her little green bottle. That little green bottle: Jane could not remember a time before its existence. It was one of her first memories. When it came out, everybody had to quiet down.

Edith opened her eyes and surveyed her long, beautiful legs in their nylon stockings, stretched gracefully down the length of the lawn chair. She spoke at last: "Again and again, it comes down to the same thing. Some people know how to act and others don't. It's not a thing that can be learned, really. People who have been deprived early in life can never get over the feeling of being slighted. They may learn to hide it, but when things get rough it erupts. It always does erupt, somehow. I remember after Elise Swan got the Dad to marry her, she tried to put on airs, act like she had come from family. But she just didn't have the *foundation* for it, and the moment there was any worry about money, she got all greedy and her manners went out the window. I really do think that's why she had all those children. She was so afraid the Dad might leave me and Izaak all his money, his real children. Well, she got her way. I hope she has been happy with all her money. She hasn't, you know. The one thing I do regret is that I didn't get my rightful share so I could have saved you from so much worry. If I had had money, I would have kept you and given you a début and you would not have had to study and worry about making your own way. I'm glad I was able to give you your trip to Europe. Maybe it would have been better if you had married that nice young Englishman, even though you would have been so far away. Oh, I do hope

John catches up with Emily and marries her. He's a nice boy with manners. I knew his grandmother, a real lady. His mother, too. Children should grow up with their fathers and mothers with them. Their real fathers and mothers. It's only right. . . ."

The boys had resumed knocking the croquet balls, arguing softly as they played at playing. Jane could smell Edith's chaste perfume, Fleurs de Rocaille, emanating from behind her long, fleshy earlobe, mixing with the smelling salts. The smells soothed and comforted her.

"I don't think I really loved him enough to marry him," she said.

"Oh, love," said Edith disdainfully. "Love is not everything in a marriage. Your mother was always one for love, and look . . . look!" She waved her left hand, with its diamond, its wedding ring, and the hated brown age spots, at the lawn of such recent violence.

John emerged from the house, looking incongruous in his white trousers and Ray's paratrooper boots. Instructed about a certain cut-off path by Kitty, he started up the mountain.

"Well," said Edith, following his unsteady progress with her hooded blue eyes for a moment, "he's not exactly a mountain goat, but he's a nice boy, from a nice family, and I do think he is helpless without Emily. It's nice that he's so much taller than she is, isn't it? Hans was shorter than I was, but I was unusually tall for a woman. Women weren't as a rule so tall as they are now; everyone eats better now, I suppose, or the race is growing or something. But Hans was a good man and he took good care of me." She opened her purse. Out came the white monogrammed handkerchief. Jane knew the handkerchiefs, too. She rested her head against her grandmother's chair and closed her eyes and smelled the familiar mixture of ammonia and spring flowers, while Edith sniffed discreetly—not loud enough to disturb her grandsons' play —in memory of her husband. She had been trying on hats in a millinery shop when he died: a heart attack at his desk, at the railroad. She still bought an occasional hat, to pay homage to the resurrection of Christ at Easter, and sometimes to a drastic change in style, but the love of hats had gone out of her, she said.

Then suddenly, in the midst of her sniffing, she said solemnly: "Though, just between the two of us, now that you *have* decided to finish up your Ph.D., I think, on the whole, it is better that *you* do not marry. Some people aren't made for the married state. And I know what I'm talking about."

Now Kitty was explaining how Edith's funeral would be a tasteful Requiem Mass, lasting exactly twelve minutes, according to Father Barnabas, and not an "ordinary funeral." "There will be no singing hymns and no testimonials and no nosy relatives filing past to gape at the body. Jack and Ronnie will serve as acolytes and the family will take Communion. Then we drive to the cemetery and that's that."

"Will the coffin be closed, then?" asked Jane.

"It will enter and leave the church beneath the pall," said Kitty. "That's what Edith wanted. She said she didn't want everybody peering down at her and thinking how much she'd aged. I told Mr. Plemmons to keep it closed at the funeral home, as well. So they won't be able to go there and gape, either. If you want to see her, Jane, or you, Emily, we'll have him open it before the funeral tomorrow morning. I won't, of course. I want to remember her as she was. And I think it's somehow indelicate to stare at . . . It's somehow uncourteous. If I were asleep, I wouldn't like to think anyone was standing over me, watching me sleep. But you girls must make your own decision."

"How about it, Pain?" asked Emily, taking a drag on her Pall Mall. A saucer from the kitchen lay beside her; Ray disapproved of smoking and allowed no ashtrays in the house. Emily's saucer had—Jane counted them—seven cigarette butts in it, and Emily had been in the room less than an hour. "Are you going to look?"

"I haven't decided yet," replied Jane. "I want to sleep on it—if I ever can get to sleep. Kitty, can't you suggest any remedy for my insomnia?" What she hoped was that

113

they would stay here in this room, talking, until she felt herself slowly drift off, as she had drifted off in the old days, to the comforting sound of Kitty and Edith talking about how they could make ends meet. She had a very definite intention of seeing Edith one more time, uncourteous or not. Again, that was Kitty's way: evading and avoiding. Jane felt sure Edith would want to be looked at by her; the two of them had always understood each other. She was sure Edith had fantasized the scene for years: herself dead and laid out in dignity, and Jane looking down at her for the last time, thinking of all her grandmother had meant to her.

"You shouldn't try so hard," said Kitty. "Say to yourself: 'What's so wonderful about sleep?' Read. Read that book you brought."

The Odd Women," said Emily dryly. "What is it about lesbians?"

"No, about women who aren't married. 'Odd' in this book means 'not making a pair.' "

"Oh," said Emily. "Do you consider yourself odd, then?"

"In terms of the definition on which this book operates, I guess I do. Why are you looking at me that way, Emily? Do you think I'm odd in other ways, as well?" For her sister was giving her a curious knowing little smile, narrowing her yellow eyes.

"I don't think anything," said Emily, maddeningly noncommittal. "I was just trying to make conversation about your book."

"I do read," Jane said to Kitty. "But don't you find that a time comes when you feel stubborn, when you say to yourself, 'Damn it, I don't want to read; I want to sleep, and if I can't sleep, I don't want to do anything'?"

"So don't do anything. Abandon yourself. Learn to abandon yourself. There's a wonderful quote, in the section on Spiritual Combat in *The Cloud of Unknowing.* Let me see if I can quote it: 'When you feel that you are completely powerless to put these thoughts away'—and he's speaking of thoughts you don't want to have; I think it can apply to insomniac thoughts, too—'cower down before them like some cringing captive overcome in battle,

114

and reckon it is ridiculous to fight them any longer. This humility causes God himself to come down in his might and avenge you of your enemies and take you up and fondly dry your spiritual eyes, just as—just as—' Something about a father rescuing his child from the jaws of mad biting bears."

"Mad biting bears," said Emily, stumping out her cigarette and reaching for her pack. "I like that. I wonder why I don't have insomnia. I'm jealous. I could use the time to memorize my briefs."

"It just doesn't work that way," Jane told her.

"Oh, yes, it would. I'd make it." Emily lit a new cigarette. Jane wondered if she was right. If someone could look into that determined little mind, what would they see: basic order, solid inner principles, a precocious maturity arrived at without the intervening stages of confused adolescence? Or some soft dangerous fear parading itself as self-discipline and determination?

Then they heard Ray coming upstairs, his Indian moccasins scuffling territorially along his hardwood floors. *Shuffle, shuffle,* down the hall. The house trembled slightly: he walked on his heels. He opened the door to Emily's room without knocking, poked his head in. "Are you three biddies going to talk all night? We've got a funeral to get through tomorrow."

As if she had received a summons from her Mother Superior, Kitty rose at once. Her interest in her daughters went out of her face and was replaced by a guilty, sorrowful look. Edith, after all, was dead. She said, "Good night, my two little girls. We should all go to bed soon, I guess. If anyone wants to go down to Plemmons's tomorrow morning, let me know." She scuffled from the room in her own moccasins, followed by Ray. Husband and wife went down the hall. The door of their room was closed.

Emily and Jane exchanged a look. Their closest moments, few and far between, included their mutual disparagement of Ray: that creature who took away their mother.

Emily sat smoking. Her yellow eyes gazed calmly at nothing.

"How is law school?" asked Jane, wanting to start an

interesting conversation in which Emily, at last, would reveal herself.

"Okay, I guess." Emily smoked on, looking briefly at Jane, then back at nothing.

Do you and John enjoy sex? How many ways do you do it? Do you ever regret not having a normal girlhood, dates, waiting in agony for the telephone to ring and for it to be a certain boy? Do you ever doubt yourself, wish you were prettier, wonder what I'm thinking about you?

"Are you passing everything as you had hoped?"

Emily shrugged. "I need to get a B in Torts. The rest is okay, I guess."

Jane was considering asking Emily if she ever read any fiction, as a way to inaugurate a confidence. From that they could move on to tastes, likes and dislikes, and who Emily's favorite characters were and why, and perhaps get somewhere. She was in the act of phrasing her opener ("Do you ever get a chance to read a novel these days?"), when Emily took a deep puff, narrowed her eyes at the stub of cigarette left, snuffed it out, and reached in her pack for another. It was empty.

"Shit," she said. "John better have brought that carton I told him to." She stood up, making no attempt to smooth her short skirt, which had wrinkled up to the line of her panties. She still wore cotton Lollipops, white and to the waist, very unbridal. Giving her "room" a rather scornful look, she said absently, "Well, good night, Calamity Jane; let me know whether you decide to look at her or not. Wake me if you do. I'll go along, too."

She went out of the room, downstairs to the guest room where she slept with John.

Jane lay for a while, pulling the covers up to her chin for comfort, even though they made her too warm. She stared at the cardboard fish making their circular pilgrimage round and round the ceiling, prodded by the air from the register. Ray kept his houses too hot. She cranked open the jalousie window beside the bed. Clean mountain air and night sounds came in. One of Ray's German shepherds was barking softly, a conversational sort of bark. From across the ridge, a hound belonging to

Mr. Creech replied. Mr. Creech was a hillbilly whom Ray hated. He lived with two women, numberless children, and his hounds in an eyesore of a shack, in plain view of Ray's new $85,000 home once the leaves were off the trees. He persecuted Ray. Ever since Ray had accidentally cut off Creech's water supply when he was putting in his own pump, Creech had devised subtle, uncivilized ways to haunt him. He would steal mail from Ray's box and keep it for a while, then put it back. Ray had complained to the post office, but they said they needed more proof. Sometimes Creech would telephone Ray late at night and breathe into the phone. Or he would send his dirty little children in delegations on scouting trips around the edge of Ray's property. They would stand just outside the electric fence, impervious to the dogs' furious barking, and gaze hollow-eyed at Ray's swimming pool. "What do you expect from such common trash?" Ray would say. "Shooting's not good enough for him!"

In 1948, Kitty was teaching English Literature at the local college. She had forty-one men in her Romantic Poetry section, all ex-G.I.s. She stood in front of her desk, wearing her dead husband's Navy wings pinned on the breast of her blouse, and read the poetry aloud to them in her soft Southern voice. She read "La Belle Dame sans Merci" and Ray Sparks understood that his Belle Dame stood before him, and he wrote at the end of his first exam that he would have her at any cost. In the spring of '48, in the lengthening light of evening, Edith suddenly became a compulsive walker. Kitty stayed out more and more in the evenings, announcing she had to go to her office at the college and grade papers. "Get your sweater on," Edith would say to Jane. "Hurry up. We're going for a walk." Up and down the streets they would go, covering blocks, Edith clenching Jane's hand tightly in her own, even though Jane was almost nine. Edith walked fast and straight, not talking, her long, thin nose pointed ahead suspiciously, sniffing something out, some rotten thing, as she often sniffed milk or meat to see if it had gone bad. She led Jane round the slowly darkening streets of quiet neighborhoods till she found what she was looking for. She always managed to come up on it from be-

117

hind: a 1947 Chevy coupe, usually parked under some trees, away from the streetlights, with two people in it. Once having spotted it, she recoiled dramatically, as though it might contaminate both of them. "That's enough. Come on, we'll go home and I'll make you some cocoa." Later, when Jane was supposed to be asleep, she would hear the two women arguing fiercely, trying to keep their voices low. "But how could you? He's twelve years younger. His people are ordinary." "But I love him." "Oh, you love him. You loved everybody. If we got all the people you loved together, we'd have to build a barracks for them to live in." "You're not going to spoil this, whatever you say. I say I love him." "And I say it's just sex."

Jane got up. She wandered round Emily's room. She sat down at the peculiar little mirror. In it, she saw a reflection of Emily's saucer of cigarette butts. There was no wastebasket, so she moved the saucer to the high chest of drawers and laid a Kleenex over it. *"When you are completely powerless to put these thoughts away, cower down before them like some cringing captive . . ."*

She continued reading for a while in *The Odd Women*. And found that, over the years, her reader's response had not changed. She still rooted for the two women for whom some chance of love was still possible. The other three she grew impatient with out of despair (as she had despaired of her student Portia): what hope for Monica's two older sisters, eating their meal of rice at a table measuring three by one and a half feet in Lavender Hill; the hair of one falling out, the other becoming an alcoholic? She did not wish to dwell with them longer than absolutely necessary as she herself lay in her young married sister's cast-off room, every other woman in this house warming herself against a man. When Monica Madden, who was still young and pretty, met the older Widdowson, a bachelor with money, in Battersea Park, Jane thought furtively, as she had thought the last time she read this novel: Oh, go ahead and marry him. Why not? Maybe in this reading it will come out better. Perhaps he will have learned his lesson and won't hound you literally

118

to your death with his jealousy. And you will have learned to be more discreet, to value a good home. Likewise, Jane counseled Rhoda Nunn, the young spinster career woman with whom she most identified: Stop playing this feminist power game with Everard Barfoot. You've proved your admirable point—that in the nineteenth century you are able to forgo the legal form of marriage to preserve your independence. And he has proved he loves you enough to give up his prized bachelorhood and marry you. Why not get married and do more interesting things than destroy your love with ideologies? Nevertheless, Jane found herself circling Rhoda's angry outcry:

. . . Love—love—love—a sickening sameness of vulgarity. What is more vulgar than the ideal of novelists? They won't represent the actual world. . . . In real life how many men and women *fall in love? . . .* Not one married pair in ten thousand have felt for each other as two or three couples do in every novel.

Was Rhoda right? Was "love—love—love" never to be found outside the ideals of novelists? But she remembered Sonia Marks saying, "Most women can identify with heroines who can learn to live without marriage; but not so many want to live without love of any kind."

Well, who the hell—if they were honest—did?

One of the dogs below bayed a mournful agreement. Mountain air chilled the room. Angry feet thumped across a floor and Ray's voice twanged through a swiftly uncranked window: "Rommel, goddamnit if you don't put a lid on that big mouth of yours right this second, I'm going to come down there and knock every one of your teeth out!" The window cranked shut. Rommel was silenced. The feet thumped more slowly back across the floor. Satisfied. The Master of the house and the hill. Jane began to shiver, but decided not to close the window. It pleased her, this small act of aggression. Ray would be furious if he knew someone had a window open in January, running up the heat bill.

She got up and searched the room for a blanket. Nothing in the drawers. Then she went to the closet. She pulled back the eggshell-colored slatted doors and turned on the light and was stunned.

She saw Edith standing there in her coat. For just a moment. As if she had been quietly waiting for Jane all this time, waiting for the rest of them to go to bed.

It was Edith's coat, her beige coat. They must have hung it here after they brought her things from the hospital. It still held Edith's shape. The collar still smelled of Fleurs de Rocaille. Tears ran from Jane's eyes. Her heart was beating from fright as she wept quietly, enjoying it a little. She turned off the closet light and stood in the closet, embracing the coat. She closed her eyes and breathed the perfume and tried to imagine what Edith would be saying to her now. She spoke in whispers to Edith and then tried to "hear" the answer.

"What did you mean, that day of the croquet disaster, when you said I should never marry and you knew what you were talking about?"

You're just not suited for the married state.

"Why not? Tell me, why not? You've got to; you knew me better than anyone. If you are somewhere around in the firmament, between death and burial, perhaps you can still reach me. I'll help you. Try. Please try."

You are like me. There's a limit to the things you can take. Besides, nothing in this world is certain. Nothing. Just when you feel everything in your life is settled and secure, someone like Elise Swan drives up in a carriage. I was in a store trying on a blue hat when they called me to the phone and told me to come to the railroad yard, and when I got there Hans was gone.

Did she really hear these things, was Edith really communicating to her, or was she making it up herself, patching together often-repeated phrases of Edith's which floated on the surface of her memory? Nevertheless, she felt Edith had sent her a message—a rather comfortless one, but a message all the same. Marriage was difficult and so was life. One was as bad as the other in that they were both booby-trapped with uncertainties. She hated uncertainties. Therefore, she was ill equipped for mar-

120

riage. Did that mean she was also ill equipped for life? And, if so, what did she do about that?

She realized that she was not making sense; her mind was taking shortcuts detrimental to sense. Besides, she was freezing. She took the beige coat from its wooden hanger and carried it to bed and covered herself. She tried turning out the lamp, but within seconds had turned it on again. Her imagination was too worked up to be comfortable in darkness, even in a houseful of family.

"When you feel that you are completely powerless to put these thoughts away, cower down before them like some cringing captive overcome in battle . . ."

In the summer of '48, Kitty married Ray. "Over my dead body!" screamed Edith when the new bride made the announcement, and lived on to witness the duration of this marriage for almost a quarter of a century. In the summer of '48, Gabriel Weeks married Ann somebody, who had now borne her married name for more years then she ever bore her own.

"Nineteen forty-eight was certainly not my year," Jane had once told Gabriel on a stolen weekend. How he had laughed. Then they had both laughed together, there in the motel room.

VI

Not one of Ray's dogs had ever made it all the way through obedience school, but he had found ways to channel their abundant energies and curiosities and send his own spirit abroad in them, in certain antics that passed for "tricks."

Kitty had tried to teach him—gently, through years of silent, reproachful looks—that it was rude to burst into rooms without knocking, especially in the morning, even if you had laid the foundations for these rooms and painted the walls and hung the doors.

At 7 A.M. on the morning of Edith's funeral, the door leading up from the basement was flung open and a herd of panting black German shepherds streamed through the house, grunting and slavering with excitement, sniffing and clicking their nails against closed doors, pawing and whining good-naturedly until their mother, the biggest dog of all, named Fritzi, stood up on her hind legs and neatly turned the knob of each sleeper's door with her muddy front paws. The young dogs, weighing from seventy to ninety pounds, burst into the rooms and greeted the members of the family with saliva, teeth, and mud. There were screams of angry delight from the rooms of Ronnie and Jack. Bismarck got to Jane first and put his paw in her eye, while Rommel skidded on *The Odd Women* and thumped his head against the bed. He turned and ran out of the room, slightly dazed.

"Fuck! Shit! Goddamn it to hell, that's so goddamn

funny!" Jane's first words on the day of Edith's funeral.

She heard Ray chuckling softly from the hallway.

"One day I hope these werewolves turn on you and tear you to pieces," she screamed, but her voice came out a mild croak. She stormed off to the nearest bathroom. Vixen, the prettiest dog, with the best markings, which Ray had once planned to sell for more than any of the other dogs from that litter, was lapping water from the toilet.

"Shit! Ugh! Oh, Christ!"

"Darling, watch your language," called Kitty's sleepy voice. "Ouch! Stop it, Rommel. Oh, you devil. Where's my little girl?"

"In here drinking toilet water."

"Send her to me." Jane gave Vixen a shove with her foot and closed the door and locked it. Kitty had made Ray keep Vixen; she was too pretty to sell, she said. Ray allowed Kitty her extravagances in return for her freedom. He built her a swimming pool and gave her French perfumes and a cleaning lady, but he did not like her to go off that mountain without him. He slightly resented her relationship with God because of the frequent trysts it required at the church in town. He knew exactly what time her classes were over at the girls' school, and if she had not returned within the time he thought adequate to drive safely home, he called the school and asked what time she had left. He and Edith were always checking on Kitty. ("Is she there with you, Edith?" "She just left, about seven minutes ago, so she should be coming up your driveway any minute." It was one of their few close times, when mother-in-law and husband combined to chart, jealously, Kitty's progress between their doors through the precarious free world.

Jane crouched on the toilet—Ray's modern toilet—and buried her head in her hands. A wave of faintness passed over her. She had not slept until five, having spent the night hours teasing herself with morbid reminders of Edith's new nonexistence, dredging up good memories so she could cry over them, reading *The Odd Women* in

123

patches, and creating disagreeable futures for herself. She had always had a talent for imagining the worst— inherited from Edith, everyone said—and her insomnia had proved an able companion, even a Muse, in assisting her imagination as it constructed grim dramas of possible futures. Starting with the basic ingredients of loneliness, poverty, ill health, and age, the two of them could spin endless stories through the night hours about future Janes until the present one fell asleep, exhausted, at dawn.

Jane continued to sit, drained of night fears but with no interest in beginning the day, critically studying Ray's newest bathroom fixtures. Everything was expensive, sanitary, always the latest. When Jane "came home" to a new house built by Ray, one of the family had to show her how to operate the water taps. With each house, they became fancier and more mysterious. The taps in this bathroom were only two: one above the blue washbasin sunk in tile, one above the tub. You pulled a large stainless-steel knob toward yourself and turned it to the right or left to adjust the temperature. The more pressure you wanted, the farther out you pulled it, until, at last, a fine spray that would hardly wet anything gushed out with the sound of a waterfall.

Inside the spacious floor-to-ceiling wall cabinets were stacked dozens of bath towels, bought by Ray any time he happened to be passing a white sale. He could not resist "stocking up" on things. He brought everything home in bulk as though preparing for a great siege, a long period of deprivation: ordinary loaves of bread, which he froze, a dozen at a time, in the big freezer in the basement, along with identically wrapped packages of hamburger meat; sheets, shirts, nightshirts, towels; and candy. He was always bringing home large grocery bags full of economy-sized packages of Milky Ways, malted-milk balls, M & Ms. "You don't know what it's like not being able to have candy when you want it as a child," he told his children, who scorned candy. At forty-seven, all his bad teeth had been capped and he ate as much as he pleased; he walked around his new houses popping M & Ms in his mouth. He took long, scalding baths in his modern tubs (never washing the tub out afterward) and never dried more than once with a towel.

The seat of Jane's present morning meditation was the latest of its kind. It had no visible tank or base, this discreetly curved slab of blue porcelain that jutted out from the patterned tiles rather like a garden seat. A slight pressure on a small enamel button concealed cleverly in the tiles would send a gentle, half-minute murmur of water rushing beneath you.

"Less than a hundred years ago," Jane heard her own voice, pitched low with a singsong skepticism, as she addressed her class, "people in London lived above their own cesspools, giving their elegant tea parties above their own stinking fumes. A simple division, it was: the perfumes of civilization upstairs; the unmentionable odors below. Things are no longer so easily separated, in life or in literature; in the moral decisions characters must make, whether they are 'real' or 'fictitious,' people—"

"Hey! Who-all is in there?" Her younger brother Ronnie, outside the door.

"Me."

"Who were you talking to, then?"

"My class."

"You nut. How about getting out so I can come in and use my hot comb?"

"Why do you need your hot comb at this time of morning? The funeral's not till this afternoon."

"Because. I'm going down to that place and look at her with you. Mom said I could. Emily's decided she doesn't want to. She's going to sleep late."

"Who said I had decided to look at Edith?"

"Oh, we all knew you would."

"Well, look. Will you kindly let me finish in here in peace?"

"Sure. But hurry up."

Soliloquy ruined, Jane reached angrily for the handle —where the handle usually was on a toilet tank—looking forward to a noisy flush. But was forced to make do with the half-minute murmur, like a faraway brook, from the discreet enamel button. She went to the pale blue sink

125

and wrenched the modern knob out as far as it would go; an explosion of spray appeased her somewhat. "I could never have a family of my own," she said. "I would kill them all before breakfast. . . ." But nevertheless she had to admit that her classroom, real or imagined, had little need of one more fashionable put-down of the status quo, however beautifully she might have worked out all the plumbing metaphors if her youngest brother had not needed his hot comb. Being an articulate denigrator, instructing in a cynical singsong, was easy. Students would be afraid to call you a fool. The risk was to be a visionary and utter phrases of unfashionable hope. Patterns of alienation, despair, disgust, denial, disintegration, and derangement lay on her desk at school as thick and plentiful as Ray's sale towels: anthologies that poured in by the dozen, gifts from publishers concerned with being relevant. No, what was needed were a few more lonely patterns of desire.

She put on her dressing gown and went to the kitchen. Ray sat by himself at the round formica table, stirring his muddy cup of instant coffee, his small dark eyes focused raptly on the morning paper. "Good morning," he said innocently, as if the incident of the dogs had happened in another house—a house like Mr. Creech's, perhaps.

"Good morning," said Jane warily. She began the series of movements necessary to secure for herself a barely drinkable cup of coffee and get several sips inside her before making conversation with her stepfather. She turned the front burner back to "high" and filled the kettle with more water. She opened the cabinet where the jars of coffee and Pream were kept. Both jars were on the extreme top shelf, out of reach. Quietly she transported a chair across the length of kitchen, stood on it, and took down the economy-sized jar of freeze-dried coffee, the economy-sized jar of Pream. She unscrewed each. Both jars were still sealed. She got down from the chair, took a fruit knife from a drawer, and neatly slit the seals on both jars.

"If you'd learn to use your eyes," drawled Ray, not looking up from his paper, "you'd finish up what's

126

opened before wasting the new." Round and round went his spoon placidly in his muddy cup. He hunched over the cup and took a long, loud, satisfied slurp.

"Where? There's no coffee or Pream opened. I looked." Her heart started beating faster with outrage. Was it to begin the first morning?

"Look on the bottom shelf. Use your eyes a little."

Jane looked on the bottom shelf and saw a tin of baking powder, bags of flour and sugar, some spices she had once given Kitty which had never been used, and two peanut-butter jars, which she now saw, were filled with freeze-dried coffee and Pream. They looked neither fresh nor appetizing in the substitute jars.

"Oh, well," she said, and began spooning from the newly opened jar of coffee.

"Put it back," said Ray. "Use the other up first. It's perfectly good."

Jane put her fists side by side on the kitchen counter. She bowed her head and closed her eyes. Inside her head seemed to be the sound of rushing water. Ronnie's hot comb began whining from the bathroom. She carefully replaced the new jars on the top shelf, turned off the front burner, replaced the chair, and went swiftly down the hall, her face stiff with fury. Kitty was coming sleepily up the hall toward the kitchen, tying her kimono around her.

"Oh, dear, what happened?" she asked in a resigned voice which indicated she already knew between *whom* it had happened.

"I'm sick to my stomach!" hissed Jane, sending a meaningful glance to her mother, then tossing her head toward the kitchen. She slammed Emily's door behind her. The cardboard fish, stimulated by the sudden burst of air, swam madly for their lives round the ceiling. She threw herself down on the bed. "Mean, rotten son of a bitch," she muttered into her pillow. Yet she knew Kitty would bring her tea and manage to pacify Ray at the same time. Jane and Emily teased Kitty; they called her "the tightrope walker." But it was not easy being a tightrope walker in this circus.

She heard Kitty's low voice in the kitchen. Guiltily she strained her ears to hear better.

"Poor Jane. She's a little sick at her stomach this morning. Did anything happen?"

"Aw, you know old-maid crosspatch in the morning. She'll never change. I just told her to use up the old coffee before starting on the new."

"She seems queasy this morning," said Kitty. "I don't see how you two manage to drink that terrible freeze-dried stuff even on your best of days." Jane heard the click, click, click as Kitty turned the burner back to "high" to put the kettle on for tea. Awesome diplomacy! It had taken Kitty many years of trial and error to accomplish this art; perhaps it had cost her the loss of other arts, but in two sentences look what she had accomplished:

1. Sympathy and humorous admiration for Ray, drinking that terrible coffee.
2. Allying of Ray and Jane—"I don't see how *you two* manage . . ."
3. Vague allusion to Jane not feeling well, thus clearing the way for Mother to bring her cup of tea without infuriating Ray.

The telephone rang and Ray answered. It is somebody from our side of the family, thought Jane, noting the uncomfortable mixture of familiarity and respect in Ray's tone. Then Ronnie, in the bathroom across the hall, turned on his hot comb again and drowned out the rest of the conversation.

I would rather die an old maid in my own private space, opening as many new cans of good coffee as I please, being as undiplomatic as I like to the morning shadows in my house, than live a "protected" life under such domination, such chaos.

Presently Kitty came with the tea, knocking first. Everything was arranged nicely on a little enamel tray. The teapot, two paper-thin cups and saucers with Oriental designs, and Jane's favorite pastry, called a "bear claw," rolled in a blue linen napkin to keep it warm.

128

"I'm a turd," said Jane, trying to suppress the look of pleasure at the nice tray.

"Where did my little girls learn such language?" said Kitty, shaking her head. But she, too, was trying to suppress a smile. Both of them were pleased to have found an excuse to shut themselves off alone for tea. Jane itched to reply "From your husband," but did not want to spoil the closeness.

"I love this smoky tea," she murmured, sitting up in bed and taking her cup. "Who was that on the phone?"

"Frances. She and Monroe just got in. They're resting up at the Howard Johnson's; then they'll meet us at the funeral home."

"Dear Frances," sighed Jane, and rolled her eyes.

"Dear Frances," repeated Kitty, and did exactly the same. She looked animated for the first time since Jane had arrived home. Then the two women laughed.

Frances, in her sixties, was Cleva's child, the illegitimate daughter of Edith's ill-fated sister who had lost her head one evening at a play and run away with the villain in it, that famous traveling melodrama passing through this mountain town in the early winter of 1905. In the late summer of 1906, Hans Barnstorff, newly married to Edith, took the night train to New York. Two days later, he returned carrying a tiny baby girl in his arms. Hans's sister Crista, childless herself and well married to a Birmingham grocer, was there to meet the train and take this baby as her own. Edith was at home, in a state of shock. Cleva's coffin had come back on the same train. In the years to come, if anyone dared to ask questions about her sister, Edith would threaten to faint, and that was that.

Frances had grown up into a model of normality, gentility, and conventionality. Her vocation became respectability and her deadly enemy had been, since she was a small child, any thought, word, or activity that stank of recklessness.

Kitty told Jane how Aunt Crista would bring little Frances up on the train every summer, "and Edith would force me to play with her. She always wore white dresses, white shoes, white socks—white everything.

Once I pushed her in the mud. I don't know what came over me. I was a model child myself."

Jane had known Frances only after she had grown up and married Monroe, a prosperous gentleman farmer who raised Tennessee Walkers. For as long as she could remember, Jane was hearing of Frances's main project: having the family history researched so that she could get into the D.A.R. and the U.D.C. Kitty told another story which always made Jane laugh—how, one day, during the time when Frances was trying to get into the D.A.R., someone from the organization had telephoned Kitty, asking her to corroborate Frances's story that a member of the family had fought in the Revolution. "Oh, yes, that would be on my daddy's side," said Kitty. "I believe our ancestor was a Prussian mercenary hired by the British. It doesn't matter which side of the *war,* does it?" Of course Jane knew Kitty had not said that, but Kitty wished she could have said it, and therefore told the story that way. Besides, Frances got in, regardless of who had said what or who had fought on what side. It would be just like our family, thought Jane, to have one on each side, fighting the other. It would be even more like our family to *create* one on each side fighting the other. Nevertheless, some token of an ancestor must have left his record at a camp along the Potomac. Did not Frances have the framed proof in her living room?

"Is Monroe going to be a pallbearer?" she asked Kitty.

"That's the trouble. I don't think Frances is going to let him. Ray forgot to ask him officially when he called yesterday, and so Monroe has only brought his sports jacket. It's a dark sports jacket, but you know Frances."

"She probably made him bring the sports jacket in order to punish us for not doing things according to protocol," said Jane. "So that leaves us one short. John, Cousin Jake, Maud and Iz's grandson, and who else?"

"Well, Ray is calling that attractive young Parker. He says he has a very nice black suit, just for funerals."

"Parker! You mean that sexy-looking construction worker on Ray's crew? A pallbearer? For Edith?"

"You wait," said Kitty. "Parker will look more respec-

130

table than any of us, in his black suit especially for funerals."

"That's true," mused Jane, who was rather fascinated by the idea. "Hired mourners and mercenaries," she added.

Kitty smiled and poured them more tea. Her eyes seemed to be turning blue again, the old human blue. "Want to hear another funny story?" she asked.

"Let's have it. Oh, I love you, Kitty." Jane leaned forward, holding her teacup to one side, and kissed her mother.

"I love you, too. This is about Beatrice. You know, Edith's half-sister, one of the steps, Elise Swan's daughter." And Kitty embarked on the story, but Jane saw that her mind was still on the kiss, her face glowing from it. Oh, it takes so little to make another person happy, she thought, and felt ashamed of her detached assessment of this relationship at the airport yesterday.

"She's really very pitiful, Beatrice; she hasn't had an easy life. And Edith was always good to her; she always talked to her when she called up drunk and wanted to cry. So when Beatrice called yesterday and said she would like so much to fix Edith's hair and do her face, I said yes. She said fixing hair was one thing she could do —you know she worked in that beauty shop for years— so I called John Plemmons and told him to let her in. She apparently went to great trouble over it, because she's called twice since to tell me how beautiful it looks. She woke up John Plemmons last night to let her back in because she had put too much lipstick on Edith and couldn't sleep because she remembered Edith never wore that much. She called me again this morning to tell me she thought Edith looked beautiful now. She kept saying, 'I was always more of a Dewar. I was never really a Swan.'"

"Oh, poor thing. Why does everyone want to be a Dewar?" Jane knew; she counted herself lucky to have got the Dewar nose, but she liked to be told again.

"So they can have a long nose, and thin, pure blood that never mixed with anything common, and worry about money all the time." Over the last two hundred years, the pride of the Dewar clan in their "blood" had increased, it seemed, in direct proportion to the decrease of their incomes.

"Poor Beatrice," Jane said, sipping her tea. "I only saw her once, when she was younger and, I suppose, much better-looking than she is now, but even then nobody could have looked less like a Dewar—unless perhaps Rommel."

"No, Rommel has a nice long nose," corrected Kitty.

The two women laughed softly. Jane sat back on her pillows and looked out the window at the mist and rain all over the mountain. She was enjoying this exclusive little tête-à-tête, at the same time totaling up, rather greedily, all the good conversations she had had lately with women: Sonia Marks, Gerda—even Marsha Pedersen could be counted, in that they got right down to it, as far down as circumstances and mutual insights allowed. In all these dialogues there had been a tacit underpinning of shared motive, of trust. Why isn't this possible with men, she thought, this getting down to it without fear of the consequences; or is it possible and I am simply not capable of it, or haven't found a man I trust to talk to as I talk to these women? With Gabriel, she often planned her conversations, sometimes weeks in advance. And edited them ahead of time of any demanding verbs or possessive adjectives or shrewish expletives. Her letters to him were, if they made it to the mailbox, austere distillations of suppressed emotion. When she was in doubt about the tone of a letter, she held it overnight. Her garbage can had been the receptacle of more letters than her lover, over the span of this affair. Last year, as Valentine's Day approached, she allowed herself, after much weighing of pros and cons, to write him a "Saint Valentine Tale," in the third person. She masked her passion in the style of Jane Austen. In cool and balanced syntax, she revealed "the very largeness of her esteem for G., her perilous hopes for the two of them," and how "J. deplored the necessity of their long separations." She spent more effort on it than she had on some term papers. Their valentines to each other crossed; on February 14th, she

132

had received Blake's lovers in the whirlwind, Paolo and Francesca blowing about for all eternity in each other's arms. "Inveterately yours, G." was penned on the back of the card. She had gone at once to the dictionary to look up "inveterately." And why Paolo and Francesca? They were doomed to Hell, after all.

"Gabriel, tell me yes or no. Do you love me?"

Why had she never dared to ask that question?

The only man in her present life she could talk to the way she talked to these women was another assistant professor in the department, named Marty, who was, like her, thirty-two years old. In fact, they were both Geminis, and sometimes, when she and Marty were having a coffee break, or lunch in the Union, she would watch the way his hands circled excitedly in the air and his eyes shot quick little lights of intelligence, beacons for his oncoming thoughts, and she would think: If I had been born a man, I would have been like this one, nervous, overexcitable, with tiny creases running up and down my pale forehead, my hair falling out prematurely, always in trouble with women, falling in love with the wrong women, who would make me unhappy, but very—oh, very —intelligent. I would never have been born a man like Gabriel, steady, private, strong, and incomprehensible.

Marty had the unchallenged reputation of being the most brilliant young teacher in the department. "Oh, he's an exciting teacher!" his colleagues would exclaim, not at all envious, because they all knew Marty was no threat in the "real" competition. Marty could not quit talking— sharing his overcharged mind, moving his sensitive hands in the air—long enough to sit down in a room by himself and write, and publish.

She found it easy to talk to Marty; yes, she could talk to Marty "like a woman." They laughingly discussed their impossible ideals concerning a love relationship, their sexual fantasies, their hang-ups. Thay admitted to each other their loneliness, how they were afraid of getting old and ugly and decrepit with nothing to show for it, nobody to love them and make it all worthwhile. One lunchtime, Jane had even asked Marty's advice about constipation. "It's been five days now. I know I'm a terrible hypochondriac, but I'm worrying myself sick already about having to wear one of those little bags around my waist for the rest of my life."

How Marty had laughed, but it was a warm, sharing laugh. He understood perfectly, he said, and he found her adorable for both her wild imagination, which had to push everything as far as it would go, and for being able to say such things to him. He recommended a good laxative with belladonna in it, and said that if things had not cleared up by tomorrow he would take her himself to see his doctor, a very special doctor whose practice was largely composed of "freaks like us."

But of course things *had* cleared up, almost as soon as she had talked to Marty. The truth was, she had brought it on herself. She had just returned from a long weekend in Chicago with Gabriel. They had shared the same hotel room, and the result was that she had been unable to go to the bathroom for three mornings because she could not bear to make the noises necessary to these functions.

She knew what Gerda would have to say about all this. Gerda would lose no time in spelling out the metaphor. "Jane, until you can let him hear you shit, there is going to be *no* free dialogue. Your shit is part of you, just like all those dirty, demanding little thoughts you edit out of your conversations and letters to him."

("But what about *romance,* Gerda?" Simple. Gerda did not believe in romance. "But the point is, Gerda, I can't find the Martys in my life attractive. In fact, I'm ashamed to say I disqualify them in my secret heart of hearts because I *am* able to tell them everything." What would Gerda say to that? "That's your problem, baby, not theirs." And Gerda would probably enjoy spending an evening with Marty much more than she would with Gabriel, anyway.)

Kitty was weeping softly, between sips of tea. "I'm going to miss her, I really am. I think I did enough for her; don't you think I did? I was over there every day these past few years, sometimes twice a day. I took her to the grocery store whenever she wanted to go. I stopped by on my way home from school, whenever I had a moment to myself, which, as you know, is not often."

"Of course you did. I have often heard her say you were a good daughter. I only wish I had written her more often."

Both women wept now. They seemed to draw their tears out of each other. When one would stop, the other would start and they'd both begin again. Yes, she's going to miss her, thought Jane. It gave her someplace to go, a reason to give to Ray for going down off his mountain.

Then Kitty said, "Oh, my goodness, what's the time? What a nice little clock; that's the one that nice couple gave you, isn't it? Nine-thirty! I had no idea. We'd better dress; we're to meet Frances and Monroe at Plemmons's at ten." She replaced the teacups efficiently on the enamel tray and her eyes became pale and impersonal again.

"They're divorced now," said Jane, getting up and going to the closet. Suddenly all her clothes seemed inadequate, out of fashion, not proper enough to wear to Edith's funeral. What could I have been thinking of to bring a skirt, a blouse, a sweater, and a pair of jeans, she thought, riffling through these items with something akin to panic. Did I actually plan to wear this plaid skirt and blouse to the funeral? What could I have been thinking of? She had not panicked over clothes like this in years; it was another era in which pocketbooks had to match one's shoes and you went to the hairdresser every week and kept your nails filed and polished.

"What? That nice couple divorced? From what you said, they had such an imaginative marriage. They did such thoughtful things for each other." Kitty lingered in the doorway, holding the tray.

"Well, now they are doing thoughtful, imaginative things for their new partners. They are both living with new people."

"What a shame," murmured Kitty, without much conviction.

"Oh, yes, lots of people are getting divorced and going with new people these days. That is," Jane added wryly, "everybody but the right people."

"Ah," said Kitty, "how is that going? I wanted to ask yesterday, but it didn't seem right somehow, not on this trip."

"Everything is exactly the same. The same old idyllic love, as always."

"Idyllic love is not something to be tossed away," said Kitty.

"All the same, I can't help wanting to see what it would be like being married to him, living in the same house, having ordinary meals, doing ordinary things. . . ."

"Ordinary," said Kitty. "See, I can tell you already, so now you don't have to go and try it."

"Mmm, perhaps," agreed Jane, not wanting to argue after their lovely moment of rapport over the tea. Suddenly she had a shift in perspective. She imagined Gabriel looking up from his breakfast and telling someone not to open the new jar until the old one had been used up. To her surprise, she could hear him say this; she could hear the exact tone he would use. It would not, of course, be Ray's twangy, self-righteous, mountain-Baptist preacher's tone. It would be Gabriel's hesitant, self-righteous, pedantic scholar's tone.

"Oh, God. Men," said Jane. She wanted, for the moment, to get back with her mother.

"Yes," agreed Kitty warmly. "Leave things as they are and consider yourself fortunate. The two of you flying out of the sky into little 'residences' all waiting for you, no two alike, and with maid service and not having to cook meals." She balanced the tray in one hand and closed the door behind her. Jane heard her moccasins shuffle down the hall and into the kitchen. She heard Kitty say something to Ray, who answered quite cheerfully.

What to wear, what to wear? She fingered through a few of Emily's old dresses. Even though Emily was taller, Jane could sometimes wear her dresses because Emily wore them so short. What about this navy-blue sleeveless —really a summer dress, but if she put her dark cardigan over it, nobody would be able to tell. . . . It would pass. Also, she could keep her coat on during the service; surely the imitation brown suède coat with the fur collar would be acceptable. . . .

Acceptable to whom?

To Frances, that was who. Frances! Illegitimate daughter of a runaway great-aunt and a villain in a melodrama. What right had Frances to make anyone worry about being proper? And yet she had claimed for herself that power. You always felt a little shabby, a little out of style; you worried about your etiquette around Frances. Because Frances noticed whether or not your shoes went with your pocketbook, and whether you introduced one person to another in the right order, and which fork you picked up and which way you pushed your soupspoon, and whether your hemline was this year's or last year's.

"My hemline. Shit!" And Jane tore her plaid skirt from its hanger and dressed in it, with her gray blouse and a black silk scarf she found in Emily's drawer. She put on dark gray stockings and gray suède shoes and dragged her coat off the hanger and went into Kitty's dressing room to inspect herself in the full-length mirror. It seemed to her she looked unbelievably tacky, but at least the hemline of the plaid skirt was this year's. Emily's dark dress had a hemline two years old.

I turn into an anachronism every time I come home, she thought angrily. I start measuring myself by standards thirty, fifty, a hundred years old. I wonder what Cleva was like. From what I've been able to squeeze out of Edith and Kitty, it sounds as though, sixty-seven years ago, she was already fifty years ahead of me.

VII

FRANCES and her husband, Monroe, were waiting in the parlor of the funeral home, talking to Mr. Plemmons, Jr.: three well-dressed adults forming a cordial circle on a gray carpet in a lamplit room with a dozen or so Dutch landscapes round the walls. The old high-ceilinged room trembled slightly from the constant traffic on the new expressway which the state had cut through the Plemmons property. There were newer, flashier funeral homes in town, but Edith's father had taken his trade to Mr. Plemmons, Sr., who was now in his nineties and lived upstairs by himself with all his best antiques and paintings, which he liked too much to have downstairs. ("When I go, let Mr. Plemmons take care of everything. They aren't fancy down there and I'm afraid Mr. Plemmons, Senior, probably is an atheist, but the Dad knew him and they're old family and I don't need anything special anyway." "Oh, Edith!" Kitty, or Jane, would protest. "Don't be morbid. Don't talk about dying." And Edith would look hurt and say, "You don't understand. I have to plan these things.")

Frances detached herself from the men and came forward on sensible stacked heels to hug Kitty, Jane, and Ray, in that order, murmuring each of their names as she did so with just the right combination of sorrow appropriate for Edith's death and of pleasure in seeing her kin.

To Kitty she said, "How are you, darling, you're looking well. You've lost some more weight, haven't you? Ray,

138

you're looking marvelous. There's nothing better for a man than outdoor work; you and Monroe are lucky in your occupations, don't you agree? Congratulations, Jane. You're a doctor now. Isn't that wonderful!"

Monroe, wearing his sports jacket, ambled over pleasantly at this point, adding, "You're looking good, Jane." Mr. Plemmons, Jr., a tall, melancholy man in his sixties who wore a dark suit and rimless glasses, hung unobtrusively in the background. Jane was already wondering why Frances had not commented on her looks; surely that must be a bad sign for them. Even Ray was pronounced as looking "marvelous." Had Monroe picked up on his wife's omission because he felt sorry for his fast-fading young schoolteacher cousin-in-law? Stop this! she told herself.

Ronnie came in. He had stayed behind in the car to finish listening to a song on the radio. Immediately he was pronounced adorable by Frances. "A real young man." Ronnie blushed and smoothed his carefully hotcombed blond hair and looked round the walls at the pictures. His small red mouth twitched with a repressed smile. Frances asked him what grade he was in now. "Eighth," he replied casually, and waited for her next exclamation, which came.

"Do you get to Chicago much, Jane?" asked Monroe.

"Sometimes. Not too often," she replied loudly, remembering that Monroe was hard of hearing. Then saw Frances wince and realized she had chosen wrong again. When confronted with a hard-of-hearing relative in a funeral home, one simply took greater care to move one's lips, that was all.

Kitty stepped over and said something in a low voice to Mr. Plemmons, who brightened instantly.

"How's the construction business?" Monroe asked Ray, clapping him on the shoulder. Rap proceeded to tell him. The two men drew away to a lamplit corner, and that left Jane and Ronnie and Frances. Ronnie, whose light blue eyes had gone purposely vacant in that infuriating way they always did when he took refuge in his childhood to get out of a boring situation, was clearly going to be of no help. Jane remembered her advice to

Marsha Pedersen: pretend you are rehearsing for a movie and you want to get the part perfect. Frances said, "How long are you staying this time, Jane?"

"Four or five days. As long as I'm needed." Pretend, she instructed herself, that this is one of those transitional scenes in a novel of manners. "Frances," a walk-on bourgeois cousin, who represents the safe traditions of her region, her society, is accosting "Jane," who might be called the intellectual representative of this family. Jane is in transit between the old values, which threaten to engulf her every time she comes home, and the new values, which she must hack out for herself. At the moment, in this dialogue, it looks as though smooth Frances is winning, but Jane, while not as practiced in this art of nonpejorative small talk, is Observing Small Details in order that, through her eyes, we as readers may form a better picture of Frances and all that she stands for.

"How sweet of you. I'm sure you're going to be such a help to Kitty." Frances stepped closer to Jane, who identified her perfume. Frances had once sent Edith a bottle of this perfume for her birthday, and Edith tried to give it away to Jane because it was too sweet. Jane had refused it for the same reason, and as far as she could remember, the expensive little bottle was still sitting on Edith's dressing table with the triple mirrors, slowly evaporating and collecting dust. "She's going to really miss Aunt, I'm afraid," murmured Frances. "They were so close, living in the same town and all."

"Yes. We are all going to miss Edith," replied Jane, wondering if it shocked Frances that they called Edith Edith. Possibly, but she would never let on. Jane admired her cousin's youthful, high-colored skin with its careful make-up, her well-preserved figure. Her skin is better than mine and she's in her sixties, she thought; but then why shouldn't it be? Her life is a round of facials and twice-daily applications of good cold cream. Would I have enjoyed being Frances, safe and secure on my husband's thousand acres, hostessing meetings and teas for the D.A.R. and the U.D.C., having my red hair washed and set each week, then my red-and-gray hair washed and set every week, my cuticles oiled and pushed back, some respectable slave at the beauty salon brush-stroking the nails with the current fashionable shade of red or pink? Perhaps. If I had been allowed a lobotomy first. (She thought of her student Sheldon Rossinger, wondered how he was using his semester break.) But Frances's life had not been perfect. She had wanted children. Like her foster mother Crista, she had been barren. As a punishment, perhaps, for denying her true mother? For when Frances spoke lovingly of "Mama," she referred entirely to the fat little widow living in a Catholic nursing home in Birmingham, whom Frances drove dutifully to fetch twice a year for a long visit; not the skeleton of a twenty-year-old foolish, headstrong girl, tucked away these sixty-odd years in the family plot where Edith would go this afternoon. Frances wore a handsomely cut dark suit, a tweedy mixture of dark colors—midnight blue and purple and black, mostly black—and a high-necked black woolen blouse, with a cat's-eye brooch pinning the tips of the collar so they stood erect beneath her well-preserved throat. The suit hung perfectly, anchored with many little chains hidden in the lining, and the hem was the hem Paris had decreed the previous fall. She wore flesh-colored stockings and plain black leather pumps that looked like thin boats on her long feet.

"Aunt was mighty proud of you, Jane. The last time she came down for a visit, she talked so much about you. She said how proud she was that you had turned out so smart."

"Why, thank you, Frances." Jane made herself return her cousin's good will. She looked straight into Frances's calm hazel eyes and gave her, not a smile—she couldn't manage that at the moment—but a look of genuine, if somewhat weary, gratitude (suitable, she thought, for the smart cousin who has worn her eyes away on books).

"We're all proud of you," continued the other. "I keep hoping one of these days you'll find that free time you keep promising and come down and stay with us for a real long visit. I want to take you around and show you off."

"I'd love to, sometime. It's just that I always seem to be so busy." She let her voice trail away, wishing to get

141

off this subject, seeing herself, the cousin in young middle age, being paraded around to the homes of fellow D.A.R.s and U.D.C.s who would exclaim over Jane's doctorate and then, after she was gone, speculate on why she had not been able to get some man.

Kitty left Mr. Plemmons, who hurried busily out of the room and off down a hall. She came over to Frances and Jane.

"Frances, Jane and Ronnie thought they would like to see Edith one last time and so John Plemmons has gone to . . . It will stay closed at the service, so if you would like to see her. . . ."

Frances paused. Her blandly handsome face became briefly turbulent with some inner conflict. Jane was granted a momentary purloined glimpse of what the dashing, troubled Cleva must have looked like: the colorful hair and skin, the almost retroussé version of the Dewar nose, a certain defiant tilt of the chin, the alive and quickly flitting eyes with little shadows in the rims.

Then, "Thank you, Kitty, but I don't believe I will. I think I want to remember Aunt as she was. Let the children go." Frances's face settled back into its peaceful contours, and Jane, who was now being motioned discreetly from the doorway by Plemmons, went along with Ronnie—the two children who had to have their gape.

"Would the two of you like to go in together," asked Mr. Plemmons softly as he led them down a hallway flanked with more Dutch landscapes, "or would you rather see her one by one?"

"I think separately," said Jane. It suddenly occurred to her what she was about to do, and she did not want a witness to emotions unpredictable to herself. "Okay, Ronnie?"

"Okay by me." He shrugged the padded shoulders of his school blazer. Mr. Plemmons beamed indulgently at him and indicated a Victorian settee in dove-gray velvet where he could wait for his sister. "It's these rooms," he whispered to Jane, opening the door for her to enter, then closing it soundlessly behind her.

The first of the two rooms, which opened into each

other, was a formal reception room. It had a narrow brocade sofa, several formal chairs, and—the only twentieth-century discrepancy—a box of Kleenex in a soft floral design on each of the small mahogany round tables which flanked the sofa. At the entrance to the second room, from which Jane kept her eyes studiously averted, pacing herself, was a little metal stand, like a music stand, which held, at eye level, an open book bound in white vinyl. The pages had wide-spaced silver lines, where visitors coming to pay their last respects had signed. On the left-hand page was penned neatly at the top, in black ink, "EDITH DEWAR BARNSTORFF."

Jane saw Beatrice's signature, leading them all. And then several names of old ladies faintly recalled from Edith's conversation. And Edith's ninety-year-old brother Iz, who lived within walking distance of the farm where Edith and her siblings were all born, and his wife, Maud. As a child, Jane had got on well with Iz. He'd take her hand and they'd sneak off to the barn, where he'd let her ride one of his pigs. "For God's sake, don't tell your grandmother; she'll slit my gullet," he'd say. She was resolving to see old Iz again, perhaps this visit, when her good intentions were squelched by the ominous threadlike scrawl beneath: *The Misses Regina and Eustacia Pinner*." God! Weren't they dead yet, those scary sisters who had won, along with Ray Sparks and several others, permanent roles as villains in the cast of her dreams. The Pinner School for Young Ladies. Closed now; it had been a two-woman operation and when they got too old to run it, it closed. But all over this town, matrons from thirty to sixty still walked with Pinner posture and spoke with the Pinner diction. Kitty's formative years had been entrusted to the Pinner School; Jane had attended for one week. It was a nightmare she would never forget. There was one other child in first grade (the school was on its way down then), a pale little girl with abnormally yellow hair, named Thora. Miss Eustacia had taught them arithmetic every day for a few skimpy minutes and then got down to business: wiping out all traces of "the unlovely mountain accent of this region." Thora and Jane had to stand and repeat from their dia-

143

phrams: "I never saw a purple cow, I never hope to see one . . ." "Caw," said Miss Eustacia. "Make your mouth a small, long O. Not a wide vulgar one. Caw, *caw*. Around here, they saw '*ka*-ow.' Get rid of those diphthongs." After lunch (this had been the best part of the day for Jane and Thora, who had exchanged lunchboxes —Jane had never forgotten the exotic taste of the special pimento cheese that Thora's mother made), the little girls were sent across the house to a room called, simply, "chapel." All Jane could remember about this room was that it had dark maroon velvet curtains, rows and rows of straight-backed chairs, and a piano called a "baby grand," which Jane couldn't figure out: it was enormous. Here, awaiting them, was Regina, the elder, more formidable sister. Eustacia perpetually smiled; Regina frowned. Regina taught them Posture. Walking, first, she taught them, undoubtedly as she herself had been taught some scores of years ago. A yardstick across the flat of their backs and hooked in the crooks of their elbows: "Chin up, tummy in; imagine someone has tied a string to the top of each ear and is now above, tugging the strings." Now walk across the room, in the narrow pathway between the first row of chairs and the baby grand. Back and forth. "Careful of that chin, Jane." Jane was imagining the string in the ears. Did that mean someone had pierced little holes to get the string in? She felt queasy. Next came a discipline created by Miss Regina and called, harmlessly, Poise. Two of the straight-backed chairs were placed on opposite sides of the room, and Thora and Jane must sit perfectly straight in these chairs for ten minutes—an eternity to a child of six—not speaking or moving. If you spoke or moved (or looked ever so slightly sideways to make sure your friend was still there), you had to start the ten minutes over again. During her fourth day of Poise at the Pinner School, Jane fainted and Edith said she did not have to go back. "You made *me* go back!" protested Kitty. "You never fainted," replied Edith coolly, with just the tiniest trace of superiority. "This child is like me; there is a limit to the things she can take." "What happened?" Kitty had asked Jane as soon as she could get the child alone. "Can you describe it? I've never in my life fainted. What is it like?" Proudly Jane tried to reconstruct the action (or refusal to act) which had bought her freedom from the Pinner sisters. "Well, I was sitting in my chair; I think I had almost finished my ten minutes, and I wanted to lie down, and I couldn't, so then I saw spots and then I just keeled over." She had liked the sound of those two last words; somehow they rang of her exemption. There had been more to it than that; she had known at her young age she was not describing it "in detail," the way Kitty said good books described things "in such detail you can feel them, see them." Yes, there had been another dimension to it, her first of many fainting spells. It had been a kind of protest, her body's rebellion against an act she had not chosen, which was being forced upon her. *I choose to die rather than submit;* for wasn't fainting a sort of little death? Funny, how fainting, swooning, was traditionally considered a feminine predisposition. It was a dark, inturned act of anarchy, accomplishing its purpose just as aggressively as—sometimes more successfully than—open war. Jung, as a child, had fainted to keep from doing his homework; she had been pleased to read this in his autobiography years later. But he had made himself stop it; he had pulled himself together after overhearing his father say sadly to a friend, "What will become of the boy if he cannot earn his own living?" Whereas Jane had continued to faint—against her will, that was the strange thing—in dentist chairs, at the moment she looked through eyedrops into the little machine which tested for glaucoma. And once in church with the family of her English fiancé.

So Jane was transferred by Edith to the local convent school, which had twenty children in its first grade and the disciplines of which included Catechism and French instead of the Diction and the deadly Poise. Jane lapsed back into the vulgar diphthongs, which had never been really bad, relaxed her shoulders, forgot about her chin—forgot, in fact, the French—as soon as each summer came. But she did not forget the Pinner sisters, especially Miss Regina, whose frowning face bending over her had been the first sight to greet her on her return from the little death. The Pinner sisters would die soon (surely they

145

would die?) but Miss Eustacia and Miss Regina, particularly the latter, would continue their restrictive educational procedures in the night theatre of Jane's dreams, along with Ray's tireless, violent efforts to keep her home, keep her back, keep her under the rule of his house.

Jane looked into the next room. From where she stood on the threshold, she could see Edith's profile against a background of white satin. Directly above the casket was a mirror, tilted downward so that it showed Edith full face, the white lace collar (a dickey she had always been fond of, had worn beneath suits), the ice-blue satin dressing gown, and her long, pale hands (with the brown spots she detested) folded loosely, just below her breasts. Edith had had nice breasts to the very last: small, well-shaped, unexploited by any baby's greedy sucking (Kitty had been bottle-fed). Jane had heard that pregnancies, even quickly aborted ones, turned nipples brown, but Edith's (Jane had spied them once) had remained a miraculous, delicate pink: symbol, perhaps, of her emotional virginity? At the convent, Jane's first-grade teacher, a small, energetic nun whose face had turned yellow from a bout with jaundice, was rumored to have been married in another life, years ago. But the Pope, the story went, had given her a dispensation and she was allowed to become a nun because "she never enjoyed it." Edith might have been granted a similar dispensation, though she would never have said so in so many words. "There are certain duties in marriage," she told Jane. "There are certain things one has to go through with because the man needs them, you see." Jane had often wondered if she herself was what the sex manuals called "frigid." Did frigid mean that you never could feel anything, never could have an orgasm? If so, she was not frigid. Or did it mean that you were unable to abandon yourself with the real man in the real moment? If so, she was frigid. For her, the real man and the real moment had yet to coincide. She could for instance, imagine Gabriel making love to her when he was not with her—and it worked. She was in control. She was the director of the scene. She could start it, stop it, say to her body, "Start

146

that scene from the beginning again," until she worked it to a furious pitch of intensity. But when Gabriel was with her, next to her body in the moment, she had to imagine him as more, or other, or saying something he was not saying: she had to put some imagined frame around the real scene, expand or distort reality in some way, to make it work. She had even been unfaithful to Gabriel in her fantasies. Her favorite one, which had yet to wear out, was of a band of extraterrestrial men, disguised as American businessmen, abducting her between flights at an airport for an experiment in crossbreeding. On their planet, it took dozens of men to make one woman pregnant, and each one who had relations with her caused her to grow an inch taller. How she enjoyed each of them, knowing she was growing out of her skin, out of her world. If it kept on, she could never walk through any ordinary door again. But she couldn't stop. She was six feet nine, six feet ten, but she had to have one more.

She crossed the room at Plemmons's and looked down at Edith. She looked elegant. Not at all like Jane's last glimpse of her at Christmas when she had been truly the "tired little old lady." This figure was ageless, queenly, invulnerable. Completed. The expression on the face of this woman who had lived out her life beset with fears about things that never happened was an expression which scorned fears. Fears were for those who had something left to lose. The dead face of Edith—waxy smooth, lips pinked too much, then wiped by the sleepless Beatrice —was a detached, cool comment on a completed existence. It was a face neither masculine nor feminine, simply regal; a face that had transcended pain, uncertainty, sex. Achieving death, Edith had rid herself at last of troublesome womanhood.

Jane did not feel the slightest urge to weep. In a strange way she was envious. She looked past Edith's body toward her own face in the tilted mirror above the coffin. It was not over for her yet. The erosion was only beginning. She had years of fear to be registered there. Her face shocked her; it always did when she faced a mirror unexpectedly. It was too alert, too tense, too transparent in what its owner felt. "You are the type of person who will

147

never be able to see your own face," Marty once said. "Your face is an infinite series of impressions, of moods. It will always give more pleasure to others than to yourself." Yet the times were frequent when Jane wished for fewer impressions and more bones. Edith's beauty had been indisputable and constant; Kitty had bones, and, even in her fifties, what the nineteenth-century novelists called "bloom." Jane was . . . a series of moods that played on those who chose to look. "You looked lonely," the Nashville traveler in the scarlet jacket had said.

How did Gabriel see her? He had never made a single comment about her looks—about anyone's looks, for that matter. His comments on faces and bodies and colors were reserved for paintings. What did Gabriel see when he lay beside her and looked into her eyes? Did he see her intelligence, her soul, the range of thoughts that widened and narrowed her eyes, creased her pale forehead, swelled or compressed her mouth? Once she had asked him, "When you are shaving, or dressing, getting ready to come to me, do you look at your face in the mirror and wonder. How does Jane see this face?" He had looked genuinely puzzled, almost sad. "No, I never have," he said.

On the days when she liked herself, she decided Gabriel had chosen to have this affair with her—his first, he told her—because he had *recognized* her, the Jane known and cherished by herself alone. He had been the first to look into the windows of her eyes and see her tender qualities, her exciting play of mind, her vulnerabilities, her nonsense, her earnest—sometimes rather tiresome— yearnings toward the heroic. But on her bad days, like today, she was sure he had simply let himself fall into this liaison because he had come to a point in his life where he needed to be admired, flattered, and she knew how to flatter his mind.

Yes, how well she had learned that. It had been one of the skills she had taught herself in the long Campaign to Escape Ray, via the fellowships and scholarships which would lead to financial independence. Intellectual flattery of teachers had become an adjunct to her scholarly activities: the impressive memorizations in grammar school, the many-drafted, idealistic high school themes ("I Speak for Democracy," "R. E. Lee: Patriot or Provincial," "Why I Need to Be a Christian Citizen in 1955," etc.), most of them aimed at the preferences or prejudices of influential teachers. Then the college term papers, carefully researched, accurately footnoted according to the MLA Style Sheet, then shaped and tinted (as other women shaped their figures with foundation garments, tinted their skins with make-up) with a delicate wit, an irresistible "spontaneous" turn of phrase which might have been worked over till three in the morning. And the dependable, but never tiresome, visits to the offices of a graduate advisers, to ask advice about choosing courses (a survey course of the eighteenth century, or a Swift seminar?) and, while being advised, to show appreciation of the replies, and whatever digressions that usually came with them, and to leave behind an unobtrusive but nonetheless charming and faintly enigmatic memory of Jane Clifford and her diligence, her subtlety—the indefinable memory that makes some graduate students more memorable than others to their weary professors as they drive home to supper, as they are asked by department chairmen to list the first three names that come to their head as deserving of next year's financial aid.

She had connived to win her degrees (and her economic independence, her release from being beholden to Ray Sparks, the Ray Sparkses of the world) partially through the charms of her sex, the way other women used these same charms to win husbands. So now they had their husbands and she had her degrees, her economic independence. That was fair, wasn't it?

Only now she could not see—as she looked down at Edith's smug closed face ("At last, I am dead. I have been making my plans for years")—what use, what joyful use, she could possibly make of this freedom. Her impetus, her goal, had been, for so long, to become her own woman, and she had followed it to its end, just as other women feel the impetus toward marriage or motherhood and follow it to its end. They marry, they have their children. Then, for years, these children have to be taken

149

care of; they grow up slowly, with much trouble and pain; they at last leave home, and then, and then—the women face the void again. Jane faced that void now. She had no children to divert her, to distract or detain her, to put off the day when the truth of the individual life must be faced.

"When I've finished raising Jane, then I can die peacefully." How often Edith had said that when the three women had lived together. But Jane had got raised and Edith did not die. When Kitty married Ray, she fussed with hurt pride and snobbishness, gradually allowed Ray to win her over, and eagerly awaited the grandchildren to help raise and spoil. "I must stay alive and do what I can for these poor children," she would say, happily refilling her days with trips to town for yarn, to crochet snowcaps, planning little lunches to tempt them to spend the day with her.

What have I to do, what urgent thing can I talk myself into thinking the world needs me and only me to do, before I die?

Jane had never believed herself to have what was called "a teaching vocation." There were too few good students and she had no charitable calling to save the masses. Her becoming a professor had been the inevitable result of finding out, early in life, she could earn money because she liked to read books and talk about them. But she felt no passion for teaching; she was not enough of an actress to enjoy contemplating her image as seen by admiring students from behind when she wrote some provocative question on the blackboard. Sometimes, it is true, she got carried away as she discussed a book that she cared about. At such times, the room faded, her eyes rolled toward the ceiling. Someone had once told her that she should practice "eye contact" when she lectured. Looking back on her own education, she decided that she had learned what she had wanted to learn and the teachers had little to do with it. Some were handsome, some were earnest, some were pitiful. Once in a while, something generative had slipped from their tongues— usually something spontaneous—which had inched her further in her personal search. She doubted whether she, or anyone else, could teach anyone much. There were those on a quest and there were those who were there because, like poor Portia, they were the hope of their family, and there were those who would learn regardless of whether they were taught. She admired the Sheldons, she pitied the Portias, she had erotic dreams, which had nothing to do with teaching, about the Howards, but, on the whole, she felt little interest in their futures. Once her friend Gerda had accused her of saving her best sympathies for characters in novels, never for real people. ("Real people are sloppy and unpredictable and often boring. You like to have constant stimulation, you like to have everything moving along. At the same time, you have to have a guarantee that everything is going to turn out in some coherent, aesthetic way before you'll get involved.") Was that true? Perhaps. She admitted that she had spent more hours of her life mulling over the destinies of Isabel Archer and Gwendolyn Harleth (what *had* those two done with their lives?) than over the majority of real people she had encountered. Except for herself, of course. She could not be said, even by Gerda, to be lacking in sympathy for Jane Clifford. What was to become of *that* personality, her constant companion, ephemeral as the dew on a morning rose under the perspective of eternity, but what about the next forty or fifty years?

A good plot, Aristotle said, goes from possibility to probability to necessity. Where was she on that scale? Was everything still possible? Was it possible that she might yet soar? Or was she at the probable stage? Well, even then, it was probably that she might—through an act of courage, a visitation of grace—be redeemed, beautifully, unexpectedly. But most people were not redeemed. Why should she be the exception? The one thing she could point to as an unarguable necessity concerning her fate was that she would one day die.

What did she really want? Today, this gloomy day, she desired the end of uncertainty, of joyless struggle without assurance of a happy reward. She had an absurd vision of

151

lifting her skirts, climbing into the coffin beside Edith, and pulling the lid down over both of them. Would the world miss anything?

If I had married, perhaps . . . Men had "wanted" her. She had received and returned James's engagement ring, in England. The two "serious" affairs she had had in graduate school had culminated in proposals: the first by an ex-seminarian, who had tried and failed to become a priest, and who tried and failed, gently and with true regret, to become a satisfactory lover to Jane; the second by a man she met in her *Beowulf* class, who worked nights in a bar to pay for his courses. She had cared deeply about the ex-seminarian. "I think I would have been so much like you if I had been born a man," she told him. They tried to laugh away his problem. They found its name in a book: "premature ejaculation." "I wish we could have been Abélard and Héloïse," he said sadly (he was gauntly, beautifully sad, this man, with deep-set eyes which had permanent dark circles beneath), "only we would have behaved ourselves." When he dropped out of school and returned to the seminary, Jane had been deeply upset. She had grieved for weeks. The *Beowulf* man she dropped, suddenly and cruelly, after she had paid an unexpected visit to his rooms one winter evening. He said, "Oh, good, stay and talk to me while I eat," and had taken two hot chicken pies from the oven and eaten them both greedily, sending nervous, apologetic glances her way, but unable to take the chance of offering her one of them.

"I think, on the whole, it is better that you do not marry," Edith had said. But she had often said something else. "Jane, Jane, all this studying. You are going to ruin your eyes one of these days. Sometimes I get down on my knees and pray that you will find a good man to take care of you, as Hans took care of me." And now she was dead and Jane could never say: "Look, Edith, which one of those statements did you really mean most?"

If I had been an artist, perhaps . . . (moving away, to let Ronnie have his turn). Art the great exempter. Like Death, it excused you from the annoyances and limitations of time. But Jane was a purist about art and artists.

There was the real thing, and there was the approximation, the imitation, and the barefaced hoax. She became increasingly convinced, more so since she had read a collection of nineteenth-century reviews praising as masterpieces novels no one now remembered and explaining why people like Hardy and Emily Brontë were flashes in the pan, that the world could not tell the difference till at least fifty years had elapsed. The real thing in any art she was not and had never tried to be. Even as a girl, when the nuns at the school assured her she would grow up to be an aritst of great talent, she had known the difference between how she painted an old man carrying his tools home through snowy woods and how Brueghel would have done it. And she had known also the difference between her overdetailed, rather rigid drawings and those of more gifted girls in the class, who perhaps lacked her craftsmanship but took chances with colors and composition with the inspired recklessness of the budding artist. "Please, Edith, take that picture down," she begged, after she stopped drawing and painting in her teens. "It's so childish and stiff. It's full of mistakes. His hoe looks like a golf club, and what was he doing with a hoe in the dead winter?" "I will not," said Edith. "You were very talented. I'm sorry you gave up your art. It used to make you happy. You could forget yourself for hours on end. All this reading makes you sad, if you want my opinion. You frown when you read. You used to hum to yourself when you drew and painted."

Many of her colleagues painted, or threw pots, or rehearsed evenings in community plays, or took violin lessons. One professor in the department, not much older than herself, wrote novels. Spurred to curiosity by an acid remark of Sonia's concerning this man and his novels, Jane borrowed the latest one from the Browsing Room. It was very short, about 150 pages, written in "takes," little blocks of prose separated by asterisks. It was called *The Country Husband*. After the dedication page (to my wife, Ilke) there followed a page of quotations.

HAMLET: Lady, shall I lie in your lap?
OPHELIA: No, my lord.

HAMLET: I mean, my head upon your lap?
OPHELIA: Ay, my lord.
HAMLET: Do you think I meant country matters?

The united praise of the whole race would be of less consequence to me than the neighing of those two degenerate Houyhnhnms I keep in my stable; because from these, degenerates as they are, I shall improve in some virtues, without any mixture of vice.
—*Gulliver's Travels.*

Man differs more from man than man from beast.
—JOHN WILMOT, EARL OF ROCHESTER,
A Satire Against Mankind.

Jane read the book with her dinner. She propped it against the sugar canister with the silver salt-shaker, so she could cut her steak and eat while she read.

Josh Horney, a poet with a wife, three children, a cat, and gerbils, leaves his apartment in New York, his analyst, the arrangement he and his wife have made with another couple to "bolster two sagging marriages," in order to take a year's job as poet-in-residence at a university deep in the heart of the Midwest.

He rents a farmhouse outside the city limits and his troubles begin. The country frightens him. The spaces make him feel inconsequential. They seem to suggest "a huge empty page whose very emptiness begins to charm you." His students are largely farm kids who have never heard of a sonnet. His colleagues are stupid and insensitive. He keeps getting lost on the look-alike roads as he drives to and from his farmhouse. The seasons terrify him. "Relentless, giant poems, *they* continued to write themselves day by day, while I wrote less and less." An enormous owl flies into the windshield of his car one early dusk and he interprets it as a bad omen. His children abandon him for the novelties of the barnyard, a family of pigs and sheep that come with the rented farmhouse. Josh becomes reattracted to his wife, who "glowed and flourished in the midst of this rural wasteland as she had never flourished in the city," but by the time she gets to bed she

154

is too tired from feeding the animals and falls asleep instantly. Josh becomes more depressed. He stops writing poetry altogether.

One foggy November evening, his VW breaks down on one of the look-alike roads and a pickup truck comes to his aid. It is driven by one of his students, Margery, the daughter of a rich farmer who is widowed and spends most of his time in Washington, lobbying for the farmers. Margery is eighteen, of mythical proportions. ("Her biceps, still tanned lightly from the summer haying, were the size of my thighs.") She lives the next farm over, which is, she tells him, half a mile as the crow flies, but three miles when he walks it through the dead fields of winter, which he begins to do frequently, after his wife falls asleep. He helps Margery feed the animals and she instructs him in country matters in her father's bed. She loves animals; she is crazy about her father, and sometimes she plays tapes of his speeches advocating the abolishment of price control, the curtailment of grain sales to Russia; and they make love "like the simple beasts" to the resonance of her father's voice.

Josh begins to come alive. His leg muscles harden from the regular six miles. He orders a pair of Wolverine boots from the mail-order catalogue. His wife and children begin to take new interest in him. His wife does not fall asleep quite so quickly every night. Josh has his hands full trying to please everybody.

One evening in early March, Josh gets away earlier than usual. His wife has taken the kids in town to an early movie. As he crosses the fields, he notices how the days are getting longer. He feels good; he has begun to like the country after all. He sees the light in the barn and decides to spy on his love as she gives the animals their evening feed. But he peeks through the window and sees Margery kneeling naked beneath her father's Morgan stallion. Her father's voice, speaking resonantly on the evils of selling our grain to Russia, accompanies her strange movements. The portable tape recorder rests on a bale of hay. "She had him in her mouth. Her strong hands moved rhythmically to the sound of the father's voice until suddenly, incredibly, the horse came."

When Margery discovers Josh spying, she is furious, "Like a wrathful goddess caught in the midst of secret rites." But then she surprises him by remaining kneeling beside the horse and beckoning to him. Josh takes her again and again, his potency seeming endless "in the shadow of that silent, brooding creature. Was he jealous? I must admit, I kept an eye on those hooves."

Afterward he tramps home through the fields. It is a clear, starry night and he thinks of many things. Margery has told him goodbye. Her father is due home from Washington and she'll have no time for visitors. Why is he not sad? On the contrary, life courses through his pulse as never before. He feels in contact with every part of his body and in harmony with this strange inchoate landscape that makes its own rules. He realizes spring is on its way, seeds of things even now pushing their way up through frozen soil, prickling the soles of his heavy boots. A wonderful poem begins to form in his head. When his wife wakes as he climbs into bed, she asks where he has been. "On a wonderful walk through the fields," he says, and is surprised to find his new potency still undiminished.

Jane skipped the details. They seemed pale after the Morgan. She tried to remember if she had ever read a sex scene that really convinced her that two people with minds, human consciousnesses, were inside each other via the flesh. What you usually got was someone "doing it" *to* someone if the book was written from the male viewpoint, or someone having "it done" to them if it was written from the female viewpoint. After her wartime success with the pulps, Kitty had tried her hand at a more serious kind of fiction, and Jane remembered how she had despaired of ever writing a convincing "love scene." Censorship was beginning to loosen, and more and more, in the late forties and early fifties, authors felt obliged to prove that they could get their characters through the sex act without flinching or omitting a single detail. Kitty's attempts had failed, largely because she sat on the fence. She would hurtle herself through a few clinical sentences and then try to compensate for her crudeness by dressing it up in the sort of romantic metaphor which had made her pulp stories of the better than average quality. Once Jane had heard her complain to Ray (it was early in their marriage, the babies had not yet come, and Kitty still believed she could be a wife and mother *and* a successful writer): "All this 'mounting' and 'grinding' and 'thrashing' and I'm sick to death of the words 'rhythmic' and 'crescendo.' " But she continued to study paperbacks in the drugstore, Spillane and the young Mailer, whatever she could get (*Lady Chatterley's Lover* would not be available above the counter until Kitty had given up writing), and tried and failed to imitate them and remain a lady as well.

In the last chapter of *The Country Husband,* Josh Horney is packing up his family for the trip back East. It is June. Every country thing is blooming. The cat is pregnant. There are more gerbils. His wife packs up their books slowly, moving with "the beginnings of a proud heaviness." And Josh has completed a book of poems, "stark, simple things; some not quite *human,* but with a new, bare honesty which I felt I could build on." He will call it *A Poet in the Country.*

Jane wrapped her leftover steak in aluminum foil, fork and all, and put it in the refrigerator. Then reexamined the novel, the Browsing Room plastic protecting its glossy dust jacket. She read the Advance Comments on the back.

Rude, Healthy, Insightful, and Terribly Funny.

I admire the hell out of this book. Josh Horney is all of us.

If Rabelais, Voltaire, and Swift went down to investigate "country matters," they might have come up with something like this.

Jane recognized the names of two of the blurb writers. One was a respectable critic. The novel was published by a reputable house.

Was there something she was not "getting"?

Was the book a hoax? The critic apparently did not think so. Did she lack a "rude, healthy" sense of humor?

Sonia Marks had been scathing about Josh Horney's

157

author. "He lives in a rented farmhouse, he has a wife and four children, he has the cat, he has the gerbils. I'm sure he's never been near a stallion. He teaches Restoration Drama and takes for granted the stupid novel-reading public will never have read *The Country Wife,* or heard of Jacob Horner, or Wycherly's Margery. He goes to bed with his undergraduate students, too, which Max and I both think is going too far."

But . . . how did the author feel about his book, this book he had written? Obviously his novels kept track of his own life, always about a year in arrears, according to Sonia, who said his previous novel had dealt with the "foursome" that had been mentioned briefly in the first chapter of *The Country Husband.* Did he know he was doing this, regurgitating his life, chapter by chapter, or did he believe he was an artist? Certainly he might believe it when he found himself compared to Rabelais, Swift, and Voltaire, and a well-known critic thought his work rude, healthy, insightful, and funny. Jane often passed him in the hall, a stocky man who dressed in the levis and hunting jackets and fisherman's boots which were so popular with Easterners who came here to teach. Had he perhaps had the experience with the Morgan? She didn't think so. Had he researched it? She imagined a letter she might send him, signed "A Country Gentleman," informing him that "what you have your filthy little girl do to that animal is impossible. He would have kicked her head off!" *Was* such a thing possible? Jane rooted around in her desk and took out the box of colored pens which she had bought over a year ago, thinking she ought to begin drawing again for her own pleasure. She found the drawing pad she had also bought that same day, and sat down on the sofa by her reading lamp, selected a reddish-brown pen from the box, and began on the Morgan. What exactly was a Morgan? A low-slung horse, if she remembered correctly. That would make Margery's task easier. Jane quickly sketched the two figures, then sat about embellishing. The finished work was not bad, except the horse stood rather stiffly, like the Trojan horse, and his penis was not quite right. It resembled a popsicle. She added a bit of red to it but that was worse. Now

158

it looked as though it was bleeding. (Perhaps Margery had bitten it?)

Jane considered leaving this drawing in the author's faculty mailbox. What would he think when he found it (unsigned, of course)? Would he be offended, or highly flattered that someone felt impelled to illustrate his tour-de-force scene? She wondered if he had ever read Stephen Dedalus's definition of improper art.

Then she thought of a way to go him one better. She moistened her lips and began a new picture. This was going to be difficult. She sketched Margery in lightly, hanging from the horse as though she were riding him upside down, her forehead pressed against his underbelly, her face toward his hindquarters. Then she had Josh kneel on the bale of hay and "do it" to Margery while Margery was doing what she had to do to the Morgan.

She worked long on this picture because its draftsmanship was a challenge. It was not every day that the human figure could get itself into such complicated positions. But as a finished work it disgusted her; it was rather pointless, just someone else's silly fantasy. She entitled the picture "Barnyard Triangle," and tore it out of the pad.

She wanted to draw a fantasy of her own. What? She drew a simple sketch of a man between the legs of a woman. This excited her more, but the architectural problems were no fun after her feat with "Triangle." The whole thing seemed tame. She flipped to a clean page and thoughtfully drafted a new picture: one woman and two men. Wait! Why not three men, four men, six men? And she began to get excited, sexually aroused, as she quickly drafted her new picture. There would be problems, of course, technical problems. There was just so much space, just a given number of apertures, for all the activity that was going to go on.

She worked long on this picture. She gave everybody something to do. As a last-minute inspiration, she made the woman, to whom so many things were being done, pregnant. Very pregnant, with huge tight belly and enormous breasts, each one attached to the mouth of a hungry man.

What time was it? She had no idea. She put down the pens and surveyed her work. Her neck and shoulders ached. Her body was throbbing with her woman's body in the picture. On a sudden inspiration, she bowed mockingly to her Southern heritage and selected a dark brown from her box of pens and colored one of the men. She titled this picture " 'What Do Women Want?'—Sigmund Freud."

She began to feel visionary, went to the cupboard and opened a bottle of wine. She took a glass and the bottle back to the living room, where she was already bursting with ideas for her masterpiece. It was to be called "Penis Park."

She poured herself a full glass of wine and drank it down. Her eyes felt hot. Her cheeks burned. She made a rough sketch of her amusement park, then realized this was a more ambitious project than she had first conceived. Conceived! Ha. She drank another glass. She felt good. No, "Penis Park" was to be a triptych, like "The Garden of Earthly Delights."

Where her energy came from, she afterward never knew. But when, finally, she put down her pens (the blue, the sky blue had gone dry, so several fluffy pink clouds floated happily over "Penis Park"; she had made the clouds faintly resemble the single shape of everything in the park) and went to look at "old T.F." The time was 4 A.M.

Suddenly she was starved. She took her triptych carefully to the kitchen and arranged it before her. Part One, left panel, "Puberty's Innocent Pleasures," she propped against the sugar bowl. A naked girl, part woman, part child, floated astride a plastic penis, rocking-horse style, in a large pond irrigated by a circle of marble statues of young men, facing outward, arms clasped about one another, pointing themselves heavenward to gush forth, in a communal geyser, the wherewithal for the young heroine's flotation. Then on she went to the Merry-Go-Round, where the steeds were flesh-and-blood acrobats (Jane did not wish to contribute further to the oppression of horses in her fantasy art) who balanced themselves admirably in precarious backbends and managed as well

160

to produce erections, painted and decorated individually like Easter eggs, for the heroine to ride. There was also a particularly lovable "Summer Santa," who sat in the shade of a tree bearing multicolored penis-shaped fruit. The young girl sucked musingly on a purple fruit as she sat astride her benefactor and enumerated her desires.

Which were granted in Part Two, center panel, "Plethoras and Plenitudes," propped against the silver saltshaker. The heroine was now in her full bloom (Santa had granted her wish to be a big girl), and partook and gave of every position imaginable to her creatrix in a landscape as colorful as a 24-color box of artist's pens could produce. Rare and wonderful, too, were the colors of her men, and of the little babies whom she paused—during the course of the panel—to give birth to and suckle (while being refertilized by another lover at the same time) beneath the cool branches of trees which hung heavy with the potent, familiarly shaped fruit.

Part Three, right panel, was propped against a tall pepper mill. It was gloomy and dark, few colors used, the same panel Bosch had chosen for his Hell. This panel was called "Piques and Penalties." The heroine—sagging and furious, a wild depraved look in her eye, no longer young, breasts hollowed from too much suckling, belly scarred and loose, legs bowed from the excesses of two and three men at the same time—first stopped to make obscene gestures at naked men trapped in small cages. On the top of each cage was a plaque which named his misdemeanor: "Jilter," "Adulterer," "Deserter," "Double-Standard Bearer," etc. Then she continued on to the Rifle Range where the felons ("Pimp," "Rapist," "Child Molester") were lined up sideways, and she, taking careful aim, shot off the offending organ. If she got them all the first time round, she was rewarded from a choice line-up of "Jaded Romps," pleasing to a woman who had experienced, many times, every species of the ordinary lustful pleasures, and was now ready for a vintage trick or two. Pan was there, in the shape of a jeering, squatty, bearded man in his sixties, who resembled an eighteenth-century professor she had once had who tried to kiss his female students when they came for conferences; and a pair of male twins who were hopelessly in love with one another's bodies and paused contemptuously to perform the duty of titillating a jaded lady; and a sphinxlike woman in a leotard, with cheeks sharp as triangles and the mocking come-if-you-dare challenge of Sappho in her heavily penciled eyes. And a few minor gods and angels and demons, languishing on shelves, picking at their private parts or playing with each other like neglected monkeys.

Without removing her gaze from her pictures, Jane opened the refrigerator and took out the aluminum-wrapped steak. She opened another bottle of wine. She picked up the cold steak with her fingers and began tearing at it with her teeth, getting grease on her cheeks, on her fingertips. It was very messy, very greasy. She laughed and picked up the wine in her greasy hand and drank it straight from the bottle. It tasted superb, better than wine in a glass! She stood in front of her triptych and tore with her teeth at the cold steak in her left hand and guzzled from the bottle in her right. She walked up and down in front of her drawings, belching once, twice, admiring her work, chuckling a little at the grace and ingenuity of her figures.

At some point, she stumbled greasily and effervescently to bed and passed out.

She woke "in the cold light" of 9 A.M., remembering she had a ten o'clock class to meet. She somehow managed to drag herself to the kitchen, put on a pot of coffee, throw away the wine bottles. She went to the bathroom and vomited, then came back and, wandering back and forth from living room to kitchen, took a baffled survey of her last evening's work. Then she began tearing up the pictures, one by one. The paper was thick and it tore with difficulty, almost as if it were mocking her, resisting her.

At last there was only the triptych left: "Penis Park," her masterpiece. She frowned at it, swaying on her feet. She was really not a bad artist. Perhaps . . . no. She took a last look at its incredible ambition, its sheer number of creatures (had she done all that last night?), its boldness of invention, its strange mixture of yearning, hate, and humor. She wondered if there had ever been a first-rate woman pornographer. She would be a good one, Jane was sure. There would be "certain womanly touches," as Dickens had written admiringly of George Eliot's work before he knew she was a woman.

She tore all three panels to smithereens. Then flushed her entire evening's work down the toilet. It took nine or ten flushings.

She was almost late for her ten o'clock class, because she had to keep lying down as she dressed; the coffee kept threatening to come up and she thought she might faint.

She returned the "Josh Horney" book to Browsing that same day.

Several days passed and, sure enough, the toilet stopped up and overflowed. Poor Marty was in the bathroom when it happened. She had invited him to supper because she did not feel like eating alone. He was embarrassed a little, but she talked him out of it, as he was later to reciprocate and talk her out of her constipation.

The next morning the plumber came, and Jane sat, on the same sofa where she'd done the drawings, white-faced, head bowed, hands clasped, waiting as sinful women await the results in their gynecologist's office.

What if the plumber was in there picking out the pieces, spreading them, with growing amazement, one next to the other, damply on the floor, fitting them together piece by piece—eyes widening incredulously—like a jigsaw puzzle?

But at last she heard a healthy flush. A second—just to be sure. She heard the taps running as he washed his hands.

The bathroom door opened, and he came out with his toolbox.

"It shouldn't give you any more trouble," he said.

"I can't thank you enough," she replied.

Two days later she received the bill: $28.65. Wasn't that outrageous? Never mind. She wrote the check at once and put it in an envelope, addressed it hastily and walked to the corner to mail it. She was glad to have it out of the house.

VIII

EARLY Sunday afternoon, the day after Edith's funeral, Kitty and Jane drove down the mountain, the back of the station wagon filled with stacks of newspaper and cardboard boxes. They were going to Edith's apartment in town to pack up her possessions. Ray had planned on driving the women down, assisting them with the packing —he adored looking through other people's things—but at the last minute a client had telephoned, and Kitty and Jane had exchanged a secret look of relief when they heard him say into the phone, "Aww, I guess not. No, you come on up and we'll go over the plans again." He could not, even for his own pleasure, put his work second.

So they had left him with his client, a pretty Air Force wife younger than Jane. The two of them sat catty-cornered to each other at the maple dining table, early afternoon sun pouring through the trees and making lacelike patterns upon Ray's beautifully drawn plans. Ray said amiably, "Well, the next time he writes from Germany about this extra door beside the carport, you write back and tell him I said if he wants a lopsided house that's what I'll build him. Out of the best materials, of course." The wife did not seem to mind this slur on her absent husband. She looked respectfully toward the Master Builder (whose name she had picked out all by herself from the yellow pages), and for an instant Jane saw, as she was leaving the house, how her stepfather looked through this young woman's eyes; a lean, competent man, short hair graying about the ears, new bifocals making him look rather scholarly, capable brown fingers with close-trimmed nails caressing his handiwork on the thick white paper with a sensuous pride.

"Do you think Ray will ever have an affair?" Jane asked Kitty as they drove down the mountain. She was slyly glad to have got Kitty alone. John and Emily had stayed behind to play poker with Ronnie and Jack.

"No," said Kitty rather wistfully. "He's not the type."

Jane wondered if Gabriel's wife thought he was not the type. "I thought the funeral went well," she said. "Even though it drizzled at the end. Edith would have been pleased with how smoothly everything went. One thing puzzles me, though. Where did Father Barnabas get that absolutely perfect handful of dry reddish soil? I never saw him stoop to pick any up. It simply materialized from his lace sleeve when he needed it."

"Father Barnabas is a magician," replied Kitty, in a secretive, possessive tone that excluded a nonbeliever like Jane from these magics.

They rode for a few minutes in silence. Jane noticed that her mother made a funny little clicking sound in her throat, as though gently choking. She had not noticed the sound before this visit. Should she bring it up?

Already she was wondering when she could leave. Would tomorrow be too soon? Yes; Kitty knew her classes did not begin till the following Monday. She could say she had to get back and grade papers, only she had finished grading them last night, in Emily's room, and bragged about the accomplishment to Kitty this morning. She had even brought the grades with her, sealed in an envelope, to mail on the way to Edith's. But she was becoming uncomfortably restless, the way she did whenever the intensities of her mental life began to dissipate— as they always did on visits to her family. Focusing too clearly did not seem to be encouraged in the atmosphere of "home." Why? Take last night, when she had decided to grade the papers, get it over with, even though wearied from the funeral. It had been *easy*, this ethical confrontation she had so dreaded only three nights before, alone in her own bedroom in the Midwest. Here, "at home," she had whisked through the whole batch in less than two hours. Portia Prentiss's *Marriage of Heaven and Hell: A Radical Poem* received a quite acceptable C minus, which would appear on the transcript as C. This paper, had it been graded three nights before, under the beam of Jane's multi-intensity lamp, would have received a D—mitigated by a personal, concerned visit to the chairman by Jane, who would explain this student's background and arrange for Portia to continue on probation, provided she enroll in Remedial Rhetoric.

Same difference, Jane had reasoned, the night of Edith's funeral, her mind suddenly gone glib under the simple 75-watt bulb beneath a frilly lampshade in Emily's room. And when she next saw the girl, "Dr. Clifford" would encourage Portia to enroll in Remedial Rhetoric. Who could or should force anyone to do anything, after all? Howard and his rice-paper poems she gave an Incomplete, rather than the F he deserved. She was weary of the struggle with him. How could she translate to him, into his Zen language, an F or a D? Those are just symbols, he would say. An Incomplete avoided the issue and left her an escape hatch. It didn't, finally, pass judgment, and there was always the possibility he might drop out of school before she had to come to terms with his second paper.

Sheldon's "Visionary Arrow Flies Backwards" got an A. No, it was good enough as it was; she would not bother to look up the Einstein stuff. She spent longest over his paper, because she copied a passage from it into her personal notebook. She was not sure whether it was unclear to her because his writing was not as clear as it should have been, or because her own taut mind had become loosely strung in this atmosphere and she could not arrest Sheldon's superior insight as it sped past in its visionary/Einsteinian velocity.

> . . . *in the time it takes a bolt to strike,*
> *fly, and be resting in the bowstring's blur—*

This is how Dante (Canto II, 23-4) describes the passage of time between the moment when Beatrice looks upward and the moment when the poet, looking at *her,* finds himself in a wondrous place, a place of new vision, from which he can look backward at the world and see earthly actions in reverse (imagine a home movie of our own daily lives run backwards). Of course, any of us who have ever practiced archery, or watched it, can apprehend the "instant" of time it takes for the arrow to find its mark, but Dante is talking about a visionary instant, which operates out of another time zone altogether. What is exciting for us about this passage is that we, too, in grasping the metaphor, are forced to turn our sights around, reverse the action of the arrow, pluck it out of its target, send it back through the fertile void of visionary air, until it rests freshly, "unmarked" by its passage through the ordinary time-space continuum, untensed as yet against the bowstring of all its possibilities. If we follow this daring hysteron-proteron as Dante meant us to, we arrive with him at the *locus* of his wondrous, as opposed to ordinary, "Newtonian," vision. And here in this *locus,* our redemption is always possible. Through a reseeing of processes, a "re-vision," which often means a re-version, or even a re-versal, we leave behind our mundane prison where "the wings of reason often do not fly-true" and find ourselves at home in this place where, as Beatrice tells Dante, "the arrows of wonder should not run you through."

Even as Jane copied Sheldon's words into her notebook as possible future guidelines to her own life, she felt a subliminal uneasiness as to the hundred-percent soundness of his grasp on the *Paradiso.* There was something a little off here, something not quite focused. Surely an A paper claiming to have defined the visionary focus should itself be truly, centrally focused. But if she could not focus on his mis-focus, how could she give him anything but the benefit of the doubt? And that lovely phrase: "The fertile void of visionary air"! Was not that one poetic line worth an A, considering the average, run-of-the-mill term paper? It inspired and soothed her. It came to her like a touch from divine Beatrice herself on Jane's insomniac brow.

She stuffed the grades in an envelope already stamped

and addressed to the secretary of the English office, and now, as Kitty turned the station wagon into the street which would lead to Edith's small side street, Jane said, "Stop at the mailbox, will you?" And she rolled down her window and stuck the envelope quickly down the chute before she could change her mind. She wished *she* were on her way to that envelope's destination. Her mind was not good here; it was not focused, not at its taut, vibrant best. She felt as if she had mailed her better half back to the Midwest, while "she" remained behind, like some dependent undeveloped wife who, when her husband goes away, taking rationality and discipline with him, has only her inferior emotions and terrors to keep her company.

When Kitty and Ray married, in spite of Edith's outcry, and took young Jane to live with them, Edith had moved to an apartment, a sealed-in side porch on the house of Mabel Cairns, a long-ago schoolmate at the teachers' college. The gray-shingled house with its gables and other Victorian pretensions presided over the few "newer" ranch-type houses on the narrow lots of the short street. "It is a respectable street, however, in spite of the tacky little houses," said Edith. "And I won't be here for long, anyway. I have outlived my usefulness." She sold almost everything from the larger apartment the three of them had shared, and kept only a few bare necessities to get her through her last days: her high double bed with the feather mattress, the dressing table with the triple mirror, a deep comfortable rocking chair, a floor lamp, an oak chest of drawers, her old sewing machine, and Jane's toy chest, which now served as a bedside table on which she kept her medicines and the radio and the telephone. She kept her china, silver, and linens, her own clothes, and three or four small cardboard boxes, which were sealed with tape and labeled "Kitty's stories and newspaper articles," "Jane's letters and little drawings," and "bills, medical, ins., etc."

As the months passed and Edith disgracefully did not die, she allowed a few things to be added to the tiny apartment which was to have served as anteroom between this life and the next. She added a second comfortable chair, so that the prodigal Kitty, more dependent on her dialogue with her mother than she had realized, could sit down when she stopped by for her daily visit. She allowed Ray to carry in with his own hands a small bookcase (also built and stained and varnished by the same hands) to be placed in one corner to accommodate Jane's books. Jane had quickly grown unsettled sharing quarters with her newly married mother and stepfather. There were too many new sounds, smells, sights that her own oversensitive puberty had trouble accommodating: the sight of Kitty, flushed and lazy in the morning, frying eggs in her bathrobe in front of this man; the new smell of Kitty; certain noises at night, unlike anything she had ever heard when the three women lived together. She chose, and was allowed, to return to Edith's for the week-nights; she could study better at Edith's, she said, and besides the school bus went right past the corner of Edith's street. So her life became halved into two manageable opposites. Week-nights belonged to the fastidious blue-curtained room where, after Edith's supper, served predictably at five-thirty, Jane threw her legs over the side of the rocking chair and studied until nine, her diligence spotlighted by the dependable lamp and witnessed by the indulgent Edith, who very often relinquished her sewing or reading of magazines in order to climb into bed and brood at her granddaughter from the shadows in her own study of possessive love.

Weekends Jane stayed with Kitty and Ray across town in their disorderly apartment, where meals were cooked only when somebody complained he was hungry, and Ray's record player was going most of the time, with Glenn Miller's "Little Brown Jug" or the Ink Spots' "If I Didn't Care." "If I didn't ca-a-are," Ray would sing in his twangy mountain tenor, picking up Kitty, who was much solider than he, and swinging her awkwardly around the little furnished room. The view from the living room overlooked a trucking company across the street. There was always the "new smell" in this apartment. Jane would look away, embarrassed at her mother, too big to be swung in this skinny ex-G.I.'s arms like a doll, and wish for Monday afternoon, when the school bus would once again deposit her at the corner of that other, chaste street.

The weekdays came and went, as did the years, Mabel Cairns, the widow who owned the house, died. Her tenant lived on, paying angry visits to the doctor to have her blood pressure checked and to be informed humorously that if she continued taking such good care of herself she might live to be a hundred. She read Dr. Molner's column in the paper, looking for symptoms of rare illnesses. When Dr. Molner died, she read Dr. Thostesen. The house was sold to a Detroit family named Wurtburg, who were rather awed to find they had purchased an original Southern lady along with their other furnishings and fittings. But the Wurtburgs were soon baffled by the social politics of this pretty town where people said soft, pretty things but never meant them; where, no matter how hard you worked or how pleasant you were to people, you seemed already to have been assigned a "place" and were expected to stay in it. In Detroit—but they were no longer in Detroit! They had left that city because it was dirty, ugly, and there were beginning to be racial incidents; there were too many black people in Detroit. But nevertheless it vexed them to come here and find the inhabitants of this town behaving as if there were no such thing as Detroit, as if the Detroits of the world were not the least little threat to them. There were plenty of black people here, but they made themselves agreeably invisible, disappearing from the back seats of the city busses into the rear entrances of their employers' homes. They stayed in their places, these Negroes. And so did the Wurtburgs. They treated Edith with a complicated mixture of subservience, resentment, and awe. She became for them the live-in symbol of the town. Mr. Wurtburg would sigh loudly when, just as he was settling down to the evening paper, Edith would step across and tap on his front door to complain there was no heat in her apartment. But he always put his shoes back on and went down into the cellar and poked loudly around in his furnace for a decent interval of time. After a half-hour or so, he would send his wife over, wearing the timid smile he could not manage after a day's worth of forced smiles to customers who came into his hardware store and said things like "Oh, are the nails kept over *there* now? When Charlie Grimes was alive, he used to have them *here*." Mrs. Wurtburg would knock on Edith's door and ask her if she was feeling warmer now. And Edith would always say, "Won't you come in for a minute," but in the tone that Mrs. Wurtburg was beginning to understand meant nothing of the kind in this town.

Often Jane was with Edith on these evenings. "Put your legs down," Edith would whisper before she opened to her landlady's knock. When Jane was there, Edith would explain to the shadow of the woman who stood in the door, "My granddaughter sits up so late studying and I didn't want her to catch a chill. For myself, I could have just gone to bed and covered up with an extra blanket, but she sits up to work, you see. They work her too hard out at that school, I think." Jane could never bear the landlady's sorrowful, hungry look at her. She bowed her head over her book. The three Wurtburg girls went to the public school in town. They were all within a few years of her, yet not once in all the years Edith shared their house did Jane have a conversation with the girls. They often passed on the front steps, coming up and down the walk. They spoke. But Kitty and Jane made cruel jokes about the Wurtburg girls. ("I saw what's-her-name waiting at the bus stop," Kitty would say. "She had her compact out and was putting on some more of that purple lipstick as I drove past.") Once Jane had passed two of the Wurtburg sisters downtown, nodded to them pleasantly, and heard one say to the other afterward, ". . . Miss Stuck-up . . ."

Just as Kitty parked the station wagon in front of the old gray house, Mrs. Wurtburg came out of the door, drawing on a pair of yellow gloves. In recent years, she had become less sorrowful, less hungry-looking. Mr. Wurtburg had sold his hardware store and bought several hamburger stands which did well with the teen-age crowd. Their three daughters were married, the oldest (that very what's-her-name who painted her lips at the bus stop) to a young lawyer from one of the town's better families. Mrs. Wurtburg, coming briskly down the front steps of her house, wearing a suit of muted green and a smart yellow hat which matched the gloves she fitted to her fingers, had achieved a certain matronly integrity in having done the best she could by her family, against considerable odds.

"Oh, dear, just our luck," said Kitty. "I don't feel like speaking to her. I had hoped to slip this check in their box with my nice little note and have done with it."

"Then don't get out of the car yet," urged Jane, turning away from the window. "Let's pretend we're sitting here discussing something urgent till she gets in her car and goes. I can't bear how she always asks me if I'm 'still doing so well in school,' and then finds some way to bring up Doris's marriage."

"No, we mustn't be cruel. After all, she and Doris came to the funeral."

"I saw them, all dressed up, snuffling away the whole time Father Barnabas prayed."

"Don't be naughty, Jane." Kitty rearranged her face and stepped quickly out of the station wagon. "Hello, Mrs. Wurtburg! What luck, running into you." She slammed the door, leaving Jane behind to marshal her slower resolves necessary to get through the forms with this woman, forms which Edith had skimmed through without a thought ("Won't you come in for a minute?"), forms which Kitty complained about, then suavely executed. It was simple courtesy. Why should she dread it so, feel so drained in advance, at the prospect of exchanging a few minutes of mournful pleasantries with Edith's landlady?

Both Kitty and Jane understood that they would cry when they entered Edith's apartment for the first time since her death. And they did, clinging to each other, making a ceremony of it, understanding that these tears meant not only a leave-taking by someone who had been important to them, but also their own farewell to certain roles in their lives. For the first time, Kitty was no longer a daughter. Only her motherhood and eventual grandmotherhood stood between her and death. As for Jane,

172

she now felt exposed at both ends of her life. She was no one's grandchild anymore, and yet she was not—perhaps never would be—anyone's mother. She held Kitty tight and looked over her mother's shoulder at her own reflection in Edith's mirror. One day, Kitty will no longer be here, she realized, and there will be nothing between me and . . . what? A reflection of a "tired little old lady"? Or perhaps, standing like a cavalier behind me, Death himself in a nineteenth-century traveling cloak, come to carry off a Romantic, a romantic little old lady.

"Let's get more light in here," said Kitty at last. She opened the curtains. "Are these theirs or hers?"

"They were Mrs. Cairns's, so I guess that makes them hers. I don't like the material much, even though they are blue."

"Neither do I. Let's leave them." Kitty went over and looked at herself in the triple mirror. "We don't have to do *everything* today," she said irresolutely. "Maybe Ray can help some tomorrow. Oh, dear, I forgot. I start teaching again tomorrow. And I haven't prepared my girls' history lesson."

"It is hard to know where to start," agreed Jane, looking around the immaculate room. So many familiar objects, never to stand together like this again. "It's sort of sad," she said, "breaking up Edith's little family of things."

"You know, I've never been able to get excited over *things,*" said Kitty. "The way she saved things, kept them up, worried about them. I've seen her gloat over a teaspoon she'd just finished polishing. Can you understand that?"

"Yes, I can. You know, I think I'm becoming like that. Honestly . . . sometimes, having supper by myself, I'll suddenly find myself feeling tender toward a silver saltshaker, or some little object on the table. I almost feel like starting a conversation with them. And sometimes I light a scented candle and just sit in my living room on the sofa, with my arms folded, looking around at all my books and pictures. I'm a great silver polisher myself. I sometimes wish I had more of it to polish."

"Well, you can have all of Edith's. That should keep you busy," said Kitty pleasantly.

"What? You don't want any? Does Emily, do you think?"

"Emily's like me. She'll stick with her stainless." Kitty folded back the flaps of one of the boxes they'd brought and opened Edith's bottom bureau drawer. "Things," she repeated, as though pronouncing a foreign word. "No, it all passes. All of it. Even people."

"All?" Jane took down the large oval-framed photograph of Edith as a young beauty, wearing an enormous black hat with ostrich plumes. She wrapped it in newspaper and decided to keep it for herself.

"Except the eternal things, of course," said Kitty.

"Do you think love is eternal?"

"It depends. *Some* kinds of love, maybe. Oh, Edith's new corset! Hardly worn. I guess we'll have to throw it away. Even the Salvation Army isn't going to want someone's corset. And two, six, ten, fourteen . . . fifteen pairs of white gloves. Do you need any white gloves?"

"I don't wear white gloves anymore."

"I suppose I can use them for church. She was more of a lady than I was and I am more of one than you are."

"I was thinking something like that in the car, when I was getting up my energy to speak to Mrs. Wurtburg. All the old forms, at least the effortless practice of the old forms, going out the window. Or maybe we'll have to rethink the reasons for them, and then find ourselves wanting to practice them again. . . . I had this conversation with a woman, a friend of mine, another professor in the department . . ." Jane trailed off, realizing Kitty did not know Sonia Marks, wondering if her mother would be all that interested in Sonia's salami story. She waited a moment, watching Kitty methodically sorting Edith's handkerchiefs, gloves, undergarments in piles. Kitty did not seem to know that Jane had stopped in midsentence. She was in thoughts of her own.

Jane went into Edith's little kitchen and poured herself a glass of ice water. But it tasted funny, probably from being in the refrigerator for so long. Then she saw a bottle of Harvey's Bristol Cream behind a stack of dishes in Edith's china cabinet.

"Aha! What's this?"

"What's what?" asked Kitty from the next room.

Jane came back with the bottle and two jelly glasses. "Look what I found! It's hardly been touched."

"Oh, the sherry. The doctor told her to take a little to give her energy. I saw her take a teaspoon once, as though it were poison."

"Want some?" Jane was already pouring two glasses.

"I never drink without Ray. . . . Oh, well, all right. Just a little, though."

"Here's to love," proposed Jane, clicking glasses with her mother. "To whatever love it is still possible to eke out of this wretched world. My love for you, our love for the memory of Edith, love of God, love of things, even silver salt-shakers if nothing else is available, love of books, love of dogs, love of—" she suddenly saw how Ray's fingers had touched those house plans, and wanted to include everybody in this toast—"one's work."

"I'll drink to that." Kitty took a sip of sherry and swallowed it slowly.

"But I want to know," said Jane, taking a fair-sized swig from her jelly glass, "whether there is eternal love between a man and a woman. I want to know whether there has ever existed in this world a lasting, lively love in which a man and woman exist, for years and years and years, taking sustenance and delight from this love, being able to do things better *because* of this love rather than in spite of it. I want to settle this question of whether we need our other half, or if that's just some old story born out of economic necessities."

Kitty shook her head, as if trying to clear her ears. Her smooth forehead above the pale, mystical eyes suddenly wrinkled.

"Why do you have to 'settle' it? What makes you think anyone can 'settle' such a thing?" She took another, larger sip of sherry.

"Because. If I could be absolutely assured that such love has never, does never, will never exist, except in books, then I would try and make a more sensible attitude and stop wanting the impossible. But if it *does* exist, then . . . I have to keep myself open and alert. I have to keep ready for my other half. At the moment, I'm divided.

I don't see much evidence for it, but yet I am collecting evidence. Look at George Eliot and Lewes. *They* completed each other. They were passionate, but neither of them exploited the other. They met in the middle of their lives when both were on their way to being disappointed people, and they gave each other back the birthrights of their best selves. The love she had for him made him do the best work of his life, and she became George Eliot because he gave her the confidence to. She was afraid to write fiction before he told her she could. They were outrageously happy, and they were all in all to each other for twenty-five years."

"Did you ask George Eliot?"

"There are passages in her letters, in her journals, Kitty. There is one I know of by heart. I like it so much, yet it hurts me, because I want it for myself. She wrote to a friend, 'We are leading no life of self-indulgence, except that, being happy in each other, we find everything easy.' Don't you love that? *Being happy in each other, we find everything easy.* As if love contained some kind of energy which freed you for your best creative work. I want that kind of love which brings such energies."

"Good luck," said Kitty. For some reason, she looked mildly annoyed. She took another sip of sherry and refilled her glass. Then she turned sideways in the chair in front of the dressing table. She frowned at her profile in one of the side mirrors. She opened the top drawer, in which Edith kept her powder, lipstick, creams, and hairsticks. She began dropping them, one by one, into the wastebasket, except for the expensive creams.

"These will make no one very beautiful anymore," she said, holding up one of Edith's hairsticks. It looked like a thick brown crayon. There were a few of Edith's white hairs stuck to it. "Curious-looking thing, isn't it? I don't know why she wouldn't just have it done when she went for her appointments. I honestly believe she thought she was fooling her hairdresser as well."

Jane refilled her glass and drank, rather depressed all of a sudden. "Oh, why can't anyone tell me the answer to these things!"

"You are such a child in some ways, darling. You're

such a good little *student*. You've always been one to look up your life in books and develop crushes on teachers who would tell you 'answers.' So she was happy, 'outrageously happy,' for twenty-five years with this man. Can anyone *living* look me in the eye and tell me they have lived with a man for twenty-five years and been *outrageously happy?* You're living in myths, Jane, to expect such things!"

"Well, if I am, it's because I am looking for myths that support the possibility of happy long-term relationships."

"The trouble with myths," said Kitty, whose face was becoming pinker with each sip of the Bristol Cream, "is that they leave out so much. They leave out all the loose ends, all those messy, practical details that make living less than idyllic. That's why myths can remain beautiful. That's why twenty-four hours or twenty-five years cannot, nonstop, be 'outrageously happy.'" She seemed to have seized on this phrase of Jane's and was determined to shrink it down to manageable size. "Honestly, Jane! Hearing you talk like this makes me thankful all that is finished for me. All that yearning. All that *choosing*. All that dreary, endless agonizing over what you cannot have."

"How can you say it's finished for you? It is finished for Edith, but not for you and me."

"Certain things are over," said Kitty. "Definitely over. Finished a long, long time ago. I don't think you understand, I don't think you are properly aware of the fact —Oh, this is silly. We ought to be packing."

"No please! What is it I am not aware of?"

Kitty set down her glass—empty—on Edith's dressing table. She looked at her daughter. For the first time in years, her eyes became angrily, selfishly alive. "Listen. There was a time when I wanted every one of the things you want. I wanted it all. I wanted love. I wanted a career. I wanted everything eternally beautiful, and with no compromise. I wanted a kind of marriage I knew my parents had not had: a marriage of passion *and* esteem. I wanted so many things it makes me sick to remember. . . .

"But nothing synchronized. The time was always just that crucial bit 'off.' The *times* were off. We are products, we are prisoners of our times, little Jane. Even your great novels will bear me out on this: look at the care in which a good Victorian novel first sets up the environment around the characters. I think I was one of those people who have the misfortune to grow up with one foot in one era and the other foot in the next. I wanted to write books, but my body got in the way; yet I wanted my babies, when they came. There were certain times I saw, almost like a vision, the virtue of selfishness, but, you see, I was brought up to believe woman's best virtue was that of renouncing herself. So I had little orgies of selfishness, followed by deep, depressing hangovers of shame. There were years when I thought I was going to tear myself in half. Now I look back on those years with—well, some pity for the poor mess I was . . . but, most of all, with a sort of sociological distance. Edith, you know, had the good luck to be born with a thoroughly contemporary soul. What she cared about was being in fashion, and that fashion decreed beauty, good manners, and dutiful, womanly behavior. As for myself, I was born too late or too early. I would have made an excellent medieval gentlewoman: you know, the ones who had their fill of courtly love—*and* fleshly—and then retired devoutly, at the same time their fleshly desires did—to a convent. I think I might also have done rather well if I had been born the year Emily was."

"What about my year?" asked Jane.

"Still a bit risky, I think. No, in my might-have-been daydreams, I refuse to compromise even a few years." Kitty opened another drawer of Edith's dressing table and began pulling out hair-net envelopes and other envelopes and papers. She became fiercely absorbed in her task.

"Sometimes I think those persons raised in the interstices of *Zeitgeists* are the ones most punished," said Jane. She refilled her own jelly glass, got up from her knees, where she'd been wrapping Edith's clock radio in newspaper, and poured Kitty a full glass. Kitty did not protest. Then Jane began throwing out all Edith's bottles of pills. So many kinds of pills! And Edith had, after all, escaped

178

all the dread diseases she anticipated, and died of old age.

When she finished, she saw Kitty pulling old photographs out of one of the hair-net envelopes and sifting through them.

"Anything interesting?" asked Jane, coming to look over her mother's shoulder.

"Here's one of Cleva, sticking out her tongue at the camera."

"Oh, let's see. Have we seen that one before? I don't remember it, do you?"

"I'm sure we have been shown every picture, at some time or other," said Kitty dryly, and Jane knew that Cleva represented the same thing in both their minds. Cleva, Cleva's tragic, colorful story had been used on both of them by Edith, to keep them in hand, the way priests use Hell on their congregations. *"You know what happened to Cleva,"* uttered in Edith's masterful sepulchral tone, had become a regular deterrent toward most of the desired adventures of both daughter and granddaughter. When Kitty, in her courting heyday, had stayed out too late with a boy; when she threatened to go to New York and study acting; when she came home smelling of whiskey; or when she wanted to buy a dress too low-cut or too revealing for Edith's standards, out would come poor Cleva from the family closet and off she'd go: first to the fatal play with her sister, *The Fatal Wedding* (if Jane had not seen the old Wilkes-Barre program with her own eyes, she would have suspected Edith of inventing that title), and then sneaking off in the dead of night on her first ("and *last*") train ride with . . . The Villain. When Jane became old enough to compare notes with Kitty, they discovered an interesting thing. When Edith was threatening Kitty, her stories about Cleva's downfall always stopped short of New York. Why, when the worst was yet to come? With Jane, Edith had indulged herself. She had taken her granddaughter and led her by the hand, through their joint morbid imaginations, into the cheapest, most dangerous sections of New York, luxuriating—insofar as Edith's sheltered life would allow (she had never been poor; she had never been to New York)—in images of the direst poverty. And Edith, who

179

never in her life mentioned "certain subjects" specifically, came perilously close to delineating what had been done to Cleva and what Cleva had done in return, to produce the final—and as far as Jane was concerned, the only provable—evidence: the baby, who had grown up to be Frances the snob; and the coffin, which came home on the train with Hans and the baby.

Perhaps, after Kitty had disobeyed Edith and run off, not once but twice, to marry undesirable men (the first wellborn but indigent; the second industrious but "common"), the mother, having failed through too much reticence, through stopping short of the city limits of the wicked city, decided to brave its dangers for her granddaughter's future good. Or perhaps (another distinct possibility) Edith recognized in Jane a similarity to herself, another similarity Kitty did not have—just as Kitty could not faint. Perhaps Edith saw in Jane her own tendency to imagine the worse. For when Edith said to Kitty, who was embarking on a date with an Undesirable, "You know what happened to Cleva," Kitty (as she reported to Jane, years later) simply said, "Oh, pooh." Not so with Jane. When, as early as the seventh grade, she confided in Edith that young Klaus Hermann, the son of German refugees who had recently moved into the same apartment house, had invited her to the movies, Edith had said: "Better not, I think. Cleva's villain was a German, you know. Von Vorst. Though I don't believe the 'Von' was authentic for a minute. Not like Hans's family, who earned theirs in the Franco-Prussian War but dropped it like good Americans when they came to this country." And Jane had immediately lost interest in young Klaus and his movie offer. "Did he have much of an accent?" she asked, fascinated. "Who?" said Edith. "You know, the villain. Von Vorst." And Edith blinked, perhaps incredulous at her good luck with this impressionable child who could be manipulated so easily through a few dramatic images. "I *think* so," she said. "Yes, I think Von Vorst distinctly did have . . . a trace of an accent." "And how did everybody know the baby was really Cleva's?" pressed Jane. Edith clouded. "There are ways

180

people have of telling such things," she said angrily. "Though, just between us, I'm like you. I was never satisfied with the so-called proof. But Frances is our family now and we must let the dead lie in peace."

Now, without Edith, Jane and Kitty studied the brown photograph of their mythical rebellious aunt. The girl was slim and high-bosomed in her wasp-waisted white dress. Her hips jutted forward, slightly provocative, as she tilted a parasol behind her and stuck out her tongue. To her right, his shoulder blocking out a square of light on her dress, was the shadow of a man, the man who was taking the photograph. He had been caught by his own camera in the act of taking Cleva's picture. Who was he? (*May, 1905. Cleva,* in Edith's handwriting, on the back of the picture.) What had he meant to Cleva? Was she sticking her tongue out at him for a particular reason (perhaps known only to the two of them) or just as a general sign of lively protest against May, 1905? Was it a form of flirtation for her? No one would ever know.

"Well," Jane said, sighing, "that's one family mystery gone down the drain without ever being solved."

"Perhaps it has outlived its usefulness," said Kitty.

"What do you mean?"

"Well, Cleva's been worn pretty threadbare, if you ask me. Her symbolism has been worn out—on our family, at least. I hardly see how her plight can be of any use to Emily. Emily would have no more use for her than she has for old silver. No, as a preventive measure, Aunt Cleva has become as outmoded as . . . certain forms of birth control. And even in her most effective years, you know, it's funny but she sometimes had the opposite effect. I remember the night I eloped with your father. We drove over the state line to South Carolina. Edith thought I was spending the weekend with my best girlfriend. I remember driving in the dark beside your father—he had a 1937 Olds convertible, black—and we rode with the top down, even though it was no longer summer . . . and my hair was blowing in my mouth, I had to keep spitting it out again, and he thought that was hilarious—we were quite hilarious that night—and the whole time, in a funny way, Cleva was with us. It was as if she was . . . patron saint of the evening, or something. The thought of her, and her villain, sneaking off on the night train together—do you know Cleva actually sneaked out of Edith's *bed* to go with him; they slept together at the college—really made me more excited. Oh, I felt very comradely toward your Aunt Cleva on my marriage night—though we weren't married till the next morning. I remember looking up at the stars and my hair blowing in my mouth and thinking to myself like a song: Here we go again, Cleva, you and I running away with our unbridled impulses. Did Edith ever tell you how Cleva disobeyed the Dad and took out his dangerous horse and the horse ran away with her? I thought of that horse. Unbridled impulses. Oh, it was quite a night. However it turned out. Your father was an exciting man. An elegant and exciting man. He drank and wouldn't get a job—he would rather play tennis—but if his ship hadn't sunk I think they would probably have let him stay in the Navy. I do not regret it and I'm glad I had the excitement of him. I felt close to Cleva that night. . . . I felt as if I were more her child than Edith's." Kitty suddenly snatched up her jelly glass and belted down the sherry, in one coarse gulp, the way barroom belles in old movies downed their whiskey. She glared round the room, eyes sizzling, all traces of the acquired "spiritual" in them gone. She looked incredulous at being trapped here, in Edith's tiny chaste blue room. She looked at Jane rather resentfully, and for a strange moment Jane felt sure Kitty was mistaking her for Edith.

"Edith did tell me a horse story about Cleva," Jane said. "But I don't think it was that one. It was the one about how she had been riding the pony all morning and her period started."

"Oh, yes!" Kitty laughed. "That one, with all the blo-o-o-d!" Kitty bayed out the word, showing the whites of her eyes. Something insurrectionary had certainly surfaced in her mother, and Jane giggled, delighted.

"We've got to stop this and pack," said Kitty, taking another sip of sherry. "He will be wondering."

"I hope we can find that old theatre program Cleva wrote the note on," said Jane. "Oh, I wish we could solve the mystery of whether Frances was Cleva's or not for certain."

"The program's here somewhere. Once I accused Edith of writing the note herself, just to make her mad. There *is* no mystery, Jane. Cleva's landlady helped deliver Frances. My daddy talked to the landlady. The baby lived, Cleva died—no mystery. It's funny, don't you think, when you consider how that poor little baby grew up to be Frances."

"I thought Edith never talked about New York with you," cried Jane. "You said she never did. You never told me about the landlady! Neither did she!"

"Oh, well," said Kitty, getting the familiar prevaricator's glaze on her flushed face, "I think it was only that one time. And she probably skipped it with you because . . . you know how queasy you are about messy details."

"It's so hard to get to the bottom of anything in this family," complained Jane. "You can't remember what time I was born and I don't know for sure the exact moment Edith died. And why didn't somebody go after Von Vorst and arrest him? God! Nobody knows anything, except what's useful for a good story at the time."

"Arrest him for what?" asked Kitty, widening her eyes. "For what crime? It was 1905, Jane. In society's eyes, Cleva had committed the crime."

"But her own father, her own sister—why didn't they go after her?"

"The Dad, you forget, had just married Elise Swan. A greedy young new wife. Cleva had run away of her own free will. He was glad to be able to disown anybody he could. Cleva had 'ruined' herself completely, you know that. In 1905. But even today you don't 'go after' people when they run off on their own free will. If Emily had run off with John and, say (oh, I don't know why we're getting so morbid), nine months later sent a cry for help —well, we'd go to the rescue and bury her if she'd died and take the baby home and raise it. We wouldn't go looking for John. (I'm imagining of course a villainous

183

John, which is rather funny, don't you think?) The last person we'd want to find would be John, don't you see, for the baby's sake. He might want to take it himself. And as for Edith, she was powerless to do anything, until she married Hans. She had no money to hire *detectives,* or anything. And nobody knew Cleva's address till the note came, on that piece of theatre program. And then my daddy did what he could, but it was too late for poor Cleva. She tried to have the baby by herself; she was too ashamed to go to a hospital."

"Ugh!" Jane made a face, imagining the pain, the mess.

"See!" said Kitty triumphantly, "you can't take it. That's why she didn't tell all. Now Edith is gone and so is Cleva; they're buried next to each other for good. Why go on dredging up gory details? Let the dead bury the dead. You are always trying to *research* everything."

"I guess I am," murmured Jane. She felt dizzy, but didn't want to say so, didn't want all this to be closed—not yet, when it might never be opened again.

"But I have always wondered about one thing," she began again.

Kitty sighed, glanced at herself in the mirror, touched her hair where the chignon had slipped slightly off center. "What?"

"How did Cleva manage to meet a man and get to know him well enough during intermissions? How many intermissions were there? The whole thing, if you ask me, was pretty fast work for 1905."

"She was stage-struck. She always went backstage and hung around in the wings when they went to plays," said Kitty. "Certain people are just more dramatic than others, Jane. They have a heightened sense of drama about their lives. Things seem to happen faster to them than to the ordinary humdrum run-of-the-mill people. Whatever the era. Whatever the year, there are always some people who are passionate and others who are not. Oh, look, here's one of you. What a serious little thing you were, always busy at some drawing, or writing little stories, or reading. You certainly knew how to keep yourself busy with your crayons and books. Do you ever draw and paint anymore?"

"No, I gave it up a long time ago. Mostly. I guess I just read now."

She wanted to ask her mother if she thought she was one of the undramatic, ordinary humdrum run-of-the-mill people to whom nothing ever happened fast, if Kitty thought she was one of the unpassionate people of her era, but she decided against it.

Through Edith's blue curtains, the winter afternoon waned. Daughter and granddaughter continued to pack, sporadically, their reminiscences and discoveries of topical objects frequently deflecting them, their efficiency diminished by the thick, sweet sherry.

At the bottom of the cardboard box labeled "bills, medical, ins., etc." they found a small brown package sealed with tape and tied with string.

"I wonder what's in here," said Kitty, trying to edge the string from the package. "Honestly! Edith was so secretive! She was a nut about privacy." Kitty gave up and cut the string with a nail file. Jane crowded close and they opened the package.

"A diary!" said Kitty.

"Oh, God, could it be possible she kept a diary?" Jane's fictional instincts were thoroughly aroused. It was entirely possible, in her mental world, for them to open the diary and find out the whole story of Cleva, everything they had always wanted to know. Perhaps Edith had had a lover, too. No. Jane was ashamed of such a thought.

"It's locked," said Kitty.

"Oh, *no!* We must find the key!"

"We'll never find it. She may have flushed it down the toilet. You know Edith."

"But why keep the diary at all, then? Why not destroy it, too?"

"The key may be somewhere, but we'll never find it. Wait a minute . . ." Kitty rummaged round in the wastebasket and found a gold hairpin. She began uncurling it. "I used to be pretty good at picking locks."

Jane held the little book while her mother picked around the empty keyhole in a rather practiced manner. "A LINE A DAY" was stamped in gold on the faded blue calf. The book gave off a promising musty smell: the odor of old secrets and information stored under lock and key.

"Ha! Got it, I think," Kitty said at last. There was something appealingly mischievous about her this afternoon. Jane was enchanted.

They opened the book. It was a five-year diary, for the years 1935 through 1939. The writing was tiny, in various colors of ink.

"Oh, my goodness," said Kitty. "Oh, my God. Well, I'll be damned. It's mine. I'd forgotten all about it. It's my college diary."

Jane was already skimming the difficult tiny writing, looking over Kitty's shoulder. "To library. Letter from Georgie—short—said nothing about being responsible for his actions Saturday." The date was Wednesday, April 3, 1935.

"Oh, can I see?" Jane said.

"Wait a minute, wait a minute. After all, it is my diary," said Kitty. She was skimming the page, too: The five April 3rds from 1935 through 1939. The last one was empty. *Two months before I was born,* thought Jane. *Oh, I have got to read this book.* She tried to turn the page, to the April 4ths, to see what more she could find out about Georgie—who on earth was Georgie? For what actions had he said nothing about being responsible for?"

"Just a minute, just a minute," murmured Kitty, busily reading. Jane decided to get what she could from the facing page, the April 2nds from 1935 through 1939. Tuesday, April 2, 1935, was crammed. Jane could not read all of it. "Town with [illegible] and Mrs. S. Dramatic Tea in afternoon. Poured. More fun. Fuss with Don. He told me he didn't love me anymore—not that I care though I pretended to, and I [cried? did?] a little, too. Most cruel. Talked to [illegible]. 11:20 Georgie phoned and was glad I refused George R. a late date. Parked at [Greyhound? No, it looked more like Gimghould]. [Illegible] Oh I love him so much. Sweet! We just couldn't [illegible] to Sig Ep House. He loves me so much—at times. If they just weren't so few and far between. Saw Don's car parked at [illegible]. I keep hoping and praying . . ."

All this on a school day?

"Let me have this a minute," said Kitty, a preoccupied new note in her voice. "Here. Let me see this." She took the book away and turned her back to Jane.

"Could you read some passages aloud, then—after you censor them?" Jane forced herself to sit down on the floor, at Kitty's feet. "Please, Kitty. I'm so interested." Why didn't Kitty write in her diary when she had been expecting Jane? When had she stopped?

"Oh, my! I'd forgotten all about that!" exclaimed Kitty over something.

"About what? About what?"

"Oh, nothing. Just something." Kitty was deep in the diary now. She giggled. Jane had never seen her like this. "Oh, I was terrible!" Another peal of giggles.

"Why were you terrible? Kitty, please. This isn't fair. Read *something* aloud."

"Oh, all right. What a persistent little thing you are, Jane!" Kitty spoke to her as if she were five years old again, begging for a story, when Kitty would rather read a grown-up novel.

"Studied all morning," Kitty read aloud dutifully. "Movies in afternoon with Mary Lib. Saw *One New York Night*. It was very good. Talked to Mother and Daddy on telephone. Worked on term paper. Nine pages now typed . . ." But Jane, watching the movement of her eyes, saw that she was reading something farther down the page to herself.

The phone rang in Edith's apartment, startling them both.

"You get it," said Kitty.

It was Ray. "Aren't you two about finished down there? Do you know what time it is? Almost six. Emily and John have to leave after supper."

"We've done a lot," said Jane. She nodded at Kitty, who was mouthing, "Is it Ray? Is it Ray?"

"Anything wrong down there?"

"Why should anything be wrong?" To her dismay, Jane started giggling, out of sheer nervousness.

"Let me speak to your mother."

Jane put her hand over the black mouthpiece and said, "He wants to speak to you."

"Oh! Wait a minute, wait a minute." Kitty rummaged wildly in the wastebasket, found a box of Edith's powder, and began powdering her flushed face with it, still holding the open diary with her free hand.

"On the *phone,* Kitty." It suddenly occurred to Jane that she and her mother were drunk.

"Of course," said Kitty into the mouthpiece. "No, don't be silly. Well, we're not quite finished. Edith had a lot of stuff." She caught Jane's eye. The two of them went into a paroxysm of giggles. "Well, if you must know, we had a little sip from Mother's bottle of sherry—you know, the one she kept because the doctor told her to."

It was all up. Ray forbade them to leave. Forbade them to drive after drinking. They must wait for him. John would drive him down and he himself would drive the foolish women home.

"Why did you have to say anything?" said Jane when Kitty hung up the phone, looking sheepish. "We could have managed."

"He would have smelled it when we got home. It would have been much worse. Believe me, it would have been much worse. I just want to keep the peace. You don't understand such things. You'd better learn, if you are ever going to be outrageously happy for twenty-five years." She burst into riotous laughter, then remembered the little blue diary in her hand. " 'Scuse me a minute. I must go to the bathroom, all this sherry," and off she went with the diary.

Jane knew, even before the toilet flushed the second time. By the seventh, eighth, ninth, she was feeling maudlin, utterly sorry for herself. Shut out from everybody's secrets. She stood at the parting of the blue curtains and looked out at the approaching winter night and remembered how Ray's red-haired construction worker in his handsome funeral suit had given her a look yesterday, as Edith's coffin was being lowered into the earth. It was a sexy look this Parker gave her, a look that indicated he recognized the woman in her and, if he had the time and desire, could stir her up a bit.

Kitty returned, her face spotty, trying to curb expressions which still veered dangerously toward rebellion and hilarity. She tossed the faded cover with the gold clasp into the wastebasket, the shell of her college diary.

"Why?" said Jane. "How could you?"

"It was mine," said Kitty. "That was another person, that girl. She's dead as a doornail. Deader than old Cleva."

"Well, I would have loved to have kept her alive," said Jane. "I think it is downright irresponsible to go around destroying things like that. I'm not sure one has the right. John Cross took out the respectable parts from George Eliot's diary and made a sort of paste-up job for posterity and threw the rest away. He had no right to do that, no right at all."

"I'm not going to be any George Eliot," said Kitty. "There was nothing of any use to posterity in my diary. Just a lot of silly old memories."

"It might have been of some use. It might have been of some use to me. How are people ever going to evolve if their forebears keep on destroying the evidence?" Jane was almost in tears; she was becoming really maudlin.

"You have to live your own evidence, dear little Jane. You cannot research everything, you know," said Kitty scornfully. She turned her back and sat down before Edith's triple mirror and began remaking her slipping chignon.

"Who was Georgie?" said Jane angrily.

"Who told you about him?"

"I saw it in the book. And George R. And what about Don? Can they all be so easily flushed down the toilet? What were they to you? Did you want to marry them?"

"I wanted to marry lots of people," said Kitty, her mouth full of hairpins, "and lots of people wanted to marry me. That's all over now and I'm glad. Be a good girl and let me forget that silly little coed."

Ray arrived. He walked into Edith's apartment, took in everything with his small dark eyes: the half-packed

189

boxes, the women with their pink faces and silly, guilty grins, the empty bottle of Harvey's Bristol Cream standing on its head on top of Edith's corset in the wastebasket.

"I'll get Parker over here tomorrow," he said. "We can finish this up." He looked with interest at the scattered photographs lying on top of the dressing table. He would go through them at leisure tomorrow, Jane knew; he liked to look through other people's things.

"I think I'll get Parker to marry me," she heard herself say.

Kitty's façade of composure cracked and she hooted with laughter.

Ray said, "I think I'd better get you two home and get something in your stomachs. Emily and John have to leave soon. I told John I wanted him to drive slow on those old tires." His voice was mature, reproachful.

Then, slowly, Kitty crumpled. Jane watched the transformation, awed at Kitty's skill. Large tears actually fell from her mother's flushed cheeks. "You couldn't possibly understand . . ."

Ray was by her side in a flash.

". . . what it is to lose one's mother. I hope yours will live for a long time to come. It was all too much, seeing her things, her family of little things, trying to separate them for the last time . . . even this bottle of sherry . . ." Kitty stooped and picked it tenderly from the wastebasket and held it like a small child. "Edith held this bottle in her hands only a week ago. . . ."

It worked. Ray took his wife in his arms. His husky arms in their plaid wool sleeves enveloped her grief for her mother. Jane suddenly saw a younger Kitty pretending to be heartbroken when "Don" told her he didn't love her anymore. Jane was pretty sure he did love her, even when he said he didn't, and that within a day or two Kitty had him back on the string, with Georgie and George R. and, eventually, her own father.

"I shouldn't have let you come down here by yourself," Ray said. "Parker and I can do it all tomorrow."

"Twenty-five years of outrageous happiness!" Jane shouted, and Ray looked at her as though she were mad.

IX

It was ten o'clock on the evening of the same day, and the permanent residents of the household on the mountain were restored to routines and sobriety. Jane, on the other hand, sat by herself in the kitchen, a glass of Scotch before her on the cleanly wiped table, going deeper and deeper into a mood she could recognize only as unfamiliar. She could not describe it: it was both frightening and satisfying. It was like letting go and being taken somewhere. She tried to trace it back. When, exactly had it started? At the mailbox this afternoon, when she had sent off her grades, telling herself she was sending her mind, "her better half," back to the Midwest, while her undeveloped emotions stayed behind like a dependent wife. One had to be careful about triggering things by finding the right words for them, she thought. Sometimes you could set things in motion purely to watch the actions imitate a group of emotionally satisfying words: "I'm leaving you" (to someone who has hurt you, but whom you do not want to leave); "Let us drink to the end of our idyllic love. . . ." Horrified, Jane watched her hand close round her glass of Scotch and lift it to her lips. I do not have to drink this toast, she thought. She drank.

After crying all the way home from Edith's apartment, Kitty had slept, first making Ray promise to wake her at nine, so that she could prepare her girls' class in Medieval History. Now Jane heard Kitty typing rapidly on her portable electric in her little study off the bedroom. She had never heard anyone type as Kitty did. It had a unique, ever-varying rhythm to it, as though she were playing different tunes on the piano. Jane remembered her own pleasure years ago, when she was a little girl, listening to Kitty type the first drafts of her stories, her love stories, on the old Remington on Saturday mornings. Perhaps she varied the rhythm of her keys to console herself for having to repeat the same old plot again and again; the plot of a girl, give or take the color of her hair, who threw everything out the window to get her man.

Emily and John were gone. "Goodbye, Plain Jane," said Emily, balancing a stack of lawbooks on her hip as she opened the door to let John go first with the suitcases. "Don't ruin your eyes." "Don't ruin yours either," Jane had replied. It was their old parting routine: the two scholarly half-sisters, whose tenderest exchange was when they were saying goodbye.

Ray had cooked supper. The boys had taken their plates to the basement, where the TV was, and had not reappeared. Jane helped Ray clear the table; he would not let her help him load the dishwasher—he had his own method, he said. "I'll have a drink, then, and watch you," she had announced, still feeling the effects of the sherry. She waited for him to forbid her; she hoped vaguely for a fight. But Ray surprised her by taking the keys from his pocket, unlocking the liquor cabinet built in above the refrigerator, and telling her to help herself. He did not like members of his family to drink without him, although the ostensible reason for the locked cabinet was a former maid, Electra Jones, who had worked for the family years ago, in another house. ("She had this mayonnaise jar, and all day long she'd drink my liquor out of it and I was never the wiser till one day she overstepped herself. She'd take a quarter-inch of gin, you see, and then she'd take a quarter-inch of bourbon, then a quarter-inch of crème de menthe—it was all the same to her—and when I checked my bottles at the end of the day, all the levels seemed to be the same. Then one day my wife drove into the driveway, and there was Electra straddling the fence post, brandishing my meat knife in the sun and calling, 'Hi, there, Miss Honey!' ")

Sipping the Scotch, Jane watched Ray step lightly about his kitchen, almost dancing on the toe-tips of his Hush Puppies to the thrum of the dishwasher, lovingly sponging the surfaces of stove and sink counter—all chosen, all set into place, with his own hands. She understood the expression on that face. It was the look of a person who is secure, a person in control of things. Why *should* he risk the uncertainty of an affair, go down into the town and find a woman who might make him miserable, when, on top of his mountain, he could be the father he never had, the provider his mother had so desperately needed, the keeper of a queenly woman who prayed and cried too much, as women do, but who sat propped beside him all night, reading books in strange languages, keeping the night from him like a mother while he slept?

Did Gabriel ever load his dishwasher? What had made him risk an affair? Perhaps *he* needed the diversion of a little uncertainty. His childhood had been secure, lonely but secure, from what she'd been able to drag out of him. Once he had said, "I'm a man of predictable habits, but that is not to say I don't like the unpredictable in my life."

Ray, unable to initiate a conversation because of the dishwasher's noisy cycles, took a large package of M & Ms from the cupboard, waved his hand cheerfully, and left the kitchen.

She sat on, nursing her Scotch, thinking, insulated by the noise of domestic machinery grinding and swishing away. Ronnie came in, opened the door of the refrigerator, and stood languidly in front of it, planning what he was going to have, a habit which drove Ray wild. Jane watched as he slowly took out a new carton of chocolate ice cream, a can of chocolate syrup, a spray can of whipped cream, and proceeded to make himself a giant sundae. Aware that he had an audience, he overdid it a bit, she thought, going importantly to the cupboard and taking out various bottles of little decorater pellets Kitty used on cakes, sprinkling them on top of the whipped cream, and then sticking Hershey's kisses round the sides. He worked with concentration on his project—this surprise baby boy of Kitty's, whose eagerness to be first

193

and best at everything had begun with his birth, so different from poor Jack's, which had nearly killed mother and son. Ronnie's labor had been the shortest of all Kitty's children, lasting a mere forty-five minutes. The doctor raced down the hospital halls and into the delivery room wearing his golf shoes, in order to catch Ronnie's head and thus nominally deserve his fee. With Jack, Kitty had been toxic. Ray had flung himself down on his knees as she was wheeled into surgery for a last-minute Caesarean. He had promised God he would never lose his temper again if He would spare his wife and this first son they so much wanted.

Ray's nickname for his younger son Ronnie was "the Little Hun." To his friends he made proud remarks, such as, "If they'll just keep this war going till *he's* old enough to join up, he'll go over there and end it in one day." But to Ronnie, he said: "Son, do you have to be so goddamned selfish and arrogant and rude? Do I have to beat you to death to teach you a little humility?" At thirteen, Ronnie was an expert on World War II. He knew more facts about it than his own father, who had fought in it. He borrowed stacks of books from the city library, researched battle tactics, the construction of aircraft carriers, what weapons and bombs were used, the internal workings of planes and explosives. He was not much interested in the people, just the machines. On the walls of his room were Scotch-taped huge drawings of skies crammed with destruction: bombs, rockets, burning planes, shattered parachutes. The things looked as if they had had the souls torn from them; yet the falling bodies of the humans in these pictures were strangely sticklike and never mutilated, impervious to the multiple injuries life could so easily inflict. In recent visits, Jane had noticed this same growing imperviousness in Ronnie. When Ray would threaten him or reprimand him at the table, he gave his father a level stare, flushed slightly, and that was all. His refusal to react had a rather sad effect on Ray, who was then driven to turn on his favorite son. Jack winced, he flinched, the tears came into his eyes—could be depended upon to come—whenever his father seriously criticized him. Jack was all sensibility, while Ronnie was all hard-nosed achievement, excellent in everything he undertook, from studies to sports, only strangely insensitive to any effort to impinge on his emotional life. And yet, thought Jane, watching Ronnie carelessly stuff things back into the refrigerator now that he had used what he needed of them, we all spoiled Ronnie, not Jack. Ronnie was so adorably open and easygoing as a baby. Once, years ago, Jane had been taking a bath when the door softly opened and a naked cherubic Ronnie stood with his arms full of boats and rubber animals, waiting to be invited into the tub. She had taken him in, toys and all, and they'd had a lovely bath. Now the dishwasher stopped and the silent kitchen was full of the warmth of this memory.

"Stay and talk, Ronnie," she said.

"Can't now. I've got to get back to my program." He took his sundae and left, eating as he went.

She snatched up the telephone and dialed Gabriel's office. He was never in his office on a Sunday night. *Please,* she willed, *be unpredictable just this once.* But the man of predictable habits proved to be a man of his word.

"Shit."

"I *wish* my children would enlarge their vocabularies," said Kitty. She came into the kitchen wearing her orange kimono. She had a sheet of paper with single-spaced typing on it.

"I have an above-average vocabulary," said Jane. "I just feel like indulging myself a little tonight. Want a drink?"

"I think we've had enough drinks for one day. We were silly, weren't we?"

"We had the best conversation we've had in years."

"Oh, dear. I wish I could remember more of it." Kitty sat down at the table, looking placidly at her sheet of paper. "I wanted to read you this. I translated it straight onto my typewriter from this marvelous little book I have, *Le Livre du Voir-Dit.* It's a love story. A fourteenth-century love story. Do you want to hear it?"

"I love a love story; you know me."

"Yes, I know," replied the other, raising her eyes. They were not quite absolved from their afternoon foray into the old world of dreams and senses: the edges were still warm and pink around the mystical blue.

In a rapt voice, Kitty read from her paper: about a young, rich, beautiful girl of noble family in 1362 who sends her first rondel to an old, poor, sickly blind-in-one eye, but celebrated poet. She invites him to enter into correspondence with her, a poetical love correspondence in which she offers him her heart. The sickly old poet re-kindles. He replies to her rondel. An exchange of letters and poems follows. After many exchanges, they decide to meet. In those days, a young lady of noble family could permit herself extraordinary liberties as long as a third party was present. The poet awaits this first meeting with many misgivings because of his unattractive appearance. But the young lady is kind and pretends to be asleep, under a cherry tree. Her maid, who is present for the interview, puts a leaf over her mistress's mouth and instructs the old poet to kiss the leaf. At the last moment, she pulls it away. A few more such "interviews" ensue, the last of which, the old French narrative gives us to understand, marks the young lady's gift to the old poet of the golden key of her honor. His good fortune ends abruptly, however. She returns to her home to be married, and he spends the remainder of his life polishing up their rondels to one another and revering her in his immortal poems. "Here, listen to this," said Kitty, really moved. She read: " 'And, my very sweet heart, are you sorry because we have begun so late? By God, so am I; but here is the remedy: let us enjoy life as much as circumstances permit, so that we may make up for the time we have lost; and that people may speak of our love a hundred years hence, and all well and honorably . . .' "

"Oh, God," said Jane. She put her head in her hands.

"That is what I call eternal love," said Kitty. She rose and came and stood behind her daughter and kissed the back of her head, misunderstanding Jane's gesture for agreement rather than despair.

"Are you teaching that to your eighth-grade girls to-morrow?" asked Jane, her head still bowed.

"Yes! Let's start the semester with love. I had the idea this afternoon while we were talking."

Jane sat on in the kitchen with her Scotch. Where was everybody? Asleep. Where was Ray? Why didn't he come and tell her to go to bed? She felt rooted to her chair. She felt she was going to do something awful.

She picked up the telephone and dialed long-distance information. The operator in Gabriel's city answered. Jane asked for his home telephone.

"Hello," he said. She had been ready to hang up if his wife had answered.

"Hello. This is the unpredictable in your life."

". . . Where are you?"

The first time she had ever called him at home. Was he thinking that, too? Why hadn't she? He never asked her not to. But it would have violated her image of their decorous affair.

"I've been trying to reach you," he said, speaking softly into the phone. Did he sound nervous?

"Oh, I'm not where you think I am."

"Is anything wrong?" A touch of irritation, just a touch, in the soft voice.

"Yes." And as Kitty had done this afternoon, Jane deflected a man's feeling of annoyance into the more manageable one of sympathy. "My grandmother died. I had to come home."

"Oh, I am sorry." All sympathy.

"It had to happen sometime. She was old. Why were you trying to reach me?"

"I had an idea. Probably not a workable one. Just an impulsive thought. I wanted to ask you if you'd care to meet me in New York. But I suppose it's out of the question now."

"New York?"

"I have to check out some things at the Met on my semester break. I got a last-minute windfall from the Art Department. I want to see those pictures one more time.

You know, for the book. But I'd have to work most of the day and you'd undoubtedly have been bored. Your family needs you there, I'm sure."

Gabriel's habit, an offshoot perhaps of his critical profession, was to set up a feasible proposal and then think up as many reasons as possible to knock it down. If the proposal concerned them mutually, it then fell to Jane to re-enchant him with his own idea by the sheer force of her own enthusiasm. She wondered if he had such a tacit arrangement with his wife. Or perhaps Ann Weeks was the naysayer in that family.

"Things are perfectly under control here," she replied quickly. "We buried her on Saturday, and Mother and I packed up all her things today. I was planning to leave in the next couple of days."

"I'm flying to New York tomorrow." He sounded uncertain.

"What airport? What time does your flight arrive?"

"Mmm, around noon, I believe. LaGuardia."

"It's simple, then," she went on, trampling down her own uncertainties to bolster his flagging resolve. "If they still run that early morning flight out of here, I can be waiting for you at LaGuardia. I'd be almost two hours ahead of you. I could even finish the book I'm reading while I'm waiting at your gate." She gave a nervous little laugh, meant to sound hearty.

"Well, actually that might not be a bad idea, except for the fact that . . ." and he embarked on a series of convoluted sentences, working into them backward, as was his style during the difficult spots of his critical articles and of his life. The "fact," embedded deep within his hesitant explanation, was that Arthur somebody from the Art Department might also be on the same flight tomorrow morning and it might be awkward if . . . he was sure she understood. He had been thinking it might be a better idea if she went ahead to the hotel and booked a room for herself. He had already written for his, last week, and received confirmation—it was before he had had his "impulsive idea" that she might join him—and it might look funny if he suddenly changed the single reservation. He told her the name of the hotel; he had chosen it from his AAA guide—good central location, sensible rates. He would join her there around one. It took about an hour to get into the city, if he remembered correctly. How did that sound?

"Lovely," she said, secretly chafing at his failure to be impatient. She would have liked it better had he pronounced himself utterly incapable of waiting that extra hour to see her.

"Very good," he said, sounding pleased. "How nice we managed to get in touch, after all. See you around one tomorrow, then! I'll give you a call in your room as soon as I arrive."

"Fine!"

"Solong."

"Solong."

He hung up, cheerfully abandoning himself to the fourteen hours of uncertainty in between, that terrible empty space—the dark side, surely, of Sheldon Rossinger's "fertile void"—in which anything at all might happen to keep them apart. Before one o'clock tomorrow afternoon, one of them might die. Ann might have to be rushed to the hospital for an appendectomy. His plane or her plane might be hijacked. There could be a snowstorm. Here, there. At some crucial point in between. He might miss his plane; his wife might oversleep, forget to wake him. (Did Ann drive him to the airport? Jane would prefer to think he took the limousine.) Fogged in: here, there, all over. Unable to land in New York, circling round and round her destination before the pilot announces they're going on to Cleveland. Who was going to drive *her* to the airport? Kitty would be disappointed at her leaving so suddenly. She would tell her mother the truth, of course. Kitty, of all people, must be sympathetic to the perennial old urgencies of having to make the train, the plane, to keep a tryst. *Here we go again, Aunt Cleva, you and I running away with our unbridled impulses.* Isn't that how she had put it? Shouldn't it be the other way round: our unbridled impulses running away with us? What if there was no seat for her on the morning flight? What if there was no longer a morning flight?

With shaking fingers, Jane dialed United. Yes to everything. She was giddy. She felt like throwing herself down on the kitchen floor and uttering a wild prayer of thanksgiving.

But the hotel. What if, after having coped with fogs, real or imagined (and both took their toll of emotional energy), untimely deaths, emergency operations, hijackings, snowstorms, all the uneasy traffickings in between, she should arrive at the good little hotel and find it filled to the brim with conventions of AAA people who had beat her to this excellent central location with its sensible rates?

After a considerable amount of trouble and no few explanations, Jane got the long-distance operator to call the hotel and charge the call to her own telephone. She would not allow Ray the luxury of complaining, as he had once done on a past visit, that she "came home and ran up his phone bill."

She booked a room with a double bed for "Professor J. Clifford."

"What time will he be arriving?" asked the night clerk.

"Around noon," said Jane pleasantly, willing to pass as Professor Clifford's enterprising wife, or secretary—or mistress. She would have felt somehow compromised to have to admit it was she, the caller, who wanted the double bed for a single person. This night clerk would be gone before she came; she would simply correct the silly mistake in sex with a cool laugh, ride aloofly up in the elevator beside the bellhop, take nonplused possession of her clandestine bed.

"The daily rate on that will be twenty-two-fifty," said the night voice in New York.

"That's fine. Thank you. Good night." Jane hung up. Everything settled. Twenty-two-fifty. Quite reasonable, considering the location. Gabriel was staying two days. Two times twenty-two-fifty . . .

Her hand went slowly to her mouth. She sat rigid for some minutes.

Then she rose and went slowly downstairs, stately as a sleepwalker, to undo the efforts of almost twenty-five years. Fickle, inconsistent "self"! No sooner was its "better half" mailed to the Midwest than the inferior stay-behind pricks up its ears, actually feels relief, at the sound of Ray's adding machine! He was still up, still awake, still available in his office.

She knocked.

"Come in!" He was sitting at his desk, going through a pile of statements. He looked surprised to see her, almost pleased. He could number the times she had visited him in his office on his right hand, which now hovered above the keys of his adding machine.

"I came to say that I have to leave tomorrow morning. Something important has come up. I know I'm going to disappoint Kitty, but it can't be helped. Can somebody drive me to the airport? I'm sorry to say, before seven."

"Anything wrong?" asked Ray, looking at her over the top of his bifocals.

"I have to go to New York."

"New York? How come you didn't say anything to us earlier?"

"I only just found out. I just made this phone call—don't worry, I charged it to my own phone—and I have an appointment in New York at one o'clock tomorrow." Why was she quaking inwardly, suddenly a teen-ager again? She was free, adult, she would soon be thirty-three years old! He could not forbid her to leave the house anymore; that happened only in dreams now. She remembered too late that she had direct-distance-dialed the call to Gabriel. Ray would have the evidence on his next bill: her lie.

Her stepfather rocked back in his swivel chair. His stubby fingertips pressed together, making a steeple. "Do you need any money?" Watching her so strangely!

"Thank you. As a matter of fact, I do. I didn't come prepared for this—extra trip. Of course I'll reimburse you as soon as I get back."

Ray sighed. He got up from the chair. He scratched his head as he shuffled to his closet and took down a gray metal box. His actions were slow, measured, almost luxurious, as though he had been rehearsing them for years. Out came the heavy collection of keys. He unlocked the box.

"Five hundred be enough? Or you need more?"

"Five hundred! A hundred and fifty is all I need."

Ray counted out five bills. "Take five hundred," he said. "Don't do things on the cheap. Your mother loves you. She values you."

"But Ray! This is ridiculous. I told you, all I need is a hundred and fifty. I don't want to carry around so much cash."

He turned on her and for a second she thought they were back in the old nightmare. He was going to take several steps across the room, his rage rising in his throat, and beat her up. But he stood there, his black eyes shining at her, taking her in as he might some phenomenon that both repulsed and fascinated him. At last he spoke in carefully controlled tones. "You take the five hundred," he said, "and you go on up to New York and you go get done whatever you have to get done right. Your mother won't be told about this money, and if you have any consideration for her peace of mind, she won't be told anything else." At the end of this speech, his eyes brimmed with tears. For what? The two of them seemed to be in two completely different dramas.

It came to her then: the comedy of it, if she had felt like laughing. *Ray thought she had to have an abortion.* Her "queasiness," reported to him by the "tightrope-walking" Kitty on the morning Jane had stormed out of the kitchen providing Kitty with the perfect cue: "I'm sick to my stomach!" And why else did modern unmarried women depart precipitously on the early morning flight to New York to keep an appointment at one? Ray had read somewhere—in his *U.S. News & World Report,* no doubt —exactly what a "good" abortion cost.

But as he continued to stand there, shining in his righteousness as he offered her those bills because she was precious to the woman he loved, his Belle Dame sans Merci of twenty-five years, Jane's comic spirit took wing and she was left with the sensational dregs of melodrama. She had to restrain herself from clasping her hand to her bosom and crying out plaintively, "But I am *in*-no-cent!"

But if she protested, he might take back his money. And what did it matter what he thought? And if the truth of the matter was known to him—oh, God, what was the "truth" of any matter any more—would it make one jot of difference to his value system (she suddenly envied him having one; this poor mountain boy had at least constructed *his* own love-and-work ethic) which of her transgressions preceded which: to take a lover in adultery, or to take the product of this love inside you on the morning plane to New York? Either way he looked at it, Ray would see himself as paying for one of her sins.

"Thank you," she said, with all the dignity she had left for this moment. "You are kind, Ray. You'll get it back the minute I can get to my bank." She took the bills from her stepfather.

"No rush," said Ray. "Send it on when you can." He went back to his desk and sat down.

She stood in his office, holding the bills. He was trying not to show it, but he was trembling a little—as she was. She would give anything to break this awful tension between them, slink back to Emily's room, pack her suitcase, and lie down in the familiar arms of her insomnia until morning. Who was Gabriel? For a minute she had forgotten.

But it was now Ray's privilege to release her, to give her his permission to leave his office and his house. And he knew she knew it.

So she waited, conceding him his victory. She held the money he had worked so hard to amass during the years she had plotted and schemed to escape the need, at last, of having ever to depend on him again.

He cleared his throat. She was prepared for one of his "Baptist-preacher tirades," as she used to call them privately; for the crudest of insults; for some truthful, insightful accusation concerning her "selfishness" which could send her to her room in tears. She was prepared for just about anything, except Howard the Hippie's harmless query, rounding off this historical exchange.

Ray said seriously, "Don't you *want* to be happy?"

Jack was lingering in the hall, just outside of Emily's room. He had Fritzi with him. The two of them seemed to have been communing about something when Jane approached, her hand crushing the bills.

"How long you staying?" Jack asked.

"I have to leave early tomorrow. Before you wake up, even. So I'll kiss you goodbye now. Jack! You're taller than I am. Down, Fritzi!"

"She wants to be kissed, too," Jack said.

"Oh, all right." Jane bent slightly so that the huge dog could slaver briefly on her cheek.

"She's almost as tall as you when she stands on her hind legs," Jack said. Then he saw the bills she'd been trying to crush smaller in her fist. "Dad give you some money?"

"He *lent* me some money," she snapped, then regretted it because of the rebuffed look on Jack's expressive face —his too expressive face. "I'm not angry with you, honey, I'm just rather tired. You know, I think you and I are alike in the same way that Emily and Ronnie are alike. Do you know what I mean by that?"

"I think I do," he said, all gratitude and happiness now. He would say he did even if he didn't, to please me, she thought. "I guess you want to go to bed now," he added, a shy, uncertain hope in his voice.

"Yes, I guess I do. If only I weren't so tired, I would say let's talk awhile. We haven't talked for so long."

"Not since that time you came in to kiss me good night and I told you about the shapes I saw in the trees at night."

"But Jack, you were just a little thing. How can you remember that?"

"Oh, I remember everything," he said mysteriously. "I can remember things that happened even before I was born. I'm psychic." And he scrunched his face in an attempt to give her a roguish wink. But the casual, flippant gestures of this world were not for him. He only succeeded in looking horribly in pain.

"Jack, if you would ever feel like visiting me, I'll send you a ticket."

"You mean by plane?"

"Of course by plane."

"God, that would cost you a *fortune*."

"No, it wouldn't. You get student rates. You might as well get something out of being a student."

"Yeah, that's the truth." Jack hated school because teachers were always comparing him with his brother, who made friends so easily and was so good at football and got A in everything without even trying. Jack had been kept back a year because he would not read. Kitty had spent an entire summer *pushing* him, as she put it, page by page, through *The Count of Monte Cristo*. Again and again she would peek through the crack in his door only to see him staring dreamily out the window, the book forgotten on his lap. Jack had great fantasies, Kitty said, about rescuing children from fires and floods, saving people from drowning, helping the police track down dangerous criminals.

"I really mean it, Jack. Maybe you could come in the spring. We could have a good time. If you have your learner's permit by then, I'll let you drive my car."

"Your *Mustang?*"

"Sure. Let's plan it. We'll write to each other. Now I'm going to get undressed and go to bed, but think about it. We'll have a good time."

"Okay. If Dad'll let me. He probably won't." Jack knelt down, pretending to have found something he must pick out of Fritzi's thick winter fur. From the wistful, resigned tone of his voice, Jane knew he did not believe in this trip, though he wanted to. I could talk him into believing it if I could spare one hour, she thought, clutching Ray's money, in a sort of paralysis of good intentions which she was too dispirited to carry out.

As she closed the door on Jack bowing over the black dog, she could not remember keeping a single one of her resolutions concerning this visit home.

X

"HE thinks I have to have an abortion," said Jane.

"You don't, do you?"

Kitty was driving her to the airport. It was six-thirty in the morning, still dark, but Jane saw, or imagined she saw, the outline of the thick curling river, the same river beside which Edith and Cleva and Iz had grown up. It was called the French Broad, and was thus the subject of many jokes as well as the setting for many novels about the families of Scotch-Irish descent, like Edith's, who had lived beside this river and identified the tempo of their lives with its seasonal ebbings and swellings, its constant movement and change, its abiding presence. But one novelist had excelled them all. He had created this town, put it on the map of the "real world" by his unsurpassed descriptions of it. The town had not existed in eternity until he wrote it out in pages, focusing lovingly on the smallest detail (many of which details had been edited and thus no longer existed), and though he had died the year before Jane was born, his vision of the town was still more accurate, more complete, than that to be found in the living eyes of anyone who lived there today. Edith's own father was now immortalized, simply because he had appeared in one of this great novelist's books as a walk-on character, walking across a single paragraph on a single page.

Kitty was still struggling with her sleepiness. Her insomnia had hardly faded before she had to break her usual morning schedule to take her daughter to the air-port. Kitty's usual routine was to sleep till nine (Ray and the boys made their own breakfasts) and then coax herself awake with a solitary pot of Earl Grey and a pastry. Then she would drive down to the Health Club, swim her mile, have her steam bath and massage, fix her hair, and drive to the girls' school, where she would have another cup of tea (not as good as her Earl Grey) and teach her single class in Medieval History. After which, she would drive to Saint Mark's, whip out her mantilla, and spend a good half-hour among the flickering votive candles and the carved faces of saints, breathing in the incense like oxygen and lighting candles herself. This morning, in order to have these last few moments alone with Jane, she would do everything backward: church first, as the pool did not open till nine, then pool, then school, and no Earl Grey till early afternoon.

"Of course I'm not pregnant. Don't you think I'm careful?"

"Well, do be. Emily is on the pill. It's supposed to be safer."

"I don't like the idea of some foreign object inside my body, messing up its natural rhythms. I like to be in control of my own body. I like that little thing—you know. I have a sort of affection for it. It's mine, it was measured for me, it lives in its nice white box. I tend it, wash it, powder it afterwards, as they advise. It's like a small friendly companion, always on my side."

"Well. Let's *hope* always. Let's hope you don't have to come to terms with some larger foreign object than the pill."

"Though, you know, I could never have an abortion. It's against my principles."

"There are certain principles that are easier when not put to the test," said Kitty. "I really cannot imagine you as a mother. You're somehow not suited, psychologically."

Jane was silent. Others had made that same remark. Was she "odd" in the sense that she would never join or pair or duplicate herself? I must remember to look up

207

that word in the O.E.D., she thought, instantly cheered by the thought of looking up something in a book that might describe her.

"Shall I go in with you?" asked Kitty, angling the station wagon into the "No Parking/Unloading Zone" at the airport. "What if my coat suddenly flew open or something, with only my bathing suit underneath."

"No, I hate long goodbyes; so do you." The buttons of Kitty's ranch mink looked securely fastened, but Jane understood there was nothing more to be said this visit. Each of them was impatient to come to terms with what had been said, refashion it to suit her own life. Jane could see Kitty's eyes already leaving her, focused in imagination on the candlelit haven of Saint Mark's. She got her suitcase from the back seat, but resented Kitty being able to abandon her so quickly. As she got out, she kept her head in the open door. "Do me a favor, Kitty, will you? Light a candle for me when you get to church."

"I do. More times than you know. Anything special today? I've already promised Emily one. She needs a B in Torts."

"Would you light a candle—one of the blue ones, if possible—that I will find—that I will find—my best life?"

"Of course, darling. Of course I will." Kitty seemed relieved. "Can you think of anything else—anything else you want?"

Jane laughed. "No, if I get that, I'll be quite satisfied."

"Consider it done," said Kitty, smiling at her daughter.

She thought I was going to say "light a candle that I get Gabriel away from his wife of twenty-five years," thought Jane. And that would have spoiled the entire tone of her morning visit with God.

"Do you think I ought to wait while you check and see that your plane is flying?" asked Kitty.

"No, *I'll* wait till it does; we both know that." Jane gave a bitter little laugh.

"Shall I send Edith's silver to you by parcel express?"

"You'd better wait. I'm not sure where I'll be next fall. I won't want to move a lot of stuff."

"What? You're going to leave your present job?"

"Kitty. The contract was for two years. In June, those two years are up." Jane's rising anxiety made her speak to her mother impatiently.

"Two years already . . ." murmured Kitty. Then with a confidence born perhaps of her own security, an assurance that made Jane want to smash her fist through the windshield: "But they'll keep you on. With that marvelous thesis and all."

"Except for you and my former chairman, dear mother, I doubt if anyone else in the world has read or will read 'my marvelous thesis.' I leafed through my copy recently and found *I* could not bear to read it. Listen, I've got to go. If the plane *does* leave, it leaves in fifteen minutes."

"I love you," said Kitty fervently. "I'm going to light two candles for you this morning. One for—what you asked. And another more practical one. I don't think God minds practical requests. After all, He puts us in a practical world."

"I'm sure He won't mind," said Jane, forcing a goodbye smile. "Hold on to Edith's silver, light my candles, swim your laps, and listen: thanks for getting up so early. I know how you loathe it."

"I would not have traded these last few minutes with my little girl for a mere few hours of sleep," said Kitty.

"Well—" Jane trailed off. She slammed the car door, and then, in a last-minute surge of self-recrimination, mouthed "I love you" against the glass, hoping the fluorescent lights from United's entrance made it visible to Kitty.

She went in and checked her bag, grateful for the exchange of a few sentences with the airline clerk, a young man who still looked sleepy himself. What kind of bed had he just got out of?

"All the way to New York?" he asked.

"All the way." She watched him carefully, upside down, as he made out the baggage checks, an "old-maidish" habit she had cultivated out of a fear of being inconvenienced—and as a result of several actual mistakes made by such clerks as this young man. It was so easy to get a few numbers wrong.

Walking slowly to her gate, her fragile self reaffirmed by the brief exchange with a person who had already forgotten her as he checked in the next arrival, she accepted what she had learned to call "the severance symptoms," which seemed to be a recurring syndrome in her solitary style of living. Always, after leaving somebody, a group, a party, any situation when she had been included or coordinated (however superficially) with the lives of other people, the remembrance of her *singleness* impinged on her in varying degrees of force and mood. Sometimes it thrust its ugly face squarely into hers, with a jeering Cheshire-cat grin: *Here we are, Janie, baby, alone again.* Other times it washed over her more softly, nostalgically, like a sentimental old tune she had learned to love. Other times it was violent, cruel. It threw back in her face every value of her life alone and walked out on her like a rejecting lover, making her dream of death. She had learned to anticipate it. Once she had almost done herself in "playing" with the anticipation of it, hoping to make it less potent by turning it into a game. Last spring Gabriel had been visiting her. It was a Saturday. They had spent the afternoon walking and talking and drinking in a little pub. Then they had come back to her apartment. There was a good supper to look forward to, and the evening together afterward, but Jane was already thinking of tomorrow. Gabriel would not be with her this time tomorrow. Gabriel went to use her bathroom. Jane stood at her living-room window, still wearing her coat, looking out at the buds of the next summer's leaves on the trees outside. Then she realized that through a trick of light at just this particular time of afternoon, around four o'clock, she could look out the window and at the same time see behind her into her own hallway and the exact mirror image of the bathroom door. Gabriel is behind that door, she thought. I will keep looking through this window and soon I will see the door open and the figure of Gabriel will come out and steal down the hall and across this room until his hands are on my shoulders. Tomorrow, at this same time, he will be gone. But I will stand exactly as I stand today and I will look out the window and I will remember. By taking away a little of my pleasure of the reality today, may I not be allowed by this foreknowledge to store up a little pleasure in the memory tomorrow? The next day came. Gabriel left in midafternoon. (Ann was expecting him for supper.) After he left, Jane washed all the dishes from their last night's supper and late breakfast that morning. Then she walked about her apartment, from room to room, straightening things up, keeping her mind as much a blank as possible. She sat down on the bed and hunted for traces of her lover: a single hair, a stain, a smell, to prove he had been there. She straightened books on shelves, walked from window to window, looking out as the afternoon waned, waiting. She was waiting for four o'clock. When it came, she put on the coat she had worn yesterday and went and stood at her living-room window, looking out. The buds had not changed since yesterday. The light was exactly the same. She saw her own reflection in the coat; she saw the hall and the closed door behind. She imagined it opening. But it did not open. She imagined his tall figure coming softly down the hallway, across the room in which she now stood. But he did not come. She imagined the touch of his hands on her shoulders, but no touch obliged, and she heard a woman moan aloud crazily and the next thing she knew she was curled up like a baby, in the empty bed, wearing her coat, screaming and crying. Somewhere, in late afternoon sunshine, Gabriel Weeks, sitting securely in the center of the present moment, was driving away from her.

Just as, this January morning, the red glow of her mother's tail-lights were receding back down the same road they had come, following the predictable curve of the river, on her way "home" to her chosen well-ordered life. She would light two candles for her first child. ("Please, God, get her a job next year, or let her keep the one she has, and then if You have any time left over—I understand the job market this year for Ph.D.s is all but nonexistent—let her, let her—how did she put it?—find her best life. Oh, dear, they are low on matches this morning. I'll light all the candles first—if it's all right with You—and then put in the requests. Excuse me just a minute. Ouch. There. Jane needs . . . what I just said. Emily

211

needs at least a B in Torts; also she would like, I know she would, the grace to give up smoking, and the will—it's going to take a truckload of it—to make John do the same. He's been smoking years longer, and also he is not, as You and I know, blessed with Emily's marvelous powers of self-discipline.")

Then seventy-five times across the length of the Health Club pool, the ritual of steam bath and massage and hair-drying, protective creaming of glowing skin, dressing slowly into Mrs. Sparks, teacher of history, driving across town to the private school for girls, the old convent school Jane herself had attended before Vatican II happened and all the nuns became none. (Ray: "Do you-all know the definition of a nun? Ain't had none, ain't got none, and don't want none!") Ray had been proved wrong; the times had changed and somebody obviously wanted something they weren't getting and struck out to get it, leaving behind the well-groomed Kitty Sparks, eyes lightened by celestial love, to charm those eighth-grade girls as, twenty-five years before, she had charmed ex-G.I.s with her own ideas of love (unrequited, sublimated, in any event incompatible with "real life," where somebody—Belle Dame of either sex—took advantage of someone else and was lyricized for it afterward).

Then she would drive straight back up her steep mountain, incarcerate herself in lonely contentment (the men would be out for hours more), and make herself a pot of tea. She'd think of her daughters. She would worry about them. That same evening, she would write each of them a letter (*I wonder whom she writes first,* Jane thought, *or does the order change, or does she force herself to be fair and alternate?*) on her portable electric, typing as fast as she could feel, hitting the wrong keys, thus creating (and sending out unread, Jane was sure; *nobody* could miss such mistakes) strange, sometimes riotous, often oddly revealing messages from her mountaintop. ("I have every confidence, darling Emily, that you and John can give up smacking. I did it, long ago, and it was easy, once my decision had been truly mad." "Take one step at a time, Jane. Far rashing decisions are always made best that way. God loves you and wants what is best for you—be-

lieve that. I love you too and wont you to be happy
...")

Jane liked neither her despairs nor her pleasures to
pounce on her unprepared. As she grew older, she noticed that the need to see herself as often as possible within the context of her whole life grew stronger. One reason
she was such a worrier was that she could not help imagining what her life might be years ahead. She did not
allow herself to take comfort from the fact that most of
her worries never materialized; but she frequently paid
respects to former fears which had not come to fruition by
speaking aloud to the old self who had had those fears.
("You see, Jane, not only did you pass your comprehensives, you passed them with honors. Go back and
study now.") As she spoke, she saw the Jane of graduate
school days, self-imprisoned in the tiny bedroom-study
of her apartment. She saw the charts, in different colors of
ink, Scotch-taped to the walls—Romantics, Victorians,
Aesthetes and Decadents; the long lists of poets and
poems—Arnold, Browning, Byron, Clare, Clough, Coleridge, Hardy, Keats, Meredith, the Rossettis, Shelley,
Swinburne, Tennyson, Wilde, Wordsworth, with a few
memorized lines from the most significant poems, snippets of relevant biography, nutshell exegeses; the rigorous
daily schedules for review—"8:30–10 A.M., Austen;
10:30–11:20, class lunch at Union (start Brontës, if no
one sits down); 1–3 P.M., Brontës, then Dickens all the
rest of afternoon, evening; go over forgotten parts of
Bleak House with supper." ("You're overpreparing, dear
girl. What you don't realize is that the stuff will be a
thousand times fresher in your head than it has been in
your examiners' heads since they took *their* exams. But
you must not know this. That is why you are going to
pass with honors.")
Because she could depend on herself to hold these dialogues with her former selves, she sometimes treated herself to listening sessions of what later Janes might be whispering to her. Once, on a good afternoon, she had lain
rapt on her bed and heard her voice of the future begin
quite matter-of-factly: "Well, Jane, little did you expect

that Gabriel would divorce Ann—who is now happily re-married—and marry you. We have been together three years at the time from which I am speaking to you. He is very good-tempered and dependable and not remiss in husbandly duties: the storm windows are always up before the first frost, the garbage cans set beside the road in plenty of time every Thursday morning. It is not *exactly* as you used to fantasize, but all in all not unsatisfactory. (Do you notice I am beginning to talk like him?) What I have learned is that just as the so-called 'exciting' people have their terrible side for which one pays, the so-called 'sublime' people have their tedious side, for which one pays. Yes, don't be shocked! I am often quite bored—a complacent, tender boredom, of course—with Gabriel. Well, dear, you wanted it and I got it for you. It took a while, and no few sleepless nights, but I got it for you. Do you still want it?"

"Yes," Jane had answered fervently. "Oh, yes." Longing for that undreamed-of distant honor of being complacently, tenderly bored.

This morning, as the mountains of her childhood receded into the valleys below, as her plane ascended toward the winter dawn and she began to believe that this latest meeting with Gabriel would come to pass, she indulged in another private game which was closely related to the one she had played through her four o'clock window, preparing herself for the emptiness of his departure. Now she primed her capacities for happiness by preparing for his arrival. She went back and recalled the beginning so that she could reaffirm the wonder, could say, "Who would have dreamed this would lead to that, and so come to this?" By going over their early history just before she saw him each new time, she could startle herself into a rapturous disbelief and make herself grateful that so much—even if it was far from *all*—had been possible.

Three Decembers ago, the Americana Hotel in New York was headquarters for the annual convention of the Modern Language Association. It was early in the second afternoon and Jane had retreated to her bed after four morning job interviews, ranging from disheartening to disastrous. She was sharing her room, for economy's sake, with another graduate student from her university —an Indian girl she did not know very well—and wishing desperately for a room of her own. She secluded herself in her bedroom whenever she felt threatened, but apparently the Indian girl, whose name was Deiri, did the same. Deiri had just ordered a shrimp curry from room service and was sitting eating primly on the side of her bed in a purple-and-silver sari. The walls of the hotel were thin. Although they were on the twenty-eighth floor, the Sixth Avenue traffic raged and scraped in their ears, and, worst of all, the suite next to them had been rented by a university for job interviews and they could hear, much to their continued disquiet, depressing snatches of the beginnings and ends of the interviews as the applicants went in and out the door.

"That sort of thing doesn't help much, does it?" said Deiri in her precise Cambridge English. She had done her undergraduate work there and was reputed to be brilliant.

"No, it doesn't," replied Jane. "That's the third one within the last forty-five minutes they've asked to wait outside because they're not quite finished with his predecessor. That happened to me every time this morning. I think they jam their interviews too close together, to make us lose our self-confidence and be ready to take anything. Listen to that poor bastard . . ."

The two women listened to the sound of a briefcase being opened in the hall and some papers discreetly rattled. "I know exactly what he's doing," said Jane. "I had to prevent myself from doing it this morning. He's checking his vita sheet to make sure he still exists."

"Did you have any nibbles this morning?" asked Deiri politely, picking at the curry with her fork.

"It's hard to tell. One sounded friendly, but I couldn't see their expressions. They had seated me facing the window and the sun was shining directly in my eyes. Another chairman told me I reminded him a lot of a fascinating woman who was formerly in his department. She went mad. There's this one Midwestern university which is looking for someone to fill in two sabbaticals of tenured people and then cheerfully leave. I think I want something more secure than that. One university was arrogant and rude, so I decided to be arrogant and rude back, since I knew I'd never get a job there anyway."

"Cornell looked avidly at my brown midriff," said Deiri. "And New Mexico inquired whether or not I would be willing to take on a supplementary course in ethnoreligious studies where I would expound entertainingly on the Hindu religion. I said not. I said my specialty was not the Hindu religion but English Renaissance Poetry. I am sure they put me down as a snobbish darky. It won't be the first time. Look, would you mind dreadfully if I ate my curry with my fingers? I'm feeling rather insecure after my interviews. I need to feel at home."

"Go ahead," said Jane, watching with interest as the Indian girl turned her quick slim fingers into the perfect eating utensil for rice. "It makes a fork look ridiculous," she commented.

"Once, when I was up at Cambridge, I was in a pay telephone box," said Deiri, licking the tips of her fingers with relish. "And all of a sudden a man came up and stuck his head in the door and said, 'Are you brown?' and then ran away."

"An *Englishman?*"

"Of course an Englishman. They're the worst."

Jane saw the possible afternoon she might spend with Deiri. They would stay in this room, dredging up vulnerabilities, old grudges, new anxieties about jobs; they would console each other. Then they would probably go out to dinner together and, over a bottle of wine, each would convince herself she had found a dear friend. The next morning each would awake to find herself as separate as ever, and feel slightly hostile toward the other for the delusion brought on by the weakness of the day before. Back at their university, they would nod nervously to each other in the halls, and Jane would feel guiltier and guiltier until she would end up asking Deiri to lunch or dinner, where they would try to reclaim, over another bottle of wine, their one shared experience.

She picked up her MLA program and leafed through the second day's schedule. There was a lecture, with slides, at three o'clock, on the Pre-Raphaelite Brotherhood. She got up and put her skirt back on.

"You're going out," said Deiri, somewhat accusingly.

"I'm afraid I must. I forgot, there's a lecture in my field that I want to hear. It starts in fifteen minutes."

"Oh, what is the lecture?"

"The Pre-Raphaelites."

"I thought you said your field was George Eliot."

"My field is the nineteenth century. That includes George Eliot *and* the Pre-Raphaelites. You know."

"Ah," said the Indian girl sadly, looking away.

Going down the express elevator, whistling past dozens of floors, Jane felt guilty at her relief to have escaped from the predictable afternoon. Did she lack charity? She had cut off the relationship with Deiri before it had begun because she knew it would be a regressive one. They would not get each other any further. She preferred to run the risk of being bored by this lecture on the off chance that a single remark, perhaps even accidental or impromptu, might trigger an interesting thought in her head. This had happened before. She was becoming increasingly reluctant to squander her energies to the demands of good will, increasingly insistent on an equal return.

Zimmer, the English professor who did most of the talking, was a small, compact man with a sinister combination of dead-white hair and black mustache. He spoke in a civilized and sonorous singsong, with little trills of irony.

Weeks, his colleague, whom he introduced playfully as "a *devoted* fan of the P.R.B., borrowed for this occasion from my university's illustrious Art Department," appeared ill at ease in the windowless lecture room, with its cramped rows of small metal chairs, its smattering of pale tense faces, most of which already wore an expression of expectant boredom. The first few sentences he uttered were broken by a stammer. The two men were so unlike, such foils for each other, that Jane could not help enumerating, as she waited for the lecture to begin—Weeks had just narrowly escaped knocking the slide projector off a narrow stack of books with one of his enormous hands

—various ways these men might play opposite each other. In an eighteenth-century comedy of manners, Zimmer would be the glib and worldly-wise City Gentleman to Weeks's unassuming, inarticulate Rural Innocent. Zimmer, in his elegant pin-stripes, fancy brocade vest, and wide striped tie, looked as if he had just tossed off a brandy and soda, his neat buckled shoe resting self-consciously against a brass rail, before coming into this room. Weeks more resembled a large, sun-flushed farmer, dutifully imprisoned in his Sunday best, a sort of Piers Plowman confronted with a subtly elegant deadly sin. He was very large, this Weeks, tall and pink and fading blond. Obviously in middle age, for his hair receded quite markedly and he had a resignation in the way he moved and spoke that comes only after youth is definitely over in one's mind. His smooth, untroubled face, however, was oddly boyish, undisturbed by lines of worry or anxiety. In a morality play, he would be Faith, undaunted by Zimmer's Skepticism.

For, as Jane could have predicted from simply observing the pair set up their show, Zimmer belonged to that genre of pedagogue who could only teach the subject of his life's work by reviling it. His style was quite fashionable at the moment with graduate students. He launched his topic today with some anecdotal remarks about the Pre-Raphaelite Brotherhood's mysterious initials. ("Some believed them to stand for 'Please Ring Bell'; others, suspecting Rossetti's membership, were certain they stood for 'Penis Rather Better.' ")

A dutiful spasm of laughter erupted in the dark room. Weeks flashed the first slide on the screen: Ruskin's chilly, sepia-dominated "Glacier at Boissons." Jane turned sideways to look at Weeks behind the projector. In the glare from the screen she could tell he had not laughed. Zimmer was now narrating how Ruskin had taken his protégé Millais off to Glenfinlas to teach him to paint like Turner and how Millais had shown his gratitude by stealing Ruskin's wife. "Old Ruskin was especially fond of rocks and stones, icy things," said Zimmer meaningfully. He paused. "Effie Ruskin got an annulment from her husband. Then she married Millais, whose paintings went rapidly downhill from that time forward." It depressed Jane at how easily her own laughter joined the rest, affirming Zimmer's cynicism.

"Ah . . . em." It was Weeks. "I wonder if I might say —ah—a few words about this painting. You see, although it is predominated—the surface of the landscape is dominated by a—um—glacier, I think you will all agree that the infinite variety of other details—that clump of trees—the careful, intricate curling of the tiled roofs in the foregrounds, the rows of young vegetables in the exact center—bespeak an intense—a passionate concern for every natural thing. Ruskin loved the world's textures —not only the textures of rocks and ice, but of winds, clouds, leaves, sky. He used a cyanometer to measure the intensity of the blue in the sky. He collected minerals. He measured rainfall. He recorded nature. It was his way of glorifying it, I think. He liked to say—he liked to say —that there was no such thing as bad weather, only different varieties of good weather. Perhaps now would be a good time to show you the painting Millais did of Ruskin on the trip to Glenfinlas to which Professor Zimmer has already alluded. I think I have it just here. . . ." He fumbled through the slide box. "Yes, now here you see the famous critic standing on an overhanging bank of dark crag, a favorite pastime of his. . . . Notice the lovely piece of worn rock, the foaming water and weeds and moss, all successfully executed by Millais in the Turneresque style which Ruskin admired. This painting is a rare example of a critic making his love of one artist reappear in the painting of another. . . ."

"He is indeed head over heels in love," murmured Zimmer from his dark corner, and the room roared. Weeks had put the slide in upside down and gone on talking earnestly without noticing.

He righted the slide with a little apology, allowed time for everyone to finish laughing and look at it, then wordlessly went on to the next. He did not speak again for some half-dozen slides.

"Ah. Here we have Millais's dead Ophelia, floating breathlessly downstream," said Zimmer. "Rossetti's mistress, Elizabeth Siddal, posed for this painting lying in a tepid bathtub for hours. She caught a chill and everyone thought she was certain to die, whereupon Rossetti gallantly consented to marry her. She recovered with alacrity and became Mrs. Rossetti. After all, he had given his word. Two years later, she took an overdose of laudanum, after a dinner party at Swinburne's, and really did die. Rossetti was heartbroken and proved it by burying his best manuscript of poems with her. However, time heals all manner of things, and several years later he dug them up again and had them published. His physical and mental decline was rapid, poor Rossetti. He filled his house at Cheyne Walk with wombats and dormice and lizards and even a Brahmin bull, because its eyes reminded him of his friend's wife, Jane Morris, whom he painted endlessly—hers is the face that most often comes to mind when we think of the Movement—and with whom he had such a long bout of unrequited love—"

"If we could get back to the Ophelia for a moment . . ." interrupted Weeks quietly. But there was a new dogged note in his voice. "It would be a shame for us to overlook the painstaking detail the artist has lavished not just on the lady's dissolving bouquet, in which every flower is separate and complete, but on what might have been left by other painters as vague 'background shrubbery': the twigs on that fallen tree, the clump of reeds . . . our eyes can make out every leaf. Millais possessed an ability unequaled in the painting of his country to extract beauty from the commonest English hedge. Getting back to the flowers for a moment, we know those flowers, we have seen them, every one, we can call them by their common names. They are no *impressions* of flowers, Millais's spring bouquet. They are the real thing. And yet, as we begin to point them out—a poppy, a pansy, a sprig of lilac, a—um—lily of the valley—we begin truly to know them. . . ."

"Excuse me, Professor, I was wondering," said Zimmer. "Could it be that the P.R.B.'s painstaking attention to detail—we might even say *hyper*-attention—is one important reason why they have failed to weather the century as well as, say, the Impressionists? Would you agree that their over-specificity contributed to the early obsolescence of their movement with the advent of good color photography?"

"Having spent almost twenty-five years of my life rediscovering the timeless qualities of this movement," replied Weeks, without a trace of his usual stammer, "I can hardly agree that they are obsolescent. If I thought so, I would not be here in this room. As to the question of photography, however good the color, I believe it allows us to see things for the second time. Art, if it is worthy of the name, reveals things to us for the first time."

Jane wanted to clap and cheer. She was as delighted as a child in a theatre at the moment when the hero does in the villain.

She completed another day of unpromising or downright fruitless job interviews and retreated with relief back to her university, to her few remaining months of safe studenthood. The university offering her the fill-in job wrote within two weeks, and she accepted from a desire to have these last months untainted by practical cares. "Who knows," she said to herself. "In two years, anything can happen. There is no such thing as security. In two years I may be dead." And there followed one of the most intensely private and serene periods of her life. Her course work was over. Though she still dreamed about exams—usually being unprepared for them—she had the waking comfort of knowing she would never have to take another one. She had passed all exams in her field. She began working on her thesis, whose topic ("The Theme of Guilt in the Novels of George Eliot") had been approved by her chairman just before Christmas. Having developed an aversion for her small off-campus apartment where she had studied for the exams, she moved her books and notes to a carrel in the library, and here she lived all day, every day, during the deep winter months. More books, picked up during prowls around the shelves, piled up around her isolating her like mountains. She brought her lunch in a paper bag so she would not have to go out into the world of real weather and conversations. The conversations she had been content to join for the past few years suddenly annoyed her intensely, whereas previously they had simply made her unexplain-

221

ably sad. She was now able to pinpoint this sadness: perhaps that was why she was more intolerant. All around her, wherever faculty and graduate students spoke, she heard what she now called "Zimmer voices," voices making light of things they really cared about, belittling great ideas, reducing to ironic trills and singsongs their profoundest hopes and fears. "Zimmer voices" permeated the very structure of university life. She realized how hard she had tried to match these voices, talking down her favorite poets, saying if she didn't get a job she'd become a waitress in a diner on Route 66 and *really get an education!* How hard she had tried to sound disenchanted; and how these previous efforts now disgusted her! So she withdrew into her carrel in the quiet of the library; she withdrew, without embarrassment, into the utter earnestness of her mind. Here she was pure and light, stripped of her usual fears about her own inadequacies, about the uncertainty of the future.

Her topic absorbed her. It suited her perfectly. The woman Marian Evans gave her courage. *She* had not found her love till she was thirty-five, nor her life's work till she was thirty-seven. Jane read her letters, she reread the novels, pored over the "quarry" for *Middlemarch,* lived all day in the social and moral universe of these people. She grew thin on celery and cheese and carrot sticks, and drank six or seven cartons of milk each day, from the library's vending machine, to keep herself from overexcitement. For the first time in her life, she was where she wanted to be; she was at one with her task. She *was* her work. Outside, it snowed constantly. One snow followed another. The campus was white and silent. Outside and inside her, all was cold, white, pure. She looked in the mirror of the library's women's room and saw a clear-eyed being with nothing about her wasted, no excess skin or energy which was not in use. Her skin, it seemed to her, glowed with a mental and spiritual electricity, like a saint's skin; she was a person operating from the center of her best will; there were no superfluities. She felt obliged to have lunch one day with her friend Lydia, who was part of the perfect couple who had given her the little Tempus Fugit clock. "You've gotten strange," said

Lydia. "How do you mean?" asked Jane. "You have this air of someone who hasn't spoken aloud for a long, long time," said the other. Jane liked this description of herself.

By mid-February, averaging five to seven pages a day, she had completed half her thesis. An unseasonable warm spell came through and melted the snows. "I hope this won't melt my beautiful frozen mind," Jane said aloud, walking to the library; and as though she had pronounced her own disenchantment, she became distracted and could not work so well that day. She kept going down to the vending machines, although she was sick of milk. At lunchtime, she took her paper bag to the Student Union and was not disturbed when a young man who had been in a Milton seminar with her, a real budding Zimmer if there ever was one, sat down at her table and began enumerating for her quite merrily all the abysmal ways he was going to fail his comprehensives the following week. Jane spoke deprecatingly about how she herself had overprepared, about her little charts in colored inks. When she returned to the library, she saw on the big clock that she had been gone two hours.

That night she dreamed she was Marian Evans, eloping to Germany with Lewes. Or, rather, she was herself, on board the *Ravensbourne* with this man who was married forever to somebody else. They walked up and down deck, dressed in matching raincoats. He held her round the waist and she could not see his face. A fierce warm wind blew against them. He said, "There is no such thing as bad weather; only varieties of good weather." *How nice it feels to lean into another person's body while you walk,* she thought. Then she woke up, disoriented; she could not remember who she was or in what century. She made herself some tea and sat staring at it and could not go back to sleep.

She forced herself, next day, to imitate, if not duplicate, her former zeal. She wrote seven new, uninspired pages of the thesis. She decided she ought to check a word she was thinking of using in the Oxford English Dictionary, and, coming back through the reference room on the main floor, she stopped beside a shelf of college catalogues and pulled out a certain one. Under the faculty listings she found "G. Weeks, B.A., M.A., Ph.D., Harvard." She went back to her carrel. She took an unusually long time copying out the information from the Oxford English Dictionary onto a note card—then decided not to use the word in her thesis, after all.

What did the "G." stand for? George, Gordon, Gilbert, Gregory?

In the evening she went to the art library, on the other side of campus. She looked through indexes and catalogues. She even got help from the man on duty at the circulation desk. She found his name, at last, on a little monograph published in 1954 by the university where he was at present. *Lessons on Love by Three Pre-Raphaelite Painters.* Nobody had ever checked out the book. On the title page, the librarian had penciled "(abriel)" over the initial "G." There was a dedication page: *To my wife.*

Jane checked out the monograph and read it through at once. A rather irate introduction, which accused his colleagues of devaluing the Movement or "resigning it to oblivion altogether," was followed by three strange, quaint essays which were unlike any scholarship Jane had ever read. They were a mixture of sermon and, it seemed, shyly personal confession, concerning three kinds of love. They took as their subject Rossetti, Millais, and Burne-Jones and explained why they were "love-painters." But, most of all, they dwelt on these highly selective loves. They discussed them as if the writer considered them to encompass the entire activity of love. There was Idyllic Love, "which is born of distances never to be crossed, distances which we suffer gladly in order to maintain the beloved on the altar of worship and unsatiated desire . . . the kind of love the aging Rossetti felt for Jane Morris." There was Sympathetic Love, "in which we lose ourselves in affirming kinship with the world's essences, its inevitable movements and changes . . . cf. Millais's 'Autumn Leaves,' 'The Vale of Rest' . . . ." And there was Mirror Love, "in which the soul, or the psyche, recognizes itself in another, and this likeness becomes the basis, often temporary or fleeting, for fascination. . . . It is no accident that Burne-Jones's pairs of lovers (Pan and Psyche, the couple in 'Depths of the Sea,' Pygmalion with his Image) have look-alike faces which could have been drawn from the same model."

Jane began dreaming about Mrs. Weeks. Once she was a huge capable Englishwoman, down on her hands and knees weeding a giant flower garden whose roots were as thick as Jane's arms. Another time she was a winsome dark woman who huddled in the shadows of a room, crying and crying. Another time she and Jane were at the theatre together. Mrs. Weeks was relating, in a whisper so loud it embarrassed Jane, the personal history of one of the actors. "You really ought to sleep with him," whispered the wife too loudly, so loudly that the actor paused in his lines and looked straight out over the footlights at them. It was Gabriel.

Her life took on the quality of fantasy. She lived all day in the nineteenth century, speaking to herself and thinking in their phrases, knowing vastly more about the art and economics and politics of Victorian England than she did of late mid-twentieth-century America. And as soon as she fell asleep at night, she became the Weekses' house guest. She roamed their changing house, sometimes perched on an arid desert site, other times shrouded in mist and heavy trees. They could do with her as they wished. Sometimes she was their daughter. Often she was part of a team in the triangle, in which she and Gabriel would steal away like naughty children from Mrs. Weeks, or in which she and the wife would gang up on Gabriel, drink coffee together in the kitchen, and laugh at his foibles and compare notes.

She went to the library's atlas one morning and measured the distance between his university and the one where she would be next fall. Just under two hundred miles.

I wonder if I am going mad, she thought. And decided that if she was it was nobody's business but her own. She belonged to nobody; it would be nobody's loss. She knew she would do it quietly enough to pass as merely "odd" or eccentric.

"Dear Gabriel Weeks," she wrote, in her carrel. She crumpled the paper and threw it away. "Dear Professor Weeks. I . . ."

225

Many drafts later, she surprised herself by putting a stamp on the letter and mailing it, in the box at the corner outside the library.

Dear Professor Weeks:

I have thought a great deal about your dialogue with Professor Zimmer at the MLA. I especially liked your distinction between photography and art. Now I have read your book, *Lessons on Love*. The essays have been most illuminating, especially regarding my own thesis (concerning the novels of George Eliot) with which I am at the moment wrestling. Your book has given me the idea that there are "love-writers," just as there are "love-painters." In fact, I am beginning to think that no artist or writer can be truly great unless he works from the raw materials of his love, whether it be for the unattainable beloved, for his own dear delightful and perplexing world, or even for his own dear reflection. I am grateful to you for not being ashamed to list and define things most of us are hesitant to speak about, except from behind our shields of Zimmerian irony.

Sincerely,
Jane Clifford

Within five days she had his reply.

Dear Miss Clifford:

Your letter encouraged me more than I can say. I am glad to hear that you were able to extract something worthwhile from that ill-fated slide lecture.

I was inspired by your intelligent understanding and application of my *Lessons on Love by Three Pre-Raphaelite Painters*. It was just such readers as yourself that I had hoped to reach when I began writing this book more than twenty years ago (when the Pre-Raphaelites were *personae non gratae* in the art world). It was, in fact, a reworking of my own thesis.
I wish you all best luck with your present endeavor.

Yours Sincerely,
G. Weeks

The letter was written in a large, slow hand which pressed the ball-point pen heavily into the paper. Jane was disappointed in it. It seemed pedantic and cold, a perfunctory thank-you to the overeager praise of an unknown graduate student. The last sentence could be nothing but a polite dismissal. She put the letter away, and her dreams about the Weekses stopped altogether. She wished it would snow again; how she wished for a thick, heavy, frozen blanket of snow to fall down and cover everything. It did snow; it was now mid-March. She returned, cold and single-minded, to her thesis, repairing the middle section, which she called "the slushy part." She set a date in her head: May 15th. On that date, barring extreme illness, catastrophe, or death, I will turn in the first draft of my entire thesis to my chairman, she resolved. It was an arbitrary date, without meaning in the university calendar. Anyone wishing to receive the doctorate in June must have three perfectly typed and approved copies of their thesis in the Graduate Office by May 7th. Her chairman did not expect the thesis till the fall, when it had been agreed between them that she would send it. She had been hired on the All-But-Dissertation basis. But she wanted to make life uncomfortable for herself. She made herself get up in the mornings before she felt like it, and she stayed in the library always a little beyond the time when she had exhausted her energy. I will not leave the building till it begins to grow dark outside, she said, and as the spring light lengthened daily she denied herself sight of the unfolding season. The eerily pure clarity of January and February she never regained. Now her mind was propelled less by inspiration and more by stubborn will as she covered each margined page (pressing her pen down slow and hard like a certain person) with words and—with a little smile like a grimace—inked in the ascending numbers at the top. When she thought of Weeks, the image now bore a "Zimmerian" tinge. Could it be possible that this man had not published a single thing since the little monograph on "love-painters," which was really a rehashing of his dissertation? She saw him as a rather sad and clumsy man who had taken his subject too seriously, who had perhaps choked his young enthusiasms to death by setting too exalted a value on them. And wasn't there something pathetic—touching but pathetic—in his seeing in her the ideal reader come twenty years too late? What could she have been dreaming of?

In the middle of April, she received an envelope with several postcards, reproductions of paintings, accompanied by a short cryptic note: "Love-Painters everywhere, up and down the centuries, once inspiration has been found again." Had it not been for the signature, she would have mistaken the packet to be an advertisement from some fine-arts society offering prints for sale. She turned the postcards over. Each had a number written in pencil on the back. Van der Weyden's "St. Jerome," extricating a thorn from a lion's paw, was marked #2. Gustav Klimt's "The Kiss" #3, and a Turner landscape #2. Cranach the Elder's "Nymph of the Spring" and Andrea del Castagno's detail of the Cumaean Sybil #1.

"What in hell—?" said Jane.

She took the perplexing little packet to the library and kept the cards and the note propped before her all day as she honored her prescribed momentum. "What in hell," she murmured from time to time, but pleased with the annoyance in her voice juxtaposed against the soft hope unfolding in her heart. She walked home slowly in the cool spring dusk.

She woke up next morning with a cold and decided to stay in bed, not go to the library. Suddenly she felt like pampering herself. The cold rapidly developed into a bad one and she welcomed it. She telephoned her friend Lydia, who came with a gallon jar of homemade soup, some miracle-drug tablets which had been prescribed for her husband's recent spring cold, and a bottle of whiskey. She made Jane a whiskey with hot water and sugar, and Jane drank it on top of the drug. She tipped off gently into a fantasy world and listened with serene distance as Lydia confided that all was not well with her marriage. "You're lucky. You can exist beautifully without a goddamned man in your life," said Lydia, starting to weep. "I wonder if it is too late for me. I wonder if it is too late for me to become self-sufficient."

228

"No," said Jane, the oracle draped against a cool rock high above the wild sea of life which crashed lightly inside her ears. "It is never too late for anything."

Lydia left, promising to return, and Jane gave herself up to wonderful dreamings. Gabriel was leading her through a field of flowers, no two alike. He told her in a rich, assured voice without a trace of the stammer that what they were going to do was pick these flowers and weave them into a blanket to put over them. "But it's so hot," said Jane. It was hot, broiling hot, though they were naked. She was too shy to look at him; she spied only the white flash of his great thigh or arm as they hiked through the flowers. And then it turned out he was right, for it was suddenly cold and dark, a frozen moon hung in a black sky, and the icy tinkle of a stream was close beside them, and they were glad for their blanket. Beneath it, Jane shyly searched till she found the center and the proof of his warmth. . . . . .

Dear Professor:

I am writing from a sickbed, so don't let me startle you with my flushes and flashes. I am at the moment irresponsible, filled with hot soup, hot whiskey, some sort of pills which go off by the hour, but I wanted to tell you how glad I am that *somebody* feels inspired, and it was nice to see proof, even in pictures, that #1, 2, 3 love has existed (and might continue to exist) in this world. This is a chilly spring indeed for me. My thesis languishes in the absence of inspiration and I wish I could make a blanket of those lovely flowers in Ophelia's bouquet and cover myself until warmed by new enthusiasm. I looked up Gabriel in the dictionary. It means God is my strength, but I suppose you knew that. How lovely to be Gabriel, the bringer of good news. I wish someone would bring me some good news.

Yours sincerely,
Jane Clifford

Lydia came by and Jane gave her the letter to mail. After it was gone, she worried if it had been maudlin, or forward, or indiscreet.

Several mornings later, when she had recovered sufficiently enough to want to return to the library, and was dressing to go, the doorbell rang. She assumed it was Lydia, who had become excessively solicitous as a welcome diversion from her own unhappiness. But it was a messenger with a box from the florist. Inside was a spring bouquet. She recognized all the flowers from the slide of Millais's painting. The card said, "Good news. Spring is here. Gabriel.'

She wrote at once, thanking him. She received a short note several days after.

I plan to be in St. Louis May 14–18 for a special exhibit at the Art Museum. Would you perhaps be interested in a guided tour of some quite exceptional paintings? If you have a car, the trip could be made (both ways) within a day. Or, if you were free for longer, you might like to see more of the city.

Gabriel Weeks

On May 15th, Jane handed the first draft of her thesis to her surprised chairman. He struggled gallantly to hide his annoyance as he told her he would try and get it back to her as soon as possible, since he and his family planned to leave for a Canada vacation as soon as all his exams and *other obligations* were completed.

On the following morning she left at dawn in Lydia's borrowed Volkswagen. She did not have a car of her own yet, and she had never in her life operated a straight shift. She drove, in terror and ecstasy, a back route flanked with fields of yellow flowers. It was as if she created the road to St. Louis as she went to meet this man whose acquaintance she had made almost totally through her own devisings and dreams.

XI

BUT today, retracing their courtly beginning did not
bring the usual end product of amazement at so much
progress in the months that followed the famous slide
show. As she emerged from the red-carpeted tube that
fed her from her plane into LaGuardia, she saw very
little progress. Wonder was replaced by exasperation, and
she regarded the world very much through "Zimmer"
eyes.

"Here we have Ms. Jane Clifford, lady pedant, peram-
bulating with a rather disgruntled step along the sterile
corridor of a twentieth-century airport. For almost two
years she has been having an *affaire du cœur* with an idealistic and proper professor, reticent in both his affections
and his publications. He is due to land in this very airport
within the hour, if his plane is on time (hers was late),
but she will not meet him at his gate because he has pru-
dently instructed her not to be (he being maritally inclined to keep his apples quite separate from his oranges).
She goes downstairs alone, and waits with a frown for
her baggage, then manfully transports it outside. . . ."

("Er—um—I'd like to point out the richness of the
cloud formations, unusual for January, above the park-
ing lots; the multiplicity of facial expressions, the great
variety of life-stations depicted in the cluster of persons
waiting for the Carey Transportation bus, the two lovers
embracing openly in the portico outside 'BAGGAGE.' In the
quality, in the clarity of this airport scene, we have de-

picted for us many separate destinies unfolding like flowers under a brisk and generous sky. . . .")

"Flowers in January, what bullshit," murmured Jane. A man in the Carey Transportation group turned to stare at her. In utter revolt against the Weeksian idealism regarding the universe, as long as nothing got too specific, she went in search of a taxi. She would spend too much money, she would arrive at the hotel too early, but what the hell. Anything to avoid "the multiplicity and variety" of the local scenery when she was more interested in the landscape of her own emotions. Suddenly she wished she could hurt Gabriel Weeks.

Her taxi driver had been stuck in the taxi circle for three hours and was in a predictable mood.

"I brought a fare out at eight and I've been sitting in the same exact spot ever since," he said angrily, hurtling them into the thick thruway traffic without a backward glance. Horns blew. Jane cringed.

"That's awful," she said politely.

"You bet it's awful. I'm not coming back here today, you can bet on that. Let's see, East Fifty-third. You want to go through the tunnel or over the bridge? You here for a vacation?"

"Whichever way is easier for you. No, I'm here to do some research." Now what was the purpose of that gratuitous little lie? It was out before she had even thought. What was wrong with being on a vacation? For that matter, what was wrong with meeting your lover? Why did she have to command respect from every hotel clerk and taxi driver?

"You some kind of student?"

"No, I teach."

"That explains it."

"Explains what?"

"Oh . . . I don't know." He laughed coyly. "You sure you won't get mad if I tell you?"

"I won't get mad."

"Well, I'll be honest with you. When I seen you coming, you know what I thought? That would be a nice-looking woman if she'd fix herself up a little. That's exactly what I thought."

232

"Fix myself up how?"

"Oh, you know. Do *I* have to tell you how to fix yourself up? You ought to wear lipstick, that's one thing, and you ought to make up your face a little. And your clothes —you ought to wear different clothes, clothes that would show off your figure more. You have a nice figure, I can tell; you just dress too old, that's all. If you fixed yourself up a little, you'd be real attractive to men. I bet you'd be married in no time."

"What makes you think I'm not already married?" asked Jane, furious with herself for having got into this conversation with an ill-tempered cabdriver named Vincent de Lucca, whose own wife had probably had plenty of opportunities to rue the day she became Mrs. de Lucca. Yet the man had strangely mortified her.

"You aren't wearing a ring!" he answered triumphantly.

"And what makes you think I even want to get married?"

"Every woman wants to get married. I don't care *how* smart. Every woman in the world wants to get married," said Vincent de Lucca rather unctuously.

The night clerk had made no reservation for any "Professor Clifford."

"But I don't understand it—I called long distance. Surely a hotel listed in the AAA should be more efficient than that." Jane knew she was taking out on the night clerk's successor the rage that had been summoned too late for Mr. de Lucca. She saw all men as inept, inferior, but nonetheless villains.

"There's nothing to get upset about. We can get a room for you; that's no problem," said the desk clerk. "It's just that you might have to wait a while."

"How long is a while?"

"Oh, an hour—better say an hour and a quarter to be on the safe side. We'll get a maid in right away to clean one of the rooms just vacated."

Gabriel would probably arrive within this time. But something in her, this morning, rebelled at the idea of waiting anxiously in the lobby, planting herself visibly so there would be no mistake, no chance of their missing each other. Her current mood also rebelled at the idea of leaving complicated, incriminating messages with this clerk, who, if he was anything like his predecessor, would forget to deliver them anyway. "Fine," she said. "If you're sure. I'll be back in exactly one hour and fifteen minutes. You do have the name, don't you?"

"Yes, lady," he sighed. "There's no problem. Clifford. Come back in a little over an hour." His tone was slightly patronizing, as if she were old, feeble, or foolish. It would get worse in the years to come: perhaps *she* would get worse.

She walked over to Fifth Avenue and headed slowly in the direction of the Park. Less than a month ago, she had been in this city, for the dear old MLA; always, before she came, she made up her mind to do many things—exploring, museums. But, once arrived, a paralyzing timidity came over her, and she stayed inside the hotel, venturing out only on Gabriel's arm—rather, not on his arm until they were out of sight of the hotel. He worried, she knew, as much as he worried about anything, about being seen by one of his "colleagues."

It was a bright, clear noonday and she looked carefully into clusters of faces in this January Monday lunchtime rush and wondered how different she was from these other souls, if her life was, by objective standards, "less real." And, if so, how much less real? Could she change it if she wanted to? And did she want to?

"You have yet to enter real life," Gerda loved to say. "I mean, when I met you twelve years ago, you were in school, and you're *still* in school. You've been in school since the age of six, except for that year your grandmother gave you in Europe, and you wasted most of that in libraries and bookstores, and getting engaged to that tiresome Englishman so you could spend nineteenth-century country weekends out of your favorite novels till you realized you were dying of it. It was too removed, even for you."

"I'm not so sure," Jane said. "He was a good person. It would have been a gentle, civilized life with him. I would be sitting by that lovely old fireplace reading a novel, and he would be out Saturdays playing rugby with his chums. The more I think about it, the more I think it would have been a good life."

"Oh, shit, Jane. How you edit your memories! I was there, you know. I came to London, after the Mulvaney fiasco, and stayed with you two weeks and had plenty of opportunity to observe the whole thing. It was his mother that interested you, basically. You let me read her letters to you. Remember that one about how the first time James brought you down, she sat up in bed all night, holding her pug and saying, 'I shall have that girl for my daughter-in-law.' You and the mother created the whole engagement; I told you then and I'll refresh your memory now. James was a nice well-bred Englishman, but he wasn't your intellectual equal and you knew it. You and Nancy Bruton joined forces to perpetrate this English idyll. she took one look at your hopelessly Anglophile soul and your romantic eyes dimming at the sight of her Tudor house and her rose garden and her very ordinary son with his blue for rowing or rugby or whatever the hell it was, and she had to have you. And you both had to have *him* to cement you, to give you the excuse for being there, and to start your drawing-room fires and uncork your sherry after the father died, and of course give you an English baby or two to carry on the family name. You and Nancy Bruton created that poor boy for your own purposes."

"You make everything sound so—abnormal, Gerda," said Jane. She mused. "By now I could have had a child nine years old! Imagine. Perhaps several children. I wonder if being a mother would have changed me."

"That's hard to say," replied Gerda. "Though, from what you told me, I don't think you would have enjoyed what you had to do to become one very much. I remember that story you told me about how he had to creep down those four-hundred-year-old uncarpeted stairs in the dark to get to your room, which was right next door to hers, and how you had to be so careful never to make any noise. You admitted yourself you couldn't enjoy it

235

because you were so afraid she might hear something. And you were so disgusted when you found out how they all used the same bathwater on Sunday mornings. That's aristocrats for you! And how furious you were when Nancy Bruton told you that in England ladies didn't order 'spirits' in pubs, only sherry or a mild bitter. You were in a rage. I remember you went out and bought a bottle of Remy Martin, just to keep in your bed-sitter to spite Nancy Bruton."

"The Brutons *were* very . . . frugal," said Jane, remembering. "Their well wasn't too deep; they only had so much water." She had tried to remember her fiancé's face and couldn't. Then she tried to remember how it had been, those nervous stolen nights in his parents' house, and for the life of her could not remember whether he had taken his pajama bottoms off or not. "They were always very pleased when they could save anything, or stretch it out. She used to unravel old sweaters for the wool and knit them into new ones. She knitted me a lovely one, after James and I got engaged. It was made out of James's old baby sweaters. I found that touching. I gave the sweater back when we broke off. It didn't seem right to take James's baby sweaters back to America. I wonder if she unraveled it a second time and made it into another sweater for his next fiancée. Yes, they loved to remember the deprivations of the war, all the bombs exploding nearby and rationing and so on. They liked to sit around a good fire and talk about the bad times they'd been through in the war and how everybody had 'taken in their belts,' and bygone rugby matches between England and Scotland. I did get aggravated by them, at times, but sometimes I wonder if I made a mistake. After all, in a family everybody gets aggravated with everybody occasionally. I wonder what it would have been like if his mother and I hadn't had that silly fight about the children's nationality."

"You need to get out of the university for a while, Jane. I sometimes think it would be a good idea for you to go and work in a factory."

"Perhaps your folks could get me a job pulling tobacco," Jane replied, then regretted it. It had been one of those days when Gerda smarted under the reality of her family.

"There's no need to get bitchy, Jane. I was just trying to help you. God! Isn't it just like you! To have a fight with his mother over the nationality of some children you didn't even have yet. Imaginary children!"

"Why do you insist on belittling my imagination so, Gerda? Why can't what goes on there be real, too? Those children were just as real to me, just as important, as—as all these ephemeral enthusiasms you throw yourself into. Your 'causes' have passed away into nothing, just like my children that I never had with James." And she had thought of Charles Lamb's tender essay, "Dream Children," an old bachelor's reverie about telling bedtime stories to the children he might have had.

"Because they're in your head!" screamed Gerda. "My 'causes' were outside, in the real world!"

"You're discriminating against the inner life, which is really beneath your intelligence, Gerda. It really is. . . . You're no better than the brutes and destroyers of civilization who rise up again and again and destroy everything because they hate the inner life. A culture, a civilization can only be as strong as the inner lives of its people."

"Oh, inner life, inner life! Of course I realize everybody has to have his and her precious little inner life. But it's not everything, like *you* seem to think. Christ! If everybody sat inside his little head and thought all day like you do, I'd like to know what would get done in the world!"

"A hell of a lot less damage and cruelty and stupidity, that's what!"

Then they had one of their worst fights. The topic was "Inner or Outer Life: Which Is More Real," but the core of contention was—and they both knew it, and fought all the harder—that each was becoming more and more repulsed by the other's life-style, saw it as a reproach to her own, was perhaps secretly afraid it might be more rewarding in the long run.

"You don't even know what it's like to be one other

237

person! You can experience nothing, nothing, except what's inside your own head or inside some worn-out old book," accused Gerda.

"Who *does* know? Who *can?*" Jane cried back, thinking wistfully of Charles Lamb. I am closer to him at this moment than I'll ever be to this screaming woman, she thought.

"You are following in Edith's footsteps," Gerda said, at bay. "If you insist on editing your memories, *I* don't forget them. You told me all about it, your favorite family myth—how she went to that Fourth of July fireworks and all the vulgar noises and all the common people were just too much for her. So she fainted, right in front of the very man who would take her away from it all. Oh, I have watched your eyes light up every time you tell that story, how she told Hans she thought life was a disease, and he said, 'Let me protect you from it.' Oh, God, how that man must have suffered from all her airs!"

"She was coming down with typhoid, you fool," Jane protested. Why had she ever confided the family history, all her tender secrets, her favorite family stories? And in the middle of her rage she began to weep like a child, for Edith and for herself (for she had always liked that story; something in it was very close to her, very close to her own feelings about the human race) and for Gerda's betrayal of her through her own confidences. She looked at Gerda's face, a face so real to her it could never fade in memory as her fiancé's had done, and she thought: That's what happens when you tell a friend the things that touch you deepest; you get them flung back in your face, as a weapon against you, the very first moment there is a fight. And she hated Gerda; she looked coldly and rather disdainfully at her friend and despised everything about Gerda's face and habits and history that made her not-Jane. That pert little face, that snub, ordinary little nose—how could people ever have got us confused, she thought. And as she looked at Gerda, she recognized the same hatred and disdain in Gerda's face.

But, of course, they made up again and exchanged as many confidences as before. Jane told Gerda about Gabrief—all of it, right from the start—telephoning it in costly installments to Chicago.

"I just can't *see* him," said Gerda; was still saying it. "He's more of a blur than your fiancé."

"You *saw* James," Jane reminded her.

"I know, but that's not what I meant. I mean I just can't get it. I can't understand the attraction. I can understand it intellectually, especially with his angel's name and all, and I suppose his remoteness appeals to you, but frankly—and I am going to be very frank—I don't see anything charming about a man pushing fifty without a single line in his face. I'll bet his wife has plenty in hers. I have a theory, if you won't get mad. I think, as you get older, you will get better and better at constructing your ideal until at last you'll come up with the perfect lover: one who is a *perfect blur,* who doesn't even exist."

At intervals, as she continued up the avenue, she would select a person out of the lunchtime crowd and sincerely try to *be* that person. She made no immodest demands on her fragile skills of empathy; she knew their limits as well as or better than Gerda did. She picked only subjects with whom she might have some degree of success: women, all within a decade of her own age, well-dressed in-turned women with something fastidious and private about them which she recognized, and she built as a beginning on this fastidiousness, this sense of privacy, as she went on to construct the choice of their lovers (not unlike Gabriel, or James) that they might be meeting for lunch, the choice of their friends, their women friends (not unlike the intelligent Sonia Marks, the straight-talking but acute Gerda), the choice of their occupations, which they returned to each day with an equal mixture of anticipation and resignation that resembled the ambivalent feeling she harbored about her own occupation. She saw a woman, about her own age, come out of Saks, carrying a Saks bag and frowning. Yet she had just bought something. Why didn't the purchase make her happy? She wore a tan raincoat and a green knitted cloche pulled down round her ears. She paused on the sidewalk as if making up her mind which way to go, and then turned in Jane's direction, bending forward into the wind. Jane could see how, as she began to walk—in a loose, long stride, as if she planned to walk miles by herself—she tucked her shoulders forward and in, curling into herself, her thoughts; shutting the rest of the world out.

Jane understood that woman, even though she could not read her thoughts.

Surely it was better to come close in imagination to a few kindred souls, traveling cautiously across a bridge built of affinities, than to plunge recklessly and indiscriminately into the weeping, bleeding, shrieking sea of indistinguishable mouths and eyes which was often called —too glibly, too ignorantly, Jane thought—Humanity.

She tried a man this time, farther up the avenue. He was thin and thirtyish, also wearing a raincoat. He chewed on a hangnail as he contemplated Doubleday's windows, lost in the books. I understand him a little, too, she thought, ducking into the store herself, as the religious are always popping into churches. Any bookstore or library was her abiding home. She had a permanent dream about one bookstore: a labyrinthine place with every known title, and ladders to reach high shelves and stairs cut into the floor to reach the very low ones. In different dreams she would find her way to different shelves (they were always, dependably, in the same place) and take down a book she needed and begin reading it, remembering the words when she woke up, words which made sense in the daytime world, and which she liked to believe gave her help in living her life. "SWEEP THE CIRCLE CLEAN, LIGHT IT ROUND THE CIRCUMFERENCE, THEN LIE DOWN INSIDE IT," she read once; another time she read about herself in another century—or rather, she read her own correspondence with another "character," the pages printed out before her eyes as she wrote to a friend about a delightful evening where "we all made music after dinner, and the birds flew round the room accompanying us." And once she turned to the end of an exciting book, which she knew was an adventure story of the soul—why didn't more people write this kind of book, she had thought in the dream—and wanted to know what happened, because she knew she was going to wake up any second, and read these words: "DO NOT BE FOOLED. THIS IS NOT THE FINAL DRAFT."

In Doubleday's, after browsing for a half-hour or so, she bought a copy of Edith Wharton's *House of Mirth*. She had another paperback of it at home, but liked this cover better, with its four large brownstones blocking all but a patch of sky, its two small saplings blooming in self-conscious isolation in the pavement, and two tiny pairs of strollers, dwarfed by the brownstones, dwarfed even by the saplings, approaching one another with the stiff awareness of the urbane on parade. The men wore top hats and carried walking sticks. The woman, with her straight carriage and wide-veiled hat and bustled skirt, lived at the same time the arrogant young woman on the cover of *The Odd Women* had lived, across the ocean, in England. Jane liked the proportions of this cover; she liked what it told her about the dangers and attractions of this city she was now visiting: the qualities which made it shimmer, decade after decade, century after century, with the illusion of miraculous and instantaneous gratification—whether in the form of wealth, fame, happiness in love or elegance in fashion—to the young of every generation: the daring, the foolish, the aspiring, the ruthless, from the days of Peter Stuyvesant to the days of John Lindsay. This novel was copyrighted 1905, the same year Cleva came here with her villain, expecting what? Hoping for what? For whatever she had hoped, it had remained an illusion, as it had for Wharton's heroine. Jane, suddenly inspired, thought: Cleva Dewar and Lily Bart were closer in nature and in destiny than Cleva and her own sister had been. She believed that she had found, unexpectedly, as she stood in this bookstore holding her purchase, a penetrable chink in the wall between life and literature; reality and imagination. Someday in the future, when the world was whole again, there would be no such walls, and people would laugh in amazement at their ancestors' ignorance in pretending such false divisions were "real."

And she went out happily onto the avenue—but Gerda's voice overtook her when she had taken not a dozen steps onto contemporary pavement. "There you go again.

241

A glossy cover of some commercial artist's stylized conception of brownstones before they got dirty and skies before they got smoggy, and old-fashioned snobs in turn-of-the-century clothes standing on the sidewalk like stick figures—since when have there been only four people in the daytime on a New York City street?—and Jane has all the New York she can stand: three times removed, through art, idealization, and time. What about Harlem, all the stabbings and blood flowing down the sidewalks of Harlem? What about all the smelly, lonely old people dying alone in roach-filled rooms and not being discovered by their neighbors until days afterwards, by the stench? What about all those people without coats, sleeping on the sidewalks? What about all the dismembered victims lying on blood-drenched cots in the emergency rooms in the hospitals of this city, and not enough doctors to go around, and one accident victim, with his head half severed, not admitted because he left his Blue Cross card at home? (He died, of course.) What about all the rapes in Central Park and the corruption in City Hall and the power failures and the muggings and the dope and the unwed mothers on welfare, and the turds unhappy dogs leave outside the brownstones, and the hungry people who cannot afford to buy a single rotting vegetable off a fruit stand and must rob garbage cans, picking among the maggots, instead? What about all the parts of New York —and there's nothing new about them—that Mrs. Wharton never even allowed herself to have nightmares about?"

Dear old Gerda. Jane shook her head and smiled as she walked down the avenue of the fallen city.

Her room was ready. It was quarter to one. She unpacked her cosmetic bag and took it into the bathroom, where she cleansed her face (wondering if Vincent de Lucca had a point about the make-up) and equipped her body for idyllic love.

At five past one, the telephone rang, just as she was hanging up the last item in her suitcase. In spite of having waited for this call for the past twenty minutes, she gave a start, dropped the hanger, and bumped her shin on the edge of the bed as she hurried to answer it. She knew what the first words from the other end would be; they never varied: Hello—em—Gabriel here.

"Hello?" she said, breathless.

"Hello—em—Gabriel here."

"Where are you?"

"Let's see . . ." and she heard the clink of his room key as he consulted it to see where he was. "Eight-oh-one."

"I'm just one floor above. Nine-twenty. At the end of the hall when you get off the elevator."

"Well . . ." he said cheerfully. "Well."

"Would you like to come up and see my room?"

They always went through this. She had to coax him every time. He had never once, in all their trysts, said the words "May I come to your room?"

"That's an idea," he said. "Let's say a quarter of an hour?"

"Fine. See you in a quarter of an hour."

They hung up.

She had no idea what he did with those quarters of an hour. At the beginning, they had driven her to exasperation: after waiting so long, to be forced to wait that much longer, when she could see absolutely no reason for it! It was another meaningless endurance test, like the deadly Poise hour at the Pinner sisters' school. Only, so far, she had never fainted her way out of this one. Perhaps she would, eventually. One day, he would say over the phone from another room in another hotel, "See you in a quarter of an hour," and she would see the spots and feel herself going. Would that be the end of their affair?

What was he doing now? How did he use his mysterious quarter of an hour? Did he unpack with a finicky, spinsterish care, as she did, putting all his underwear in the drawer, hanging up his suits, aligning his shoes on the closet floor, his little bottles and brushes on the bathroom shelf? Did he go out for a quick walk? Did he eat one of the apples he always carried with him? Did he sit quietly on the side of his bed, back straight, hands folded, and meditate on the spheres for fifteen minutes? He was good at staying in the same place for long periods of time; he was expert at lapsing into the present moment and staying there. He would have been Regina Pinner's teacher's pet! *He* could have driven that old woman to madness, sitting patiently, unmoving, in her torture chair forever.

She imagined herself another lover: who, upon hearing "I'm just one floor above," would fling down the receiver, not bothering to hang it up—leave that for the maid, who would be summoned to do it by the switchboard operator!—and rush up the fire-exit stairs, three at a time, like Douglas Fairbanks, Jr.

But such a lover was not her Gabriel. Would she want such a lover? Gerda would say not. ("One lover who takes *hours* to creep down a flight of rickety old English stairs, one lover who waits fifteen minutes before creeping up one floor in an elevator . . . that gives you plenty of time to arrange him in your head.")

She wished Gerda would get out of her head just now. Gerda and Gabriel did not mix well together. The whole day was going wrong, because she had the wrong people in her head: first Zimmer at the airport; and now Vince de Lucca and Gerda Mulvaney.

So she went to the mirror and waited there for him. She looked at herself through his eyes, tried to "be" Gabriel seeing Jane. Did he see her in segments and layers, as she scrutinized herself: a nose, straight and long, a little bit too long if you weren't impressed with family noses; large, blue-irised eyes with pale whites and a faraway look that came from nearsightedness; a face which, in nineteenth-century novels, would be described as "drawn," or slightly past its bloom; a mouth with rather wide lips, unpainted, her only sensuous feature. Or did he see her as she saw him, more as an organic unit that represented a dream, a experience that was more than its parts—perhaps more than a person, even? Did he see someone who, were she shown this image on a screen, would be a perfect stranger? People looked different to themselves in mirrors, she knew. As a child, she had often watched Kitty getting ready to go somewhere, doing herself up in front of the mirror. And she had wondered: Doesn't Kitty know she doesn't look that way at all? Once she had said to her mother, "Why are you puckering your mouth up like that?" "Like what?" asked Kitty, annoyed. *"You* know. You're trying to turn yourself into someone else," said Jane. "You're trying to look like a sad princess or something, and not my mother. "I'm not *just* your mother, you know," Kitty had replied, and Jane could not understand the anger in it. "And I'm not *just* Edith's daughter. It's time some people remembered that."

Jane looked at her reflection and tried to ascertain what would stay the same when she turned away. Her hair, perhaps. Her eyes, she had been told, were not always blue, not always large; sometimes, in certain lights, certain moods, they were gray or green, or even small. Her face, she knew, showed dozens of expressions to others that it would deny her always. The Jane of her mirror was almost never the Jane of photographs. But her hair—he probably saw it as she did: fine-spun, rather electric, more of a texture than a color, though on her passport it was "LIGHT BROWN." It had been blond when she was young, blond as a thistle, a pure, ethereal color that people were always commenting upon. Once an old German nun at the convent reached out and grabbed a chunk of it in her fingers and called it angel's hair. "Little Jane has *Engelshaar,"* she croaked in her old, accented voice. "The hair of an angel. It will soon turn dark. Yes, my dear, as the soul losses its purity, the *Engelshaar* must go dark." Within months, Jane had witnessed, horrified, the old nun's prophecy fulfill itself. Her hair became dark the winter she was in the fourth grade, the first winter she spent her weekends with the newly married Kitty and Ray. And there was worse to come. Soon, on other parts of her body, dark hair began to grow as well. She was alarmed and shaved herself with a razor and got down on her knees at night and prayed it would not come back. It came back. Darker and thicker than before. Her guilt pressed upon her. One week-night, while trying to study at Edith's, she had looked so glum that Edith—expert at detecting guilt—said, "What's wrong with you? Have you done something?" Jane broke down and told her secret. "I guess you'd better let me see," said Edith, who took her to the bathroom, where Jane pulled down her panties and Edith looked. "You stay in here," she ordered. Then she went and telephoned Kitty, across town. Jane listened through the door. ". . . a *mother's* job to explain . . ." she heard. " . . . might have cut herself with that razor . . ." Then Edith came back. "I listened through the door," confessed Jane, utterly infested with guilt. "I thought you might," said Edith. "Let's go and have some cocoa." The two of them sat in Edith's bedroom, sipping the cocoa. Edith said, "Now I'm going to ask you something and I don't want you to be afraid." "What?" whispered Jane, barely able to swallow. "Have you—now don't get upset—noticed any little spots of blood down there, on your panties?" Jane shook her head, appalled. "Well," said Edith, "I think it's better to be warned about those things and I'm going to tell you. It will probably happen soon. It happens to every young girl, and it's better to be prepared. I remember how Cleva came home one time; she'd been riding the pony hard all morning, and the whole back of her skirt was *covered*." "In blood?" asked Jane. "Mmm," said Edith, "but she hadn't even noticed. That was like Cleva. The Dad saw it. He said, 'Well, what do you know, the little filly has become a mare.'" As Edith imitated her father's words, her face curled down into an expression of disgust Jane had seen before, the same expression she got when smelling milk or meat that was "off" or when, in those former evening walks, she had discovered Kitty and Ray necking in Ray's Chevy coupe. "We just didn't know these things and there was nobody to tell us nicely. If our mother had lived it would have been different. If our mother had lived, she would have kept Cleva in hand and she wouldn't have lost her head . . . and lost everything else in the bargain." At that moment, Jane was disgusted with her budding womanhood. She wished more than anything to have it over with, to be respectable and old, with no taint of men and the blood that seemed to go with them, like Edith was.

There was a soft tap at the door. Jane glanced at "old T.F.," which she had already set in place on this latest bedside table. Exactly twenty past one! His punctuality still astonished her. As did his predictability. There was

246

something mysterious about it, something both mechanical and godlike.

She opened the door and stood a little to one side, so he could whisk quickly past her into the room. Then she closed the door and his big hand was on hers as she fastened the night latch. Exchanging a shy, silent greeting, they ducked into each other's arms. Jane's face pushed against the warm roughness of his wool jacket. He was wearing the same suit from the slide show, two years ago. He had very few clothes; such things did not concern him. She loved him for this. She imagined some aggressive female taxi driver saying to him: "If you'd fix yourself up a little, you could make yourself attractive to women." Well, he's here, she thought, trying to enter the present moment and be with him in it. But "reality" had eluded her again. Fifteen minutes ago, she had been ready for him. Now, in his arms, she was a little girl again, with Edith, trying to understand the menacing relationship between blood and impurity and a dead aunt she had never seen, who was done in by her womanhood.

"It's so nice to see you," he said, his chin resting on top of her hair. She tried to imagine what he was seeing as he stared down the part in the center of her head. His voice was young today and full of expectancy.

She looked up quickly, hoping to surprise him in his own reality, to check the real man against the image she carried in her head. What surprised her was that he was better than her memory of him. Delighted, she reached up a finger and touched the line of his cheek, the curve of his ear, which was pink with living blood flowing through it; she touched his hair, the soft, radiant hair that ebbed from his temples. The years had brought to him what hers had taken away: the *Engelshaar*.

He bent quickly and kissed her. His mouth tasted of apple, and she giggled.

"What is it?" he said, drawing away and smiling. "You're in a good mood today."

"Yes, I guess I am. I've missed you."

"I'm in a good mood, too. I feel wonderful." And, as

proof, he picked her up easily, so that suspended in the air, her face was level with his. His eyes went back and forth upon her face, as if he were reading her like one of his books. Some shadow passed behind his eyes. She wished she could arrest it by saying, "What were you thinking just now," but that was not their way. Then he gazed at her gravely and gave a slight nod. She nodded back. This was their ritual, which they had slipped into from mutual shyness and from a reticence natural to both in these matters.

Shyly, they separated and, back to back, began to undress. She wondered how it might be if they could undress without self-consciousness, as each surely undressed alone, and lie naked for a while beside each other, talking first instead of afterward. She had never tried this with anyone. It seemed to her it might be better: each slowly filling the other in on whatever had passed in the interval, emptying out for the other the preoccupations of his or her individual life so that they could truly come together in the present moment. She heard him folding his trousers, and wished she had a little pill she could pop secretly into her mouth and swallow, to anesthetize all her creatures of past and future which made her anxious when she wanted to be spontaneous, cynical when she wanted to be sentimental, distracted when she wanted to be intense. Did he have such creatures with him now, swarming round inside his head like those figures in the many "Temptations of Anthonys" they had looked at together, tugging him away from her, whispering to him of of other times, other places, other selves?

But, climbing first beneath the covers, watching him remove his wristwatch and smiling vaguely to himself, she did not sense any such creatures. As he performed these gestures she knew so well, there was a single-mindedness about him, a suspension. He was not anywhere if he was not here, in this room, and this was one of the things that reassured her when they were together and infuriated her when they were apart. For she believed that Gabriel, more than any other person she knew, belonged entirely to the moment in which he lived. If she was in that moment with him, he was hers; if she was not, he wasn't.

And now, as he crossed to her swiftly, veering slightly on the balls of his feet as one unaccustomed to walking barefoot, but gazing totally at her and nothing else, she believed she had at last solved the mystery of him: his patience, his predictable endurance, which, in the progress of their affair as well as in their lovemaking, always gave her enough time to construct whatever fantasy she needed; his open, unvarying, untroubled countenance, ✓ which, each time, amazed her with its freshness. . . .

(". . . I don't see anything charming about a man pushing fifty without a single line in his face.")

Why should he have lines? Lines came from frowning over one's past and squinting into one's future. If you did neither . . .

Each of the good angels, said Thomas Aquinas, *rushes to the embrace of God unhindered and with all the intensity of its being.* While the Catholic children had their Catechism lesson at Jane's old school, the Protestant children were made to practice Penmanship . . . by copying out the Catechism book. She had loved to write those lines. Saint Thomas had written an entire chapter on angels. Another sentence she had liked to copy was *Not even a child is puzzled about how an angel gets its clothes on over such huge wings.*

As Gabriel slipped beneath the cool sheets and aligned his long, warm body down the length of her own flesh, she took him in her arms, gripping his shoulder blades, and closed her eyes and wished a sort of prayer: Please God, let the present moment enter me and stay there, through the act of love with this person. Let me rush to this embrace unhindered by all my phantoms, and with all the intensity of my being. Gabriel and I will be angels together, lovers soaring in the present moment, which *is* the embrace of God.

She often made up prayers when making love, even though she no longer believed in the sort of God she prayed to. With James, her fiancé in England, during those clandestine, nervous joinings beneath his mother's

249

roof, she had strained so hard to abandon herself, and often prayed to help herself along. She had prayed for wild and dramatic transformations which would change her utterly; most often, with James, the transformation was to be in the form of a baby. It would transform her from a free young girl into a mother, and she could never leave James. It would swell her into another destiny, make her part of a larger, impersonal process, obliterating her finicky, finite self-love. And yet she continued to practice birth control.

With Gabriel she had never prayed for such a thing. She had become either too practical in her fantasies or too decadent. For as Gabriel rocked against her, pacing her tides, serenely husbanding the mental drama in her to its own fulfillment, she recalled, even in her fantasy, that another wife and another life awaited him outside this room. Often, therefore, he was angel, like his name, who lived in disguise as the husband of a woman named Ann, but revealed himself only to Jane in his divinity. And each time he took her into his divine secret, he immunized her against ever feeling passion for a real man; she was becoming inoculated with every thrust against any real flesh-and-blood male with hair on his chest and lines on his forehead and a head haunted by troublesome embarrassing creatures like her own.

He was above her now, his smooth chest rocking upon her undecided breast, smiling down on her, already a little question in his eyes. (Was she with him yet in the moment?) His endurance continued to amaze her, but she knew it was not limitless, and she had better make up her mind. The angel was not "working" today, and, anxious to enjoy their reunion, she snatched at one of the many creatures swarming upon this bed, competing with the "real" Gabriel: her Aunt Cleva's villain. She would try a villain today, not an angel.

What must it be like, slipping aboard a train, leaving everything you knew, everything that had heretofore been *you,* to go off with a stranger with whom you'd somehow said the few necessary words (*what* words?) between the acts, a person you knew chiefly from his role as a villain in a play? (What was the play about? What had he done, your villain?) And how would he treat you once he'd got you on that moving train with him, no escape possible, going down the mountains that had ringed round your childhood, out of these mountains aboard a moaning night train, into regions north and unfamiliar, full of strangers with different habits and different heritages? What would he say when he got you with him in the berth and drew the heavy green curtains? "You're with me now, little girl. There's no going back. Why are you so shy there? Don't you know what we are going to do? We're going to unfasten your dress, rustling together in the dark; we'll keep the shade up so we can see the lands of your childhood whip past you like remnants of dark ribbon; and now all these layers of pretty things that wives take off by themselves while gentle husbands lie waiting for them in the sanctioned bed. I am going to husband you, but with no sanction. It will be better this way, the excitement will be greater. Don't worry now, it will hurt a little bit, but you will be changed forever; let me stroke you a little, little kitten; you don't even know what all your own softness is for, do you? But you will, you will. You'll go down these mountains, the train is taking you with it, it can't hold itself back, speeding faster and faster into dark, new, strange territory; we'll go together, you can't separate yourself from me from this minute on . . . from this minute on we are one flesh, although neither of us knows it now, I am planting new flesh in you, now, this minute, now, as the train shudders and we hurl over the trestles together above the gulch, and now we are on the other side of your lands, little girl, we are in the new lands, and we shudder together in darkness and irrevocably joined flesh, and there is no going back for you, never, no, never again."

And Jane heard the train moan, high in the night, obliterating the lost girl's cry of baffled capitulation to forces she could never go back on. She shuddered and was still. Her eyes were tight shut.

"I think we must have missed each other quite a bit," she heard the man's gentle, pleased voice say, at last.

She opened her eyes and, for the sake of the trusting self-confident voice whose owner had found her out so

251

little all these months, looked forward almost seventy years into his calm eyes, which rested, lovingly upon this present woman in present time.

"Yes, I think we really must have," she said, tracing a drop of human dampness from his warm forehead, and streaking it like paint through his angel's hair.

XII

"GABRIEL? How's the book coming?"

Now was the time when they talked.

"Oh, it's adding up."

"You mean in quantity or in making sense?"

He laughed. "Both, I hope." He lay on his back, a long, white figure, stroking her hand which he held captive against his stomach. "As of last Friday, I had filled eleven shoe boxes full of note cards. And it has pretty much taken its final shape, I think, even the divisions I'm going to use. I've decided against chronological divisions. Time seems to take second place in this subject. I have decided to divide the book according to the type of love discussed, a different type for each chapter, regardless of the century or the school of painting."

"How many chapters will there be?"

"Um . . . six long ones."

She couldn't help but wonder if he planned to give a chapter to their kind of love. What kind was it? What kind did he think it was? She wondered if she dare ask, and was about to begin working into her approach, when he said, "I really do believe—if I should get that thing—I could have a good first draft within a year."

"That thing" was a Guggenheim. She had talked him ✓ into applying for it. "I stopped applying for grants years ago," he had protested. "I'm not the sort of scholar who gets grants." "Why not?" she had asked. "Because. I'm not interested in making loud, sensational splashes. I'd rather be just a quiet, enduring swimmer. I've dedicated my life to looking at good pictures and trying to see what they're telling me. That's more important for me than rounding up a bunch of old essays and slapping them into a volume with a catchy title, just to get a grant—or a raise, for that matter. Though I wouldn't mind a raise."

"I hope you get that thing," she said now, a strange little division working itself into her consciousness. She both wanted him to and didn't. If he did get one, it must rouse her to new actions and a new way of thinking about him. And they were dangerous. Marian Evans went off to Germany in 1854 with a married man, but Jane did not think she had a tenth of that woman's courage, even given the relaxed moral structure of a world a hundred years older. And Lewes *had* given Marian his heart openly, wanted to live with her, and did live with her openly for twenty-five years; whereas Gabriel only suggested nine months of secrecy in London.

Her second ambivalence was more difficult to accept. It made her seem small and ignoble. If the Guggenheim Foundation were to recognize Gabriel as an outstanding scholar, she would feel threatened. Why? Was she afraid that if the world loved him more, he would need her love less?

"I've been having optimistic twinges lately," he said, smiling at the ceiling and stroking her hand. "After all. I have a good angel now."

Once, months ago, she had asked him: "Why me? When you asked me to come to St. Louis, did you have this in mind?" "Oh, no," he said, and looked surprised at the suggestion. "I don't go in for that sort of thing." "Well, *what* then?" "I felt *you* coming towards me," he said. "And all I knew was that, whatever it was, it was good. You started me writing again, before I even met you, or knew what you looked like. That was good. You gave me hope. If there is such a thing as sin in this world, I think it must be shutting oneself up against hope. I think I had begun to do that." "Hope for what?" Then he had smiled that calm smile, that mystifying, infuriating smile. "Hope does not necessarily have to take an object," he said. "You're the English teacher. You should know that. I am speaking of a state of mind you brought me.

If an angel has the good grace to fly down and give me her company, I'm certainly not going to ask whether she's brought me any presents as well." "You are *my* angel," Jane had said. But he hadn't liked that. He had stroked her hand as he did now, imprisoning it palm-down against his slow-breathing belly, and said: "No, I'm not. I'm an ordinary man whose mother named him after a bachelor uncle with money. It didn't do a bit of good, either. Jane, Jane, I think I must teach you what the old paintings knew: you don't recognize an angel by his name, but by the luminous quality around the space he inhabits. My space, since you have chosen to visit it, is distinctly transformed." This was the closest he ever came to telling her he loved her, and in her good moods she believed it was better than the mere "I love you," which could be tossed off so lightly from less cautious, less articulate tongues.

"Well, let's hope your optimistic twinges are radar signals for the approaching good news. When did you say you expected to hear?"

"Sometime in late March or early April . . . I think. Brooks, a young fellow in our department, had one several years ago. I suppose I could ask him exactly when, but he's so arrogant as it is; and I haven't told anyone—except the chairman, of course. I asked the chairman to write me a letter of recommendation, you see. . . ."

"What has this Brooks done?" Now she was completely on Gabriel's side, like any adoring wife, jealous of her husband's competitors in the unfriendly world where many must always lose in order that a few may win.

"Oh, slapped together a sort of ménage, Bosch and Ernst and Blake and that Escher in California, all the favorites of the young, which they believe they have just discovered for all of us; then he has little snippets from Baudelaire, on opium, and Rimbaud, on hallucinations, and some snippets from Norman O. Brown's book of snippets, and some McLuhan . . . you know the sort of thing. He called it *Vision, Hallucination and Apocalypse*. It has sold something like a hundred thousand copies, I believe." Gabriel smiled. His face, which Jane watched closely, contained not a flicker of visible disdain, envy, or anger. He was simply stating an interesting fact, as he might remark, "There's a rice shortage in Japan."

But Jane shot up in bed. "Christ!" She snatched the pillow from beneath her head and punched it savagely with her fist. "Oh, God, how sick I am of all this fourth-grade stuff passing for seriousness! And how even sicker I am of my contemporaries, my colleagues, people who call themselves intellectuals, eating this pablum up as if it contained some youth fertilizer, throwing hard-earned skills and disciplines and languages and anything that requires sustained effort or more than a cat's span of attention out of the window, *maiming* themselves in order to squeeze a few dazed 'wow's and 'man's and 'cool's out of a bunch of semiliterate, spoiled children. I hate them! I hate this goddamned fashion. It is turning the curriculum into a syllabus of comic books!"

Gabriel chuckled and hooked her round the waist with his elbow. "Come back down here," he said. "Fierce one."

"I'm not finished. How can you be so calm about it? This snippet-master, this collage-creep, getting a free year to go off to Italy or Greece or somewhere warm, in order to cut up picture and poetry books and paste them up again."

"You mustn't make so much over it," Gabriel said. "It isn't important. Brooks isn't important. Under the eye of eternity, Brooks and his book matter very little. Besides, good people get rewarded, too—occasionally."

"How can you always be so sublimely fair? *You* are not the eye of eternity; you're a man with a limited life span who has a project to do and a living to earn. How can you lie there and smile when a fool with a fake project takes away time and money from you?"

"We're having our first married quarrel," he said, still smiling.

"But it's not fair," she persisted, luxuriating, however, in this word he had just used (Did he and Ann argue about money? Did Ann beleaguer him about getting a raise?), in the attentions he was giving her, stroking her hair, her face. "It's not fair that people like that should win."

". . . 'the race is not to the swift, nor the battle to the strong . . . nor yet riches to men of understanding, nor yet favor to men of skill' . . ."

"That is the gloomiest book in the Bible! I hate it worse than Job. I think its message is almost as damaging to human progress as the Beatitudes. If the meek shall inherit the earth, why should the strong go on trying to be strong? If the race is to the slowpokes, why should the swift go on running? Everyone should just lie down and stop trying and be blessed for it. Job at least persisted in his stubbornness. He knew he was good, and he got back on his feet."

"You're confusing weak with meek," said Gabriel pleasantly but with authority. She supposed he must be something like this arguing down a stubborn student in class. "And neither of those books, as far as I remember, advocates lying down. Oh, no. 'Whatsoever thy hand findeth to do, do it with thy might . . .' It does not promise Guggenheims for trying, but the message is pretty clear."

"You're so good at memorizing," said Jane. "I wish I could remember more of my favorite things like that. I don't know why I always get so furious over this subject of weak versus strong, but I seem to. I remember, in convent school, when grades came out every month, there were two kinds of rewards. There were Honor Cards for the smart people who had all A's and B's on their subjects; and there were Merit Cards for the dumb people who didn't do so well in their studies but got A's in all the 'virtues' at the bottom of the card. Patience, Self-control, Courtesy, and Neatness. I remember how unfair I used to think it was that an all-A student could be kept off the Honor Roll if she had just one B in Patience. But a student with A's in all the virtues would not be kept off the Merit Roll if she had a C in Math or English."

"You're confusing honor with merit," said Gabriel, in the same pleasant, matter-of-fact teacher's tone. "Honorable people simply have to try harder, that's all. *Noblesse oblige.*" Then he laughed delightedly and rumpled her hair. "I'll bet you sometimes got less than an A in Patience, am I right?"

She admitted it. "But it's not nice of you to say so. I'm

much more patient these days than I ever was before in my life. Oh, I think I am *very* patient." And there was a little threatening edge to her voice, which she knew he would probably choose to ignore—or deflect. He deflected.

"Yes, on the whole, Jane, I think you are a very patient person. After all, you've put up with me for almost two years."

"I wonder if we'll make it till our second anniversary in May," she said dangerously, unable to stop herself.

"That's up to you," he said, not smiling now. "As for myself, I would be very sad if we didn't."

What right have you to say such things! she wanted to scream. *What right would you have to be sad!* And she heard Ann Weeks, during some bedroom impasse, musing sadly, "I wonder if we'll make it till our twenty-fifth anniversary," and Gabriel answering gravely, "That's up to you. As for myself, I would be very sad if we didn't."

Where did he get eleven shoe boxes in which to store his note cards for this project of his, the project he had told her she had inspired through that first letter? Nobody had eleven shoe boxes of his own in the house, unless he collected shoe boxes over the years. Gabriel had only two pairs of shoes that she knew of. Perhaps a third at home, an old pair, years removed from any shoe box, which he wore for mending the roof or mowing the lawn. Women were the seasonal shoe-buyers. He was keeping his note cards in Ann's shoe boxes, that's what he was doing! And the thought was as if Jane had surprised him in adultery. Ann's shoe boxes! She pictured them from the shoe boxes she had had herself: shoe boxes of various widths and glosses and colors, with jaunty Italian names scrawled attractively across the lid. Did Ann buy lots of shoes, spend away her husband's modest salary in decorating her feet? Was Ann vain? What size shoe did she wear? Did she have long boat-shaped feet like Cousin Frances, which looked best sheathed in a black, unobtrusive I. Miller? Or did she have a tiny, short foot with sexy toes, which she showed off through little straps and thongs? Did she paint her toenails in the summer, carefully placing a cotton wad between each toe and the next? Did Gabriel sit fascinated, in some room Jane had not imagined, or on a summery patio or porch, watching his wife paint her small toes?

Suddenly miserable, Jane shut her eyes tight and pushed her head into Gabriel's armpit. "I want you to help me stop wanting things so badly," she said. "I want you to tell me how to be detached, as you are. Surely it is something I can learn. I have always been an excellent student. I have always been able to learn from a good teacher. Please, teach me how to take things or leave them, to take *people* or leave them."

"That's not an easy assignment, even for a good teacher," he said. "I know you think I have a maddening approximation to self-sufficiency. I suppose, compared to most people I know, I do. There isn't the dimension of longing in me, I'll admit. Was I always this way? I don't think so. I can remember wanting things with an almost physical pain—though I don't remember what they were anymore. It may be that I've just closed off so long ago that it has become my nature not to want things."

"You really *don't* want things, do you? If you get the Guggenheim, you'll be pleased, but if you don't get it you won't go to bed and cry."

"No, I don't guess I would go to bed and cry about anything. At least, certainly not the fact that somebody else's name got drawn out of a hat rather than my own. Of course, it's more than a lottery, but in the long run most things amount to the same thing."

"How I wish to God I could get rid of *my* dimension of longing!"

"I'm not sure it would be right for you to get rid of it—even if you could. The loss has its practical advantages, I must admit, but I can't help thinking it is a deficiency on my part."

He looked at her, but his eyes had gone distant. When she looked into them, trying to fathom his whereabouts, she saw only two reflections of herself, lit by a bluish winter afternoon light coming in through a hotel window: pale, frowning face drawn into a tight, tense mask of longing.

Gabriel suddenly laughed.

"What, may I ask, do you find funny?"

He stroked her head. "Poor Jane. Please try and forgive this maddening person as long as you can stand the relationship. I wasn't finding anything funny. I was just suddenly charmed by you all over again. I was thinking about you."

"What about me? What were you thinking?"

"Well, I was thinking that the thing that gives you the most trouble is in some ways your best quality."

"That's comforting to know," she said bitterly. "What is my best quality?"

"Your resilience, your pliancy. The thing that makes you bend softly into each new situation, but with your eyes open, questioning it every step of the way. I don't know if now is the time to give the English teacher another vocabulary lesson, but the word you were abusing a few minutes ago, in its original, pure sense, describes you. 'Meek' means pliant and gentle, Jane. It does not mean weak. And in the pure, good sense of the word, I do believe the meek shall inherit the earth: those who can bend with all its movements and changes, without breaking. It is the rigid and unbending and inflexible— perhaps persons not unlike myself—who are the real losers in the long run."

"If you really believe such a thing, why don't you change? Or do you get some sort of satisfaction out of thinking of yourself as a loser?" (She sometimes thought that he did.)

"No, I don't particularly like the thought of myself as a loser. I don't think, really, I am a loser. I have, I'll admit, a soft spot for the underdog. I like to champion unpopular causes. Maybe that's what made me pick the Pre-Raphaelites when I had to pick somebody in 1948."

That's not the only thing you picked in 1948, she thought. *Was the other thing you picked also an underdog, an unpopular cause?*

"Nobody would touch them," he went on. "There was not a single monograph written on them after 1903. They were a lost cause in those days. The art establishment had pronounced them dead, and was ready to pronounce any young scholar dead who dared to take them out of the closet and brush them off and refurbish them." He smiled a strange little smile, rather smug, but was there also just a touch of pain in it? "Though I sometimes *have* wondered if it wasn't something else as well that made me choose them, some deep-seated arrogance which disguised itself in the nobler motive of wanting to champion the underdog. I wonder if perhaps what really appealed to me was the idea of being the only one. Better to be the uncontested authority in a field nobody else wanted than to be a second- or third-rate authority in a popular field: the Impressionists, for instance. They were the in thing, in those days."

"But don't you see," said Jane, suddenly becoming excited, "you *aren't* rigid or inflexible. If you can still question yourself like that, you're not rigid."

"But questioning one's past is not quite the same thing as questioning one's present, as you constantly do. There comes a point in each person's life where certain choices harden into the irrevocable. After that, they can't be changed. Perhaps that's why I spend so little time these days indulging in this sort of questioning."

"So you don't think you can change any of . . . the life choices you have made." She watched him carefully. "They are all irrevocable?" And waited between breaths for his answer.

"Irrevocable but not irredeemable," he replied maddeningly, taking her in his arms with a desperate suddenness unlike him, nuzzling her face, her hair, her neck, as though they gave off some elixir of renewal. She was slightly shocked to feel, pressing against her, his resurrected passion. And she was a little angry. Now! When she would rather go on talking about his past, which they did so seldom, and ferreting out clues for their future together; yet here he was, offering her himself in the moment again. She imagined herself jumping out of bed —even as she was curling pliantly to him—she imagined herself doing what she had never done with him: causing a scene, shouting: *"It is time to make another life choice, here in room nine-twenty of this AAA-approved hotel, Gabriel Weeks. Who do you want in your bed for the rest of your life, Ann or Jane? Either the apple or the orange has got to go."* What would he do? What would he say? She had to suppress a little laugh as she imagined his passion withdrawing, courteous as the rest of him, furling back into itself like a day lily, as he said: "I know, I know, I am a maddening companion." But he would never cry about it; she could refuse him (which she never had) or she could accept him, and "under the eternal eye," what would one time, more or less, matter "in the long run"?

But how *pliantly,* how *resiliently,* as though his description of her had broken some evil spell, she found herself bending with him. It took her by surprise. How quickly, how easily, after all these years—and all these months with him—after all the abetting fantasies, she suddenly let herself go into a brand-new experience.

Which was: synchronizing wholly with the man she was with, in the moment she was with him.

And yet he had described her so accurately when he said she bent softly into new situations, "but with your eyes open, questioning it every step of the way." She held this real person in the closest embrace she had ever known, she shuddered with the knowledge of him, and yet simultaneously her mind stared and questioned. Perhaps it would never rest; perhaps it would always remain insomniac, monitoring all her bendings and abandonments and loosenings, questioning, as it questioned now: how could this be happening when nothing is resolved between you and him, nothing more than this moment? A moment ago you were talking about Guggenheims and the Beatitudes, and then—suddenly—this! Why? Why now of all times? What has caused it? Did some topic set it off? Some word? "Irrevocable," perhaps? You used "irrevocable" in your last fantasy, your villain fantasy; irrevocable is, as you know, a good word to help yourself along. Yet there is something self-destroying in abandoning yourself to words like irrevocable. Was it the other word, then? Or, rather, words: not irredeemable. Dearest Gabriel! Of course he would insulate such a dangerous word of hope and grace within double negatives. How like him!

She held him, she held to him, to this man in the center of her life, this champion of lost causes (and of found?) who, for all his cautious double negatives, knew the meanings of words she would do well to look up again, this real man of flesh and blood who had made her so miserable and so happy in adjoining instants, and they fell asleep that way, locked together in an afternoon moment of blue winter light.

When she woke, he was fully dressed, kneeling beside her bed. A lamp had been turned on.

"I was getting worried about you," he said. "You really slept. I have never seen you sleep like that."

"Insomniacs have to surprise themselves into sleep," she said, opening her arms to him. He bowed his head on her breast and she kissed the top of it. Soft, evanescent angel's hair. If their relationship lasted for many more years, she would find herself kissing a head as smooth as a baby's. Would she mind that? On the contrary: the thought made him vulnerable; waves of tenderness came over her. "What time is it?" she said, to keep from saying "I love you."

"Almost seven. How about some dinner?"

"I'll get dressed."

"Take your time. Then we'll go out and find whatever food we feel like eating, and maybe afterwards we'll walk for a bit. How are you feeling?"

"I feel wonderful."

"I do, too. Oh, dear Jane, dear Jane." He put his cheek against hers. It was warm. He does need me in his life, she thought; he would be very sad if I went out of it.

He stood up. "I'll just go down for a few minutes. Will a half-hour give you enough time?"

He always left her alone to dress, even when they had shared a room. He would say, "I'll take a short stroll," or offer to go and refill the ice bucket, or something. She had always appreciated his tact, because she was unused to dressing around another person; she liked to feel unobserved. But today she didn't want it. She felt she would like to try more intimacy, to have him watch while she moved about the room, slipped on her stockings, combed her hair. She wanted him to know her as she knew herself.

"Why don't you stay here? I won't be long," she said.

"Well, actually, I think I ought to make a call," he said. His face, until recently so happy, went so long and woebegone that she saw he was not looking forward to it; it was all a matter of duty, it would take nothing away from her. And though she felt her usual fury reserved for this subject stirring potently inside her, she got out of bed and stood on tiptoe and resolutely embraced his fully clothed body.

"Of course," she said. "Forgive me. Come back in half an hour."

She felt him relax. "Wild horses couldn't keep me away," he said. He touched her beneath her chin, cocked his head thoughtfully. She looked at him. His face, unlined as it was, suddenly looked its almost half-century. But his eyes shone at her.

"You are a treasure," he said.

After he had closed the door behind him, they all came out. If was as if they had been waiting under the bed, patiently biding their time while she slept in his embrace; suppressing their cackles as she played to the last dregs her Understanding Mistress Scene. Now, out they came, all the naysayers who lived inside her head, supplying her with a running cynical commentary on her life: Gerda, Zimmer, the entire editorial staff of the magazine for swinging women that specialized in titles like "So You're In Love with a Married Man and You Think Your Case Is *Different!*"

RATE YOUR MARRIED LOVER (AND HIS CHANCES FOR GETTING UNMARRIED . . . . AND REMARRIED . . . TO YOU!)

After you and your ML have spent the afternoon in a hotel bedroom, does he:

a. Excuse himself to "make a call"?
b. Suggest dinner?
c. Call you a treasure?

If a., you are wasting your time; if b., he is at least a

gentleman, on an expense account, or very hungry; if c., he MAY BE GETTING SERIOUS, *unless* he says it after you have not made a fuss about a., in which case it means he is guilty, and grateful to you for not making a scene.

"Here we have Ms. Jane Clifford, same lady pedant, performing certain post-coital, pre-dining ablutions in the bathroom of a medium-priced hotel, circa 1970. For the past five and a half hours, she and her professorial *amore* have lain together, interlacing their physical congress with the sort of conversation two professors in bed think they should have. The topics discussed were:

"1. His hopes of receiving a coveted fellowship in order to gain a free year abroad in the illicit company of his bedfellow, filling an infinite number of ladies' shoe boxes (belonging to his lawful wife) with note cards for a quixotic project, this project being the interpretation of the entire art collection of the Western world as expressions and manifestations of various kinds of love, which he has enumerated, with true Procrustean economy, as being six in number.

"2. How the Undeserving Manqué always receives the laurel and the olive, while the Swift, the Strong, the Understanding, and the Skilled must make do with sour grapes. This paean to the True Deservers being heavily ornamented with quotes from the Book of Ecclesiastes. The lady appeared particularly fetching when, naked and flushed with indignation, she attacked a pillow with her fists, blaming outwardly for her rampage the fake scholars of the world and the Third Beatitude, but actually railing against her own unacknowledged position in various fields of endeavor.

"3. A bit of etymological foreplay, employing the words "meek" and "irrevocable," in which the art professor managed to forestall the lady's grievances *re* their equivocal relationship by decking her complimentarily, with a rather earnest wordiness, in the first adjective, after which he cleverly managed to divert some embarrassing questions (*re* their equivocal relationship) by clothing the ugly "irrevocable" in the more flattering garb of "redemption." . . . Thus, wooed by his wordplay, the lady of letters stripped away her inhibitions with a hitherto-un-equaled zest, attributing it to a magical word. (Which word? Does it matter? Everything for her is measured in words.) Also, it is this scholar's humble opinion that she, being of the old-fashioned "discipline" school of pedants, was impressed by his rather dull feats of memorization. . . ."

"So," said Gerda as Jane began brushing the tangles from her hair, attempting to remold it into some reasonable sort of bun, "you finally made it. You finally—"

"Shut up," said Jane aloud to the hotel mirror. "I won't have your jargon ruining my finest hour. At least not yet. I want to think about this thing that has happened to me without the benefit of current coinage, if you don't mind." For in the last issue of Gerda's circulation-soaring *Feme Sole* had been a lead article written by Gerda herself and entitled "Home Remedy," which had enumerated with painstaking directions ("Always be sure the head of the vibrator is clean; it is also a good idea to take a towel to bed. . . .") the various politically acceptable (i.e., without a man) ways of accomplishing this goal.

Was Gabriel's project quixotic? For almost two years, she had vacillated between thinking him a nearsighted fool and a farsighted genius. How could she tell? Surely there must be a way to measure it, but how? After the fact, it became a bit simpler. For instance, in the field of literature, of literary criticism, she *knew* Northrop Frye was a genius—even though some respectable scholars like Sonia Marks's husband detested Northrop Frye. Frye's ideas made sense; they rested on valuable hypotheses; they lit up the entire realm of literature for you. After you had read Frye, you thought of your favorite books as parts of a large family. You not only saw them as you had before, but you saw behind them and in front of them. It was like meeting someone, forming an opinion about this person, then being privileged to meet the person's parents and grandparents, as well; and then being privileged to meet the person's children, and grandchildren! Of course, someone like Max Covington would say, The person himself, alone, should be judged. What do his parents have to do with it? What do his children have to do with it? They only confuse and diffuse you from the proper study of the object, which is: the object itself.

She had tried to lift her assurance about Frye—as one might gingerly try to lift an anchovy from its tin and place it, undamaged, on a plate—and transfer it toward her wavering confidence in Gabriel. Surely, during the forties and fifties when Frye was painstakingly filling his wife's shoe boxes with note cards for *Anatomy of Criticism,* Mrs. Frye had had an occasional qualm. Or had she? After all, Frye had done *Fearful Symmetry* first. She had that to build on. She knew that first closetful of shoe boxes had come to something. Whereas, with Gabriel, there was only the queer, eccentric little monograph, published half a lifetime ago! And how did one transfer the standards of excellence in literary criticism to the standards of excellence in art criticism? She had consulted art books, found temporary respite in Panofsky. Intrinsic meaning! Essential Tendencies of the Human Mind! How she had welcomed these standards for judgment in Panofsky. They reminded her of the way Gabriel talked about pictures. *The meaning of this picture* . . . And *essential tendencies of the human mind* . . . wasn't Panofsky limiting things, too, in that statement? Just as there were (she had not finished the book, but was sure Panofsky had enumerated, or at least intimated the number)————number of essential tendencies of the human mind, there could surely be————number of kinds of love. But her hopes were dashed at a Christmas party, given by Sonia and Max, when she met an art professor, who held a chair at an Eastern university, on loan to the Midwest for a mere semester. Safely ensconced in the Renaissance, a former *student* of Panofsky's, this professor had sat kindly in a corner with Jane and explained, at her request, why, first of all, the Pre-Raphaelite Movement could never be taken seriously, could never be more than a fad, even if it became a re-resurrected fad.

"The Pre-Raphaelite pictures," he said, "are too meticulous, too sterile. They are *illustrations*. They tell a story, *one story,* and that is why art scholars need not waste time applying their tools of iconography. In Pre-Raphaelite pictures, there is not a hint of the atmospheric vibration of the coming Impressionists, not a single hint of the synthesizing of the coming Symbolists. The Pre-Raphaelites existed in a vacuum. They had no bearing on the art continuum, and, as such, cannot be treated seriously by a serious art historian except as a curiosity. Now I can well understand your own interest in the movement. You are a scholar of literature, of nineteenth-century literature. And the Pre-Raphaelites were more literary than they were artistic."

"I have a student," Jane went on, allowing him to refill her drink and come back while she fashioned the lie that would serve her best, "I have this graduate student, very bright, who did his undergraduate work in Art History. He wants to do a term paper on the kinds of love, and how these loves have been represented in Western painting. Is that a valid subject, do you think? I must admit it interested me."

"Ah, it interested the Renaissance courtiers! It became a sort of Cinquecento parlor game, rather like those parlor games in psychoanalysis people were playing in the forties. Everyone was going around trying to add up and categorize the kinds of love. It was, of course, a vulgarization of Ficino's system. If your student wanted to do a paper on Neoplatonic paintings which in some way deal with love, and then connect them to Ficino, that might be valid, except Panofsky's already done it. But that would hardly serve as a paper in a course on nineteenth-century literature, unless you were really stretching a point. Of course, there are so many young teachers willing to stretch a point these days, I sometimes think they are made of elastic—*eroded* elastic—but you don't strike me as one of those."

"I try not to be," said Jane. "What were Ficino's kinds of love? Did he actually enumerate them?"

"Of course he did. Let me see, he had . . . ah . . . *amore divino, amore umano, amore bestiale.* Then Pico, who was less medical—Ficino was also a physician as well as a Platonist, you know—connected the three forms of love with the three psychological faculties of *intelletto, ragione,* and *senso.*" The eminent man got a great sensuous pleasure, it had seemed to Jane, in rolling out his Italian words with a languorous facility which proclaimed his frequent sojourns in the Cinquecento capital. But she had to have all that he could give her, and was willing to be humble.

"I think my student means to focus on the *amore umano,*" she said. "But I don't think he has divided it up in quite the same way as Pico. So far, he has, let me see," and she inserted just a touch of irony in her recitation, in spite of herself, "Idyllic Love, which, I guess, might be related to *amore divino* . . . certainly platonic in nature. . . . Then, let me see, there is, in my student's system, what he calls Sympathetic Love, which is a sort of world love, love for the universe, a bit like the Transcendentalists; and Mirror Love, which is rather narcissistic, but also fleshly; I think he said something about it being a kind of love in which we recognize ourself in another, which doesn't *have* to be a bad thing; then he is going to add some more . . . some more kinds of love."

"Good gracious, what a mishmash!" And the eminent man laughed. He put his arm around Jane in a fatherly way, and she felt—guiltily, disloyally—pleasure in being aligned with the established, the esteemed of the world. "Let me give you a word of wisdom," this man said to Jane, in the confiding tones of a teacher. "You are young at your profession. And when we are young, we are easily impressed. You said, I believe, that this student was bright. But the truly bright are cautious in their systems; they know that the big things are not so quickly and easily categorized. The farther one can see, the more he understands must remain vague to him. I have found it is, by and large, the nearsighted boob that goes in for grandiose systems. Or the megalomaniac. I'm not saying your student is either, but what I am saying is that you may want to encourage him towards a more modest, a more realizable project."

So you don't think his project could be realized," repeated Jane, inwardly stinging for poor Gabriel. *Nearsighted boob. Megalomaniac.*

"Perhaps for *himself* it could. Yes, there are many who spend their lives creating weird systems to baffle and confuse other people. But objectively it would be a waste of time. His system would be useless to anyone else."

"But how does one *judge?* What if this were, say, fifty years ago, and I was standing here telling you about a brilliant young student who wanted to do an ambitious paper setting down laws for iconology, and this student later turned out to be Erwin Panofsky and the paper turned into *Studies in Iconology?"*

"Setting down laws, if we must put it that way—though I'd rather say 'postulating workable criteria'—for the universal judgment of acclaimed works of art is not in the same class with . . . that other madcap thing you described; what was it? You see, it's so mad I can't even remember it properly. It's too subjective, don't you see? The world is certainly too complicated for anyone to attempt to enumerate the kinds of love and then apply *his* categories to painting . . . or even literature, for that matter. Ficino was not trying to do such a thing. He was trying to harmonize the vast writings of Plato and the 'Platonici' with the Christian religion, trying to find similarities, agreements between two *established* systems. He wouldn't have dreamed of digging around into his own subjective ideas about love (he was, by the way, a chaste and abstemious man; thought it suited the dignity and preserved the health of a scholar) and then sticking them onto an established tradition, a body of ideas accepted by most of the world. Am I making myself clear? You look uncertain, my dear."

"I think I'll suggest he try for a more workable topic," said Jane.

"That's the girl," said the eminent professor. "I'm happy to have been of help."

Later, Jane had asked Gabriel, casually, what he thought of Ficino's categories of love; and of Pico's refinements. When he had frowned, temporarily blank on these categories, she had a moment of horror, remembering George Eliot's Mr. Casaubon and his worthless lifetime project, The Key to All Mythologies, and how Will Ladislaw had told Dorothea that her husband would have done better to have learned German; most of the work he was slaving over had already been surpassed by the Germans.

But was she being fair? What if Gabriel, during a stolen weekend, had suddenly turned to her in bed and asked, "Oh, by the way, what is your opinion of————," and sprung on her some obscure literary influence of the Renaissance? Specialization was, in both their fields, very much limited to a century, and she and Gabriel were nineteenth century, for better or for worse.

"Is it true," she had asked him, "that a Pre-Raphaelite painting tells only one story?"

"What's wrong with that?" he had answered. "If it's a good story."

"If a movement has no successors, if it doesn't generate a coming movement, does that mean it can be no more than a curiosity, an anachronism only?"

"If a person has no children, does that mean he can be no more than a curiosity, an anachronism only?" Gabriel had no children either.

In so many ways, thought Jane, brushing her hair in front of the bathroom mirror in room 920, brushing it till it radiated out from her pale face in little bands of light; *in so many ways Gabriel and I are curiously wedded.*

"Such sentimentality," said Gerda. "It sure must be *curiously,* when he's downstairs calling his wife. Why must you insult your intelligence by such soft-soaping sentimentality, just because you finally—"

"Out," said Jane to the mirror. "I want all of you out of here." Her eyes burned at themselves. At the moment they were an intense blue green. Her mouth, without lipstick, seemed softer and pinker than usual. Would Vincent de Lucca think she was so bad if he were looking at her now? And her hair! Her hair had not looked so alive in years. She should brush it more, pamper her body more. They were not such bad things. Feeling suddenly lovely and desirable, she decided not to pin it back, hide its light under a bushel, but to wear it down, rippling and flowing, catching what light it could. And it looked lighter, it suddenly seemed to her; or was it only the light above the bathroom mirror, which fell differently from her light at home? Never mind, it looked lighter *now*. It had regained some of the young luster that the old nun had caught, like sun motes in her old hand.

"Today has done me good," said Jane, to the mirror, to the silent bathroom, evacuated of creatures. "And I intend to enjoy what is left of it."

XIII

But she couldn't let herself. As she and Gabriel walked hand in hand down Second Avenue, trying to relocate the Lebanese restaurant where, less than a month ago (thanks to Ann's father's cataracts), they had enjoyed an urgent "stolen" dinner before Gabriel took the nine o'clock bus back to Montclair, very little of her was with him.

She remembered how she had once stood behind two men in O'Hare airport. One had joked to the other: "Gotta call home. That once-a-day call that keeps you out of jail, you know."

She was Ann Weeks in an old bathrobe, having just washed her hair and left it in the towel while she ate leftovers, feeling a little sorry for her poor husband, who, on this January night, was forced to go out, like a stray cat or dog, in search of food.

"You're very quiet," said Gabriel.

"I'm hungry. Are you?"

"Oh, boy, am I. I think I remember now where that place is."

"I'm going to order the couscous this time. I was so jealous of yours the last."

"Hmm. That's an idea. I might have it again myself."

"Then," she said sharply, "I'll have to order something else. Otherwise how can I be jealous of yours?"

Gabriel laughed uncertainly and squeezed her hand. He was not used to her infrequent eruptions of sudden bitterness. She was surprised at herself. Usually she managed to keep them hidden from him. Once he had asked her, "How do you manage always to be in such a good mood?" She, Jane, always in a good mood! But she had smiled modestly and replied, "How do *you*?" "Oh, goodness. I'm not," he said. "In fact, I'm often a grouch, so I'm told."

So I'm told.

Jane imagined a woman walking toward them, on the same side of the street. They would not be able to see her face till the last minute, and when they did it would be Ann Weeks. What would Gabriel do? Drop her hand like a hot potato?

What if she should write an anonymous letter to Mrs. Gabriel Weeks: "Have you never truly imagined what your husband does before and after his phone calls to you? Do you really think he eats alone—walks down dark streets in cities you've never visited with him, to eat alone —munching thoughtfully and looking at paintings in his head? If so, you are editing something out. This is perhaps not your fault. But would you agree with me there are too many lies abroad in the world? Wouldn't it be better for all of us if you could see him, unedited, now, and I could see you, imagine you as you are?" She saw Ann Weeks begin to frown as she read this typed anonymous letter. Frown and then . . .

What? She hadn't the least idea of what Ann would do next.

("You don't even know what it's like to be one other person!" Gerda had screamed.)

But she was trying, she was trying now, to the exclusion of Gabriel himself, to feel as the wife of Gabriel would feel and not as the mistress of Gabriel would imagine his wife to feel. What if she had been the wife of this man for almost twenty-five years? How would she feel about him? Would she see him at all as "Jane, the other woman" saw him? How would the marriage have changed her? How would twenty-five years with this man have altered her from all the other possible women she might have been had she not married him?

Perhaps, Jane thought, with a triumphant little surge of cynicism, if I had been married to him twenty-five years,

I would be quite content to have this evening to myself. The reason I'm not imagining a mistress walking beside him down Second Avenue is quite simple. I'm not thinking of him at all. There is no need to edit anything out, because it matters so little that I'm not thinking of it. My thoughts are entirely somewhere else.

But where?

("What do you think she's like?" Jane had asked Kitty once. "What does it matter?" said Kitty, as she had said about the unsolved mystery of Aunt Cleva. "That shouldn't concern you. It's not your business. You knew he had a wife when you started this thing. In fact, you once said you liked it better that way; it kept it eternally fresh." "Did I say that? I'm almost sure you said that, Kitty." "Oh, I can't keep track of who said what," replied Kitty airily. "Anyway, I distinctly remember the *feeling* of those words in that conversation, the feeling that your love will go on for years longer if you see each other only once a month.")

And Jane had played it that way. Her affair had been a measured, stately waltz in which each partner focused on the dance in progress, and did not, by tacit mutual consent, appear to notice or—God forbid!—discuss the wife waiting patiently on the sidelines, chaperoned by the dowagers of Habit and Law. She had had almost two years to ask Gabriel some straight questions and she had not asked. She had not wanted to break the smoothness of the dance step, pit her jarring voice against the elegant music. So wasn't she, then, an accessory to the crime? Hadn't she, by consenting for almost two years to deceive, forfeited all rights to demand a showdown, insist on the truth? What would happen if she did? Ah, was she afraid he would leave her if she "broke step"?

That gloomy Ellen Glasgow story, "The Difference," where a mistress writes to the wife and the wife of twenty years puts on her walking suit and gloves and hat and veil and goes to see her. The mistress asks the wife to "give him up for the sake of *his* happiness," and so the wife returns home and tells her husband, "I won't stand in your way if you love her." "Who said anything about love," he answers, extremely put out by the whole unnecessary discovery. He says immediately, "Of course I won't see her again," and picks up his wife and carries her into the dining room where the servants have laid a fine dinner. "You must try to eat a good dinner," he says.

But that was Glasgow, whose favorite theme was men's inhumanity, men's inferiority to women. Glasgow, who created a heroine in *Barren Ground* who could live without love, a heroine whom Sonia Marks's students could not identify with because they were not ready to live without love. Ellen Glasgow, Sonia had once told Jane, had been in love, most of her life, with an inferior human, a rather inhuman, vain man. And so she had projected this image of her beloved on all the male characters in her fiction. Jane could not live her life according to Glasgow. ("You have to live your own evidence, dear little Jane," said Kitty. "You cannot research everything, you know.")

Gabriel loped along beside her, oblivious to her insurrectionary thoughts, his warm, dry hand trapping hers.

"What are you thinking, right this moment?" she suddenly asked, accusingly.

"What am I thinking? I'm thinking that if my memory serves me right, our restaurant is just around the next corner."

She looked up at him, this person who managed, as no other person she knew, to keep abreast of the present moment. *His* thoughts were not flying wildly abroad, knocking one another down, flinging themselves against impenetrable windows, barriers of other times, other places. He was with her, walking down Second Avenue. It was she who had deserted him, this beautiful unweary man, his coat collar turned up around a dark blue scarf, a soft wool scarf; she had noticed it as they left the hotel, and wondered if Ann had given it to him. Ah, there he was, predictably as always, pressing forward, never into bad weathers, but only into different varieties of good.

"That's a lovely scarf you're wearing," she said. "Wherever did you find it?"

"Well, I ordered it," he said. "Out of the Marshall Field catalogue. Actually it looked a navy color in the catalogue, which is what I really wanted. But when it came, it turned out to be this color."

"Well, why didn't you send it back and tell them they had misrepresented the color?"

"Oh, I don't know. This color's not so bad. In fact, I've grown rather fond of it. The more I grow used to it."

Apples and oranges. In fact, I've grown rather fond of ———. The more I grow used to———.

"My memory did serve me right," said Gabriel, squeezing her hand, pulling her into a side street.

There was their Lebanese restaurant, its exotic colored sign winking at them from the midst of an otherwise dark street. Here they had come a month ago—not quite a month ago. They had been celebrating how they had met—or, rather, how Jane had first seen Gabriel—at the last New York MLA, three Decembers ago.

We were happier the last time we came together down this little dark street, thought Jane. Much happier. And yet nothing has changed since that other time. Gabriel had a wife last month, just as he has her this month. And tonight, unlike the last time, he does not have to leave on a bus. And a month ago, we had never experienced—I had never experienced—what I experiencd this afternoon. So why are we not even more happy tonight?

Why am *I* not as happy tonight? He is the same as always. It is my attitude that is coloring tonight; it has nothing to do with him. If he had not happened to mention that call, which he always makes anyway, my attitude would have been different and I would be enjoying the moment.

Several weeks ago, in the library, she had read an interview with a new, revolutionary psychiatrist. His theories were so impossible, yet so fascinating, that she had copied out phrases into her personal notebook, the same notebook into which she had later copied Sheldon's passage on "the fertile void of visionary air."

Only in the ego can we go mad, he said, *and only through the ego is pathology possible. Hence all of life is an evil struggle for the person nervously strong in his ego; all of life is a fight, a competition, a ceaseless and disas-*

trous attempt to make permanent what is so obviously impermanent, to define as an entity what is only a process, a flow, an event. . . .

But are you saying there is no ego? asked the interviewer. That there is only "a process, a flow, an event" where we have always thought the ego was?

Yes, I am saying that.

Then perhaps you would explain how it is that people go mad. You said—am I not correct?—that people can go mad only through their egos.

That's right. It is because they are trying so desperately to hold on to, to keep in shape, something that cannot be held on to, that has no shape. That is why they go mad. The paradox, of course, is that they do not really go mad. There is no madness, just as there is no ego.

Do you think people will ever accept this . . . this proposition of yours?

It's not a proposition. It's a reality. People, some people, have been accepting it for centuries. The mystics accept it. Certain truly creative people, who have gone beyond personal needs, have accepted it: I mean those rare artists and philosophers and scientists who are more interested in the Entire Event, of which they are only small parts, rather than trying to control or arrange for their own personal uses the little, passing ephemeral events.

Would you say you qualify for this . . . rare group? Have you gone beyond your ego?

I will say that I don't at all experience myself as an entity, a "person," but as a process, the "ego" of which has consciousness and some intelligence, and some "vision," if you like, in the sense of being able to look around and calculate, but the Entire Event is much larger than "myself," and "my" only responsibility is to attempt to find out, to figure out, what the assignment is, what the destiny is, how high "I" should attempt to go with the "ego's" peculiar resources. The main responsibility is to live up to, or live into, one's destiny, or one's DNA-programmed future.

Excuse me, but I notice that you keep using these

278

words of things you say don't exist, even though you are careful to stress them in quotes, so to speak.

That is because we are having the kind of conversation we are having. It would not be necessary to use these words if you and I both accepted what I am telling you many have already accepted . . . and many more—one day the whole universe—will accept: that there isn't any struggle essentially, except what our self-created ego tells us is a struggle. All the disharmonies, conflicts, conversations, love affairs and failures and death are superficial events. None of them are significant, really. The only significant thing is how we enjoy the moment, our attitude towards the moment. One should simply give himself up to the moment, enjoy it, even if it is horrendous.

Are you saying that if a person is getting murdered at a certain moment, he should *enjoy* that moment?

Why not? Why not enjoy it? It's his last moment, the last personal, superficial event in his finite life. Sure, why not enjoy it? What else better is there to do?

What else better is there to do? she thought as they were seated in their old corner. The same table, just like last time. Only, one must not read any significance or continuity into that. The same table is really two tables, two separate events. The fact that we sat here almost a month ago is irrelevant. In that case, why not look at all the moments in Gabriel and Ann Weeks's marriage as separate moments, unconnected to one another, adding up to nothing? Oh, God, I wish I could talk to that son of a bitch, that psychiatrist. I don't believe him; I don't want to believe him. Yet I don't *not* believe him. And there is even a little part of me which would be so relieved, able to rest at last, if what he says is true. How nice to sit back and enjoy this moment, to have done with significances, to forsake this terrible task of personality, to let myself, with the help of my intellect, be DNA-processed towards my destiny, to join the Entire Event willingly and stop laying up for myself selfish little treasures, stop collecting things and ideas and people for my paltry little "entity," which may someday be proved never to have existed. And Jane thought of all her friends and family and even her favorite characters in novels, which were also friends and family; she thought of their painful strivings, their absolute certainty that they were who they were: "Dorothea," or "Isabel" or "Jude," or "Ivan," working so hard to make sense of that "entity," with all its disharmonies and conversations and conflicts and love affairs and failures and ultimate death, perhaps not thinking once during the course of their whole life that the "entity" was only a process. And she tried to think how their lives would have been different if they had lived by that knowledge: If Kitty had lived by that knowledge and Edith . . . and Gerda . . . and Sonia . . . and . . .

Could it be possible that Gabriel was doing just that? Could it be that Gabriel was one of these fortunate "new" persons, one of the rare outstanding persons of his era (just as there were, Kitty had told her, always some people in any era who were more passionate than others) who had already become a member of that select country club, The Entire Event, which she might die without having joined, without ever having even glimpsed, she who was so "nervously strong in her ego."

The waiter laid their table with many little dishes: hummus, taheeni, pita, a salad of chopped tomatoes and spring onions and parsley. A pleasurable greed welled up in both of them for this exotic food, for the variety of it, and they tore their pita in little pieces and dipped it first in hummus, then taheeni, then took a bite of the pungent, agreeably sharp salad, then back to the taheeni or humus: it was the choice, the being able to go from one to the other, that was so pleasurable; it actually stimulated the appetite longer than if there had been only one dish.

It would be like giving up humans for taheeni, or the other way round. . . .

It was quite possible Gabriel was one of the "new men," one of those lucky people who had got beyond all the trivial, depressing needs. Just because Jane could not imagine, could not experience for herself, this higher state in which conversations, love affairs, strivings, etc.— in short, all the stuff of novels—were no longer seen as significant, that did not mean such a state did not exist.

She remembered her student Howard, his odd little smile, apologetic and forgiving at the same time, as he told the class, "It's simple, really. When we try to lay our bad trip of 'personality' on the angels . . . they just aren't having any."

And dear old Thomas Aquinas, simplified for the fifth-grade Catechism, which she had copied out, whole chapters, and knew by heart. There had been a chapter on the angels, quite specifically describing the angels. *It is an awesome thing to be loved or hated by an angel . . . nothing will arise to change that love or hate, there will be no belated discovery of goodness or evil, no error of judgment to be corrected, no rival to detract from the totality of love's embrace or hatred's spleen. The angel loves or hates instantaneously, with all the intensity of its unimpeded nature, irrevocably, with utter generosity or malice, in a roaring flame of consummation of its desire . . . .*

It was quite possibly—no, it was quite probable that she had selected Gabriel, fallen in love with Gabriel, precisely because of his refusal to deal in finite concerns. Not for him the petty Zimmerian chitchat about what artist stole what critic's wife, reluctant marriages, remorseful widowers, overdoses of laudanum, dinner parties, eccentric behavior—all the stuff of gossip: all those tempests in a teapot that yielded nothing, ultimately, nothing except hangovers of the spirit, that kept most of the inferior beings of the world swirling in the minor passing weathers of their "egos," while above all this, unnoticed by them, the Eternal Eye beamed its eternal varieties of Good Weather—if only they could see that there was "no such thing as bad weather, only different varieties of good"!

(Are you saying that if a person is getting murdered at a certain moment, he should *enjoy* that moment?)

Why not? Why not enjoy it? It's his last moment . . . why not enjoy it? What else better is there to do?

What if this were my last moment, thought Jane. The last "personal, superficial event in my finite life"? This moment when Gabriel and I are sitting here . . . I can feel his knee against mine, under the table . . . the room is warm and softly lit, the waiters are smiling and friendly, there is a poster of some crowded exotic city with golden mosques shining in the sun, a city totally different in appearance from the one we are now in. And all these varieties of food on the table. And a person sitting next to me whom I chose to love because of his beautiful restraints, his admirable distance from all that is small and petty and ephemeral in the world, and he doesn't even hate me; there is no malice in him, no "hatred's spleen." In fact, I *know,* in the part of me that accepts the over-all existence of good weathers, that he does love me. This man with his soft, pale angel's hair and his serious face, so smooth and grave, who said, "My space, since you have chosen to visit it, is distinctly transformed."

What more do you want, Jane? Like Aquinas's good angels, nothing will arise to change his love. He will go on loving you for as long as you let him, as long as you keep moving to the stately, eternal music, your eyes lost in his eyes, not darting around like the eyes of those insecure people at cocktail parties, darting to the sidelines to see who else is there, what they might be missing by not being every other place but where they are. Would you really want to change places with anyone on the sidelines? Would you really prefer to be Ann Weeks, waiting in the Midwest for "the man she owns" to return, if this were the last finite moment of life, if there were no more after this? Or would you rather be here, eating a good meal in a warm, attractive place with a man you love and who you know loves you? You aren't even going to get *murdered* in your last moment. Gabriel doesn't have to catch the nine o'clock bus back to Montclair, as he did the last time you were sitting here. You'll have him all night. So will it be so very difficult, spoiled child of the nervous ego, to enjoy this moment?

"I'm going to have the couscous again," he said. The waiter was standing over them, waiting. "How about you, Jane?"

"I want it, too," she said, smiling.

He put his big hand on top of hers, on top of the tablecloth. The waiter smiled indulgently.

"And two beers," said Gabriel.

"I have to ask you something," she said.

"Ask." The hand, still covering hers. She looked and saw herself in his eyes again, her hair hanging long and loose, shimmering a little on top, with a sort of rosy halo, from the way the light fell.

"What if someone said to you, 'Gabriel, there isn't any struggle essentially. There is no struggle, except what our self-created ego tells us is a struggle.' What would be your reaction?"

"My reaction? Well, I think I would want to hear more."

"So it interests you, it attracts you?"

"I think there is something to it, yes."

"Do you think it's true?"

"On a certain level, it's true."

"What level?"

"Well, you know. You really do know. We were talking about it much of the afternoon."

"Yes, I do know. I mean I know in an instinctive way, but I want to put it into words. *Where* is that statement true, in what realm, what kingdom? What is the name of the level? Do you think an ordinary person with a well-meaning intelligence could live by such a statement?"

"Oh, I think many people do. They may not all be able to put into words what they are doing, but they are doing it all the same."

Jane sighed. "Start over, go back."

"I can't name the level; no one can name it—you know that, too. It isn't like—well—naming a city like Pough-keepsie or Akron or Cleveland. I guess you could give it a symbolic name. Many people have done that. The Kingdom of Heaven, Beulah, the empyrean, Olympus, Nirvana, Valhalla, Falak al aflak . . ."

"What's that?"

"That is, most likely, our waiter's name for your level. 'The highest heaven' of the Mohammedan religion."

"Where do you learn all those things, Gabriel?"

"Ah," and he picked up her hand and pressed his lips against her fingers. "You've been taken in by a bunch of words. The words mean nothing in themselves. They are written, spoken symbols of something that can't be written or spoken. In art, in painting, this level is often depicted by a circle—something circular. . . . Do you know Klee's drawing, the one called "Limits of Understanding"? No? I'll send you a postcard of it. It's simple, really, yet it's one of the most spiritually eloquent statements I know of—a complex structure of ladders and lines, all sorts of crisscrossings of linear focus on the bottom half of the picture. And at the top half: a circle. A circle, partially obscured by a cloud. The level where your friend's words begin to make sense is after one gets past all the confusion of the ladders and partitions and finite focusings and up there with the circle."

"Well, how do you get up there?"

Gabriel burst out laughing. He took her hand in both of his and, with the top one, stroked it, all the time looking at her fondly while he laughed. She felt like an adorable child who had just said something so innocent it was clever.

Laughing a little herself, she persisted: "Have you ever been up there, Gabriel. Please tell me. Have you?"

"Mercifully, yes. Not permanently, of course, but—occasional small leaps."

"What happens? Can't you at least describe that? Or is that also something that can't be written or spoken? I'm beginning to feel excluded, or something, I really am."

"Oh, yes, it can be described. But my words wouldn't represent your experience, or the words of all the people who have and do describe it wouldn't represent mine. . . ."

"I haven't had this experience yet, Gabriel. . . ."

"Oh, yes, you have. Jane, all we are talking about is that 'level' or state of mind—or state of soul, if you like —where—providentially, chemically, for whatever reason, the ego stops rushing about from one desire to another and comes to rest—for a blessed minute or second —though time is not important here—in the wholeness and stillness of the self."

"What do you mean by 'self'? Isn't 'self' just another way of saying 'ego'? I'm speaking generally, not in any Freudian sense. Simple *ego* as meaning 'I.' "

"Well," Gabriel said, frowning with concentration. (He

let go of her hand and began tearing a small bit of pita into smaller and smaller pieces.) "As I see it, the self is what is left of us which can't be destroyed, what is there after all the impurities have been burned away—not that they ever are. In the self, a person knows everything. It is all there, inside the self. The whole universe, the whole Kingdom of Heaven—and Hell—is there, available, to the self. It *is* the self. The self is like a great warehouse, where we can go and take whatever we need—or like a library, a perfect, complete library, which contains all the volumes, all the thoughts. . . ."

"Are you saying we are all basically alike? Interchangeable? Indistinguishable from one another?"

"Oh, certainly not. Certainly not. Remember how we compared Moreau's 'Temptation of Saint Anthony' to Bosch's? That's it. Think of those two paintings. Put them inside your head now, and look at them. Totally different representations—but of the same devils. The devils that are always there in the self. The *representations* are the work of the ego. . . . By ego, I now mean that part of the person which experiences the external world through the senses, which records and transcribes. And Moreau's recording equipment was different from Bosch's. . . ."

"Do you mean," asked Jane, who was beginning to get a headache, "everyone has the same devils? A lot of people would disagree with you there."

"The devils are always there," said Gabriel. "I haven't counted them all. Different people see certain devils at different times. You and I are not harboring the same set of devils at this present time—at least I don't think we are." He laughed, rather nervously and abstractly, and Jane was tempted—then thought better of it—to ask him to describe his inner guests.

Their couscous came. The aroma of chicken and spices made her feel faint. Ah, to capitulate totally to food, to silence, to the everlasting little circle with its dozens of ethnic names; to climb out of the labyrinth of crisscrossings which made images of themselves on one's flesh, one's forehead (but not on Gabriel's!), to scuttle divinely up all ladders, slapping and swatting away the swarms of devils, whatever portion of the eternal repertoire of devils that happened to be after you at the moment, and to arrive at . . .

But "Can two selves have a permanent relationship?" she had to ask, before she'd even swallowed her first mouthful of the delicious chicken steeped in spiced juices. "Can two selves, do you think, after they have cleaned themselves up, got their 'egos' in hand, can they then have a permanent love relationship, say; a kind of love that—that exists in a permanent, eternal way?"

Gabriel waited until he had carefully chewed and swallowed his mouthful. "No," he said, simply and matter-of-factly, as though he had long ago thought out this question and come to terms with it. "Art can exist in eternity, but relationships can't. A relationship, by its very nature, is transient, because it is made between people, and people change."

"Oh," said Jane, crestfallen. "Do you think I could have another beer?"

"Of course!" Gabriel looked absolutely relieved to be asked at last for something tangible that he could deliver. The waiter was summoned and soon returned with an open bottle, frosted with cold, and a clean glass.

They walked back to their hotel without talking much. Once inside Jane's room, however, she burst into tears.

Gabriel was bewildered at this unexpected turn. "What is the matter?" he exclaimed. "Jane, Jane, tell me what it is." All concern, he put his arms around her; he helped her to the bed and made her lie back. The more he did for her, the harder she cried. Truly exhausted, she felt she had come to the end of something. She did not want to think or try anymore. She only wanted to be allowed to go on crying until she had cried herself away. Wasn't the body 90 percent water, or something near that? She would like to cry herself down to a dry husk, her dark little ego bobbing away on the stream of her tears. Whoever wanted it could have a present of what was left, that final dry husk, absolved of all earthly needs, a sort of trophy to remind him of the old, complicated, troublesome Jane.

"You must tell me," pleaded Gabriel, sitting beside her. He stroked her head, pushing the hair back from the temples. He took out his handkerchief and patted uselessly at the streaming eyes. "I've never seen you like this. Are you in pain?"

He had not even taken off his jacket. She looked at the pattern in the jacket, the same jacket he had been wearing the first time she saw him. And she noticed now an extra color. There was a tiny dot of red in the pattern, when she had thought it was only grays and browns. The way the jacket creased at the waist as he sat bowed over her made her cry more, for some reason.

"Well, just nod your head then. Are you sick?"

She shook her head.

"You're not sick? You're sure? You didn't eat something that was bad?"

"N-no . . . it was a lovely meal," she managed to blurt. Then she looked up at him, this kind, worried man in his rather ill-fitting tweed jacket, shapeless where it should have clung, a bit too short at the wrists, looking gravely down upon this person in distress, and she remembered the kind man in tweeds on the flight from Nashville, the man who didn't sit next to her because of scarlet jacket, and how he had supported, so tenderly, the old man who needed the oxygen mask; and she luxuriated, in her exhaustion, that she had someone now to support her tenderly. It was very comforting indeed.

"Has something upset you, then? Have I upset you? Something I did, or said?"

"What makes you think that?" But she was curious, waiting to hear it. He seldom spoke in this way.

"Well, it wouldn't be the first time. I mean, I often—I sometimes—I have been told I can be very upsetting. In fact," he said, his tone turning suddenly bitter, pessimistic, "it's been rather remarkable that you and I have managed to go on so long without my seeming to upset you."

She started to cry again. But now her crying was not a flushing out, from exhaustion and resignation, of all the impurities of the day, all the tiring, troublesome strainings of her ego; this new fit of weeping engorged her, soaked the old ego into her again, making her turgid and defensively alert. She was back on her guard, and for your guard you needed your ego. What so competent as the ego to assess the strategic losses and negotiate back lost points?

"I've ruined it," she wept gloomily. "I've ruined our perfect idyllic relationship. Now you think you are upsetting to me. I've become a drag on you; you feel sad and dragged down by the whole thing. I only darken your space now, clog it up, and make it bitter for you. I know, I've ruined everything, but—oh, hell, what does it matter? Relationships can't last, anyway. Only art can last."

"Oh, I see," he said. "I'm beginning to see."

"Well, you said it, you know," she reminded him accusingly.

"I thought I said something else. That was quite a heavy discussion we were having there, Jane. I had no idea either of us was taking it personally." He was patient, forbearing; she could imagine him talking to his upset wife in this slow, careful tone. "As I recall, you asked me if two people could have a relationship that existed permanently, sort of fixed for all time, in eternity, and I said no. I do think relationships, all relationships, change. The longer they continue, the more they change. The more they must change. Relationships go up and down a spectrum: from the barely tolerable to—the quite satisfactory. But I said nothing, to the best of my memory, about them not *lasting.* . . ."

"You said they were 'by their very nature' transient. That means impermanent, doesn't it?" But his last words started a new cold fear growing in her heart: she almost wished *some* relationships *were* transient, not securely anchored in their spectrum like abacus beads on their timeless little wires.

He sighed. "Perhaps it does mean that. It has been a long day of words, hasn't it? But I ought to take more responsibility for them around someone like you, I suppose."

"Ah Gabriel, you're tired. I've worn you out with words." She tried to joke, tried desperately to think what Kitty would say to a man at this point. Gabriel was "on the defensive" in the way people get when they are really on the offensive. "Why not take off your jacket?" she coaxed.

He took it off and laid it on the back of the chair as he had done this afternoon. But how different their mood had been the last time he had done this. Then he came and sat on the edge of the bed, deadly quiet, inturned. Would he say, "It's been a long day. Would you think me unforgivable if I went down to my own room and got a good night's sleep?"

"Here," she said. "Lie here." She made a place for him on the pillows. *Where on the "spectrum" was Ann now? Gone up a notch?*

He lay back without a word. He seemed willing to change places, to become the comforted. He lay, in his shirt and tie and trousers, rather stiffly, down the whole length of the bed. She loosened his tie, carefully watching his face for signs, and when she saw none she unknotted it completely, slipped it from his neck, and folded it carefully and laid it beside her. His face was blank, abstracted, with a slightly grayish color around the cheeks and jaw. She unbuttoned the top button of his shirt, a light blue shirt with a thin white stripe. She ran her hand apologetically across his forehead, brushing her fingertips up into his cool, silky-fine pale hair.

"I'm beat, I'll admit," he said, at last. He lay so still, his face so immovable as he spoke that it was as if a male mannequin, lying on its back on some department-store bed, had suddenly spoken.

"Yes, yes," she said, trying hard to brush away her own needs, her own protests, as she stroked, stroked, stroked him back into the Gabriel she knew. This impassive, rather defeated-looking male mannequin frightened her. His face reminded her of the faces of businessmen in airports, or on commuter trains, already set in gray masks, no light or movement behind the eyes, as if they had become merely the occupation they rode to, already machines. In an odd way, Jane felt she had killed Gabriel.

"It has been such a long day," she said. "You must have been up *so* early. Yes, it has been an exhausting day for you. . . ." She stroked with phrases and with fingers, giving in to the simplicity of repetitions: "A terribly long

day . . . exhausting . . . yes, we are both exhausted. . . ."
No more metaphysical dialogues and entomological discourses, just these simple, soothing repetitions . . . if only he would look at her again with quickening affection: his Jane, who lit his space.

"I don't, as a rule, bring up my childhood, my personal life, all that sort of thing . . ." He began slowly, staring up at nothing.

She waited. She did not even dare say, *"yes?"*

". . . but I just now thought of something. It might be of use to you, regarding—well, I'm not sure regarding what. Only that I sense I have hurt you in some way—by a sort of characteristic omission I seem to be capable of. I was lying here wondering why I am so maddening to people sometimes, and then I thought of—well, I thought of my mother, I remembered this—I started to say incident, but it's not an incident, really; it's more like an experience, a sort of continuing experience. Not even an experience so much as a style of knowing—a way of knowing another person. If you'd be interested . . ."

"Oh, God—of course. Please go on."

"Well, my mother was a music teacher, you see, although I don't think she liked it very much. Being a music teacher, I mean. She had lots of students, schoolchildren, from the first through the twelfth grade. They came to our house every afternoon, a different bunch of them every day of the week. I liked to answer the door. I got to know their faces, the little girls with their morning ribbons gone slightly limp, and the awkward boys with their braces, and the grubby stacks of schoolbooks and the music books—the shiny red covers for the beginners and the dull yellow covers for the advanced—but this is beside the point. In they'd come, slightly disheveled, even the neatest of them, for, after all, they'd been in school all day, all their best energies were used up; for most of them this music lesson was just one more thing they had to get through before they could go home and play that hour before supper, in the back yards and streets with their friends. Anyway, in they'd come, one after another, like an assembly line, from half past one in the afternoon till half past five. My mother would teach them patiently, often giving the same lesson to three students in a row. Often they didn't even get to the piano. She had a card table set up and the two of them, my mother and the student, would sit across from each other and they would do finger exercises, to strengthen the fingers. Then, afterwards, the lucky ones got to go to the piano, and they would play through their assignments. Very few of them played straight through anything. I got so that I would cringe even before the halt came or the mistake was made. I got to know exactly at what point a particular student at a particular time would stop—or make his mistake. I'd be upstairs in my room doing my homework, when suddenly, of their own accord, my shoulders would draw up and I would close my eyes and make a sour face and cringe. And I knew that my mother, at the exact moment downstairs, was also cringing, inwardly, mentally. She would never have shown it.

"At six o'clock, the last student left. My father arrived home every evening precisely at six-thirty. After the last student had gone, my mother always reserved for herself a sort of sacred quarter of an hour, a little time to herself before she began preparing our supper. Do you know what she did? She played music for herself. Beautiful music, with no cringing stops and no wrong notes. She gave herself back what had been denied her all afternoon: completion, beauty, perfection achieved through art. There was a favorite she had that she played more often than anything. It was my favorite, too. It said just about everything about a certain way of feeling. I don't know a thing about music; I never was gifted that way and my mother didn't force it, but I still hear snatches of that piece today. It was in four parts; the entire thing could be played well within my mother's quarter of an hour. It began—it began with a chord that deepened and got persistently stronger, but kept a certain stately beat —like a heartbeat, I thought as a boy. Then against that chord the melody began. The melody was like a single voice singing its pain, insisting, rather eloquently, on expressing its pain, up and down the keyboard, while, all the time, the 'heartbeat' kept on and on. At the end of that first part, there was a sort of statement. It was as if the composer said wisely, 'And that's how it is, but I have made it into this.' A sort of signature on that first movement. Then came a fugue; I can't remember it too well. And after the fugue, in another key this time, came a restatement of the first theme: that melody and that deepening chord, the singer and the heartbeat. But then things changed! The melody began playing with its own possibilities. Taking the same notes it had used to 'complain' in the first movement, it now used those notes to—well, to *frolic*. It actually hopped and skipped around the upper ranges of the keyboard. As if—as if somebody were retracing his sorrows the way a child would leap from stone to stone, over a brook. Playfully re-leaping your agonies. Then there was another fugue, which took the first fugue and reworked it, turned it around, once more reversing the *mood* of things, but within the limits of its given structure.

"I listened to my mother heal herself at the end of every day. I understood this as I listened from upstairs; I knew exactly what was happening with her, even though we never discussed it. She never discussed feelings, and I suppose—I suppose I must take after her. I believe it is possible to know everything about another person—I don't mean facts, statistics, things like that, but everything that really matters. It is possible, if we can be silent, if we can just listen to the 'given's of that person and hear how they play and replay themselves, experimenting a bit, improvising a bit here and there, but always within a given structure. I have understood this for years, though I don't speak of it much because—I find it is generally not understood. I remember—once my mother and father were having an argument, and I heard him shout: 'But can't you just *tell* me what's wrong? Can't you tell me how you *feel*?' I remember listening to this argument and wondering how it was that my mother's husband, the person supposedly closer to her than anyone else in the world, could not understand these things."

"Do you still find that you can know people like that," asked Jane. "In that same silent way that you knew your mother, knew her soul?"

"I still believe it is *possible,* but I'll admit I haven't had

292

very good luck with it since—that time I speak of. Perhaps I outgrew the capability. Perhaps, I've often thought, one has to be very young, pure in heart—or perhaps you have to love someone very much. Nevertheless, it makes me sad whenever I think of it. Not that I do think of it all that much; it's only because tonight we seem to be delving into quite a few profound corners." His left hand reached across his body and found her hand, automatically, as if by its own motivation.

She was weak with relief.

"Perhaps one could do it," he went on, "but it takes a certain amount of tacit understanding, a certain amount of silence, even. . . . People generally fall all over themselves to tell you how they're feeling about this and that"—he laughed quietly, rather bitterly—"though often they don't feel that way at all. They may feel just the opposite, but they want to feel the way they say they feel, or they think they *ought* to feel a certain way . . ." He trailed off, gone deep into himself again.

Jane had at least a dozen questions on her tongue, but was rebuked. She did not want to expose herself as one of those people who "fell all over themselves," talking and telling, speaking of feelings. She was afraid some of her questions would reek of "facts, statistics," things that didn't "really matter." She felt very low indeed, a very low member of the species. Like Gabriel's father, she, too, had been guilty of wanting to force into words what should be allowed to grow in silence.

She looked at him. Now he had closed his eyes, though his hand continued to stroke and press hers, testing the fingers, rubbing the backs of the fingers. Perhaps he was trying to read her through her fingers, if she would just shut up and be silent. What would her fingers tell him? Would they tell him something she didn't know herself? *I would like for him to know that I love him,* she willed her fingers to communicate to him. But perhaps she didn't love him at all. Perhaps she was only telling herself she loved him because she wanted to love someone like this, because it suited her purposes.

". . . *or perhaps you have to love someone very much*" before this tacit form of knowing could be practiced. If that was true, then he might be feeling nothing at all now, except a complicated structure of small bones, gristle, and skin. And—she faced this possibility—if she had really loved him, if she really loved him now, he would not be a mystery to her at all. She could lie here next to him, this long, weary man with his eyes closed, whose left hand stroked and tested her fingers as if of its own volition, and she would know everything important about him, everything that mattered, as the child Gabriel had known about his mother.

Never had she so completely doubted every form of reason; never had she doubted herself, all that she had based her life on, so completely. What was the use of "knowing" anything if you happened to think you loved someone like Gabriel Weeks? What was the use of reading or reasoning or constructing hypotheses on the known in order to find out what you didn't know?

Experimentally, she tried to hypothesize what it would be like, say, if she loved Gabriel as much as was necessary to practice this subtle, unspoken form of knowing? She would let her mind go blank of "word-knowledge" and try to feel him out, track him to his own very heartbeat, find, at last, the shape, as a blind person might hollow out for himself the interior of a certain cave and then translate this knowledge to his mind, the shape of Gabriel's "given structure."

What would she know about Gabriel if she loved him enough? If, just if. Imagine, postulate. But don't get "mental," don't get "wordy." Just be silent and hear his melody. What is it he "plays and replays, experimenting a bit, improvising a bit here and there, but always within a given structure"? Follow him, feel him out, track him to his lair. What is it about him that you keep telling yourself you don't understand—and it has nothing to do with Ann's "statistics" or his "statistics," either—that is really as obvious and as palpable in its shape as the man lying beside you now?

She struggled against the mode of thinking that had been her life: adding evidence to other evidence, comparing and measuring things against other things, remembering words said in a past moment to predict what might be said in a future moment, trying to apply one person's remedy to another person's situation—listening to all the voices, in short, except the "still, small one."

His left hand slowed in its stroking, slowed and slowed, until, at last, it simply held her hand loosely within itself. She closed her eyes, still trying to empty herself of a lifetime of preconceptions in order to approach what she could not figure out in words about this man. She felt his pulse, the slow rhythm of his blood, through the contact between their hands. She was in contact with his heartbeat, the chord of him now . . . and what of the melody? What of that? She must listen, lie there beside him, hand in hand, and let his melody work itself through her, playing out its possibilities through her as well. She had the chord now; that was easy . . . the chord, the stately beat that would move, slowing and quickening its tempo, as long as he lived. But the melody . . . why could she not hear that yet?

Because you are trying too hard to hear it. Let go, leave it. Let the melody come in of itself, whenever it chooses, against the chord.

So she lay very still, eyes closed, letting her hand rest against the beat of his pulse curled around her flesh. She emptied everything out, everything of her own will—not that it was easy, but there was nothing else to be done.

Did she imagine it, was she "willing" it, when, against the pulse, at first exactly synchronized with its beat, she felt another beat, like the beat of wings, as if one *were* the wings, beating, pushing against gravity, pushing their heaviness against this other heaviness in order that one might separate from the other, that the wings might push away and rise . . . rise where, to what? Never mind, *don't ask!* Stay close within the wings, beneath their shadow, and be carried . . . breathe with the wings, synchronize your breathing with the pumping, the tireless, enduring pumping of the wings. . . .

It became easier, lighter somehow. Everything was lighter; the surrounding air was the soft, light, downy, misty gray of the underside of the wings. . . .

The air and the wings were one.

The beat and the air and the wings were one. The distinctions fell away, and so did the heavinesses. If there were no distinctions, there were no heavinesses, no pushing and pulling away, no gravity, nothing to separate from or push toward. It was all there, in the air, in the wings, in the blood; everything beat inside you with its own blood rhythm. . . . No, it was not necessary to articulate something when there was no distance between it and you, no separation between it and you, only a tacit, silent understanding. You and it experienced each other, you're you and it's it, but *you have not articulated it yet,* the time has not come when you see it as "not-you," as something set over against you and not yourself. Stay beneath the wings as long as you can! Feel the movement and continuum of all things "not-yourself" and for as long as you do, all things are yours, because all things *are* you.

What things are mine? Show them to me. How big? How many? What color? Is it wet or green? How is it different from me? For how long is it mine? Will it always be green? Will that hurt me? Is it dangerous? Does it love me?

May I take a picture of it? I would like to photograph that. What do you feel? For God's sake, why can't you *tell* me what you *feel!*

There was a time when I knew everything; everything was seen purely, of itself, in its own element, *for the first time* . . . only those words, "for the first time," were not necessary . . . just as photographs were not necessary . . . just as words were not necessary.

In the beginning was the word . . .

NO! NO! NO!

Stop stuttering

I'm n-not.

How do you *feel?* What is wrong with you? For God's sake, can't you tell me how you *feel!*

"Rossetti was heartbroken . . . though penis rather better . . . stealing Ruskin's wife . . . after a dinner party at Swinburne's . . . overdose of laudanum . . . proved it by burying . . . rapid physical and mental decline . . . icy things . . . probably impotent, you know . . ."

NO! IF WE COULD JUST GET BACK TO . . . COULD WE
PLEASE GET BACK TO . . .

"I don't want to make you uncomfortable, but how can
you love both of us? Don't you get confused? Do you
need both of us? Tell me how we are different. That
would make it about 2030. If I live till 2030, will
you . . ."

HE LOVED THE WORLD'S TEXTURES . . . NOT ONLY THE
TEXTURES OF ROCK AND ICE . . . OF WINDS, CLOUDS,
LEAVES, SKY . . .

". . . gallantly consented to marry her . . . given his
word . . . wouldn't you agree that the over-specificity contributed to the early obsolescence . . . good color photography . . ."

Do you love me? How long will you love me? Will you
stay with me the rest of your life, till one of us dies?
What are you thinking? What are you feeling? What did
you have for supper? What did you mean by transient?
Why did you say that? You said it, you know! *Why won't
you tell me how you feel?*

PLEASE! . . . LISTEN! . . . HAVING SPENT YEARS OF MY
LIFE REDISCOVERING THE TIMELESS QUALITIES . . . HAV-
ING SPENT THE LAST TWENTY-FIVE YEARS OF MY LIFE
REDISCOVERING . . .

Rediscovering what? Jane opened her eyes and lost it.
Gabriel was asleep. His mouth was slightly open and, for
the first time, she heard him snore. She hadn't thought
him capable of it. She lay, not daring to move, even
though her neck was stiff from having lain for so long
propped at an odd angle on the pillow, and watched him,
fascinated and a little repelled. Shouldn't she shake him,
turn him over? There was something embarrassing and
rather comical, that rattling wet sound that came through
his nose and throat.

Had she slipped off herself? Fallen asleep briefly without realizing it? Was it possible she had actually *succeeded*
in experiencing Gabriel as he experienced himself? No.
She had been conscious the whole time. Even at the
height of her "flight," the old ego had been following
along beside, like a film director and crew in its little

dirigible, calling out the appropriate words, snapping film like mad.

In fact, she had probably ridden in the dirigible herself, she and her ego entertaining themselves with the appealing little fantasy that her "pure self" was getting acquainted with Gabriel's "pure self," that she was "entering Gabriel's pulse," "listening tacitly to his soul-song." She and her darling ego, inseparable twin—her precious, invaluable recording equipment had most likely trumped up the whole thing, building their "vision," their "mystical experience" out of data already stored and on hand for such an occasion. Just as they had stood together in the closet in Emily's room, embracing Edith's beige coat, sniffing the Fleurs de Rocaille and pretending to themselves they were "conversing with Edith's spirit."

She edged herself carefully from the bed and stood looking down at Gabriel, wondering whether she should try to undress him. He looked so incongruous lying there, the strange little gurgly rattle coming out of his mouth, like a life-size man-doll arranged stiffly on a bed, a little recording of a snore placed deep inside his neck to make him seem more lifelike. Like a robot, some machine created to look like a real man, on which Jane had been "practicing love" for almost two years, fulfilling her need to have a lover, the idea of it, from the same escapist motives that Gerda advocated taking a vibrator to bed, a plastic vibrator which could be switched on and off and washed and dried by yourself, instead of the real and hurtful man.

She bent down and unlaced his shoes. They were heavy, wing-tip lace-ups in an oxblood color that had been repaired with Cat's Paw rubber heels. For some reason, this touched her to the depths.

She set the shoes, side by side, beneath the chair on which he had hung his jacket.

How did you meet her, in 1948? Were you very much in love?

What about the trousers? She would surely wake him up if she tried to take off his trousers, but it suddenly occurred to her that this might be the only suit he'd brought with him and he would not want to spend the

298

day in the museum tomorrow walking around in a rumpled pair of trousers.

She sat down again on the bed, as gently as she could manage, and waited. His breathing changed. His mouth snapped shut and the snoring stopped. Then he continued to breathe, deeply and evenly. She wondered how he had looked as a boy, how his mother had seen him when she came into his room and looked at him sleeping. Did his mother know that her son felt he understood her better than her own husband? What would she have thought if someone had told her that?

Is your whole trouble nothing more than an Oedipus complex? Did you want to sleep with her, your mother?

Jane unbuckled his belt.

Do you ever dream about her, dream you are inside her? Do you hate your father? What was the name of that piece she played during her "sacred" quarter of an hour? Who wrote it?

"Gabriel, if you can lift up, I'll take your trousers off so they won't get creased."

He arched his back obediently, lifting up one leg at a time, as sleepy children allow themselves to be undressed. His eyes were closed and his deep breathing did not miss a beat. She folded the trousers carefully, laid them across the seat of the chair.

What I want to know is . . . everything. Do you still sleep in the same bed with her? Do you still make love? If so, how often? Are there parts of her body you like better than mine? Can she stay in the moment with you? Why don't you have children? What are the little habits, endearing and annoying, that have grown up between you? Can you see someone age if you live with them every day?

His shirt. Should she try to get that off, too? There he lay, so helpless, those long legs, so pink, not much hair. His undershorts were blue, like his shirt. ("He used a cyanometer to measure the intensity of the blue in the sky.") The big body was completely at her mercy, like a doll. To dress or undress, to throw cold water over, to strangle, to sit astride and try to seduce . . .

Where is it now on that spectrum, your relationship

with her: down towards the barely tolerable or creeping up again towards the quite satisfactory?

She covered him with a blanket, in his shirt and shorts and socks. She turned off the lamps, took *The Odd Women*, and went to the bathroom and climbed into the tub with a pillow. Let whoever could find sleep find it; and whoever could not could always read.

XIV

FATE of five "odd women"—1890:

Monica Madden. Marries old Widdowson for security, then fights his morbid possessiveness. Has disastrous flirtation with rogue. Dies giving birth to Widdowson's daughter.

COMPROMISE-REBELLION AGAINST ONE'S COMPROMISE-DEATH.

Virginia Madden. Becomes severe alcoholic. Voluntarily enters institution. Plans, when if released, to help sister Alice open school for young children.

ESCAPE THROUGH DRINK—PARTIAL REHABILITATION TO "A USEFUL MEMBER OF SOCIETY."

Alice Madden. Undertakes complete care of Monica's baby. Returns to Clevedon where she and her sisters were born and raised.

STARTING ALL OVER AGAIN IN A CHILD. RETRENCHMENT.

Mary Barfoot. Continues her work with young women. Menopausal age. Besides, she gave up wanting things for herself years ago.

FINDING "FULFILLMENT THROUGH OTHERS."

Rhoda Nunn. Ruins her love affair with Everard Barfoot through her "fatalistic idealism," as he calls it. He marries another woman, pretty, rich, wellborn, "feminine." Rhoda and Mary Barfoot start a feminist newspaper and expand premises. When asked how she fares, Rhoda replies gamely: "The world is moving!"

SUBLIMATIONS OF PERSONAL DESIRES AND FURIES INTO A "CAUSE."

Jane wrote these thoughts slowly into her notebook. She was sitting up in bed, in room 920, wearing the tawny silk robe which Edith had given her. Gabriel had yet to see this robe, the most elegant garment she owned. Perhaps he never would. Elegant robes did not seem to have a place in their relationship.

From time to time, she paused in her writing and took a sip from the coffee or grapefruit juice she had ordered from room service.

It was Tuesday morning. In a week, she would be standing in front of a new class, teaching this book. A week ago, Edith was still alive. She had been with Gabriel less than twenty-four hours. In less than twenty-four more, they would have packed their suitcases; they would have gone their separate ways for the fourteenth time during this affair.

She did not hate these statistics. Time passed, space altered, but she located where she was, what endured in her, by amassing these facts, setting them up like toy soldiers and marking off their formations as they radiated, in neat little lines, to and from the fortress: herself. She sent them out and called them home again. What was wrong with that?

She took a sip of juice. Sharp, like her mind. Slowly and thoughtfully, she underscored: "COMPROMISE-REBELLION AGAINST ONE'S OWN COMPROMISE-DEATH." Then she wrote quickly in the margin, beside Monica's fate: "Theme of literally dozens of 19th century novels—the 'Emma Bovary' syndrome. Literature's graveyard positively choked with women who chose—rather, let themselves be chosen by—this syndrome; also with their 'cousins,' who 'get in trouble' (commit adultery, have sex without marriage; *think* of committing adultery, or having sex without marriage) and thus, according to the literary convention of the time, must die."

She was running out of margin, writing smaller and

smaller. In tiny letters she scrawled: "Lily Bart, Anna Karenina, Hetty Sorrel . . . Cleva Dewar . . . etc., etc., etc."

Gabriel was downstairs in his room, checking his notes over before he set off for a day in the museum. He would call her at five-thirty and they would meet for dinner at six. Perhaps he was eating an apple, for his breakfast, down in his room. He thought things like room service were extravagances, he said, when she asked him should they have coffee sent up. So she waited till he was gone before she committed the extravagance. As he dressed, he told her cheerfully of how he had once made a mince pie last for three days on a train; he had not had to go to the dining car once. She laughed and questioned him about the size of the pie, while she wondered what it would be like being married to a man who thought room service and meals on trains to be extravagances.

She was not sorry to have the next eight hours to herself. Although he had wakened restored, all the gray gone from his face, blood circulating merrily through his earlobes again, apparently harboring no remorse for having told her a personal story about his childhood, she had not yet housecleaned her spirit from the emotional orgy of last night.

What was all that emotion? Where did it come from? What had it all been for? She felt like a cried-out child, who sits limply in a corner, hiccuping, from time to time, a dry sob; so exhausted from its performance that it has forgotten utterly what it wanted, what had brought on the sobs.

Why that incredible flow of tears? What had set it off? Some words about the transience of relationships. She remembered that, but now she could not connect the words to those tears of utterly abandoned hope. She remembered what Gabriel had said and she saw the Jane of last night, weeping herself into a frenzy. But now it was as if it had happened to someone else.

Over lunch, once, Sonia Marks had told Jane about "the black fights" she had with her husband, Max. They had named these fights "the black fights," after Churchill's "black dog" depressions, because, Sonia said, it was as if a large black beast came from somewhere and sat on Max and herself, monitoring and encouraging their fights, sending its own wild, savage energies into them so they could get on with a violence neither of them could ever later explain. And she told Jane that what was so awful during these fights—she and Max had agreed on it afterward—was the *love*. "If it weren't for our love, the beast couldn't get to first base," Sonia said. "It's as if— oh, this is impossible to explain—the beast feeds on our love, uses it as a raw material. He chomps it up inside himself and spews it out transformed into *weapons*. Max and I have been almost torn apart at times, and all because of this love that we have to carry between us like —some kind of saddle pack. I feel saddled with it, too, during a fight; I want more than anything to throw it off, get rid of it; it kills me, you see, when we aren't in harmony. And he feels the same. Once, during the worst of one of our black fights, I saw Max give this horrible little shudder, like—like a dog who is trying to shake the water off himself. And I knew exactly what was going on: he was trying to shake himself free of his love for me so he could live. . . ."

This story had intrigued Jane. It had bewildered her. Had she ever felt this terrible emotion for anyone in her life? Even for Gabriel? She had to admit no. Last night was the nearest she had come in her adult life to violent abandonment. And it had, after all, been not so violent and not—completely—abandonment. ("There are always some people who are passionate and some who are not," said Kitty.)

One Saturday afternoon, when Jane was about four, Kitty had dressed herself in a rayon-silk print Jane had never seen before and announced she was going out for the afternoon and evening. Kitty looked like a different woman in this dress, a stranger, and—Jane couldn't remember what had led up to it—suddenly she had attacked her mother, like an animal, using her teeth, and ripped the dress from her hip, tore a huge gash in it. Kitty's white slip lay exposed beneath the gash. That was all. She vaguely remembered Edith's saying, "Now look what you've done! Your mother's new dress! And with the war and all . . ." She could not remember if Kitty had stayed home, or changed dresses and gone out anyway.

Any more violence? No. If not, it was long-buried, long-forgotten. Or perhaps only imagined. Like the time Jane had detested a girl in third grade, at the convent school, because she told lies and had put a piece of chewed chewing gum in Jane's coat pocket. "I pushed Susan Ledbetter down on the ice today," Jane came home and told Edith. "You *what?*" "Pushed her down. She fell on the ice and something cracked, I heard it." Edith was already on the telephone to Mrs. Ledbetter, who answered, quite friendly. "Jane has just told me about—about Susan falling on the ice." "What?" said Mrs. Ledbetter. "Susan, come here. Did you fall on the ice today? Mrs. Barnstorff, it must be some other little girl. Susan would always tell me and she said she didn't fall. But thank you for calling!"

I think I would like to be a passionate person, Jane thought in room 920, wearing her elegant robe. *Is it too late to change?* And, oddly, she reclaimed these two little memories; she held on to them as something special, just as she held on to what had happened between herself and Gabriel yesterday afternoon. *That happened:* nothing can take it away, however "transient" our relationship may prove to be.

And yet—oh, God, how she looked back with nostalgia, with admiring nostalgia, on that single-minded winter, that frozen, pure winter when she lived all day in her mind, writing her thesis in the library, her image in the mirror thin and burned clean, like a saint. She may not have been passionate during those frozen weeks, but she had been contented.

But who had pronounced the "thaw"? She had pronounced the words herself, melting herself back into the messy world. "I hope this won't melt my beautiful frozen mind," she had said, whereupon, like magic, the spring *drip, drip* began. Oh, there was no doubt about it: words contained magic, all right.

And so she created Gabriel.

She went to the shelf of college catalogues and looked

him up in a book, and traced the initial "G." to the art library, and took his name and his words home, where, over a period of weeks, she carefully dreamed him: first through his wife Ann she dreamed him, a multiplicity of Anns, and then Ann gave her permission to sleep with him, and so Jane had fashioned in another dream a blanket of spring flowers for the two of them.

And the spring flowers arrived in a box, a real box on a real morning. She still had these flowers, dried and pressed, in her biggest dictionary.

Yes, if you believed in words, if you lived by words, *you had better be careful which words you say and how you say them. You had better be careful what you look up, which words, which names.*

But she wanted to go beyond words, too. She would like to live those moments when words were not necessary. ("I saw Max give this horrible little shudder . . . I knew exactly what was going on. . . .") ("I listened to my mother heal herself . . . I knew exactly what was happening with her, even though we never discussed it.")

Perhaps one got beyond words only through love. Having finished all his volumes of ponderous *Summa,* in which God, the Trinity, Creation, the Angels, Man, and Man's World were described in wordy detail, Aquinas folded his hands over his huge belly and contemplated the love of God. "There are some things that cannot be uttered," he said, whereupon he rose several inches from the ground and spent the remainder of his life prayerfully suspended, in utter silence.

". . . perhaps you have to love someone very much," Gabriel had said.

Or Gerda, screaming: "You don't know what it's like to be one other person!"

Were they all trying to tell her something?

Perhaps I created Gabriel to teach myself how to love. Even in that lovely frozen library, I looked into my saint's eyes and saw they would burn themselves hollow if I didn't yearn again.

So now I have yearned quite adequately for two years. What comes next? I can't seem to see the way forward, and I don't want to get "frozen" again. It's too late to refreeze. Yesterday and last night made refreezing impossible. I don't want to regress. I don't even want to retrench.

She took another sip of juice and drew a line through the word "RETRENCHMENT." Then, more quickly, positively, through "DEATH, COMPROMISE" and, God, yes, "ESCAPE THROUGH DRINK."

"STARTING ALL OVER AGAIN IN A CHILD." Someone once told her—or had she read it?—that only when a woman becomes a mother or a man a father can they truly stop seeing themselves as the child. Was she, then, doomed always to be her own child, the "only lonely"? Kitty obviously thought so. ("I really cannot imagine you as a mother. You're somehow not suited psychologically.") Why not? Perhaps nobody was "suited psychologically" before the fact. Did she want children? In her twenties, especially when she'd been engaged to James, she had taken it for granted she would have them, had defended their unborn nationalities in that famous fight with Nancy Bruton. And when she and the ex-seminarian were in love, they had discussed their future children eagerly; it was the time, Jane now recalled, when he had been happiest about the necessity of what you had to do to get them; yes, after she'd had a few children, after he'd seen the blessed results, perhaps his problem would have cleared up altogether. But what would that have made her? A baby factory. And yet, in her sexual fantasies before Gabriel, it was just that, being made into a baby factory, that had the power to excite her most. Now, as her early thirties crested inevitably toward their middle, she sometimes had the fear that she would not be allowed the choice. And yet wasn't it just that, not being allowed the choice, that disturbed her most? Or was it? She found it easy to draw a line through "STARTING ALL OVER AGAIN IN A," but, somehow, taking her ball-point and cutting a thin line across "CHILD" seemed too much like cutting the—whatever they had to cut or puncture when they performed an abortion. She was moving inexorably toward the last of her childbearing years; she was in love with a man who had shown no signs of leaving his wife and marrying her. He and his present wife had no chil-

307

dren, which could be because he was unable to have them. But though she could with impunity relinquish the satisfaction of razing the mess she had made of herself to the ground and building a nice clean one in its place in order to justify her own disappointed existence (starting all over again in a small, fresh creature), she didn't think she had the right to close all doors of her mind to the possibility of such a creature someday knocking. Kitty had conceived Ronnie, after all, because she had believed herself to be "past all that." Who knew, who could know about the future? Some adorable little creature—perhaps a little like the smiling, naked Ronnie, with his arms full of rubber animals and boats, wanting to share everyone's bath—might be waiting even now, in the place where all inconceivables waited patiently to be dreamed. And who knew: though she might never conceive him, she might dream him, sitting in front of her old-maid fire, as Charles Lamb had sat in front of his, telling wonderful stories to her unborn child.

"FULFILLMENT THROUGH OTHERS"? Was the capable of such unselfishness? She had a brief—a very brief—vision of visiting Portia Prentiss's blind mother and postman father, sitting with them in their home and discussing Portia's future. She saw herself coaching a dozen or so Portias in Remedial Rhetoric. She crossed off "FULFILLMENT THROUGH OTHERS."

That left "The world is moving!" How are you, Jane? "Oh, the world is moving!" She thought of Gerda burning her black candle, signing the death warrant for romantic love, now signing income-tax forms for the employees of *Feme Sole.* She crossed off "SUBLIMATION OF PERSONAL DESIRES AND FURIES INTO A 'CAUSE.'"

On the bedside table, Tempus Fugit said 10 A.M. Gabriel would be at the museum now.

Seven and a half more hours till he called. *Seven and a half more hours to get through,* she caught herself thinking.

No, absolutely not. That was worse than regression, worse than anything on the list—except death, perhaps. It *was* death: nullifying yourself while a man lived his life away from you; pacing yourself, like a cat with the poor dried food of yourself, waiting till your "owner" came back.

She got out of bed at once, put away the notebook, and began to dress. She would go to a museum herself. She would go walking, browsing, something. She must, would, go out and have a day of her own.

Carelessly, she dragged down her plaid wool skirt and a jersey blouse she'd had all through graduate school, and began to dress. She put on her gray stockings and the comfortable gray suède shoes and stood in front of the full-length mirror on the back of the bathroom door. She didn't even have a full-length mirror at home. The only thing she could see of herself in her apartment was her head and shoulders. Only a month ago, she had gone to a dinner party and her hostess, helping her out of her coat, had the tactfulness to exclaim, "What a lovely skirt! Only, I believe it's not zipped in the back. May I do it for you?"

This morning, she zipped everything up quite firmly, checked it against the mirror image. There, everything buttoned and zipped. A perfectly self-respecting member of society. The plaid skirt dipped a little in the back. Vincent de Lucca's shadow hulked in self-righteous masculinity just to one side of the mirror. "Aw, you can do better than that," he said. "Why not fix yourself up a little? Make yourself attractive to men. That skirt for a start. Hangs way down where it ain't supposed to. Down below your coat. You know it does—you've noticed it yourself. Makes you look like an old lady schoolteacher. I don't care *how* smart—"

On an impulse, Jane decided how she would spend her morning—and afternoon, if necessary. She would go shopping and buy herself some attractive clothes. She would use Ray's "abortion money" to refurbish her image. The symbolism seemed very right, somehow. Redemptive. Escaping Ray via her brains, she would now redeem her physical appearance through the money he had forced on her.

She became rather excited at her project. It was a change, it was a purpose. And who was it said: "Wear your part, you'll become it." Well, she'd go down to some elegant store on Fifth Avenue and buy herself the next Jane. She had not bought clothes—not seriously, making an art of it, as Edith did, since . . . why in almost ten years! It was Edith who took clothes seriously, who saw to it that Jane was well-dressed. "We must outfit you for your trip to Europe," she said, and seven months later, when Jane came home from England, having let a fiancé slip through her fingers, "We must get you the right clothes for graduate school. You'll need things a little more dignified, sophisticated. . . . We'll call Mr. Blum."

Edith always called Mr. Blum to announce her impending visit to his store. She called him when he was in his eighties, a prosperous retired merchant who was no longer "on call," who came into his store and sat for a few hours every day in his office, smoking his cigar and reminding his sons that he was still a force to be reckoned with in the empire he had created: Blum's for Quality Fabrics & Distinctive Apparel.

"Do you really think we need to?" asked Jane. It always embarrassed her, these peremptory announcements to Mr. Blum that they were going to patronize his store. Plenty of other people patronized it without calling him first.

"I've always called him. He knows what we like."

And, while Jane cringed, or went into the next room, Edith made her call to Mr. Blum.

"If we were going to buy out the store," Jane would say, "that would be one thing. If we were going to spend thousands and thousands of dollars. But we never buy more than a few things, Edith."

"The right things," replied Edith. "And Mr. Blum understands the difference between quality and quantity, Jane. I have bought all my important clothes from Mr. Blum since—well, never mind when. A long, long time. I bought my first grown-up clothes there. The first thing I got from Blum's was a beautiful mohair walking suit. Oh, I wish you could have seen it, that mohair suit. A rich camel color, fully lined, and I had a hat with a peacock feather, a matching hat, and I wore the little topaz brooch the Dad gave me for my sixteenth birthday."

Edith had an astonishing memory when it came to her

clothes. She used her wardrobe to fix past events the way some people use Presidents in office, or baseball scores. "That was the year I had that blue linen, the one that didn't sit well. I never went to that dressmaker again." Or, "Let's see, her children must be in their teens now, because I remember she was pregnant for the last time that Easter when it turned cold and I wore my plum wool with the velvet cuffs and collar, which was at least thirteen years ago. . . ."

Sometimes, weather permitting, Mr. Blum waited outside the store for them. Their taxi pulled up to the curb and they'd see him, tasting his cigar, belly forward, legs wide apart, wearing checkered trousers and a brilliantly colored silk waistcoat with gold watch chain. He was a very dignified old man, rather regal as he stood there, so immobile in his fatness, a critical old patriarch with heavy-hooded eyes, which swept lazily back and forth, like the eyes of a wise old frog surveying the teeming pond from his lily leaf; back and forth, slowly, Blum's eyes would go, up and down the people who went in and out of his store, taking in their shoes, their hemlines, their trouser and jacket cuffs, noting the cut and the fabric of their clothes, whether they had been bought from Blum's.

"How are you, Mr. Blum," Edith would say graciously as Blum handed her out of the cab (as he perhaps long ago handed ladies out of carriages). "We were so lucky to have caught you in your office. My granddaughter is taking a little graduation trip to Europe and she needs a few things. Mr. Blum, do you remember this cape? I bought it from you that winter when capes were so big. Hasn't it held up well? I took a chance and had it dry-cleaned and it came out looking like new. Capes aren't in style at the moment, but I adore this cape. There is something eternal about a cape, I don't care what anyone says."

"Botany," said Blum. "It can't be surpassed. You're looking extremely well, Mrs. Barnstorff. A cape never goes out of style. Your daughter was in yesterday. With her little boy. Mrs. Meecham helped them."

"Oh, dear. I hope she bought him the little *tweed* car coat."

"I'm afraid the corduroy," said Blum.

"It won't last the winter!" cried Edith.

"Oh, yes, it will," replied Blum, a touch of admonishment in his voice, defending his quality fabrics.

In the old days, when Blum still made the buying trips to New York, he would "look out for things" for Edith. "That man knows my taste inside out," Edith would say. Only once had he erred. Once, after Edith was widowed, in her fifties, still unable to forgive herself for having been trying on a hat when Hans died, convinced that, were it not for having to raise little Jane, her life might as well end, Mr. Blum had actually telephoned. He had just come back from New York, he said; he had brought back a sea-green-and-silver-brocade hostess gown, cut Empire style. The head buyer at Saks had wanted the gown for a favorite client of his own, a real princess, exiled from somewhere in the Balkans and living in New York City. But Blum had said he knew a lady at home, a Southern lady, for whom this gown was made. Blum assured Edith he would have no trouble selling the gown; every woman in town would think, like Cinderella's sisters, it was made for her. But he insisted that Edith had to see it first. She had to come downtown and try it on first. So Edith had gone and tried it on, a widowed princess in her fifties, in Blum's store. The salesladies gathered to watch. "Mr. Blum came down from his office, with his cigar, and when he saw me he started nodding. I could swear there were actually tears in his eyes. I told them I couldn't possibly buy it. I must admit it did fit me awfully well, but where would I wear such a gown? Oh, it was perfectly beautiful, that sea green and silver; it did suit my coloring, it was like something out of a fairy tale. But me, a widow, with nowhere to go anymore—of course I couldn't possibly and I told Blum so. Being careful not to hurt his feelings. He always has thought I wore clothes well, and I think I kind of represent something to him. I am the embodiment of something for Mr. Blum. But really that was silly of him. He sold it, of course, so I didn't put him out any. But he wouldn't be satisfied till I had seen it first." Edith went about the house feeling womanly again, looking at herself whenever she passed a mirror. For the first time since Hans had died, Edith allowed herself to admire her reflection in mirrors.

When Edith took Jane to buy clothes, Blum escorted them to a chosen saleslady and said, simply: "Mrs. Barnstorff and her granddaughter would like to see some things." Or, "Miss Jane is going for a graduation trip to Europe." "Oh, Europe!" said the saleslady, "Isn't that wonderful. You'll need things that don't crush, won't you, dear?" "Thank you so much, Mr. Blum," said Edith. Mr. Blum bowed and wandered gently off into the mist of his own cigar smoke.

But between them, Blum and Edith, they somehow managed to transform the ordinary clothes on the racks into just the right things for Jane. She felt sure that if she had gone into Blum's store alone there would have been nothing. But because this fat, patriarchal old wizard pronounced a few magic words, linking Jane to the saleslady, sanctifying these words with a puff of aromatic smoke, and because Edith stood there, august in posture, impeccable in her own dress, *insisting* that things be of the very best taste, certain dresses on the rack—quite ordinary dresess, mass-produced in the garment district of New York—felt inspired. They struggled within their seams to fulfill the expectations of these two. Certain of them quivered, Jane imagined, like flowers in a garden, wanting to be picked, and Edith's quick, pale fingers, flicking fastidiously through the rack, had plucked them to their best destiny.

"This is a nice little print. . . . What is this material, Mrs. Monteith? I think it's challis. Wait . . . yes, it certainly is. Challis would be perfect for England, Jane, where it's never really hot or really cold, so I'm told."

And the challis print would be singled out, chosen, separated from its less fortunate sisters, and carried by its hanger, with certain other contenders, to the dressing room, on the crook of Edith's finger.

"It's all right if you step into it," Edith would whisper. "She's not looking and you won't mess up your hair. . . . No, no, I'm afraid not. The waist is too short. I hate a short-waisted dress. You have a lovely long waist."

The poor challis print, to have come so far and missed its chance.

Once, in her early twenties—before the European trip, in fact—Jane was standing in her bra and panties in a dressing room at Blum's, when she suddenly noticed certain little ripples in the skin of her upper thighs. She stood fascinated and horrified, studying these ugly little waffle marks, the first signs on her body of age, of imperfection. "What are you doing?" asked Edith, who was seated in the dressing room and had noticed how Jane's mood so abruptly changed. "These—these awful ripples . . . what are they?" Jane saw no use in ever buying another thing. Why bother to clothe age and ugliness in new garments?

"They are nothing," said Edith. "They are these new lights, these harsh lights. The influence of Blum's sons. They'll ruin this store as soon as he's gone, you wait. These lights are too harsh; Blum's sons don't understand a thing about running a store like this. Blum uses a rose-tinted light, not these unnatural phosphorescent things. Try on that dress—that one, I think it may be what we're looking for. When you get home, I promise you, you'll look in the mirror and your legs will be perfectly beautiful, as they always are. Also, a harsh, unnatural light shining above is the worst light possible. It makes everything look like it's hanging."

Jane wore the dress they bought that day for many years. It was a beige color with an aquamarine figure in it, very quaint, like some old wallpaper pattern. The waist was long and the soft fabric clung about her hips. She felt feminine in the dress. She felt she could forget herself in it, because it had secured Edith's imprimatur. ("Now that suits you. The blue goes with your eyes, and the cut brings out your slim figure.") Jane was wearing that dress when James, her English boyfriend, took his mother's advice and proposed.

And, sure enough, when she and Edith got back to Edith's apartment, Jane had pulled up her skirt and looked hard at her legs in the triple mirror, turning this way and that, and though she could see where the ripples had been, in Blum's, they did not seem so bad anymore.

Jane went to Saks.

Somehow she had not expected it to be so big. It was going to be no easy thing finding what you needed, she realized, studying the directory posted beside the elevators. Saks was going to be more difficult than Blum's.

She noticed the other shoppers as she waited with them for the next "up" elevator. They were, the majority of them, a certain kind of woman: the kind of woman who has leisure to shop at ten o'clock on a Tuesday morning. There were no office girls, no working women, waiting for these elevators. Their hour would come at noon. There would be a feeling of frenzy about them as they struggled to clothe themselves and feed themselves, cramming everything into a lunch hour.

There was no frenzy about most of these women, in their fur coats and pants suits whose cuffs hit exactly the right spot on their leather boots. They sported chic leather purses, which hung by gold chains from their shoulders; many carried canvas shopping bags as well, or Saks bags from former shopping trips. They would be the ones returning and exchanging things.

Which floor? There were dresses, suits, casual clothes, separates collections, on so many floors, and no way of telling which might have something that would suit her. Jane was sure every other woman but her waiting for this elevator knew what floor she was going to. She picked out a woman whose honey hair swung loose to her shoulders, dressed in a black wool pants suit, with gold loops through her ears, gold bracelets, and a wide flat wedding band. A nice spicy perfume emanated from her. She had a huge black shoulder bag of soft leather, and carried, in addition, a Louis Vuitton carryall and an old Saks bag. She looked as though there were no doubt in her mind which floor she wanted.

So when they all pushed into the softly lit elevator (everything seemed the color of soft brown in this store), Jane decided to get off at this woman's floor.

The honey-haired woman got off at the seventh floor and walked straight toward the far end, through a series of alcoves, each featuring its own special clothes. Jane felt a moment's uplift. It looked like a pretty good floor. She let her guide disappear, with a smart little military *whisk,* around a corner, and lingered at a promising selection of suède and leather skirts, all made by one "name." She touched the materials skeptically, as she had watched Edith do. Then, because she knew that the saleswoman was watching, Jane inspected the skirts to see that they were fully lined. They were. Jane lightly fingered the tag. The skirt was $75. Well, she could afford it. She could afford four of them, with Ray's money (which she still planned to return to him as soon as she could get to her own bank).

But she didn't need any more skirts. Wasn't that the whole point? For the past several years, she had been dashing into campus shops and quickly trying on and buying tweed and plaid skirts, another sweater or blouse; it had seemed easy. They fit and she bought them and wore them. They looked all right. They looked, in fact, quite good as she abstractly ran her finger over a salt-and-pepper tweed while she sat at her desk listening to a student explain why his term paper might be a little late; as she admired the elegant silky lining of a jacket she was hurrying into, to rush across to the Student Union and get a good cup of coffee, not out of the English Department machine, before her next class. Her clothes, bought randomly and casually as they were, were always *good*. Edith had taught her that.

But today she was supposed to be outfitting herself. Refurbishing her image. *Making herself more attractive.* Today she must attend to the whole picture, create herself in full, in front of a mirror. Stop looking at her head and shoulders only, or admiring a piece of material: parts of the whole.

She went on, toward the next alcove, which featured a large number of very similar dresses, shirt dresses made of some light jersey-type fabric, in spring colors. (It was late January; stores were therefore encouraging these women, who had long ago bought their January clothes, to look toward April.) There were quite a few women inspecting this array of pastel-colored dresses. Ah, that must be a good sign. She heard a saleslady say, "Limited shipment . . . unpacked late yesterday afternoon." Jane saw how these words stimulated the women. Their fingers darted rapidly up and down the dresses, squeaking the hangers against the metal rail; like greedy birds, the pale hands reached in, snatched, plucked out one, two, three dresses. You had to be quick to get the one you wanted, in your size; otherwise it might be gone! Limited shipment. The urgency of these women communicated itself to Jane. She, too, began pushing quickly through the dresses. . . . This one? This? So many colors and designs, so many choices. The right dress might be there: the right design for you, the right color, the right fit. Only, you must hurry and grab it before somebody else did. She felt as if, any minute, an ominous buzzer would ring and a voice would call, "Ladies, your time is up!" And who would want to be the one "caught out," the oddball, the woman who had failed to find her dress? Jane selected several in her size, and was looking about for the dressing rooms when she heard a calm, older, slightly sarcastic voice nearby say, "Come on, Melanie and Susan, let's go down to three and look at the Anne Kleins before you get all excited about these."

She turned and saw an elegant woman, in her fifties or early sixties, accompanying two debbish young women. At once, the young women put back the dresses they had taken down to try, and off the trio went, back to the elevator, to go down to three and look at the Anne Kleins. The older woman was, clearly, a veteran of successful shopping. Something about the way she carried herself reminded Jane of Edith. Jane considered following the women down to three, then decided to stick it out on seven with the honey-haired woman of the earrings and the Louis Vuitton carryall. She looked at the three dresses she had plucked from the rack. They seemed cheaply made. She saw dozens and dozens of them, in all sizes, up and down the length of the little alcove. Thousands of them were probably manufactured within walking distance of this store. Limited shipment! She turned up the hem of one as she might have curled up her lip. Unlined.

Jane put the dresses back and moved on to the next alcove, which was coats. She paused briefly, not because she needed a coat but because she was beginning to feel strangely exhausted. She caught sight of a woman in a

317

brown imitation-suède coat whose skirt dipped at least two inches in the back. The woman was rather slump-shouldered and had a strained, uncertain expression on her face. Jane would never follow such a woman in Saks to see where she would get off. The woman clearly did not belong in Saks at ten on a weekday morning. The woman was, of course, herself.

Suddenly, she wanted to be invisible, simply to slink unobserved through the store, without the burden of being looked at, until she could learn how women went about outfitting themselves. How could she have reached her thirties without learning how to shop? It seemed incredible. It suddenly seemed *important*. There she'd been, stoop-shouldered and tense, reading her eyes out under the lights of libraries, while all these women had been mastering the skills of making themselves poised and competently beautiful. They knew, they had understood early, that it was the work of a lifetime to achieve the approved face of the American Woman, the layers and layers of healthy sheen, the groomed, poised total of Fashion.

She would not look in any more mirrors for a while; she would simply move, unobtrusively, humbly, about this store, observing how other women did it. Already the prospect of researching something made her feel better. She went in search of her guide with the honey hair and black pants suit, and found her, in a deep alcove of separates, conversing earnestly with a young and pretty salesgirl. ". . . I want a skirt and a top . . . maybe a top in several parts. . . . I saw that ad—you know the one with all the little sweaters, the lightweight sweaters, one on top of the other—and then I saw a pair of jade-and-turquoise earrings down on first. They would go beautifully with this lime here. . . ." She caressed a scoop-necked Angora evening sweater she had removed from her old Saks bag. ". . . sort of coordinate the whole thing, if you see what I'm getting at." Of course the salesgirl saw! Her young face flushed and glowed as she looked admiringly at this customer. They spoke the same language. They read the ads and understood the importance of coordinating all the parts. How she must admire this customer who knew what she wanted, who was obviously a mistress of coordination, who could shop on two floors at the same time, holding a pair of jade-and-turquoise earrings in her mind's eye against a lime Angora evening sweater! Jane imagined how this salesgirl might take an inspired lesson from the honey-haired young matron in black; how, on her own lunch hour, she would hurry down to one and hope there was another pair of those earrings left, which she could buy at an employee's discount, or put aside on layaway, to go with the lime Angora she would also buy in admiring imitation of her customer. Women observed one another, learned from one another. (". . . let's go down to three and look at the Anne Kleins before you get all excited about these.")

Oh, Edith!

But Edith was no longer here to say an emphatic no to a short-waisted dress, to explain away an unprepossessing appearance as a trick of light. Edith was dead, and so was Mr. Blum. No kindly old wizard would puff his way beside Jane through the intricacies of Saks, sanctifying her relationship with salesladies, waving his cigar-wand and turning ordinary clothes into Jane's own clothes, clothes in which she might live her life and forget about how she looked, clothes in which she would get proposed to.

She entered a large room to the right and wandered slowly about, shaking her head a little at the dozens and dozens of racks on which hundreds and hundreds of clothes were crammed waiting for the right woman to come along and transform them, slip her proud flesh into their emptiness so they could fulfill themselves. All these poor, look-alike clothes waiting for a destiny.

Jane felt like crying.

"Is there something I can help you with, dear?"

An ancient little old lady had come up to Jane. She was looking up at Jane, her face about the level of Jane's shoulder. She was an Englishwoman; Jane recognized the accent at once. She wore bifocals, chained to her with a long gold chain that fastened round her neck, and her shoulders, in their dark, plain dress, were frail and bent. "Anything I might find for you, dear?"

"There's simply too much," said Jane. "I get confused —all these clothes . . ." She waved her hand helplessly toward the multitude of racks.

"Were you looking for anything in particular?" asked the little woman. "Was it a dress you wanted, or a two-piece suit—a pants suit, perhaps?" She seemed timeless she was so old, very unhurried and patient. Unstylish to the point of wisdom. Yet she was saying, "Was there anything in particular you were needing today?"

"I need everything," said Jane. "But I know one has to start with particulars. A dress, perhaps . . ."

"We have lots of nice dresses," the English saleslady said helpfully. "I could show you some. What size are you, dear?"

"Or a pants suit," said Jane. "Yes, perhaps a pants suit. I've never had one, but I've seen such attractive ones. I saw a lovely black one—would you perhaps have a black pants suit?"

"Black, no. We have lots of other nice colors. It's the spring collections now, you see, dear. We got in a nice mauve pants suit. Would you like for me to show it to you?"

"Mauve . . ." repeated Jane. Exactly what color was mauve? Was it more of a pink or a blue? She felt she ought not to ask. "No, I don't think mauve suits my coloring."

Miraculously, the little saleslady did not protest. "Doesn't it, dear?"

"I really need dresses," said Jane. She will soon think I am crazy, and if not crazy, then certainly a waste of time. "I don't want to waste your time. Perhaps I should just look around; then if I see something I'll call you. I don't know where to start."

"That's all right, dear. What are you, size ten?"

"Ten, nine, twelve. I don't know. Probably ten."

"Let's step over here and look at the tens."

Jane followed docilely alongside this tiny, unperturbed woman. She stood gratefully by while the woman's old fingers moved knowledgeably through her stock. "This is rather pretty . . . do you like this? No? Neck too high. I see. This is a lovely color. Lavender is popular with the girls this year. Going to be very big this year. This is a nice little dress. You could wear it to town—for lunch in town, that sort of thing."

Jane let her pick out several dresses, this patient soul who had all the time in the world. She did not look like a typical saleslady in Saks; she looked as if she belonged in some other milieu, perhaps sitting quietly in an English rectory, in some obscure Midlands village, patiently mending her brother the clergyman's surplices, the tireless English rain falling softly outside.

But I do not look like a typical shopper in Saks, either. We are strangely paired, this old bird and I.

The old lady led Jane down a long row of curtained dressing rooms, hung up the dresses in one, and said she would be nearby. "The thing to do, dear, is try one of them—any one—for size. Then, if you need another size, I can be finding it for you."

"Thank you," said Jane. "You are being very helpful."

"Not at all, dear." She departed, frail and patient, leaving Jane and the dresses behind the curtain.

Jane put on the first dress, the one she liked the most. ("It's all right if you step into it. She's not looking and you won't mess up your hair.")

She wriggled in, pulling it up round her hips. So far, so good. Maybe it was going to be easy, after all. It was a good dress. She saw herself wearing it to dinner this evening with Gabriel. They would have a "cool" evening tonight, she had decided. No metaphysical and emotional orgies. They would sit across from each other, soft candlelight between them, and the distance between would be restful, healing, after last night. Tonight she wanted to observe Gabriel in his own space, get to know him without blurring her knowledge with what she needed from him. Just let him be . . . and learn what that being was.

The arms of the dress were too tight. Oh, well.

She stepped quickly out of it, hoping she wouldn't be caught tramping on it by the nice old lady. She rehung it carefully on its hanger. No use making extra work for this obliging soul.

"How was it, dear? Any luck?" The kind face, peering through the curtain.

"Oh," said Jane. "I liked it, but the arms were too small. It fit everywhere but the arms."

"Let me get a twelve for you."

Alone again, Jane tried on the next dress. The arms were fine in this one, but the print, small and floral and "busy," made Jane look like the contemporary of her Cousin Frances.

The twelve of her first choice was brought to her by the saleslady. The arms fit, but the rest swallowed her. I wonder if my arms have gotten fatter or something, she thought, and longed in vain to be told of course not, it was this store, these lights; when she got home, everything would be perfect again in her own private mirror.

She grew depressed as she tried on dress after dress, her little lady making tireless journeys up and down the long row of dressing rooms, bearing away the mounting collection of "no"s, always coming back with another size, something not quite like what Jane had wanted but something that "might do."

She found herself becoming so relieved when something fit that she forgot to ask whether she liked it or not. Whether she wanted it. This might do, she found herself thinking about a dress she did not particularly like, simply because it had the courtesy not to make her conscious of some part of her body.

This might do.

This isn't all that bad.

This would do as well as anything I've seen.

An angry, hoarse woman in the dressing room across from her called: "Hey, where's my lady? Hey, look, you'll have to bring me a fourteen. This is much too small; this is a very cheaply made item, if you want my opinion. I may have gained weight this winter, but I know damned well I didn't gain a whole size." The voice of the saleslady, a more expedient saleslady than Jane's, assured her customer that she looked exactly the same, and a size fourteen in the dress she wanted would be the equivalent to a size twelve in this particular make.

Choices narrowing down. Clothes choices, life choices. As one got older, heavier from other choices already taken on. As some parts grew and others sagged or atrophied.

As one grew old, or fat—or odd. One could curse and continue to fight the irrevocable, pretend it hadn't happened yet; or one could find soft, tactful retreats, dimmed to the specifications of one's diminishing hopes.

But were those the only alternatives when you arrived at the point where, as Gabriel had put it, "certain choices harden into the irrevocable"?

That one step further was what interested her. ("So you don't think you can change any of the life choices you have made. They are all irrevocable?" "Irrevocable but not irredeemable.")

I must look up "redeem," again. So many words I thought I knew, words I didn't know at all.

Feeling hot, nervous, she hurried into the top of a two-piece "dinner outfit," made of some shiny material. She would never use a dress like this, but it was the next thing waiting to be tried and she had a compulsion to see if it fit. She was beginning to think nothing would ever fit her again—not really. There would always be some loose part or tight part, or else it might fit her but she wouldn't want it.

On this particular top, there were no buttons or zippers; the only way in was over her head. Halfway in, she got stuck, and was choking and beginning to panic when she was rescued by the little Englishwoman, who had brought two more dresses.

"Try these, dear. One of them might do nicely."

"Thank you, I'll try them." Jane was breathing heavily.

"Hey! Hey, could you come in here a minute?" The hoarse woman across the way had cornered Jane's little saleslady. "Can you get my girl for me? I don't know where the hell she went. And you can take this thing back, while you're at it. I'm surprised at Saks, making such skimpy junk."

"Yes, dear. Could you hand me the hanger for it, please? I'll see if I can get your girl for you." So patient and polite. Probably somebody's grandmother herself.

Jane looked at the price tags of the two latest dresses. The less expensive one was $48.95. She was flustered, distraught. It occurred to her that in the history of this store more than one woman may have gone mad in just such a dressing room as this. Having tried and failed to fit into numerous clothes, simply pulled the curtain securely and took the only way out: of her head.

She took the $48.95 dress off its hanger and draped it across a chair. Then she stood, in bra and panty hose, taking deep breaths, breathing as she had read was good for you. When you inhaled, your diaphragm should expand; when you exhaled, it should hollow out. She noticed a little bulge, like wrinkled tissue, just above the elasticized band of the panty hose. Her flesh looked slightly blue in this light. Her lips had gone very white.

The little saleslady came back, looked discreetly in. "How did those work out, dear?"

Jane snatched up the dress she had draped across the chair. "I found one, at last," she said. "Could you put it in a box for me? I'll be out in a minute to pay for it."

"Very good, dear. This is a nice dress. I think you'll enjoy it. Will that be cash or charge?"

"Cash."

The little lady took the dress and went away.

Jane reached up and pulled the dressing-room curtains securely shut. She unhooked her bra. She peeled off the panty hose. She put these externals on the chair, on top of her purse and glasses, the discarded skirt and blouse, the coat.

She faced the mirror, arms flat at her sides, the way models in medical books posed.

There was a mirror reflecting the mirror she faced. She could see front and back of: female, white, age app. 30–33, height 5'6", weight app. 120–125, eyes blue-green, hair light brown, mole on upper inside quadrant of left breast.

If she were found murdered, naked and murdered, all identification stripped away, these words would suffice, for all intents and purposes, to describe her. A few policemen and detectives and a medical examiner would stand in a cold room with tiled walls, gazing down at her, on a slab, and this is what they would see.

Not a professor, not a schoolteacher, not a "lady pedant."

Not a "bookworm," an intellectual.

Not a woman in Saks, slightly past her prime, who failed to fit successfully into any dress, but bought one nevertheless so as not to hurt the feelings of a patient little old lady who might be someone's grandmother.

Not a mistress, not a daughter, not a granddaughter, not a friend of several other women.

Not an "ego," or a "personality," or "an oddball"; not even a "flux" or "process."

Simply: white female, 30–33, 5'6", 120–125, blue-green, light brown, mole on left breast.

So what was all the fuss about?

What did a few ripples in the flesh matter when, all too soon, now or later, that flesh would be making its return journey to dust?

The world she knew, took for granted, now dissolved in nuclear holocaust . . . Saks gone . . . all universities . . . London, New York, Hong Kong indistinguishable heaps of radioactive cinders. . . . Years pass . . . centuries . . . a curious visitor from another planet, with archaeological interests, picking through the rubble. Picks up some part of her . . . could there be anything left after radioactive centuries? Imagine yes. Picks up a Jane-piece: bone sliver, shard of molar with silver filling . . . what is this?

This is a . . . He would never have heard of the word "Jane"; he would never have heard, perhaps, the word "bone," or "molar," or even *Homo sapiens."* . . . Perhaps he would never have heard of words.

This is a . . . what? Valuable? Can something be valuable if not describable? If there is no hope of putting it into words, ever?

If the curious visitor to these cool ruins were a scientist, perhaps he would put the Jane-piece in his pocket to mull over later, should future information come to light. If she were lucky, she might take her place among a shelf of interesting fossils, alongside moon rocks and . . . pieces of other things as yet unbroken, in places as yet undreamed of.

If the curious visitor were not scientifically inclined, well . . . he would look at the Jane-piece, perhaps wonder, but not for long, then . . . toss it back, into the indistinguishable rubble.

The thing as yet unbroken, composed of millions of Jane-pieces, began wrapping various pieces of clothing about itself in a small cubicle, one of numerous identical cubicles, on the seventh floor of an edifice as yet standing on an island bought for $24 worth of beads.

Jane went back to the room full of racks and dresses, and found her little old grandmother. She reached in her purse and handed over a little more than twice the price of the island on which she was now standing, for a dress she had not tried on.

"I hope you get a lot of enjoyment out of it, dear."

"Thank you, I'm sure I will!"

She walked, not looking at anything, to the elevators. Other female *Homo sapiens,* carrying identical boxes and bags, stood watching the progress of the arrows moving up or down a semicircle of numbers above the elevators. A red light would flash above one of the elevators, and within a second or so that elevator would open. There would be a rush of female *Homo sapiens* toward the open door. But the elevator would be full already, having collected its load from above. Only a few were allowed to squeeze in. Then the whole process would begin again. The unsuccessful female *Homo sapiens* would stand nervously eying the progress of the arrows, edging their way toward the next possible red light. A door would open, and a few more would be herded into the already packed car. Where had all these herds come from? How tense they looked, how determined to squeeze their bodies into the next available car. She would never get in!

Jane began to feel faint. She knew the first signs all too well: the cold dampness on the surface of the skin, the queasiness, the rising horror at the prospect of having the self she knew and kept track of dissolve into nothing.

She found an EXIT and began walking down flights of cement stairs, taking deep breaths to the regular thump, thump, thump of the cardboard dress box bouncing against her leg. She thought a sort of litany: *Hold on, hold on, hold on,* each time the box touched against her leg. She held on to that last precious piece, the final Jane-piece—bleached white as ancient bone, the ultimate reminder of whatever she was—which had withstood all holocausts and ravages of time, all passing fashions and styles. Hold on. She concentrated on keeping the piece clean, buffing it against her leg, polishing it and warming it. She would focus on that last piece.

The main floor. The enormous brown-tinted room with its slabs of wainscoting reaching to the ceiling, its cases of jewels and scarves and handkerchiefs and perfume and gloves . . . the soft mixture of scents and the murmurs of female voices, making their transactions, coordinating all the parts, creating a glossy, packaged whole of suèdes and silks, jades and turquoise, leather and Cashmere and Angora. A smooth, effortless-looking, expensive package, an American package composed of all the desirable animal-and-vegetable-and-mineral-pieces of the world, into which they would stuff—unknowingly—all the millions of pieces which would be reclaimed one day by the very earth on which they—unwittingly—still stood, the earth hundreds of feet beneath the subway tunnels under these polished floors, which gave them back, so reassuringly, the mirror tap of their expensive shoes and boots.

They could buy everything in this store if they had enough money and credit. But the pieces of themselves were on loan and must eventually be returned. Jane imagined their bewildered faces, looking up from the various counters, should a voice suddenly boom from a hidden loudspeaker: "LADIES, REMEMBER: THE PIECES OF YOURSELVES ARE ON LOAN."

At last, the street. Still breathing the deep breaths and inwardly reciting the ritual *hold on*. She knew, though she was sweating and trembling, that it was all right again; she was herself, she was not going to dissolve—not today. She understood when it was all right again; she had, over thirty-two and a half years, at least acquired that much understanding of her pieces.

A cabdriver was signaling to her. It was Vincent de Lucca!

She went at once and climbed into his cab. How pleased he would be to see her Saks box and learn she had taken his advice.

"I thought you wanted a cab. The way you stood

there," he told her. It was not Vincent de Lucca. It was another collection of pieces, resembling de Lucca, only this collection had another Italian name. Bernard Cavalcanti. A nice name. An ancestor of his might have been aboard the *Santa María,* in the waning autumn of 1492, plotting to mutiny against the captain because the men had waited and hoped for so long, and the idealistic bastard had failed to produce any New World.

"What?" she said. He had asked her something.

"I said, where to?"

How could she tell him the truth that she had seen in the dressing room: that there was no destination for her in this city that was due to collapse with the rest of the world in a matter of centuries anyway. She had no right to impose her pessimism on the Cavalcantis, who, even now, were in process of achieving the New World, and whose wives and daughters still believed in their ability (aided by cash) to conquer Saks.

"Where to?" he repeated, slightly impatient.

She thought of the one place where she was sure to feel at home, where dowdiness was the norm just as chic was the norm in the store that had almost done her in.

"The Public Library," she said.

"The one at Forty-second?"

"Yes," she said, assuming he knew his city better than she.

XV

ONCE again, in the catalogue room, it struck her: *Everyone seems to know what they want today except me.*

Here I am, in my fortress of fortresses, The Library, she thought. If I can't orient myself here, where? Gabriel had said the self, the basic self, was like a warehouse, or library . . . "a perfect, complete library, which contains all the volumes . . ."

She stood near the entrance of the room and watched how easily other people approached the reference desk with their requests. She had no requests. She couldn't even think of something she would like to look up in the card catalogue.

A young man and an older woman were on duty. They dealt efficiently with each new query. Jane heard a woman wearing a nurse's stockings and cape ask how she would go about finding a guide to carnivorous plants. The young man was able to help her at once. A nice old man, the kind of old man you would expect to find feeding pigeons from a park bench, asked the woman behind the desk if he could see all the New York *Daily Mirrors* for April 1917, and she very carefully told him all the old newspapers were at an annex, the newspaper library. When he looked frightened and asked, "Where is it? Far?" She drew him a little map on the back of a slip of paper and said, well, frankly, she would not walk it herself; she would take the crosstown bus at . . . and told him exactly where.

If I were in a familiar library, what would I do, Jane

thought, and tried to reconstruct her graduate school wanderings, when, exhausted from sitting so long in her carrel applying herself to the same books, she would "reward herself" with a casual half-hour roam through the open stacks. Where had she roamed? As often as not to Jung: the shelf of black books with gold lettering, slowly completing itself, thanks to the Bollingen Foundation. She liked Jung's titles. They shimmered with the promise of ultimate revelation. *Symbols of Transformation. The Secret of the Golden Flower. Aion. The Archetypes and the Collective Unconscious. Mysterium Coinunctionis.* How often she had stood before this growing, imposing collection, and thought: If I were systematically to attack these volumes, one by one, reading carefully from beginning to end, I could solve my life. I am sure I could solve it, once and for all. But the old man wouldn't let her, the magician who had posed so successfully in Zurich as a psychiatrist. She would check out, say, *Aion,* and take it home and try to "attack" it, and the message which had seemed so certain in the library dissolved in front of her eyes. It was only print, a lot of words about old things. She tried to approach the book responsibly, as she had done with difficult books in graduate courses, reading it chapter by chapter, no matter how bored or distracted she became, taking notes on each chapter, reviewing and coordinating the notes as she went along. But Jung eluded her: snippets she could have, but no formula, no solution to her life. Sometimes she believed the spirit of the dead man was playing with her, leading her on a wild-goose chase of little starts and flashes of intuition, a mere peek at the luminary, a hint of alchemical gold, shining his mirror at the sun and, when she tried to follow too seriously, turning himself into the wind, or a tree. *You can only have me in flashes,* Jung seemed to be telling her; *you have to learn to trust your own intuitions—as I have trusted mine. After I broke with Freud, my life was filled with uncertainties. What should I do next? Thereupon I said to myself, "Since I know nothing at all, I shall simply do whatever occurs to me."* And he had done just that; Jane had read about it in his autobiography. A medical man and father, pushing forty, he had stooped down again like a child and played childish games, building little villages out of small stones. And over the weeks and months, playing the game he had most loved at age eleven, Jung's thoughts clarified and he saw what came next in his life's work.

The clock in the catalogue room said eleven-forty-five. Almost six hours to go until she could pick up the phone in room 920 and let Gabriel save her from herself.

She remembered that time as a child when she had asked Kitty, *Why not write a story about people like us,* and Kitty had replied she could only sell stories about girls who could throw everything out the window when the man came along. "There must be nothing too permanent, or heavy, in their lives."

Is there nothing in this entire library, the largest public library in this city, that I want to look up?

What if this was my last chance, my only chance to take what I needed from that library that is the citadel of the self?

Various possibilities came to mind. I could look up "love" in the Oxford English Dictionary. Or "redeem." Or even "odd." I could see if they have Gabriel's monograph here. I could pay a friendly call on my old standby Jung. But nothing seemed urgent. It could all be thrown out the window.

She became aware that she was being watched, peripherally, by the man behind the reference desk. How long had she been standing in just this one spot? Perhaps he thought she was a crazy woman, or was about to be ill, or cause some trouble, do something not habitually done in libraries. And Jane, who could not stand being thought crazy or eccentric by strangers, walked up to this man and said what had providentially flashed into her head. She would *play* at wanting to know something, since there was nothing she could think of that she wanted to know.

"It's just come back to me, the title," she told him. "The title of an old play. Where would I find information on a melodrama called *The Fatal Wedding,* which was performed around the turn of the century?"

It worked. Now he understood. She ceased to "stand

out," and became normal and invisible again. A nice fulfillable request, as grounded in normality (perhaps even more so!) as wanting to know which plants ate meat, as grounded in chronology as all the New York *Daily Mirrors* for April, 1917.

"What you want is the Lincoln Center Library of the Performing Arts," he said. He told her how to get there. "They're sure to have what you want!" he assured her.

As she climbed into her third taxi of the morning, she realized that she had left her new dress behind in Bernard Cavalcanti's cab. It bothered her amazingly little. The dress had never really belonged to her anyway. It would belong to Mrs. Cavalcanti, perhaps, or her daughter. Or maybe the chic mistress of the next fare, who would pretend the Saks box was his.

Before Jane had started to school, she had often played with another little girl, who lived in her apartment house. Her name was Sheila and she was the daughter of a policeman. Jane and Sheila would sit in the lobby of the apartment house, with paper and pencils, and Jane would say: "I know what. Let's do some shorthand." And both little girls would scratch away like mad with their pencils, making useless marks across page after page of clean paper. Neither of them had learned to read or write yet. "Look, we've already done five pages of shorthand!" Sheila would exclaim, and then Jane would look down at the mess of useless symbols and wasted paper and know it was all a fake. And she felt ill and wished Sheila would go away, back to her own apartment upstairs. When is my life going to start, she had thought—even then, at age five. And she was sure it would start when she began going to school and learned how to read and write real, meaningful marks that told all the things she couldn't know.

Now, as she sat in this elegant new library, "researching" an old melodrama, she kept remembering those frustrating playtimes with Sheila, sitting there on that old wartime sofa, making useless marks on perfectly good paper, because she was still a "child" and was waiting in the lobby for a more serious life to begin. And today she knew that what she was doing was only a time-passer.

It was not the same thing as her beautiful frozen winter when she had been writing her thesis.

"Be More Interesting! Have Things of Your Own to Do!" That's what the magazines told you. "Have a Hobby! Read the Editorials! When He Comes Home from an Exciting Day, He Doesn't Want a Drudge!"

Only a way to pass the time, to be more interesting. So that tonight at dinner, exhilarated from his own meaningful day, when Gabriel asked her "What did you do today," she would have her cool little offering for him. "Actually I spent the day reading up on an old melodrama that came through our town in 1905. My great-aunt ran away with the villain in it, and was never seen alive again."

And yet—she would be fair to herself—what a queer thrill it gave her when she was assured *in print* that Edith's sensational cautionary tale was based on reality; when, in a book called *The World of Melodrama,* she came across:

Prominent among the new writers corralled as stock authors by Sullivan, Harris, and Woods was Theodore Kremer. He worked closely with his producers, as the other authors were to do. There was a fairly well-fixed routine. Woods would dream up a snappy title, the posters would be designed and printed, and finally the play would be written and rehearsed. Prolific like all his kind, Kremer ground out scores of dramas for this and other managements. His masterpiece, and Harris' greatest hit, was *The Fatal Wedding,* given in 1901. It filled the old Grand Opera House for months at one dollar top, and there were five road companies, the star of the second one being Mary Pickford. The plot dealt with a nefarious conspiracy by the villain and his paramour to wreck the peace of a happy home by means of false accusations against the blameless wife, leading to a divorce.

She felt a little like a detective when she came across the word "villain." As if she had tracked the nefarious Von Vorst one centimeter closer to his hiding place, undoubtedly now in a graveyard. And how interesting, that they actually designed the poster before they wrote the play. She would tell Gabriel; he would be amused.

The Fatal Wedding had run for fourteen years, to packed houses all over the country. "The villain and the villainess hissed and the wronged mother sobbed through four acts of *The Fatal Wedding* at the Avenue Theatre Sunday, to the great delight of two packed houses," reported the Detroit *Journal* on January 19, 1914. It must have been sensational if it took World War I to put it out of business.

And it had had four acts. Four acts and three intermissions. ("That must have been a play with a lot of acts if Cleva met him and made all her plans during the intermissions. Pretty fast work, don't you think, for 1905?")

Whatever the year, there are always some people who are passionate and others who are not.

At the moment, Gabriel was standing before some painting, making notes on the tint of a woman's skin, the shape of a cloud; afterward, he would collect all his shoe boxes full of note cards and turn them into six kinds of love.

At the moment, if Sonia Marks had finished grading her papers, feeding her children, and loving and fighting with her husband, Max, she might be in her neat study, with the shelves and tables painted white, working on her long-term project: comparing James's 1908 revisions of *Portrait of a Lady* with the 1881 text. She had already discovered that James's first Henrietta Stackpole had been highly sympathetic; but in the second edition he had decided to make her ridiculous. Sonia would publish this bit of news in a famous scholarly journal.

Gerda, the New Employer, was probably filling out income-tax forms for the employees of *Feme Sole*.

And I? What on earth am I doing here, killing time till I can go and have dinner with my married lover? Has all my reading and writing and thinking led me to *this*?

Even the Enema Bandit seemed better off in terms of having something worthwhile to do. At least he got excited about what he did. He took chances in order to go out and do what he felt he must do.

But then, in a file folder full of old clippings, she came across a photograph of the villainess, faced by the wronged wife at the altar, just as she is about to steal away the misguided husband. How sensational it all was! No wonder Edith had enjoyed building her own stories on the melodramatic form. "Cora Williams, the jealous cat," read the caption beneath the picture, "seeks to break up the marriage of her best friend, Mabel Wilson, to Howard Wilson. With the help of Howard's best friend, Robert Curtis (the villain), who surprises the innocent Mabel in a passionate embrace just as Howard enters the room, she succeeds. Howard divorces Mabel, who is forced to live in a garret with her starving children. But the day Cora and Howard are to be married, Mabel faces them at the altar and busts up the party. Cora takes out a gun and shoots Robert Curtis dead."

How simple it all was back in 1905!

Jane imagined how she would get Marty—her friend Marty—to conspire with her for the hand of Gabriel. Marty would go to Ann's house, surprise her in a passionate embrace just as Gabriel walked in to supper. . . .

And there it stopped, of course. In a Broadway play in the nineteen-seventies, the husband would say, "Oh, I didn't know you had somebody with you. Just a minute, I'll go get Jane. I left her in the car with a McDonald's hamburger. Then we can all swing."

The real Gabriel might very well say, "Oh, I'm sorry. I seem to have interrupted something, I'll go down to the office and make a few more notes. Under the eye of eternity, it matters very little."

But her excitement was equal to any "real" scholar's when, in a Robinson Locke scrapbook, she found the program. She remembered that program—a torn-off page of it, at least—with its cast of characters and its desperate note, scrawled in pencil: *"Sister I am in grave trouble please can somebody come the villain has left me,"* and an address.

Two things about that piece of program had impressed the child Jane. One was that Cleva hadn't used any capitalization or punctuation where she should have. A person must be in deep trouble if they forgot to capitalize and punctuate. And she remembered that ad, down in the corner of the torn-off page:

Louis Hirshowitz, Watchmaker and Jeweler
Money Loaned at Low Rates

"He who knows most, Gives most for wasted time."

Now, for the first time, she saw this piece of evidence (evidence that if you were a woman and you didn't take care, some villain would come along and get you in grave trouble) in its entirety. A theatre program, "The Opera Glass," from Wilkes-Barre, Pennsylvania, for December 4, 5, 6, 1905." "THE FATAL WEDDING: *Ben Kahn presents Sullivan, Harris, and Woods' International Success, a touching story of heart interest by Theo. Kremer.*"

Here was the rest of the maimed program which Edith had wielded as a "preventive measure" on daughter and granddaughter. Under an advertisement for Stegmaier's Beer was a Synopsis of Acts. Jane was able to reconstruct from it the outlines of the melodrama watched by young Edith and Cleva almost seventy winters ago. How fast things went, how fast the "jealous cat" Cora had worked, if Scene One, Act One, took place in "the happy home of the Wilsons," and Scene Two "the New York Divorce Court." No two years' tact for Cora Williams, waiting around for the man she wanted.

If Cleva had run away with the villain in November, then she must have been with Von Vorst—yes, there he was, listed right there in print:

ROBERT CURTIS, A MAN ABOUT TOWN—Hugo Von Vorst

She must have been traveling with him in early December. She was undoubtedly in the Wilkes-Barre theatre, holding one of these very programs, glancing down at it, with a complete lack of ironic distance, to read the coming attractions:

Girl of the Streets, Dec. 7, 8, 9
Lured from Home, Dec. 11, 12 13

Why Girls Leave Home
(or: *A Danger Signal
in the Path of Folly*), Dec. 14, 15, 16

Jane thought of the note Sonia Marks had once written to her about soap opera. "Too many women's lives conform to its pattern. Do you think the soap opera follows life or do we pattern our lives with their innumerable crises and catastrophes and shifting casts of characters on this model?"

Cleva's case seemed almost a dramatization of the above statement. Ridiculously clear-cut, in fact. You wondered how she could have missed seeing it. But the Age of Ironic Distance had not arrived in December of 1905 as a Southern girl, raised on a farm, a little in arrears of her *Zeitgeist,* waited in a theatre in Wilkes-Barre for her villain, looking down at "coming attractions" and failing to connect them with her own future.

It was easy to have the wisdom of ironic distance in retrospect.

Jane imagined her own grand-niece, some seventy years in the future. A young woman, Emily's granddaughter, poking around in the family history some rainy day, or to kill time while waiting to do something better. *Oh, here's a picture of old Aunt Jane,* she would say to her mother, Emily's daughter.

Oh, God, yes. Old Jane, the mother would say. Perhaps laugh.

What was she like, anyway?

Oh, I don't think she was very happy.

Not happy? How did she manage that? Everybody knows how to be happy now. God, people must have been stupid in the nineteen-seventies!

No, in every era there are some people who know how to be happy and others who don't. Your grandmother knew how. She was not at all like poor Great-Aunt Jane.

I find that incomprehensible. What was wrong with her? Couldn't she see that it's all a matter of . . .

And Emily's granddaughter would go into the sort of tirade Jane's students sometimes did. "How stupid of Anne Elliott to listen to Lady Russell, not to marry

337

Frederick Wentworth when she loved him. Couldn't she see he had the makings of a captain? Where was her faith in herself? God, young people were spineless back then! If Anne Elliott had only *seen,* she wouldn't have had to suffer for two hundred pages!"

"And we wouldn't have had *Persuasion,*" Jane would reply in the mock-ironic tone she sometimes used to re-assert herself, to veil the uncertain part of herself, with all its potential ecstasies and vulnerabilities, from those scornful young students, so bold in their wisdom of retro-spect.

But, oh, if she could only project into the future and listen to Emily's granddaughter summing up, with the careless wisdom of the young, what simple matter left un-tried would have made all the difference to poor Aunt Jane's happiness!

She closed the Robinson Locke scrapbook and returned it to the desk. It was almost three o'clock and she was ex-tremely hungry. She would go and reward herself with an enormous meal, with wine, and then go to the hotel and sleep it off till Gabriel called. Playacting at "re-search," she nonetheless had a feeling of accomplishment, and over veal scallopini and a second glass of wine, she suddenly replied "Oh, can't I?" when Kitty's inner voice said, "You cannot research everything you know."

The two men at the next table turned to stare, and Jane thought, but not without amusement, *I really must watch it. Sooner or later someone is going to mistake me for a crazy person.*

Back in 920, she took off her shoes and skirt and crawled into the freshly made bed and napped. She had been going to take a bath first, so as to be ready when Gabriel called at five-thirty. But no: as she slipped off drowsily, she thought, He'll just have to wait a few min-utes. For once it will be I who says, "See you in fifteen minutes, okay?" And she felt rather pleased and smug, having come through this day alone with honors, even managing to crowd things right up till the five-thirty re-lease.

The phone rang at precisely five-thirty. Gabriel was

338

calling from a pay telephone, near the museum. "Things have taken a rather complicated turn," he began awkwardly, and went on to explain in a series of lengthy, broken sentences which he worked into backward, as if tackling a controversial point in an essay without wishing to offend anyone, that the very same Arthur Parsons whose possible presence aboard the morning flight had prevented her meeting him yesterday had shown up at the Metropolitan Museum today instead and insisted on Gabriel joining him for dinner. "He's alone here in New York and hates his hotel—and—he thinks I am alone, too—so it would have been problematic. . . . We are colleagues, after all, and I see him and his wife socially sometimes, as well. . . ."

"I" and who else, thought Jane, holding the receiver pressed against her ear. She was shivering suddenly, in her blouse and stockings beneath the bedclothes. Her happy stolen nap, the luxurious drowsiness into which she had abandoned herself, vanished from the room, leaving her an alert prisoner in it. *Not coming! After I'd looked forward to it all day! Our last night! Couldn't you have told him no? What am I going to do for three more hours? Oh, I can't go through this again. Who in hell is Arthur Parsons!*

But the habits of the two-year-old stately waltz died hard, and Jane said in a slightly choked voice, "Oh, what a disappointment, Gabriel, and on our last night together."

"I know," he said. He did sound sorry, even miserable. Perhaps if she were to be very still, hardly breathing on her end of the line, he would become so miserable he would reconsider. Who is Arthur Parsons, he would be saying in a moment; who in hell is Arthur Parsons to come between us and our last night?

But, "I'll try and make it quick," he was saying. "I'll try and get back early."

"About what time?"

"Oh, let's see. If we eat early—and I think I can manage it; neither of us are drinkers—I might even be back about eight-thirty or so. That would give us some time. . . ."

"Yes," she said reluctantly.

"But what about you?" he said. "You must have something to eat."

"Oh, it doesn't matter." She did not tell him she had just eaten a veal scallopini. Why should he get off so easy? Let him worry. "I don't like to go out alone," she added, really playing the martyr, and succeeding so well that she blinked back the first tears of pity for herself. Oh, what a soap opera!

"Why not try the hotel restaurant? It might not be so bad. I'd rather you didn't go out alone, either."

What right have you to "rather" I didn't do anything?

"Don't worry about me," she said. She was imagining Gabriel and Ann Weeks, in dinner clothes, going slowly up the walk to the Parsonses' front door, on a soft Saturday evening. Gabriel would take Ann's arm lightly, absently, with the habit of years of courtesy; he himself would press the bell. The door opened. She imagined a vile Arthur Parsons, grotesquely bourgeois, a loud bourbon clattering in his fat fingers, a stupid jovial welcome on his jowly countenance: "Annie, you're looking gorgeous! Gabe, boy, what'll ya have? The wife's just out in the kitchen. C'mon in, lemme take your wraps!" *C'mon in out of the cold, Annie and Gabe. Leave the Other Woman out there with a McDonald's; she'll be okay.*

"I know this is upsetting," Gabriel was saying, not sounding very upset himself, "but let's try and make the best of it. I had a pretty lucky day, all in all, at the museum."

"Oh, I'm so glad, Gabriel." Another point gone. The Understanding Mistress had failed to get there first with her understanding question: How did your day go, dear?

"What did you do?" he asked. "Did you have a nice day?"

"Oh, I—"

There was a beep, beep, beep. The operator broke in. "Your time is up, sir. Signal when through."

"I haven't got any more change," said Gabriel.

"Please try and call as soon as you can," she begged, hating herself. "I'll wait here for you."

"I will. I'll give you a call as near to eight-thirty as possible. And, Jane?"

"What?" she said bitterly.

"Thank you for being so patient."

They were cut off. She slammed down the phone. She hurled herself from the bed and paced the room like a demented soul. She wished she could smash everything in the room. Her face in front of the mirror frightened her, it was so ugly and full of failure. It was tensed into lines and folds of poisonous, hateful disappointment. She would not like anyone in the world to see this face of hers. Someone like Emily, or one of her students, or a stranger. The sight would make them sorry for her and fearful for themselves, as the sight of a student in a wheelchair often ruined her mood as she crossed campus. She remembered a photo of Indian women, raped by enemy soldiers and then abandoned by their own husbands because they were now "unclean." Their faces were blank. Simply blank. Whatever unimaginable disillusion they were harboring in their broken hearts, they had the dignity—the dignity of the true sufferer—not to inflict it on the camera, and thus on the world.

She picked up her hairbrush and began brushing out her hair, in fierce, burning strokes, till each hair was standing out on its own, electrified. She looked at this strange creature of the moment: head bristling live wires, pale tense face with panicked, angry eyes, body clothed in a gray flannel blouse and gray panty hose; it looked like a wildly perplexed creature from another planet, neither male nor female in its odd gray spacesuit garb. Perhaps all people would look like this in future. She had read somewhere that even things like hair and eyelashes were on their way out, would be gone from the bodies of humans within a hundred years. Would a globe full of pale, bald creatures in identical gray spacesuits be able to comprehend through the wildest stretch of imagination the problems that had beset one Jane Clifford on a Tuesday in late January, circa 1970? What would it mean to them: her confusion in Saks, her rushing around in taxis, losing a dress, squinting over old newsprint, going to pieces because a lover had phoned to say he would

341

not be able to have dinner, after all? Would there be such things as "lovers" in a hundred years?

She brushed and brushed until her hair crackled and the poison drained from her face. What right had she to compare her plight to the betrayal of those Indian wives? She had not been betrayed. Not at all. She had, all but legally, contracted to this arrangement with full knowledge of the circumstances and conditions. She had accepted the invitation—no, she had done most of the inviting herself—to perform a certain slow and restricted dance with a certain sort of man. She had known in advance the formation of the dance pattern and the type of man. As Kitty had said, "You knew he had a wife when you started this thing. In fact, you once said you liked it better that way; it kept it eternally fresh." Had she said such a thing, after all? Was this what she had wanted: this stately dance, leaving her mind free to construct its fantasies around this cool man? And, in the interims between dances, did she enjoy another kind of fantasizing, a playacting at "hoping for more," watching herself play the abused mistress hoping gamely for a future that might change everything? ("Jane, you're going to live through your nineties. . . . You are indestructible . . . . That's what I like about you." "That would make it about 2030. If I live till 2030 . . . I suppose you might marry me." "That might well happen," he had replied, smiling.)

In 2030, Emily's granddaughter would be in her thirties. She might be Jane's own age now. Clearing up with her own mother, perhaps, the old, perplexing but beloved debris of dead Emily's aftereffects *"Oh, look, all these old lawbooks. Should we keep them? They might be valuable. What funny laws! Mother, do let me read you this quaint old law. . . . Here's another picture of Great-Aunt Jane. What ever happened to her, Mother?"*

Jane paused before the mirror, hairbrush suspended, in her gray outfit, waiting to hear the answer.

"Nothing happened to her—I don't think."

"Nothing? How do you mean nothing? Well, did she happen to anything, then?"

"No, but she was very patient."

Jane watched herself. She was packing. Yes, she had her suitcase on the bed, open, and she was folding things, putting them in. She made trips to the bathroom, wrapping a toothbrush in Kleenex, zipping up a travel kit full of tubes and little jars.

So this is what I am doing now, she thought, making these trips. But *how* am I doing it? Am I packing, making ready to leave this scene? Or am I "packing" in order to watch myself playact at leaving Gabriel?

She didn't know.

She decided to go on with the act, since there was nothing better to do. Give the audience its money's worth! If the abused mistress is really packing to leave the scene of so much abuse, what does she do after she's finished packing? For Jane had finished packing.

Call the airlines, of course. Jane called United and asked for flights to Chicago for the rest of Tuesday. There was one every hour. The last flight left at 10 P.M. from Kennedy.

"Do you wish to book a flight now?" asked a friendly male voice.

What would she answer? The audience quivered in suspense. Jane said, "Is it really necessary to book? Can I just take a chance? My plans aren't certain just yet—"

The voice said of course it was always better to book, but she might be able to get on at the last minute; it was up to her.

The audience sagged a little. Ah, that Jane Clifford. Coming from such a nice dramatic family, couldn't she ever rise to a dramatic act herself?

Well, did she happen to anything, then?

Since she could not, it seemed, make a bold, dramatic leap into the future, she decided to act, at least, by reclaiming past losses. She leafed away from United toward Yellow Cabs, from the bravely visionary to the more accomplishable mundane. Perhaps she could track down her lost dress, left in Bernard Cavalcanti's cab. Between United and Yellow came the "V"'s. Still in the grip of her afternoon "research," she traced her finger down the "Von"'s, not knowing what she would do if she found a cousin or a son, but curious, all the same.

343

There was a Hugo Von Vorst who lived on West Forty-fifth Street.

The audience was gripped again as the heroine dialed the number, saying to herself (because, after all, this was the "realistic" drama of the seventies, not the melodrama of 1905), "It's probably a son, or a grandson, or no relation at all. Things like that don't happen in our world."

"Hello?" said a very old, deep voice. The true basso profundo of convincing villains, only wavering a bit.

"Hello . . ." She didn't know what on earth she was going to say. "Is this—Hugo Von Vorst?"

"Speaking! Who's calling, please?"

"Could you by any chance be the Von Vorst who played in a—play in 1905, called *The Fatal Wedding?*"

"Yes," he replied, delighted. "You must have seen the article, did you?"

"What article?"

"In the *Post*. It was called 'The Last Villain Reminisces.' In last Saturday's *Post*. Saturday was my ninetieth birthday."

Is this happening? she thought. The proof was that he was on the other end of the line, waiting for a reply. "No, I didn't see the article—I don't live in town—but congratulations on being ninety. That's wonderful."

"Oh, it has its ups and downs. May I ask who's calling?"

As Jane introduced herself, she had an image of Frances's face upon learning that her scholarly niece had poked around in a library until she had unearthed her natural father. "Actually, I'm a professor of English, but I've recently become absorbed by the topic of melodrama while engaged in a—certain research. I was over at the Lincoln Center Library today and I saw you played the villain in *The Fatal Wedding*. You were on that Wilkes-Barre tour, I believe, and had come from—farther south on that particular tour. . . ." She trailed off significantly. Did he scent the hounds of detection already, she wondered. Would he hang up?

"Oh, yes! I died one hundred and eighty times in that play. Lately, in my spare time, I've been adding up all the times I died. In performances, that is. As you can hear, I am still alive."

"You were shot in *The Fatal Wedding*."

"Right you are! I am talking to a professor, all right, Miss—or is it Mrs.? Or does one say 'Doctor'—I was never sure."

"Oh, Miss. I guess. I mean I'm not married or anything."

"You sound very young."

"Oh, well, I'm not," said Jane, then fell into an embarrassed silence. He was imagining her, no doubt, this old-maid professor who called up strange men. She must end this call, tactfully.

"At my age, everyone seems young. How long will you be in town? Perhaps you will come and visit me. I could show you that article. I have had a few thoughts myself on melodrama."

"Thank you so much, Mr. Von Vorst, but I'm afraid I can't. I'm leaving the city tonight. Actually, it was only by the strangest coincidence that I called. You see, I was just looking through the telephone book for the cab company—I did the silliest thing today; I bought a dress and then left it behind in a taxicab—and on the way to the 'Y's I came across your name. I couldn't resist seeing if you were the same Von Vorst I had"—she almost said "been hearing about all my life"—"read about only this afternoon."

"Oh, I see," he said. She heard the disappointment in his voice. "Yes, Miss Clifford, I understand. Rather, I must have misunderstood. I thought you were doing some serious work on melodrama, and, of course, I would be only too happy to oblige. Of course you must try and find your dress before you leave. And it was a cheerful surprise for me, your calling."

She heard the reproachful dismissal in the old voice. She saw herself as he must see her: not only an old-maid professor, but a flighty one, as well, who leaves dresses behind in taxis and raises false hopes in others through her egocentric whims.

"Oh, the dress isn't important," she said. "I wasn't

345

even going to bother about it; then, at the last minute, I felt I ought to at least make a sort of 'duty' attempt to track it down. The truth is, Mr. Von Vorst, I would be charmed to visit you if only I weren't leaving so soon. But I had made up my mind to take a flight out of here tonight, and—"

"What times does your flight leave?"

"Well, actually, there is one as late as ten, but—"

"You might come for a *little* while," he said encouragingly. And Jane tried to imagine a seventy years' younger version of this voice pleading charmingly with an aunt she'd never seen: "You might come to New York for a *little* while."

"Well . . . all right." She laughed nervously. "Yes, I could come for a little while. Only, what about your supper? I don't want to interrupt you."

"Oh, come now. By all means. We've already eaten. Where are you?"

Jane gave him the location of her hotel, wondering who "we" might be. His wife still alive ? Mrs. Von Vorst? Perhaps he had had a wife in 1905 and that was why Cleva had to die.

"Not far at all! If you want to risk another taxi," he said, laughing. "you could be here in no time. Mine is the ugly new apartment building about three doors down from the old Martin Beck Theatre on Forty-fifth Street. You can't miss it. It has a garish sign painted on the side of it which says 'NOW RENTING.' But inside the rooms aren't too bad. Yes, come on over, Miss Clifford, and we'll have—we'll have a cordial!" He sounded so pleased she was coming that she felt the tears start again.

"I'll be there. I'll be there in about"—and she thought of Gabriel's famous quarter of an hour—"a quarter of an hour."

After she hung up, she checked Tempus Fugit. Not quite six. Then, automatically, she wrapped it carefully inside a blouse and placed it in a corner of the suitcase.

Wait! What was this? Was she really going to walk out? Had she been serious, packing angrily away for the "audience"? Poor Gabriel, he would call this room "as

346

near to eight-thirty as possible" and what would he think, if she didn't answer? She had *always* answered! How worried he would be! The thought gave her a moment's pleasure, but she rejected it. No. She would play fair. She would leave a message: *"Took flight tonight. Don't worry."*

But how sad he would be. Their last night. Even now he was probably hurrying through this unwanted dinner with Parsons to hurry back to her, back to her arms.

She ought to at least have the courage to tell him personally. She could whisk over and see Von Vorst, whisk back, and be in this room, hotel bill paid, bag packed and shut, at eight-thirty. The phone would ring—Gabriel was extremely dependable; when he said "as near to eight-thirty as possible," that meant anywhere from eight-thirty-one to eight-thirty-five—and she would answer and say, "Look, I've decided to leave tonight. It's difficult to explain, but I need to go off and think about our relationship coolly, and decide what future it has. . . ." She might even lighten things up by telling him of her visit to the villain, the same villain who lured her great-aunt into sin in 1905.

No, she was enjoying this too much, looking forward to it. If she got into conversation with Gabriel, he would say, "Try and put up with this maddening person tonight. Let's have this night. I don't know when I'll be able to get away again. And I want to hear about your evening; it sounds fascinating."

Decide, damn it!

The audience was waiting, urging her on in whispers: *"Pick up that suitcase and leave! Pay your bill! Walk out without a backward glance! Let him eat oranges the rest of his life! Go see your villain, then make that plane!"*

The deafening roar of applause—she could feel it, emanating from her own love of a good story, when she picked up that bag and made the sensational definitive break!

She zipped her suitcase shut, remembering her brother Jack, so shy, so accommodating as he went to wait beside "BAGGAGE": "I'll get your bag. Is it still that same old black one with the zipper?"

347

Same old bag, same old Jane.

Leaving the suitcase on the bed, she took her purse and coat and left room 920. She went quickly past the desk, dropping off her key. And out to the sidewalk, where she hailed another cab.

"Aww, no! What a letdown! What a cop-out! Why didn't she walk out and leave that bastard? I want my money back."

This is my scene, she thought, looking at the back of the driver's head. This one was a Negro. It was too dark to see his nameplate. And I am going to play it as I see fit. It is all I have, and I shall honor it with the consistencies on which, so far, the drama has been constructed. A good plot goes from possibility to probability to necessity, and I have not yet felt, deep in that place where my most vital instincts live, the necessity of leaving Gabriel. I regret it, of course; it would be so much neater, so much cleaner. I would be a heroine of clear bold lines and colors. I would be sensational.

As she was driven through the dark streets of early winter evening, she thought of how Bernard Shaw had once said that the only thing to do with family skeletons was to take them out of the closet and dance with them, and she liked the idea so much that here she was—unsensational and cautious in her heart—on her way across town to have a cordial with the family villain, at last.

XVI

Von Vorst's building was not the sort to sport a doorman. Meditating vaguely on what she would do if accosted by a mugger, Jane went cautiously through the abandoned lobby with its dim wattage and rows of aluminum mailboxes. The single piece of furniture in the small area was a sofa which had been, at some happier point in its life, "modern Danish." Now it was slashed beyond all function, its mutilated foam-rubber stuffing spilling out of the muddy-orange upholstery. Going up the slow elevator, Jane shook her head at all the angry, semiliterate obscenities scratched into the metal walls. Some of it was in an unknown alphabet, with lots of dots and curlicues. It looked angry also. Von Vorst's apartment was at the top. It would have been cruel of her not to come, after arousing his curiosity. Old people did not, as a rule, expect hordes of visitors, but perhaps, more than others, they hoped for the miraculous, unexpected visitor. She remembered how Edith, in her last years, had developed the habit of hovering, shy as a young girl, behind her curtains, looking out hopefully at the uneventful street. Even when she had company, she would suddenly become "absent," rise from her chair as if someone were calling to her, and waft to the window, plucking softly, discreetly at her curtains, peering out.

"Who are you expecting, Edith?" Kitty had asked, once when the whole troop of them had dropped by for a visit. "We are all here. For heaven's sake come and sit down, you're making me nervous." "Oh, nobody," Edith would say. Ronnie, who was very small then, seized on this, delighted. For years afterward, whenever he was there and Edith went to the window, he would cry: "Is Nobody coming yet?"

Von Vorst is only four years older than Edith was last week, thought Jane, going toward his door. And Cleva was a year older than Edith, so in 1905, when Cleva was twenty, Von Vorst was a villain of twenty-three. Younger than my student Howard!

She knocked softly, not sure she would be ready for whatever revealed itself on the other side of the door. Footsteps scuffled nearer on the far side of the thin walls. Light, womanly: old Mrs. Von Vorst approaching softly over a worn carpet?

A slight, scholarly little man with green-tinted glasses looked up at her with surprise. "Miss Clifford? How prompt you are. Well!" Still gazing up at her. What was it he hadn't expected? Did he see a family resemblance? Was Cleva coming back to haunt him in the shape of a great-niece?

"Yes, the taxi came pretty fast." She entered the room talking, putting comfortable, mundane words between herself and this yet unknown factor, this stately little man who was, just now, bowing her so charmingly into a lamplit room which resembled a small greenhouse. "There was a traffic jam around Sixth, the last of the rush-hour traffic, I guess. . . ."

"Yes, yes," he agreed happily. "Let me take your coat. That chair—I think you'll find it the most comfortable." It was clearly his chair. Everything was arranged around it. Reading lamp, evening newspapers, which had been re-folded neatly and laid on the carpet beside the chair, a footstool with a petit-point swan floating calmly inside a circle of roses (worked by Mrs. V.?), and a round mahogany table containing various useful items arranged within easy reaching distance upon a plastic place mat: a magnifying glass, a ball-point pen bearing the name of a fire-insurance company, a little glass bowl with paper clips, thumb tacks, Scotch tape, nail scissors, some stamps, and a needle with black thread in it. Facing toward the chair was a small framed photograph that looked as if it had been cut out of a book with the same nail scissors. Even Jane recognized the white-haired woman with her noble face. In this photograph she was sitting indomitably upon a wooden staircase, a rifle slung across the lap of her long skirt. The same woman, young and beautiful, at the budding of her career, looked down on Jane from an old yellowed poster tacked on the wall to the right of the chair. She wore a large black hat, much like the hat in the oval-framed portrait of Edith as a young woman. *"Charles Frohman presents Ethel Barrymore,"* said the writing on the poster.

This was obviously Von Vorsts's "corner" where he lived his inner life, watched over by the legendary actress, against his backdrop of greenery. There must have been a hundred potted plants, at least, crowded upon every free inch of surface, sprouting healthily down window ledges, sending thick rubbery shoots up from the floor, overflowing in clumps of dense spidery foliage from the ceiling. An avocado plant twined its tendrils boldly up a fan of grocery string stapled to the wall beside Barrymore's poster. Jane suddenly understood, from the orientation of this room, that only one person lived here.

Von Vorst had disappeared with her coat into an alcove, and now she could hear him running water into a sink, opening something with a can opener. He must be in his tiny kitchen.

"I *hope* I haven't interrupted your supper," she repeated, at a loss for something new to say.

"Oh, no!" came the disembodied basso profundo. It sounded much bigger than the wisp of old man. "Ethel and I had already eaten when you called!"

Jane stood looking uncomfortably from poster to small framed picture. Oh, no. She should have known. She heard herself telling Gabriel later: "And then it slowly began to dawn on me, he lived quite alone . . . only *he* didn't see it that way. . . . He looked remarkable for ninety, very thin and straight; he still had his own teeth and most of his hair, except right on top. He reminded me of those spry little professors emeritus you see at every university, walking to the library on nice days . . . but the disintegration in Von Vorst was where it couldn't be seen —in his mind. . . ."

He still had his Christmas cards standing on an old oak buffet. She tiptoed closer and peeked inside the nearest one. "Love and Happy Christmas from Val Winters and the cast of *Last Shadows,*" was written in red ink below the season's greetings. *Last Shadows!* Why, Edith used to watch that. It came on in the late afternoon, just about the time mothers would be preparing supper. It was a strange mixture of adult soap opera and children's horror story (and most likely designed to be both, at such an hour), which presented the everyday episodes of several families in a small village in the foothills of the Catskills. One of these families, of German descent, had a streak of vampirism running through its male members and it was this extra touch which had sometimes attracted Jane, if she happened to be at Edith's at the hour of this program. "Oh, this is silly; why are we watching this?" Edith would say. "Let's turn it off and talk. It's one thing when I'm alone—I kind of enjoy it because it *is* so ridiculous—but now you're here." "Shh," Jane would say. "Let's just finish this one scene."

There was an old steamer trunk in the room. A curious greenish fur had been left on top. A cape? No, perhaps a muff. She did not have her glasses.

("And then, while he was still out there in his little kitchen, another possibility occurred to me. I saw the trunk, the kind actors keep costumes in, and the fur wrap, and I began to wonder: Is Von Vorst 'Ethel'? Did he dress up in turn-of-the-century gowns, moth-eaten furs, wide hats, and wigs, and become, in the privacy of his small lonely apartment, the great Barrymore herself?")

What fetish is waiting for me, she wondered, round the corner of the next century? In 2030, or thereabouts, what secret thing will I be doing? Please, God, *let* it be secret. Let it be something I can do with dignity, within the four walls of my rented rooms.

Von Vorst emerged with a tea tray. He really was sprightly. Jane noticed he wore Hush Puppies, like Ray. The tea tray was lined with a clean cloth that had crocheted edges. On it were a very small bottle of Drambuie with the seal still on, a green bottle with no label, two exquisite little wineglasses of red cut glass, and a Chinese bowl full of salted peanuts.

"Please sit down, Miss Clifford. Do take that chair!"

Jane sat down in Von Vorst's chair, resolving to get through this hour with a mad old man as graciously as possible. She was touched by his prompt offering of refreshments. She recognized that urge she had often felt herself—as soon as company came, to get something in front of them at once, to make sure they would stay.

"Oh, how nice . . ." she began.

"I'm sorry, Ethel, dear, but you will have to move," said the old actor, tugging at the handle of the steamer trunk. "We need this as a coffee table."

The greenish fur slowly unfurled itself. Two yellow eyes glowed toward Jane's chair. The largest cat Jane had ever seen slowly swelled into standing position on the moving trunk as Von Vorst navigated it across the carpet and between the two chairs. Then she arched her back like a showy Halloween poster cat and plunged straight into Jane's lap.

"Shame, Ethel. What if the lady doesn't like cats?" Von Vorst put down the tea tray.

"It's all right," said Jane. "I'm flattered. Ethel, you are so trusting!" She stroked the animal, who set up a loud mechanical purr, folded her front paws neatly in half, and settled in like a stone.

"She *is* trusting, though she has every right not to be. When I met her she had just narrowly escaped death at the hands of two child actors who dropped her out of a third-floor studio over at C.B.S. to see how she'd sound," said Von Vorst. "She landed on her feet, didn't you, Ethel?"

The cat narrowed her eyes. She opened her mouth in a pink soundless *miaow*.

"That's because her voice box is gone," explained Von Vorst. "She shrieked herself silent on the trip down, so the little fiends got their 'sound.' Naturally, that was the end of her career. Ethel's voice, you see, was her living. Or so they say. I never heard it. So when I died in *Last*

Shadows, I took Ethel and we retired together. Will you have some Drambuie? I hope you like it. Ladies prefer sweet liqueurs, don't they? I went down to my corner place after you called, and it was a toss up between Benedictine and this. I do hope I chose right."

"Oh, I would love some Drambuie." Jane hated it.

"That's fine, then," said the old man, looking pleased as he peeled off the seal. "I think I will just stick with slivovitz. It's homemade, actually. Against the law. Don't tell anybody." He chuckled, poured Jane her Drambuie; then popped his own cork, rolled his eyes wickedly, and tipped a healthy dollup of a clear liquid into his own glass.

"Let's drink to your project, Miss Clifford, whatever it is." He clicked glasses with her. "I am hoping you will tell me more about it." Taking a deep draught from his glass, he added: "It's my one wickedness, this slivovitz. But at my age don't you think a person is entitled to a wickedness or so?"

What other wickednesses, Mr. Von Vorst? How about 1905?

"Oh, absolutely," said Jane, sipping convincingly at the thick syrupy liquid.

"I sometimes have the sneaking suspicion I'll live forever," said Von Vorst gaily. "I have survived so many deaths. I've been dying in one form or another since I was seventeen. Poor Ethel and I, they can't kill us off."

"I've watched *Last Shadows* a few times," said Jane. "I wonder if I ever saw you. Though I'm sure I'd remember your voice. It's very memorable."

"Thank you. I have been told so. I was old Uncle Drew. I've been playing old somebody-or-other for decades now. I was supposed to be part werewolf. Nobody could ever see me in mirrors, that kind of thing."

"No, there was no uncle in the episodes I saw. I do remember the Drew family, of course. Actually, I watched it with my grandmother. Whenever I would go South on a visit." And Jane named the town, watching him carefully.

Von Vorst blinked. He was giving her that *surprised* look again, the way he had done at the door. Jane was embarrassed. She felt she had come too close, too soon.

"Have you played mostly villains during your career, would you say?" she asked.

"Predominantly villains, yes." Von Vorst crossed his thin legs and rearranged himself proudly, aloofly. He held his glass rather theatrically, becoming the important celebrity who condescends to be interviewed. Oh, God, thought Jane, what if he thinks I am doing some definitive study on melodrama and gets his hopes up, thinking I plan to immortalize him or something? "I talked about all that in my article," he said. "Please don't let me forget to give you a copy. I had some made. It really was a nice article. Even though the fellow was put on to me by the scriptwriter who wrote me out of *Last Shadows*. He felt bad about it, and he should have. It was a perfect part for me; I could have gone on forever. Everyone knows werewolves live for centuries. But no, he had to 'reform' me so I could die a good Christian death. The sponsors demand that sort of thing every so often. So I was out of a job again, and they're not easy to get at my age. Parts for dying old men are not easy to come by. Whereas villains are always in demand. I was never out of work when I was a villain. Yes, everybody loves a villain."

"Do you think that is true? I have often wondered about that very thing. Why is it, do you think?"

"It takes the strain off. There's a part of us that gets tired of being good and goes looking for trouble. If that part can be satisfied through an entertainment form, all the better for society. I remember when I played Sikes in *Oliver Twist*. First I dragged poor Nancy round the stage by her hair (really a powerful wig), and as I did so, I looked up deliberately at the gallery. My own innovation, that. As if defying them, you see, defying the forces of justice to stop me. And, as if on cue, they howled and cursed me. Whereupon I dragged her round the stage again, more defiant than ever, and they howled and cursed even louder! We were working together, that audience and myself. Sometimes this went on for five or ten minutes; I would drag it out, you see, depending on the audience. Some audiences are more responsive than others. Then, at the climax, I covertly smeared her with red ocher—she helped me, actually—and dashed her brains

355

out—right on stage. Then you understood about the side of us that wants trouble! How they shrieked! How they howled! How they hi*ssss*ed!" and Von Vorst hissed so menacingly that even Ethel was aroused. She rumbled her appreciation from Jane's lap, opened her mouth in a second silent *miaow,* and rolled over on her back; her large paws began treading in some invisible substance. "Hundreds, *thousands* of enraged voices!" boomed Von Vorst, working himself up in this lamplit room, brandishing his slivovitz. "Pure Bedlam! Deafening! The roar of a thousand escaped menageries!"

Jane was infected. She took a large sip of Drambuie before remembering she didn't like it. Huge Ethel was so warm on her lap. What on earth was she pushing at with her paws like that? Jane had never owned an animal in her life. It suddenly occurred to her that this was a loss. Well, there was still time to end up an old maid with her cat.

"After Nancy was dead," went on Von Vorst, in a whisper now, "bloody and battered, lifeless—a mere heap of lifeless flesh on the stage—I came forward, right up to the footlights, and took my bow. That was the practice for a villain, you see. And you should have heard them then! Every person in that theatre became his own villain —in the cause of justice, of course, which made it all right. You should have heard their language, their vile epithets! They shouted at me all the terrible things they would like to do to me, tear out my entrails—worse things, things that wouldn't be good enough for what I deserved. And at the end of the play, they all left the theatre mild as lambs, purged of all their violence."

"Oh," said Jane. "You make me sorry I have only *read Oliver Twist.*"

"Yes," concluded Von Vorst, a slight tremor in his voice from his declaiming. "Villains had their use."

"But there are villains today, too, aren't there?"

"Well-l-l," drawled the old actor. "Yes and no. Now they are so believable. Today, a villain always has a *side*. He's no longer all bad, all wicked. He affects no waxed mustache, no stealthy step nor evil eye, no hollow voice. He no longer consorts with other vile degenerates in foul and frowzy dens of iniquity. Your today's villain is often a sympathetic character who has a perfectly good psychological excuse for wrecking the lives of others. He may murder or heartlessly seduce or blackmail or extort, but he pays his psychiatrist and insures his life for his family, you can bet your boots. And this kind of villain throws off the whole process of catharsis, don't you see?"

"Yes, I do," said Jane. When, when was she going to learn that nothing was ever quite as she imagined it was going to be beforehand? Far from "humoring" a mad old man, she was being instructed.

"He's too realistic, your modern villain," said Von Vorst. "That confuses the audience. 'He's an ordinary Joe like me,' they say; and off they go—you read it in the papers every day—out to perpetrate his colorful crimes on the real world. The merit of melodrama, you see, was its exaggeration, its very *un*naturalness. For, with all of its sweeping gestures and grimaces, its declamatory style of speech, it succeeded in duplicating our fantasies, our primitive instincts, our night fears. Our dreams, I have come to believe, are pure melodrama. We are always declaiming, exaggerating, stomping and running about, hamming everything up. Melodrama," and Von Vorst paused dramatically, looking intently at Jane through his green-tinted glasses, "melodrama is the naturalism of the dream life."

"Oh, I want to remember that. I wish I had brought a little notebook I have," she said.

"Your notebook," he murmured, and there was something in his tone which indicated he would have expected her to bring her notebook. "Well, never mind. Most of what I just said can be found in my article, which I shall present you with before you go. As I think I have said, I have thought about these things quite a bit. What exactly *are* you doing on the subject, anyway, Miss Clifford, if I can be so bold to ask?"

"Well it's—nothing world-shaking," she said. "I mean, it's not a huge book, or anything like that. I've lately become interested in drama, the way drama relates to the way we live our lives, the parts we act, even if we have never taken a bow before the footlights. More and more,

Mr. Von Vorst, it seems to me, we are always in some play or other. Some of us move about, trying different plays, others of us stick doggedly to one role throughout our lives. What I am interested in is: do we create the roles, or do they create us." She paused and took a long sip of Drambuie. To her surprise, she had finished it. Von Vorst still had half his slivovitz. To cover her embarrassment, she ate a handful of nuts, hoping to distract him from noticing.

The perfect host, he simply uncorked the little bottle, refilled her glass, then refilled his own to the brim. "Do go on," he said. "It isn't often I am stimulated, mentally. And you get so excited about things. You should have gone on the stage. Did you ever consider it?"

"One of my colleagues tells me she thinks teaching is three-fourths acting," Jane said. She took a sip of the new Drambuie, then plunged on. "No, the only person in our family who had acting aspirations was my great-aunt Cleva. Cleva Dewar. She came to New York in 1905, on the train." She ducked her head, stroking Ethel for reinforcement. "Is the name at all familiar to you?" She was hot in the face and could not even reap her reward, catching him red-handed, letting him see that she saw his guilty face.

"*Do*-er. How is that spelled? Like the Scotch whiskey? Can you remember what she played in? Did she have any big parts?"

"No big parts," said Jane, looking up now, straight into the old villain's face. (*Sister I am in grave trouble please can somebody come the villain has left me.*)

But there was nothing. The old eyes behind the green-tinted glasses were calm, meandering along with his mind in a mild, polite curiosity as he said, "Cleva. What an unusual name. I don't believe I have ever heard it before. It would make a marvelous stage name. What does it mean?"

"I don't know. I never thought about its meaning before now."

"Cleva Dewar," repeated Von Vorst, testing the words slowly on his lips. "No, I don't think I recognize the name at all."

"I don't believe she ever had a major role," said Jane. "She probably has no interest for anybody, outside the family. Besides, she's been dead since 1906."

"What a shame," said Von Vorst. "Was it typhus? I had a brother die of typhus in 1906. It was very sad. He was only twelve and my poor mother never got over it."

"Is—Von Vorst a German name?" pursued Jane, but listlessly. Her "detective work" she considered at an end. Von Vorst was either a superb actor or he had truly forgotten Cleva. She imagined a very old Gabriel, many years from now, with someone asking him, "Does the name Jane Clifford mean anything to you?" *"Jane Clifford,"* he would say, perhaps spelling the last name. *"No, I don't think I recognize that name at all."*

"Von Vorst is my stage name. My father was in vaudeville, you see, when I began playing the melodramas. He didn't want us confused. So I made up Von Vorst. 'Sir Worst,' some of the actors used to call me. It sounded sinister, *foreign.* More foreign, I mean, than Varga. My father was a Hungarian Jew, but he was born here."

"Oh, I see," said Jane, remembering Edith's entreaty about staying away from little German boys who wanted to take her to the movies, because the villain had been German. "I wonder, do you think your—villainy onstage ever tempted you to be villainous offstage?"

"Not really," said Von Vorst. "That's a very common misunderstanding people have, however. You're certainly not the first. No, Miss Clifford, you will find that, offstage, the most famous villains have been the mildest of men. The celebrated O. Smith, for instance—he was before your time, of course—was in private life the shyest of mortals. For his own amusement he painted watercolors and collected butterflies. Yet onstage there was no one more gruesome than he!"

"And Von Vorst, who bashed out brains onstage, in private life cultivated many varieties of green plants and took in unemployed cats," said Jane.

This delighted the old man. "Do you know, that's what the young fellow who wrote the article said! In more or less the same words!"

"Well, there must be some truth in it, then, mustn't there? Did you—in those days when you played villains, did you ever find that young ladies were frightened of you offstage?"

Von Vorst laughed merrily. "Quite the contrary, I'm afraid. I will make a confession to you, Miss Clifford. Offstage, I never frightened anyone, and especially not young ladies. In fact, how I wished, in private life, to *be* more frightening, but it was not to be. And, of course, now it matters very little. 'Give me bless'd Age, beyond the fire and fever,/Past the delight that shatters, hope that stings, and eager flutt'ring of life's ignorant wings.' I love that little poem more each year. Sir William Watson. No, it matters very little now. Socrates was said to have been pleased about getting old, no more fire and fever. Though I didn't go in for Socrates' sort of delights. I never married, however. Sometimes I wish I had; more often I'm relieved I didn't."

"So you have no family?"

"None, except Ethel."

Jane thought of Frances. It was in her power to reconcile these two, father and daughter, in a sentimental Dickensian embrace. And the audience inside herself who went in for sensational dènouements was indeed whispering: "Tell him, tell him. Make something happen! Think how exciting it would be." But she saw Frances's lips tighten as she made her way up in that obscenity-annotated elevator, clutching her pocketbook to her breast like a mother protecting her child. Jane could read her thoughts, going up in that elevator: "Oh, dear, of course it is my duty . . . I wonder if he will want to come and live with us . . . or will he want a lot of money? . . . Perhaps he's not even my real father; perhaps she . . . I can't call her my mother, I can't! I never even knew her! I love my other 'Mama.' Oh, why—oh, why couldn't that earnest little cousin of mine have kept her nose in her books, where it belongs, instead of putting it into my business?"

"We make out all right, the two of us," Von Vorst was saying. "Human things matter less and less, I find. Perhaps that is nature's way of getting us ready to say goodbye to them. Though I must admit she's taking her time with me . . . and Ethel. Eh, Ethel?"

The cat twitched her right ear.

"She knows we are talking about her. Ethel is fifteen years old, Miss Clifford. For a cat to live to fifteen is as rare as for a man to live to one hundred and five, did you know? In cat years, Ethel is one hundred and five years old."

"You named her after Ethel Barrymore, didn't you? Were you a great admirer of hers?"

"I knew her. Do you see that little picture? That's Miss Barrymore in *Farm of Three Echoes*. I did most of the lighting for it. That's when I got to know her. What a warm and witty woman she was! I will always treasure our chats together. She played a ninety-seven-year-old woman in that play; it was a melodrama, of sorts, about South Africa. She told me how she painted her teeth white to make them look false and how a psychiatrist wrote to her that her performance was the most magnificent portrayal of senility he had ever witnessed. She was so pleased over that, I remember. . . ."

Von Vorst yawned. Then remembered he had company and tried to turn it into a sort of jaw exercise. "Slivovitz is so relaxing," he murmured.

Jane made up her mind to be out of there in five minutes. She had not yet decided what to do about the Frances thing. If what Von Vorst said was true—about human things mattering less as he grew older—what right had she to foist Frances on him, Frances who was all too human? They seemed to have done all right without each other up till now. But: to deny him the family he never had, when only a few words . . . But what if he denied Frances, as he denied Cleva? I'll think of something, thought Jane. I'm not—I have never been—a spur-of-the moment person, so why should I be now when it's not even my own life in question?

"How do you make slivovitz?" she asked. "Ethel, try and loosen yourself from your beautiful comfort. The visitor has to catch a plane."

"Come, Ethel!" called Von Vorst. "You don't have

361

to rush off so soon, Miss Clifford. You just arrived. You haven't told me a thing about yourself. I've done all the talking. I make it with cherries, though some people use plums. Cherries, sugar, and—well, ordinary denatured alcohol. I wouldn't advise you try it. You won't, will you? Val Winters, the producer of *Last Shadows,* insisted on wresting the secret recipe from me and almost succeeded in killing himself and his wife. It's a special process; it takes patience, which most people don't have. Since then, I advise people to buy it at their local package store."

"I promise I will not try any experiments in my bathtub," said Jane, nudging Ethel. The animal looked up, twitched her ear, but refused to budge. "I'm afraid I really must *begin* to get ready to leave," said Jane.

"Here, let me rescue you," Von Vorst said. He rose and plucked Ethel from Jane's lap. She immediately fastened herself to his frail shoulder and began purring like a motor. "She sleeps a lot these days," said the old actor. "Well, perhaps I will, too, when I am her age. I do beg your pardon about the way she's imposed herself on you, but, you see, she thinks of it as her chair, no matter who's in it. The person matters very little. It's like an extra cushion on the chair."

"Human things matter less and less to her, too, perhaps," suggested Jane.

"Exactly!" cried Von Vorst. "Miss Clifford, I'm very, very sorry I never had the privilege of being a student in your class. I'm sure I would have learned many things. You know, a friend of mine has a theory—I wonder what you'll think of it. He says the dead feel the need to go on learning; they feel short-changed if there was knowledge available in their lives that they didn't take advantage of while living. One night he heard sounds in his library, and he got his gun, thinking it was a burglar, and crept downstairs, and there was his dead mother ransacking his Encyclopaedia Britannicas. She'd been dead for almost fifty years, but there she was; he said she was reading three of them at one time and the pages of all three were turning by themselves! He fled upstairs, locked his door, and spent the rest of the night shaking. By the next morning, he had convinced himself it was a dream. But when he went down to check his Britannicas, they were all out of order; one of them was even put in upside down. Now what do you say to that?"

"I don't see why not," said Jane. "As for myself, I certainly hope somebody will allow me the use of their library after I'm dead. I will certainly want to look up all the things I didn't know when I was alive." She stood up. Time to go, before he yawned again.

Von Vorst stood looking up at her, Ethel slung over his shoulder like a fur. For the first time, Jane saw that he was really very short. Perhaps five feet two, or three. Yes, maybe he had wanted to frighten a few women in his time, only to find that, offstage, they no longer looked up to him. "What a shame you don't live in the city, Miss Clifford. I would like to see you again. Perhaps we could even become friends."

"I get to New York occasionally. May I call you again the next time I come?"

The old man beamed. His eyes behind the green glasses sparkled, almost brimmed. "You wait," he said. "Just one minute!"

He went to the oak buffet and opened a drawer and fumbled about with some papers, folding and fussing. Jane saw him put a small piece of paper to his lips. Ethel uncurled herself from his shoulder and walked slowly down the line of Christmas cards. One by one, she knocked them to the floor with a neat sweep of her paw. At the end of the row, she sat down, pulled herself up regally, and turned to her audience.

"Brava, Ethel," said Jane. She clapped.

"Yes, brava Ethel," repeated Von Vorst. "You see, there will always be some discerning souls in this world who recognize a superior talent. Now did I understand you to say you were leaving on an airplane tonight?"

"I had planned to, yes."

"Then I would like to give you a little gift." He went to the shelf beneath his window and selected a small ugly green plant in a pot too big for it. "I transplanted it," he said, "from this," indicating a giant of a thing growing in two directions from a huge pot on the floor. It was so heavy and grew at such an angle that it had to be supported by wire. There were several pink flowers budding from its tough leathery dark-green leaves. "Don't worry about traveling with this. It endures superbly. It needs very little water, isn't fussy about light, and it lives forever." He laughed. "Like some people. It is very hard to kill this plant. It's from the *Crassula* family. Grows very slowly, but if you bear with it, you'll have one like this"—he gestured toward his monster with the pink flowers—"before you reach my age." He handed her the pot with the small ugly plant, an envelope with a stamp on it and a label bearing his name and address, and a Xerox copy of the *Post* article "The Last Villain Reminisces." She saw at a glance it was not a big article. It had a one-column photograph of a younger Von Vorst—in his fifties, probably. Running her eyes quickly down the print, she recognized, almost verbatim, several of the best things he had said tonight.

"You're very kind," she said. "I'll look forward to reading this, and I'll try not to kill the little plant. I've never had a plant before."

"Then it's time you did. I love my green things. We are not the only living things in creation, you know. And I hope you'll drop me a line in the envelope provided, and perhaps include a copy of the project about melodrama."

"It may be some time before I finish it. Actually, it's mostly in the planning stages, Mr. Von Vorst. I hope I might drop you a note before then, just to see how things are with you."

The old man bowed. "I would be honored. This has been an unexpected surprise for me. I can't begin to tell you how I've enjoyed it. If you insist upon going I'll just get your coat and a little plastic bag for the plant. I watered it yesterday, so it should be all right till next week."

"Every time I water it, I will think of you," she said, then added, with perfect inspiration, evolving out of the gift itself: "And just as it has its big relative in New

York, I hope you will think of me, Mr. Von Vorst, as a sort of relative. I am in a way, you know."

"Bless you, Miss Clifford. I wonder if I might kiss you."

Jane offered her cheek to the old villain. He stood on tiptoe and kissed her. A strong odor of camphor emanated from his sweater.

He went away, stooping a little, to get her coat. She heard him blowing his nose in the little kitchen. Then he had a coughing spell. He returned, fussed considerably over a plastic bag and rubber-band arrangement for the spindly *Crassula* plant. Ethel had slumped lifelessly on the exact spot of her last bow on the buffet. Her eyes were nowhere to be seen. Once again, Jane saw a queer, moth-eaten, greenish fur flung down carelessly upon a piece of furniture.

Von Vorst walked her to the door.

"You looked at me so strangely when I came," Jane said, trying one last time. "Why was that, Mr. Von Vorst? Did I remind you of someone? You seemed surprised, somehow."

"Oh, did I? I suppose I did." The old eyes blinked behind the large green-tinted glasses, very slowly, like eyes under water. "It was because—well, to be honest, Miss Clifford, because you were pretty. I somehow hadn't expected that from our conversation on the telephone. Will you forgive an old man for such brashness?"

"There's nothing to forgive. Thank you. I'm glad you think so." She was genuinely pleased, though she didn't want to be. It canceled out Vincent de Lucca. "Just a minute," she said.

All right, Cousin Frances, you are to be spared. The U.D.C. and the D.A.R. need never know. I'll take on the burden of my own research. I found him and I'll keep him.

She went into her purse and tore off a piece of blank check, which had her name and address printed on it. "If you ever need me, Mr. Von Vorst, I'll be available."

He had trouble with the small print. Then she remembered the magnifying glass on the mahogany table. "It's my name and address," she said, "where you can

365

reach me." She wondered how much he did see, even with the aid of all his lenses. Perhaps that was why I seemed pretty, she thought.

"I think I'm going to be very sad in a few minutes," said Von Vorst, folding the piece of paper carefully. He looked as if he were about to fold, himself. The harsh light from the hallway ceiling truly made him look "like death warmed over." Had it all been tricks of light, then; the subtly maneuvered focusings of his audience's eye by a skillful old performer; an act of sheer energy and will which he was capable of sustaining for a limited time? He seemed to be crumpling before her eyes. She took his hand and squeezed it quickly, and they said their good-byes while he was still able.

He watched her all the way to the elevator, leaning against his doorframe, and when the slow thing came and she was, mercifully, on her way down, she heard his door close, and the click of a Yale lock. She imagined them, the two old troopers, wrapping themselves, exhausted, in each other for warmth, folding themselves back into the old steamer trunk with a sigh, and sinking into ancient, immobile hibernation: their long intermission, embalmed in camphor and mothballs, until some unexpected future audience happened along and summoned them for another command performance.

XVII

THE desk clerk handed her a message with her key. She started toward the elevator, reading it. *"Will try and be there at ten without fail. G."*

She stopped. The elevator came and went. So did the next one.

She went back to the desk.

"Yes, Ma'am." The clerk, a rather sullen-looking older man, had just sat down again. He was reading a detective novel.

"Could you get my bill ready? I have to check out."

He suppressed a sigh. "What room, please?"

"Nine-twenty."

He took his time in leafing through a file. When he pulled it out, he said with a little touch of malice, "I'm afraid I'll have to charge you for the full day, which ends at noon tomorrow."

"Of course," said Jane. She pulled the bills from her wallet. Ray's abortion money was dwindling considerably, with all these taxis and the lost dress. She had tipped too much for her Italian lunch, too. The clock above the desk said a little before eight. "Do you happen to know what time this message came in?"

"I really don't know. The operator takes those. It should have a time on it."

"Well, it doesn't."

"I'm sorry. But it's not my fault. Why don't you step around the corner and ask her? She's new—she probably forgot to put it on. This is not the Pierre, you know."

"No, I guess it isn't. I'll ask her." The man's seedy bitterness made her ashamed for him. She did not want to have to imagine the road he had traveled to reach this job.

The switchboard was abandoned. Two remaining slabs of peanut brittle lay in a pile of crumbs on a spread-out paper napkin. A tiny transistor radio was playing rock-and-roll. Jane waited for several minutes. Two circuits were ringing angrily. Then she turned with a shrug and headed for the elevator.

Back in 920 (she did not bother to close the door), she took a sheet of hotel stationery.

Dear Gabriel, The frustration is beginning to outweigh the joy of this affair . . .

She crossed out "affair," wrote "relationship" instead. Then crumpled the paper and took a fresh sheet.

Dear Gabriel: It has been quite a day for me. I have gone through many strange moods. Perhaps one day I'll tell you about this day. Among other things, I have thought a lot about how you said relationships must change if they are to continue for long periods of time, and I think, in some way yet unknown to me, ours is due for a change . . .

That was not true. She had not thought "a great deal" about what he said about relationships. Not today.

Dearest Gabriel, I have decided to go off by myself and think about things. It is not your fault, but I am becoming bitter. It seems there is always one more *restraint* on us that I hadn't bargained for. Also, I am not as "patient" as you would like to believe . . .

Of course it was his fault. If not, whose? Well, certainly it was partly his fault. And partly hers, for "being patient" so long.

Dear G. Have decided to take the 10 P.M. flight (United) from Kennedy . . .

368

Oh, Jesus!

"Dear Gabriel," she wrote on the last piece of hotel paper. Five sheets to a customer at this modest hotel. If she had been a guest at the Pierre, she might spend all night composing possible notes on an endless supply of elegant paper. *"I decided to leave. Jane."*

If she really meant it, that was all she needed to say.

She stopped off at his floor and slipped it under his door. Then out into the winter evening to hail yet another taxi.

On the way to the airport it began to rain. A terrible depression came over her. She pulled up her coat collar and sank into her coat, into the seat. She closed her eyes, listening to the hiss of wet tires, the steady thump-thump of the windshield wipers, and the click of the meter, eating up Ray's money which she would pay back as soon as she returned. Von Vorst's little plant in its plastic wrap was a nuisance. It kept falling over when she balanced it on her lap. She sank further into her coat and saw perfect sense in a life where you simply sank in a heap at somebody's feet and said, "I give up, you take over; life is a disease." And she thought of Edith, who had done this so successfully, first to Hans, and then to gentle death; Edith tucked away in her favorite blue robe, securely, for all time. The idea that she herself might have to wait for such eternal peace for decades—till this spindly plant, not yet three inches high, became the size of a small tree—seemed cruel to her.

Phrases that she recognized to have the sentimental, self-pitying, high-flown quality of bad acting homed in clusters to her mind.

Nobody's life would change drastically if I disappeared from the face of the earth.

I shall always be a stranger and alone. . . .

The only thing I can put my trust in is death.

A wet highway, an oil slick, headlights of oncoming cars distorted by rain . . . driver brakes and swerves, a sickening squeal of tires, collision . . . darkness. The world goes on in its usual routines. Gabriel nods politely at some departmental anecdote being related by Arthur Parsons

369

at the moment the state trooper searches through the dead woman's purse for identification, name of person to be contacted in case of emergency: Mrs. Ray Sparks. Kitty and Ray at home, perhaps going through Edith's things, old stocks, old railroad insurance policies, Hans's watches, handbook of Masonic rites, etc. Phone rings. Ray answers: he always answers first if he can. "Yes, this is her husband. What? I see. Are you sure, Officer? No, she's right here, but I'd better tell her myself." Ray breaks the news carefully, gently, going slow, watching his Belle Dame for signs of shock, perhaps making her drunk on brandy before he puts his capable arm around this woman who's had too much to bear already this week, and says (cannily selecting the Ally most likely to rate with Kitty), "I want you to remember, darling, this above all things: the Lord works in strange and mysterious ways . . ."

Back "without fail" at ten, Gabriel would find the note, *I decided to leave,* slipped under his door. He would feel sad, puzzled, hurt, perhaps, until he remembered the eye of eternity. Perhaps console himself with an apple, shake his head slowly as he climbed between the cold sheets by himself. After a few weeks, still unaware that she had ceased to exist altogether, he might dial her number. "I'm sorry, sir, that number is no longer a working number." "Ah," he would say to himself after thanking the operator politely, "I guess she meant business, after all."

Jane felt as if she had died. As a punishment for not living life fully while on earth, she was doomed to travel perpetually back and forth between airports. Her ghost would be visible only in the rear-view mirrors of taxicabs, in airports and aboard planes.

When we perform acts that change our lives, there is a certain mad quality like a dream. She heard herself telling this to Sonia Marks, telling Sonia the whole story about herself and Gabriel. "For almost two years it was idyllic. It was enough, even with all the built-in restraints of our situation. I saw this man standing in a small lecture room—he was too big for his petty surroundings—and then the lights were turned off and I heard him calmly and stubbornly battle the forces of petty, deadly irony, and

370

I felt as if I were watching a morality play between Pessimism and Optimism and I chose Optimism for my hero, pessimistic as I am. Then I went away and dreamed about him and I wrote him a letter and he came into my life. I dreamed him and then summoned him with words and he answered, he responded. For almost two years we floated down together, wrapped in idyllic love, until, one January night, we touched the earth again. It was a rainy, winter night, and I lost sight of all good weather. I wrote him a note and then slowly began to undream him."

She opened her eyes, disgusted with herself. She was far from being dead. Here she was rehearsing for a future scene.

Sonia would want to hear more. "How beautiful and sad and—well, I'll have to admit, interesting, Jane. What different lives we lead! I have never lived alone and seen your dark fish surface in an ominous moment of circular time. I have never dreamed or undreamed a lover. But wasn't it difficult leaving like that? Just walking out? How did you make up your mind to do it?"

"I can't say. I'll never be able to put my finger on the exact second. All I know is that, within two hours, something shifted. At six o'clock one evening, I couldn't have done it, and at eight o'clock the same evening I did it. A few small factors intervened, but nothing monumental. It was simply that the grains of salt piled up, I suppose, in my cup of grievances, till there was no more room in the cup. Or . . . I don't know. Perhaps it started much earlier. I remember, after my grandmother's funeral, I was sitting by myself in the kitchen, drinking Scotch, and I suddenly felt like saying some words. The words were 'Let us drink to the end of our idyllic love.' Then my hand raised the glass to my lips and I found myself drinking this toast I didn't even want to drink. Or at least I told myself I didn't want to."

"But you did! God, the fascination of the psyche," Sonia would say.

But then she remembered Gabriel, the reality of Gabriel, and this premeditated victory chat with Sonia Marks fell flat. Victory over what? She saw, as if it were before her, his grave, smooth face, the way it shined on her, took her into the moment with him, and the way they had been together in the blue light of yesterday afternoon. I would rather have had fourteen meetings with him than a lifetime with any other man I have met in my entire life so far, she thought. And she went over all the good things he had said to her, all those phrases that had reverberated for weeks and months afterward, phrases good enough to keep her hopeful for months alone, because they stressed the things that didn't fade, the things that went on existing in the one eye that really mattered: the good old eye of eternity. She dwelt gratefully on his patience, his dependability, his punctuality—which had never once failed her before that night. Perhaps this very failure was a gift to her, a way of letting her know he would understand if she felt she could not take anymore of this idyllic love. And she thanked him in her heart for appearing to her at that hour in her life when she could have gone either way—why, if he had not asserted how important it was to believe in something and go on researching it, however unfashionable it was, she might now have joined the Zimmers of the world, the great majority, who went around defiling all that they secretly held dear.

If it was so good, why don't you go back? Tell the driver you've changed your mind and please will he turn around and take you back. You can explain to the desk clerk that you missed your plane or remembered an important engagement, and besides you are paid up until noon tomorrow. Then up to 920, fling down your suitcase, back down to sit outside Gabriel's door, and when he comes you laugh and say, "I wrote you this insane note. I must insist that you let me have it back." "Well, of course," he will say, looking curious, but not desperate to know, as is his fashion.

What is this, anyway? Do you really want to be here? Speeding away in the rain, with nothing but two long boring flights and an empty apartment waiting at the other end? It's not too late to reconsider. What is this drama? Did you choose it? Or are you letting some facile director, eye on the sensation-loving audience, force you into this premature dènouement? Where do *you* really want to be at 10 P.M.? On a plane bound for O'Hare, or in the arms of the man who taught you to believe in good weather?

I want . . . Oh, God, I don't want to be *patient* in somebody's eyes. I want to be *first*!

And thus she found herself at the airport, early as always. Almost an hour to kill. And she was informed at the ticket counter that her connection out of O'Hare was nine o'clock tomorrow morning.

A wraith in a brown imitation suède coat, balancing a spindly plant on her lap, watched her reflection against the clear plastic of the phone booth as she dialed a long-distance number.

"Gerda? I hope I didn't wake you."

"Who is this—Jane? God, no, I haven't been to bed for days! You wouldn't believe what a mess everything is here!"

"What's the matter? Did your apartment flood again?"

"No. Natural catastrophes I can handle. No, it's the paper. I can't tell you the mess I'm in. We were all pasted up, and then this bitch chickens out and withdraws her article. It would have been sensational! She's the wife of a very powerful union leader here. She opened her mouth and told all, we taped it and wrote it up and I sent her the proofs, and that goddamn husband of hers told her—do you know what he told her? Listen to this: 'As far as I'm concerned,' he said, 'if you want to be separate but equal, you are going to find yourself equal but separate from me!' So the fool chickened out and now we have three fucking columns of empty space. I've been up for forty-eight hours, writing a filler. I'm calling it 'One Hundred and One Ways He Uses You Every Day.' I'm only on fifty-two and the dummy's due at the printer's tomorrow at ten. Well, where are you? How did it go?"

Jane asked Gerda if she could put her up for the night. "I wanted to go straight through, but there's no flight till morning. I could be there around midnight."

"Oh, God. What a minute. The trouble is, I've got this woman staying with me. The awfulest thing—Eleanor Tibalt. Her husband is the famous neurosurgeon here, Francis Tibalt. Well, my dear, true to form, he took her out of medical school thirty years ago, to support

373

him and raise his four boys, and now he's left her and gone and married a beautiful young student, an intern who is going to go into neurosurgery. She's a wreck. A friend of mine at the University of Chicago told me about her and I called her up, thinking she might want to contribute her story to *Feme Sole,* but she's too reticent for that sort of thing. . . . Anyway, we got along fabulously and she's moved in. She does the cooking and makes the coffee for the staff. . . . She is a gem, though she can't get out of her wife-and-mother role. You'd like her, she's a perfect lady, but Jesus fucking Christ has she ever been had. Anyway, the trouble is she's got your bed, the bed where you always sleep, but you're welcome to the couch. Where are you, anyway?"

Jane told her.

"But why are you there? I thought there were flights from your mother's place straight to Chicago."

"Well, I met Gabriel. He had to come to New York at the last minute and he asked me to come."

"Ah," said Gerda. Jane could tell she was a little miffed, that a friend of hers was still debasing herself in a relationship with a married man.

"Actually," said Jane, not liking herself very much, but wanting a warm welcome at midnight more than her self-respect, "I have just left the son of a bitch. Forever."

"Good girl!" shrieked Gerda. She put her hand over the phone. Jane heard her shouting something, then other voices shouting. "Come on," Gerda said, coming back on the phone. "We'll make a place for you. God! You finally went and did it! You finally woke up! Maybe you can help us with our hundred and one ways. Listen! Be thinking on the plane, okay?"

Jane said she would and hung up. She felt nauseated. She went in search of a "LADIES," passed a newsstand. The February issue of the magazine for swinging women was on the stands. A woman in amber sequins, amber earrings, amber hair, and amber lipstick offered a dècolletage that plunged like a pointer straight into the month's leading article, advertised in white capital letters:

SIX SEXY WAYS TO RECOVER FROM A BROKEN AFFAIR!

Jane turned to the table of contents, then leafed through till she found the page. "Number 1: Find a new dress, the sort of dress that makes you look in the mirror and say, 'I would never DARE look like that!' Do dare! Buy it! Wear it!"

She remembered Marsha Pedersen. ("Then I tried it on again at home and said no, it was too low. He said I was the most maidenly woman he had ever met and this dress was just not maidenly.")

*You are the most maidenly woman I have ever met.
Thank you for being so patient.*

You are the most patient woman I have ever met; you are the most————woman I have ever met, because that's what I want you to be, by God.

Jane replaced the magazine and hurried in search of the ladies' room. Just in the nick of time, she got her dime in the slot, put down her purse and the plant, and threw up her triumphant Italian lunch and Von Vorst's Drambuie. Then she washed her face, rinsed her mouth, and found her gate. She sat down with her back to the people and stared through the large glass. Huge planes taxied in and out, to and from the runways. Blades of rain cut across their lights. The great machines nosed docilely into their slots, were emptied and filled with human cargo, then pushed out again. For all the powerful, expensive machinery which equipped them to soar thousands of feet above the earth, they lacked the ability to back up on their own. She found this touching and strange.

Gerda Mulvaney, nèe Miller, who was at the moment between number fifty-two and fifty-three of the "One Hundred and One Ways He Uses You Every Day" for her feminist newspaper, had walked into Jane's dormitory room one early spring evening twelve years ago, sat down on the plaid Bates bedspread, lit a cigarette, and said, "Do you know Bobby Mulvaney? Judge Mulvaney's son? The one who wears a brace on his leg and walks with a cane? I've been thinking. I might marry him."

"I didn't know you knew him that well," said Jane. She did not know what else to say. She had known Gerda four months and that was long enough to know she was capable of doing what she now proposed. And Jane also knew, from the conversations they had had, most of the reasons why.

"I've had coffee with him several times. After class. We have Economics together. He's extremely bright. He's already been accepted in the law school here for next fall. I like it here. I think it might work out very well. He's a very manly person; I think he will be very important someday. After all, F.D.R. wore braces on his legs. I've been thinking. We could get married in June, just after we both graduate, and then next fall we could get a nice apartment here and I would do all the things for him he has to do for himself. You know, he is planning to live in a *dorm* next year, because it's close to the law school. But I could drive him to classes from our apartment. I might take some economics courses myself, graduate courses, or, I don't know, at the moment the idea of just being the indispensable wife appeals to me."

"It might work out," Jane said, trying to sound positive. "Yes, I've seen him. He does have a good manly look about him. And who knows, maybe his legs will get better. But look, has he said anything?"

Gerda whooped with laughter. "No, his legs aren't going to get any better. There you go, off into one of your novels again. He's had therapy since he was twelve. The very *best,* I can assure you. No, he hasn't said anything yet, but I can see how he looks at me. I only decided on this today, about wanting to marry him. I thought I'd ask you first, before I started things rolling."

"Me? I'm not going to marry him. As a matter of fact, I have no idea what I'm going to do in June. I don't even want to think about it. I like it here, too. I wish I could stay forever. Why are you asking me?"

"Because. You're my Doppelgänger. The nice one. I just wanted to check with you to see if I was being too awful."

Jane and Gerda had become friends through being mistaken for each other. An ambitious, silly girl, campaigning for next year's Student Council, had made each increasingly aware of her "Double" by hailing Gerda eagerly every time she saw Jane, and calling out chummily

"How goes it, Jane!" every time she ran into Gerda on campus. Both of them were fair-skinned, with light eyes and curly, thistle-textured hair, which they wore in the currently popular style: teased into a crown of fluffy waves on top, cut short as a boy's on the sides and back. A saleslady in a store, leading them to the size tens, might easily take them as sisters, or confuse one with the other if they came in separately. Or a girl with politics on her mind, bent on shouting a name every time she saw a face, might do the same. There it stopped, however. The features of the two were quite different. Gerda's tended to tilt up, Jane's went down. Also their expressions. Gerda affected, quite often, a sly, mysterious half-smile. Jane wrinkled her brow into various lines of puzzlement, and people were always telling her to stop frowning. But the two girls liked this idea of the "double" and cultivated it in their conversations, and purposely made it a symbol in their friendship. It gave each of them a secret feeling of expansion, of being more than one person. "Miss Jekyll and Miss Hyde," Jane would joke. "The Girl Every Boy's Parents Hope He'll Bring Home and The Girl They Pray He Won't," Gerda would quip. Each girl seemed bent on exaggerating the side of herself described by the other, as it became clear that Jane was shy and cautious and guilt-laden, hanging back from things when she would most like to reach out for them, and Gerda, who seemed to have had guilt left out of her, operated directly, sometimes ruthlessly, out of her primal needs and desires. They had even discussed the matter of "class," how their social class had shaped their personalities. Once, when Jane expressed shock after Gerda had shoplifted a twelve-dollar book on existentialism from the campus bookstore, Gerda said: "Honesty is in reality a form of snobbery. Only the very rich and the very secure can afford to be authentically honest. The bourgeois, the socially ambitious, who are really insecure as hell, like to affect honesty, in the same way they like to hang up those phony coats of arms in their living rooms." "I don't think that's true," said Jane, but the remark had stayed with her. It had made her question her own standards. *"Nice People don't act that way"*: Edith's favorite disciplinary sentence. And

Jane, who had never had any doubt in her head about wanting to belong to the group who knew themselves as Nice People, had responded. Was she *really* honest? What if she had been the daughter of tobacco hands, like Gerda? Why, it spoke miracles for Gerda's intelligence and determination that, coming from such a background, she would *want* a book on existentialism enough to steal it. Indeed, Jane usually considered Gerda her evolutionary superior. She had started so much lower, and here they were together, at the state university, on the same identical scholarship. Every month, each girl received the same check for the same amount of money from the business office. In the eyes of the award-granting world, Jane and Gerda were equals. Worth $280 a month, after the government took its cut.

And now Gerda had it in her head to marry Bobby Mulvaney, Judge Mulvaney's son. Well, why not? The drama of it appealed to Jane. She would like to watch such a love story happen. Perhaps it would work out. Perhaps in thirty years' time her eyes would be wet with tears as she watched on television as Bobby Mulvaney dragged himself to the podium to make his Inauguration Speech, a modest but well-dressed Gerda, who could now afford the virtues, smiled encouragement through her own tears.

In June, after graduation, Jane could go home and "rest" at Edith's. Edith had even suggested a little graduation trip to Europe: she had put aside money for this, she told Jane; she and Hans had planned to go to Europe, to visit his relatives in Bern, if he had lived, but now she had no business in Europe, whereas it might be just the thing for Jane, put the finish on her education. Jane had not told Gerda about this possible trip. She was afraid Gerda would say, "Well, how wonderful. You're all right, then. I wish I had a grandmother to send me to Europe, to 'Put a finish' on *me*."

In June, after graduation, what would Gerda do if she did not pull off some miracle marriage which would lift her out of "Millerdoom," as she sometimes cynically called it? Well, Jane thought, let's not be maudlin about this. Gerda, with a B.A. in Economics, does not have to rush home to the Miller shack, roll up her sleeves, and begin pulling tobacco. She could get a good job, in economics, perhaps devote her education to abolishing the very conditions that created "Millerdoom."

And yet she knew this as the unappealing, however noble, alternative it was. Like buying a pair of sensible shoes when you had been wanting, and not been able to have, an outrageously frivolous pair all your life.

But she wished Gerda had not asked *her* advice. The whole thing made her uneasy.

"But look, Gerda, don't you think there has to be a certain amount of mutual attraction for a marriage? I mean, say you did get him to fall in love with *you,* and ask you, do you think you could make it stick?"

"I don't see why not. Look, I already *like* him. I would be bringing him something and he would be bringing me something. I'm not a novel-reader, Jane; I'm not a starry-eyed romantic like you. I'm an *Economics* major. I believe marriage is an economic proposition; the whole world did, until literature confused the issue. Oh, yes. I learned that from you, from your A paper on how the troubadours from Provence changed the course of civilization, how they celebrated courtly love and nobody was satisfied anymore with sensible marriages. Though old Judge Mulvaney will see it as anything but sensible. Did I ever tell you my parents came up before him in Domestic Court when I was a little girl? My brother and I went, too. Did I ever tell you about what he said to my father?"

"No! What?"

"Well, my father and mother used to have these awful fights. He would beat her up and then she would swear out a warrant on him and he'd have to go before the court and pay a fine and then he'd come home and they'd cry together and screw. [Gerda never said "fuck" in those days; it was not yet fashionable.] And then he'd get drunk and hit her again and the whole thing would start over. Well, finally, Judge Mulvaney summoned the whole family. He said he wanted us all in court. I still remember being dressed up, along with my brother, and then we all took the bus into the county seat. My mother kept telling us, 'Please, you children, act like ladies and gentlemen before the judge.' She was so nervous, so embarrassed. Of course that's what the old son of a bitch wanted. When we got there, he had us taken to a private room. There was my father, looking sheepish, and my mother and us, and two welfare workers. One of them was the meanest-looking woman I have ever seen. Then Judge Mulvaney began talking to us, to the children. He asked us all the things children like to be asked: what grade we were in at school, what our favorite subjects were, what we wanted to be when we grew up, did we like animals. He was so soft-spoken and he had on this white suit; I had never seen a man in a suit so elegant, and the room was too warm, and as he talked to us every now and then he'd take out this neatly ironed handkerchief with his monogram on it and sort of *touch at* his face—never wiping it, or anything so vulgar. My father, of course, had no handkerchief and was sweating like a pig. My mother looked as though she was going to pass out any second. The welfare workers looked ready to whip out a net and whisk us out of our parents' sight forever. I remember thinking, I must not be taken over by this man, even though he talks so nice. My brother was long gone. I think he would have left my parents for the judge right then, just taken the judge's large, well-manicured hand and walked right out of there forever. I won't go over, I remember thinking. And I didn't. But I was terribly impressed. I knew he was different from us. And from the way everybody in that room was acting, I understood that he was supposed to be, that he was considered to be, by most people, better than my father. Then, in this very elegant, dramatic gesture, Judge Mulvaney put one had on my brother's head and one hand on my head. 'God has blessed you with two beautiful, smart, well-behaved children, Harvey Miller,' he said. 'Don't you think you ought to try and live up to them, be a good father to them, make them proud of you? Don't you think these two beautiful young people would be worth the effort of trying to behave like a decent man?' My father began blubbering. He was ready to have himself cut up in pieces and offered to us, he was so desolate and repentant. But I saw what that son of a bitch had done. I hated him. And yet I was attracted to him. He was like some sort of king or nobleman. I was seven years old then. And the judge had a little boy at home, little Bobby Mulvaney, who was the same age. He was a healthy, wealthy little boy then, able to run around and play. I've been thinking about this all week. How funny, that in that heat wave which brought on the last polio epidemic in our county, the rich safe little boy on the hill should have gotten it, and dirty Gerda and her brother, down in the fields, should escape. Don't you think that's strange? I've been thinking about it all week."

Jane agreed yes, it was strange, there were some strange coincidences in this story. She began to grasp widening, somehow chilling dimensions in Gerda's plans for Bobby Mulvaney.

"Still," she persisted, "I think you ought to love him."

"Well, who knows," said Gerda. "Maybe I will. It's perfectly possible, all things being equal."

Jane was in Switzerland paying a visit to a Barnstorff cousin, a widower who owned a jewelry store in Bern, on the first of July. He served her an impeccable tea in the back of his store, asking in correct, uninspired English after all her family, and showed her how to look through his little eyeglass and tell a real diamond from a fake. Jane kept watching the clocks in his store, counting off the hours till Gerda's wedding.

At American Express in Paris, she found a postcard from Gerda, sent from Nags Head, where she and Bobby were honeymooning in the judge's cottage. "We are making each other extremely happy. How is Paris? I'm going to get B. to take me someday. Write me c/o The Hon. Terence Mulvaney, Dunn, N.C., after July 21, Gerda."

Jane crossed the Channel to England. She calculated how soon she could return home without hurting Edith's feelings. She had discovered she did not like traveling, the process of travel. Her nerves were always on edge, she worried about making trains on time, and whether she was tipping enough or too little in these confusing foreign currencies. She went through agonies of embarrassment every time she tried to order a meal in French, or ask directions of a stranger. And felt guiltier and guiltier that she was not enjoying herself. Edith had not saved a thousand dollars so that she could mope around Europe, wondering why she could not behave like a happy-go-lucky young woman enjoying her graduation gift. She dutifully collected postcards at art museums, menus, little souvenirs—more for Edith than herself. She would wake up in strange rooms, to strange noises of morning in a foreign city, and her first thought was *When is my life going to begin?* She dreamed constantly that she was back at the university. Her unconscious seemed not to have caught up with the fact that she had graduated. Once she dreamed she and Gerda and Bobby Mulvaney were on a picnic together. Only, Bobby was not crippled; on the contrary, he was leaping country fences. "Don't you think he does well with his handicap?" Gerda asked Jane.

But London was different. Jane recognized it at once. She knew it intimately. It was like coming home, to your soul's home. She never got lost—not once. It was as though she carried a map of the city inside her head. If she wanted to see the courtroom where the case of *Jarndyce v. Jarndyce* was heard in *Bleak House,* she took a bus or a tube and went to Lincoln's Inn. If she wanted to sit in the church of Saint-Dunstan-in-the-West, where a vicar named Donne had preached every Sunday, she went to Fleet Street. The Carlyles lived on Cheyne Row, reachable by either a 19 or a 22 bus, and most of her favorite authors resided in Westminster Abbey. She looked in vain for George Eliot in Poets' Corner, was disappointed, but so much else was there. London was Jane's city.

She lost her shyness when she discovered that English people, not even Englishmen, did not look at her. She became bolder as she felt increasingly invisible. Yes, London was safe. It was like wandering around in your own imagination. She went into pubs and ordered warm beer and ate Scotch eggs and pickled onions right at the bar, poking them into her mouth with her fingers, washing them down with the gentle beer. She looked openly at people, studying their faces, their gestures, their clothes. The men wore bowler hats, just as the books said, and she knew from novels that "vests" here were worn under men's shirts and not over them, and that if she wanted to look at sweaters she should ask for "jerseys," and that "biscuits" were sweet and "cotton" did not grow in the fields here but was threaded through needles.

She wrote to Edith and Kitty that she was enjoying herself more than she had expected. She leafed through her traveler's checks and was thrilled to find she had been so stingy in Switzerland and France. She decided to spend the remainder of the summer in London, and checked out of the little Russell Square hotel and rented a bed-sitter in South Kensington out of the *Evening Standard*. Nothing was difficult for her here. The printed word transformed itself obediently into reality whenever she called upon it.

A large blond man with red cheeks came up to her in a pub. He sold real estate and played rugby for London Scottish on Saturdays. He invited her to a practice match. The season had not started. At tea after the practice match, he introduced her to a teammate: a shy solicitor's apprentice just down from Oxford. His name was James Bruton. He blushed every time he spoke to Jane and kept cracking his knuckles, which were raw and red from the cold, damp day. She told him how she had looked for George Eliot in vain in Westminster Abbey. "I shall ask my mother," he said. "I'm running down tomorrow. She knows where everyone is." He took Jane's address. She had no telephone because she hadn't been able to afford the twenty-five-pound deposit.

On the following Tuesday, Jane received a postcard from Kingston-on-Thames. "Dear Miss Clifford. My son has told me you couldn't find George Eliot. She is buried at Highgate Cemetery (because of her irregular alliance with Mr. Lewes—rather a shame, such narrow-mindedness!), but Karl Marx is also there, in Highgate. I should be pleased to see you at Willow Run Cottage any time you might be free to run down with James. Sincerely, Nancy Bruton."

James visited her Tuesday evening, and she agreed to drive down to Kingston-on-Thames with him on Saturday.

After it became clear to Jane, as it did with alarming

speed, that Nancy Bruton was determined to have her for a daughter-in-law, she remembered (and smiled to herself) Gerda's quip about "The Girl Every Boy's Parents Hope He'll Bring Home and The Girl They Pray He Won't." How true they were running to form! Almost too true. Before the end of the summer, Jane wrote to Gerda of her engagement. She and James would be married the day after Christmas—"Boxing Day," they called it. "How fast things happen to us," Jane wrote to Gerda, care of Judge Mulvaney's home. "And yet, like you, I think all is for the best. I feel I have known James for years." She missed Gerda. She longed for one of their "no holds barred" conversations. She kept waiting for English people to say something indiscreet, confessional, dangerous, to go too far in a conversation. But they never did. James spoke more in gestures, in feeling. He would bring her a small gift and his face would go beet red. Or very formally suggest a walk down to the river before tea, and then take her behind a willow and kiss her, reddening at his own boldness. She had her physical life with James and her mental life with his mother, and vaguely wondered if she was being peculiar in some way. But why not? She liked the idea of a shy young husband with his hard masculine body and a nervous, cultivated older woman who was so fascinated with human society, who loved to gossip about the same characters in novels. Jane thought the contrast was charming. And she did not want James's hard, pure masculinity to be dissipated into nervous, gossipy chatter about the Bennet girls or Marian Evans and Mr. Lewes. Mrs. Bruton also seemed to accept the division as perfectly natural: men were for husbands, other women were for talking to. She admired her own husband; she served him, even. But Captain Bruton, a retired naval officer, went his own way. He poured their sherry, (and port for himself and James), went on walks with his setter, and closed himself after lunch in his study, where he read naval histories. James and Jane spent every weekend at Kingston-on-Thames. James was cramming for his solicitor's exam. When his head was stuffed full, he would go off tramping in the woods with Captain Bruton and the dog. And Jane and Nancy Bruton would peel potatoes or mend socks and talk. During the week, the engaged couple ate supper together at Indian restaurants or took fish and chips back to Jane's bed-sitter. Later James went back to his own flat in Putney. Jane liked being with him, eating with him. He accepted her so easily as what she wanted to be, and did not go poking round in dark corners. With him she could be safe enough to do her own poking, in the privacy of her own mind. Such divisions did not bother her. Why inflict your nastiness on others? She hated to see him go and felt sorry for him when he got out of her bed around midnight, dressed himself in the chilly little room, and went back to Putney to study. They had both been virgins. They crept tenderly together, on these evenings, into the after-embrace, each repeatedly grateful that the other had not demanded more passion, more wildness. And yet Jane liked being alone in her bed again. She often read after he was gone. Or lay with a small lamp on, thinking about how softly she had slipped into her destiny, how unobtrusively her "real life" had begun. It had a very *English* beginning, my fate, she would think. During days, she went to the Tate and looked at the roomful of Blakes, or to the British Museum. James had managed to get her a pass. She was becoming fascinated with George Eliot. Most of her manuscripts were in the British Museum. Jane looked forward to years and years of going through them, learning the inner life of this tough-minded woman. She saw herself pursuing George Eliot's dramatic overcoming of her insecurities in the un-dramatic security of her own adopted English life, studying this braver woman's passage through the cold world while she herself sat in front of cozy fires, banked by a devoted and tender James, and marveled at Eliot's intelligence and stamina.

One November night, when James had left early, there was a knock at Jane's door. She thought he had come back for something. But it was Gerda, swathed in a huge fur coat and laden with luggage.

"Thank God!" she cried, wild-eyed. "You're home. I won't have to sleep on the streets. What's with you? Why don't you have a telephone? I tried to call you from the airport. Listen, do you have any change? I will die if I don't have a cigarette, and who is going to cash a twenty-dollar traveler's check in this deserted little neighborhood?"

Jane went with her to the tobacconist shop. She was shivering in her raincoat. It was cold and foggy. But part of her shivering was from sheer excitement at the way her wild-eyed friend had so beautifully disrupted the placid Kensington evening. Gerda's strident, demanding entrance somehow brought America back to Jane: the America English people hated and that Americans were always nervously defending. Jane was sure that *something would happen* now that Gerda was here. She was almost positive Gerda would tell her something shocking.

"Did—did Bobby come with you?" she asked as they entered the dingy little tobacconist shop. Knowing that he hadn't, somehow.

"God, no!" said Gerda loudly. "A pack of Luckies, please. No, wait. Look, can you spare enough for me to buy two packs? I'm a complete wreck. One pack won't last me the night. No, that's all over. Bobby Mulvaney and I are divorced."

Jane winced inwardly as the man behind the counter winced outwardly. There it all was in one outburst, he was thinking: Their noisy demanding, their impulsiveness, their greed, their exaggeration, their public airing of their dirty laundry. Then a surge of patriotism, suppressed during these last weeks when she was convincing herself she was becoming English, shot through her system like adrenalin. How small and dim and musty you are in here, she thought, you poor British stick-in-the-mud. She looked at Gerda in her fabulous fur coat dismissing his look, tumbling a handful of change absently into his resentfully outstretched palm, and she anticipated Gerda's dreadful news with an excitement unlike anything she had felt in a long time.

They sat up till dawn talking. "It's freezing in here. Can you put another shilling in the meter?" Gerda would say. And Jane would hurry out of the nest they had made of Jane's blankets and Gerda's coat, deposit a shilling with a *clang,* and the little bars of the small electric heater would glow again. "It's warm in this room for the first time," said Jane. And hurried back to cover herself in blankets and coat. "So, go on."

"Well, like I said, it started off surprisingly well. I really didn't expect it to go so well. The honeymoon was a bit of a drag, because—you know me. I like to show off at the beach and all that, and there was poor Bobby. My husband, in his new swimming trunks and leg brace. But at first I found his brace sexy. I have heard about women who get excited by going to bed with a man whose body has been damaged in some way—amputees, even. And, you wouldn't believe it, but Bobby Mulvaney was superb in bed. Really! He always satisfied me. He would go on all night, holding himself back, till he did. It was very gentle, very therapeutic . . . a bit boring. But I'm being horrible, please stop me. Oh, Jane, I'm going to end up in a horrible mess someday. I wanted this to work so much and in spite of myself I ruined it. Then we went to spend the rest of the summer with the judge. Oh, God, do you know that after Bobby would fall asleep at Nags Head, I'd take out my paperback copy of Amy Vanderbilt and go over my manners and which fork to use and red-wine glasses and white-wine glasses and so on. I was determined to make that arrogant son of a bitch fall for me and admit I was a good catch for his son. And we ended up hitting it off—for a while. We really became quite chummy. After dinner Bobby liked to read; he had already begun studying cases out of his father's lawbooks, he was so eager to get started in law school, poor thing. And the judge and I would play poker. I was a match for him and he liked it. He liked it when I beat him. I won two hundred dollars off him one night. Do you know, when I was growing up, two hundred dollars was a month's pay for my father? And then he insisted I take tennis lessons so he would have someone to play tennis with. He was astounded at how quickly I took to the game. We were playing real well before the summer was over. Bobby would lie in the hammock beside the court and smile at us from time to time. He'd have on his reading glasses and look up from his book, and he looked so handsome my heart would almost break sometimes. I was really contented, Jane. I can't tell you. I had everything I wanted. Oh, God, I hate myself for messing everything up! If we could only have stayed at the judge's forever! If only Bobby's law school hadn't started! If only we hadn't moved to that cramped little apartment!"

"But what *happened?*"

"Oh—" and Gerda got a funny smirk on her face, partly rebellion, partly shame. "Oh, I slept with someone and ruined everything."

"Ah! You found someone!" exclaimed Jane, understanding. "You found someone else."

"No, he was nobody. He was nothing. That's the whole point. It had nothing to do with him *or* with Bobby. I just had too much time and unused energy to myself—Bobby spent his whole existence studying those goddamned lawbooks—and so I went looking for trouble and I found it. I tried to explain that to the judge, but the bastard wouldn't listen. Oh, Jane, you should have been there for it. My day of downfall. Bobby calls me, about eleven o'clock one morning. I'm just on my way out to meet Si—that's the man. He was nothing; he wasn't even good in bed. Just a cheap know-it-all ex-Marine that wanted to get into my pants. He thought he could write poetry. Ha! 'I wanted to tell you that I won't be coming back,' Bobby says. I can tell he is crying. The old bastard was probably standing right behind him, prompting him with his lines. 'I've arranged to move back into the dorm,' Bobby says. 'It will be better that way.' Then he really blubbered and started to say something else like 'Oh, Gerda, why—' but the phone went dead. About a half-hour later—needless to say, I did not go to my rendezvous with Si—the judge knocks at the door of our little apartment. He's looking his usual elegant self, in a vicuña coat and gloves. 'Gerda, get your suitcase packed,' he says. 'We are going to have to make a one o'clock flight out of here from Raleigh-Durham. I suggest lightweight things. Do you still have those dresses you wore all summer? And take a raincoat, or a light-weight coat of some kind, and your marriage certificate. Oh, and better take your birth certificate. You have all those, don't you?' Well, my dear, before that day was over, we were in Juárez. He took a room next to mine and stayed close as a bodyguard till the whole thing was done. The law is terrifying, Jane; it's swift and mysterious and cruel, unless you happen to be on the right side of it. He tried his best to make me give up the name. 'I'll need it,' I said. 'I'm going to go to Washington and get a job.' 'Don't go to friends of mine,' he said; 'I'll see to it they cut you dead.' 'Okay,' I said, 'I'll go to your enemies. Or I'll get a job scrubbing the toilets in the Russian Embassy and make sure everyone knows my name is Mulvaney.' He died laughing, the bastard. 'Oh, Gerda, why did you have to be foolish and ruin it all,' he said. 'I had such hopes for you. You could have been a great asset to Bobby. You're the real stuff. You're tough as nails and pretty, and by the time I finished with you nobody could have told you were born Harvey Miller's daughter. Now you've gone and done this foolish thing and hurt my boy considerably. I'm sorry to lose my poker companion, but you have nobody to blame but yourself. Now I'll make a deal with you. Five thousand if you become Harvey Miller's daughter again; one thousand if you insist, against my wishes, to remain my daughter-in-law in name.' I took the one thousand. I said his name meant more to me that a measly four thousand, or even ten thousand. You know, he was secretly pleased. I could see it in his eyes. He stayed on in Mexico; he went to Acapulco to go deep-sea fishing with the Mexican finance minister. He knows everybody. And now I know nobody again. Except you. So here I am. I thought I'd come and talk to you and get myself together again. Can you put me up? This goddamned flight really bit into my 'bribe money.' Oh, God! When I think what a fool I was. He had pictures of me and Si—everything. It was almost as if he was waiting around for me to make a mistake. I was lucky to get the thousand. But look, I won't be a drag on you and James. I know you're engaged and I hope to hell it will work out for *you!* I can sleep on the floor and I'll buy my own food and cigarettes. I just need to get the image of myself back again, if you know what I mean."

"I know what you mean," said Jane. "Sure, you can

stay here. James will be delighted to meet a friend of mine."

"Oh, God! Wait a minute!" Gerda screamed. It was dawn. Day was beginning to show itself over the rooftops and chimneys of South Kensington. Jane shivered at Gerda's strange cry and pulled the thick fur coat up over her knees. She wondered if Judge Mulvaney had given Gerda this coat. "I've seen something! I knew I would understand things if I could come over to London and have it out with you! Do you know what I've just realized, Jane? Be prepared for something awful."

Jane said she was prepared. In fact, she thought she had already guessed.

"I HAVE JUST REALIZED IT WAS HIM I WAS IN LOVE WITH! I'VE BEEN IN LOVE WITH HIM SINCE I WAS SEVEN YEARS OLD!" Gerda began sobbing.

Jane put her to bed, where she slept without waking for sixteen hours. When they talked again, Jane said: "It's for the best that you left when you did. Think of the havoc you would have caused. The judge might have returned your love eventually, then think of the ruin. Perhaps *he* had already thought of it and wanted to get you out of there. This Si person was nothing, but the other would really be the end for Bobby. You were generous to go without a fuss when you did, Gerda. Try and think of it that way."

"Yes, I will try," said Gerda.

She stayed in London two weeks, was treated to meals by James and Jane, had her say to Jane about James. ("He's very nice. I think there's every chance you'll be happy. He's not *quite* your intellectual equal. You don't mind my saying that, do you?") Then James and Jane took her back to Heathrow airport and she embarked upon Washington. "Terrific things are happening here," she told them as they waited for her flight. "It's a new era. Youth and beauty and brains have hit Washington with this new administration."

"*Will* hit," James gallantly corrected, "a few hours from now."

Then Jane drove back to London with her fiancé, in his Mini-van. It was a smoky late November evening.

everything suddenly looked small and bare and dingy, disenchanted. Jane envied Gerda flying up and out of here, to mesh, within hours, with terrific happenings, the youth, beauty, and brains she considered her birthright. Gerda is flying *home*, Jane thought, homesick.

And then she fainted in church one Sunday, kneeling between James and his mother in the historic little Norman church. "Drink His blood," the old priest said, beckoning them to the cup. Jane had felt the English life closing in on her like a shroud, had seen black spots, had felt herself whirl away, and came to with James and his mother bending possessively over her. A week later, she quarreled irrevocably with Nancy Bruton over, of all things, the passports of her unborn children. "You'll give up your American citizenship won't you," said Nancy, "so the children can travel on your passport." "But I don't think I want to give up my nationality," said Jane. "And I want them to have the choice. They can become Americans, if they want, if I keep my citizenship." But James had sided with his mother, and this had led to an intensification of Jane's feeling of being closed in, of being taken over, and the engagement had ended soon after.

And here we are, twelve years later, she thought, paying off another taxi at West Irving Park Road. A blast of cold, wet air came to her from the lake. All the lights were on in Gerda's basement. She saw shapes of women moving on the other side of the frosted windows. *Here is Gerda Mulvaney née Miller, having written off Phil with the popular expletive of her day, and gone on to put words together for the feminist cause for a paper named* Feme Sole; *here is Jane Clifford, having written off Gabriel with the ambiguous declarative "I decided to leave," and gone back to the Midwest to put words together before a class listed Women in Literature, Section II, beginning with a book called* The Odd Women.

It would be interesting to consult with the good old *Eye of Eternity,* she thought, going down the steps, past a row of garbage cans. The shadow of a cat slunk as quickly past. *What would He/She/It say?* "One ran in circles, the other stood still, and they both ended up in the same place. One flung herself into the current, the other hid her head in the sand, and they both ended up on shore: where one had started from and the other stayed. The thinker had a lot of thoughts, but the flinger had more fun!"

Jane rang Gerda's bell. It jangled shrilly inside. "That's her now," she heard Gerda say. Scuffle of bare feet, swish of jeans. "Pound hard on it, will you? It's stuck!" cried Gerda.

Jane pounded hard and fell into the room. Gerda caught her. Several women laughed. Jane was aware that their faces, blurred by her nearsightedness, looked toward her expectantly: this latest renegade, hurling herself into their solidarity, after having fled through the cold night from the enemy. This was the voice on the other end of the phone that had said, "I have just left the son of a bitch. Forever." She had the feeling that she should do something dramatic, to give them a break from their weary labors. Leap up on the painter's platform where Gerda still displayed, under a spotlight, his nude of her in vivid rose and gold. Sock her fist into the air as she had seen cheerleaders do. Then what? Let loose a joyful stream of Elizabethan obscenities, after which she might snatch the scissors from the table where the dummy of *Feme Sole* was now being pasted up, and cut off her hair. Exaggerations, perhaps, but as she moved closer, into the range of the three women who were not Gerda, she did see clearly from their very different faces, one very young, the other two middle-aged, that something was expected of her. Something positive, something symbolic. They knew that she had just flown a third of the way across the United States, having walked out on some man, and they were prepared for the appropriate gesture which would punctuate such an act. She would be, too, if she had been laboring for hours under these harsh overhead lights that killed the eyes (the painter had worked under fluorescent lights, unable to afford daylight) to get this young paper to bed, to tuck away this latest offspring, which was the phoenix of their blasted hopes. She, too, would want to see dramatic proof that it was all making sense, that all her eye-killing basement toil was, after all, illuminating the friends above.

She put down her suitcase and went shyly over to the dummy. "So this is what one looks like," she said. "I don't think I've ever seen one before." The moment was past. She had disappointed them. Their faces became pleasantly blank and tired again. Each returned to what she had been doing. The young one wore a Mickey Mouse wristwatch. It said 1 A.M. Two A.M. in New York, in a certain hotel room. Was Gabriel, this very minute, sitting with his head buried in his large hands, those hands that had almost knocked over a slide projector the first time she had ever noticed them. Or was he fast asleep, his face utterly emotionless, like a mannequin: the way she had seen it last night. Was it only last night? How could so much have happened since last night? She stared at the girl's wristwatch, trying to remember something. What? It seemed important, but when it came it was just that old ad from the theatre program, Louis Hirshowitz, Watch-maker . . . "He who knows most, Gives most for wasted time."

"Yeah," said Gerda. "I'll bet you've never seen one with a hole so big when it has to go to the printer's at ten."

"Oh, of course. How is that going?"

"We're on seventy-five. We thought we'd leave the last twenty-six for you." Gerda plucked a smoldering cigarette out of a saucer and laughed. Jane hoped she was joking.

"Could I . . . do you think I could make myself a cup of tea?" she asked. "Don't worry, I know where every-thing is. I'm feeling kind of weak. I threw up my lunch at the airport." She shrugged out of her coat, then realized she had been clinging to Von Vorst's plastic-wrapped plant for so long she had forgotten it was not part of her.

"Lunch?" said one of the women, one of the older ones. "You mean you haven't had dinner?"

"Now, Eleanor, don't fuss," said Gerda. "Jane never eats properly, just like most of the rest of the world, except for your family. Your former family. Jane forgets to eat

393

when she's involved in something." Then she said to Jane, "This breakup really must have upset you some, huh?"

"Oh, it's nothing. I don't care," said Jane, starting toward the kitchen. She had realized suddenly, with a recurrence of the nausea, that the last thing in the world she felt able to do was "rap" about Gabriel with these women. Her heart sank when the woman called Eleanor followed her into Gerda's kitchen. Well, nobody could make anybody talk. Jane remembered how Edith was so adept at freezing out strangers who asked personal questions. And how Kitty, who had her own style in this matter, simply turned it back on them, asking *them* all about themselves. ("Get them on their favorite subject," said Kitty, "and they forget everything else!")

"I just made coffee a while back," said Eleanor. "The kettle's still warm. I'll heat it up again." She turned on the gas, then went to the cupboard over the sink, both of which were painted red and bordered with various nude and flower designs by the painter. She was a wide-hipped, motherly looking woman. Her jeans did not look right, somehow. She had pulled her shoulder-length, lanky, graying hair into a sort of low ponytail. She took down a clean coffee mug. Gerda's shelves had never looked so orderly. New shelf paper and everything. Jane suspected this to be Eleanor's work.

"You're very kind, but please don't wait on me." Jane took the cup and tried to smile gratefully but be firm at the same time. "I'm used to doing things for myself. Please." Then she added, feeling she may have rebuffed this kind soul, "Just stay and talk, if you like." Then wished she hadn't. "To tell the truth, I'm beat. I've been running around New York since morning. Do you think Gerda would be furious if I just drank a cup of tea and curled up on the couch and slept for now? She wasn't serious about saving those last twenty-six for me, was she? I couldn't think of twenty-six *numbers* in order, I'm so tired."

"Why not take the bed?" said Eleanor. "I'll go and make it up with new sheets."

"Oh, no. It's your bed now. I couldn't. The couch

will be fine. The floor would be fine at the moment. I mean it. Please. Don't trouble yourself."

"No trouble," said the woman cheerfully. "It's programmed into me. There are the tea bags. Milk in the refrigerator, sugar on the table. Or if you prefer honey, I think there's some left. I think it's in one of these cupboards. . . ."

"Sugar is fine," said Jane quickly.

"Fine," said Eleanor. "I'll go and get your bed ready."

Before Jane could stop her, she had gone.

Gerda came in. She flung her pack of cigarettes on the kitchen table and collapsed into a chair. "Oh! I'm ready to die. I'd like to draw a big obscene birdie, to fill up the space and be done with it. 'Up Yours, Gentlemen, and Good Night.' But that wouldn't be tasteful. My patron would be disappointed in me. I'm beginning to think I sold out by promising to be tasteful. The more I work my ass off in this airless basement, the more I realize that tastefulness is a cop-out when you're really trying to make something move. Can you imagine a 'tasteful' riot, for instance? Or a 'tasteful' strike that achieved its purpose? I wish to God I'd been born black in Detroit, sometimes. Honest to God, I do. My anger would be so much cleaner. Do you feel yourself trapped, Jane, when you least expect it, in all that old myth they sold us about Southern womanhood, having to be 'soft and feminine,' and all that crap? I do. The other night, I had dinner with my publisher again. I was wearing a new dress and I looked terrific. I passed myself in the mirror on his arm and I thought, Heh, heh, heh, who would ever know this sexy doll runs a feminist newspaper out of her basement. I was so satisfied with myself for being able to do both. Just like we once thought it was the height of something to be able to hold down a job and a man at the same time. I felt shitty. Then I came back here and talked to the others about it. They all agreed, except for Eleanor, that the next time I had dinner with him I should show up at the restaurant in exactly what I had on. See if he'd take me to dinner then. Test him. What do you think?"

"I think I agree with Eleanor." Jane poured boiling

water over a tea bag and stirred some sugar in. She considered milk, but didn't have the energy to get up again, once she had sat down.

"Oh?" asked Gerda with dangerous sweetness. "Why?"

We are going to quarrel tonight, thought Jane, unless I'm careful. She's tired, she's angry because she hasn't finished her work, and it's much more gratifying to have a fight with an old friend than with new ones, especially when you know the old friend is leaving tomorrow and you must go on working with the new ones.

"Nothing would be gained," she said. "And besides sex doesn't come into it. It's a business deal. If you were a man invited to have dinner at a nice restaurant with the firm's senior partner, you wouldn't go in your gardening clothes." Suddenly she remembered the time Kitty had tried to convince Emily that Jesus, contrary to apocryphal rumors, did not have any brothers or sisters, that Mary had remained chaste after his birth. "It's like this," Kitty had said to mocking, yellow-eyed Emily. "You wouldn't use your very best wineglasses, the ones you kept for very special occasions, to drink ordinary water out of. Or you wouldn't drink a Coca-Cola out of the gold chalice Father Barnabas serves Communion from."

Now Gerda looked as convinced as Emily had. "I could take that from Eleanor," she said, "but not from you—not from someone of our own generation."

"I don't think I belong to any generation sometimes," said Jane.

"Of course you do. It's just more romantic to think of yourself as the lonely traveler," said Gerda. "I'm sorry. I'm being bitchy. Did you really vomit at the airport? I thought fainting was your thing. I'd love to have seen his face when you told him. How was it? Angelic and unlined as always? Or did he burst into tears? You never can predict people, even when you think you know everything about them."

"I didn't see his face. I left him a note."

Gerda raised her eyebrows. She tapped a cigarette from the pack with the tip of a blunt fingernail with dirt inside the rim. Jane thought about all the cigarettes

396

Gerda must have smoked in her presence, about the countless times she had seen Gerda perform just this gesture with varying lengths of nails, in varying colors.

"What are you thinking right this second," Gerda demanded to know.

"I was remembering you, that time, when you sat on my Bates bedspread in McEvoy dorm and tapped out a cigarette and lit it, just as you are doing now, and told me about Bobby Mulvaney."

"Oh, that. Why bring up that now?" Gerda looked annoyed.

"And I guess I was also sort of subliminally thinking about that funny girl. That girl running for Student Council who kept mixing us up."

"Ah, what was her name?" cried Gerda. "Was she ever stupid! Those big pop eyes and that squeaky little voice. So pleased with herself when she could rattle off a name every time she met somebody, even if it was the wrong name. Patty something. Some double name like Patty Marie, Patty Ann, Patty—"

"Patty Beth!"

"Oh, God, yes. Patty Beth Pomeroy! What a dope!" Gerda laughed. She blew smoke from her nose. "I wonder whatever happened to old Patty Beth Pomeroy."

"She's probably happily married to a textile manufacturer, has three adorable children, and is president of the local Women Republicans," said Jane.

"Yes! Campaigning her head off to get reelected. Still getting everybody's name wrong."

Gerda and Jane were silent, Jane sipping the hot tea, Gerda smoking, having managed to avoid the argument—which waited, even now, in the smoke-filled air of the painter's kitchen—through the mutual mockery of Patty Beth, who had brought them together. Jane wondered if Gerda still thought of this flat as belonging to the painter, if she ever thought of him at all. She remembered Gerda, younger and thinner, giving that weird hurt shriek at dawn, as the two friends huddled beneath her thick fur coat in South Kensington. I'VE BEEN IN LOVE WITH HIM SINCE I WAS SEVEN YEARS OLD!

Her heart had been sick for Gerda that terrible dawn. She remembered wishing she could take part of her suffering on herself, share it. That awful realization of love. And yet (whatever this was worth; perhaps nothing to anybody but a "Romantic" like herself) Jane had felt the humanness of Gerda when she uttered that terrible shriek and then slept like a child for the next sixteen hours. Gerda felt, Gerda loved, and Jane had felt warm toward her as a result. She might be "hard as nails" but she could suffer because she loved. Jane had been relieved, that morning, to know that her friend was capable of being hurt, as sadistic as that might seem.

"Now what?" said Gerda dryly.

Jane looked up at this woman, with her shaggy pigtails, regarding her so cynically. She thought, She doesn't like me anymore! "I was wondering—" She was going to say, *if you ever think about the judge anymore,* but Eleanor walked in, which was probably for the best.

"Wondering what?" asked Gerda.

"If Patty Beth saw us today, if she would still confuse us."

Gerda snorted. "Not likely." She watched Eleanor squeeze out a sponge and wipe some spilled sugar from the table. "Fuss, fuss, fuss, Eleanor." But her voice was amused, protective of the older woman. "Come and sit down. Did you know, when Jane and I were Southern belles, matriculating down there in the old home state, people used to confuse us? Do you see any resemblance, Eleanor?"

Eleanor sat down at the table and scrutinized the two of them, as if she had been set a definite assignment. "Your features are different," she said, at last, "but—well, you are both very attractive young women." She smoothed back a lank strand of hair which had drooped into her face, and, from the darkness that passed quickly behind her eyes, Jane knew she was thinking of herself when she had been an attractive young woman. She probably dwells on such comparisons now, thought Jane, too much for her own good. Eleanor had long, bony, strong fingers. Jane could imagine them tenderly and capably poking around in someone's open brain, and regretted the woman's lost vocation. Ah, why couldn't people have everything!

"Oh, attractive," said Gerda meditatively. She smoked. Her eyes wandered restlessly. She seemed to be running after a number of thoughts and catching none of them.

"Your bed is made up," Eleanor said to Jane, smiling at her.

"And I belong in it. It was very kind of you, Eleanor. This is the end of the kind of day that makes a freshly made up bed truly appreciated. Gerda, I know you have this deadline. I'm only distracting you." She took the last sip of tea and stood up.

"So you're deserting me," said Gerda mockingly. "Well, why shouldn't you? It's not your responsibility, this goddamned newspaper." But something in her voice said it clearly was.

"Oh, Gerda, I wish I could think of something. I really do. But it's two in the morning! And this has been a terribly long day for me. Perhaps the longest of my life. I don't think you realize—Look, couldn't you call your piece 'Seventy-five Ways He Uses You Every Day?' Why does it have to be a hundred and one? The number is arbitrary, isn't it? At the airport I saw an article in a magazine called 'Six Sexy Ways to Recover from a Broken Affair.' The six didn't really matter, except that it made the title alliterative. I mean, it could have been twelve sexy ways, or twenty or sixty-two. Who knows, perhaps the person who wrote it *meant* for it to be sixty-two and then ran short of time like you did."

"Because, stupid, I have a certain amount of *space* to fill up," said Gerda. "Each of my 'Ways' is a one-liner. And I have twenty-six lines to go. And, frankly, Jane, I could do without your comparing my piece to a piece in that foolish magazine. 'Six Sexy Ways to Get Over a Broken Affair!' Ha, what a crock of shit. The 'Sexy' gives the whole thing away. It means they want you to turn around and start the whole asinine process over again. Tell me one 'sexy' way you plan to get over *your* broken affair, if you can. That is, if you really have broken it. What exactly did your note say? Look, will you sit down;

you make me nervous, hovering like that. For Christ's sake, keep me company five more minutes. Something you say accidentally may give me an idea."

"I seriously doubt it." But Jane sat down. "It was a very short letter, Gerda. I said, 'I decided to leave.' "

"That's all?"

"Well, I put 'Dear Gabriel' at the top and signed my name at the bottom."

"Just your name? Or did you put 'love' or something?"

"No, just Jane."

"Hmm," murmured Gerda, slightly critical. Probably thinking of her own, more explicit letter to Phil.

"Do you really think you'll be strong enough not to see him again?" asked Eleanor. She clasped her hands and leaned toward Jane, across the table. "I hope you don't mind my asking. It's just that lately I've become interested in these things." She gave a sad little laugh.

"I don't know, Eleanor. I mean, I wish I did know. I'm not so dramatic as Gerda, I guess, but, as mild as it seems, it really was a beginning for me—a way of *starting* to tell him goodbye. If I hated him, it would be easier, but he's not—easily hateable. You'd have to know him to understand what I mean, probably. . . ." She trailed off. Both Gerda and Eleanor were watching her strangely, as if waiting to see the first signs of a disease break out on her face, a disease they did not want to catch again at any cost.

"So what did he finally do," asked Gerda, lighting up another cigarette, "to make you walk out. If you have walked out, that is."

The overhead fluorescent light stung Jane's eyes. She had a momentary shift in vision in which she saw these two women as adversaries, inquisitors, who would not let her go to sleep until she had proved to them that she, too, had forsworn the race of men. *I don't have to take this,* she thought. *I could plead nausea, utter exhaustion, and simply walk out of the kitchen.*

Instead, she heard herself telling them about this long day, begun after the night of tears, how, this morning—but no, it was already yesterday morning—she had sat up in bed preparing her class notes on *The*

Odd Women, crossing off, one by one, their solutions to the predicaments in which they'd found themselves in 1890. She took them, Gerda and Eleanor, through her day, noting their responses. She saw how Gerda's mind plucked and discarded, seized greedily upon, then dismissed, possibilities for twenty-six more one-liners which would demonstrate "ways he uses you every day," and how Eleanor, like an earnest student who had missed some of the lectures, clutched at clues to help her understand her own situation. When Jane described her experience in the dressing room at Saks, Eleanor gave a soft groan and said, "Exactly—oh, exactly . . ." Neither of them seemed very excited about Jane's discovery of the old villain. "He's the one that Jane's great-aunt ran away with," Gerda put in, "and then he knocked her up and vanished and Jane's grandfather went to New York and took the baby home—and the mother in her coffin." "Ah," replied Eleanor. But neither was much interested in the redeemed Von Vorst, almost seventy years older, rushing down to his corner liquor store for a tiny bottle of Drambuie, his affection for a retired acting cat, or his thoughts on the naturalism of the dream life.

It's a wonder that anyone ever really communicates with another person, thought Jane as she narrated these events which had led her here, and saw two other versions of her story reflected in the eyes of these women. And yet telling it aloud gave her new insights. She said, "And what probably brought things to a head was that I put so much effort into getting through the day on my own, trying to avoid the image of 'the waiting woman,' and then—to have him say, announcing one more postponement, 'Thank you for being so patient,' and then, several hours later, send word of another delay. . . . I think that's when I saw the writing on the wall."

"You mean," interrupted Gerda caustically, "when the writing on the wall fell down and hit you over the head."

Eleanor, who had been frowning with concentration, asked suddenly, "How old are the children?"

"What children?" said Jane.

"The children of—your lover and his wife."

"They don't have any children."

"Ah, how interesting!" cried Eleanor.

"Why? Why is it interesting?"

"I have often thought . . ." Eleanor hesitated. "Do you mind if I speak my thoughts? It won't upset you? Well, I have often had the notion—based purely on my own circumstances . . . How can I say this? I want it understood that I adore my children. I wouldn't have missed having them for anything. . . ."

"Yes, Eleanor, we understand," said Gerda wearily. "Go on."

"Well, I have often thought couples without children stay *couples* longer. I mean, children displace the privacy of a couple. The interests all shift towards the child. He is the thing that must be considered first, nurtured, looked after. And as the couple looks more and more after the child, they look after each other less and less. Of course, it's the natural way. It's biology. And every sensible person knows"—she laughed bitterly, softly—"That biology is irrevocable."

The word shimmered meaningfully in Jane's tired mind, but she had given up making connections. Apples and oranges, irrevocable but not irredeemable, thank you for being so patient—what did any of it matter?

And yet when Eleanor went on to say, "I have often thought recently that childless couples remain truer to each other longer, because they are more things to each other," Jane's heart stung with another connection she would rather not have made: Ann and Gabriel Weeks, Marian Evans and George Henry Lewes—childless couples.

"That is why," Eleanor went on, becoming suddenly flushed and animated, "I think Nan Frampton may be doing herself in by being so ambitious and wanting everything. I mean Nan Tibalt. I must remember to get that right."

"Nan Frampton is the young neurosurgeon that Eleanor's husband married," explained Gerda.

"No, she is still just an intern," corrected Eleanor sharply. This fact was obviously of significance to her. "Just an intern . . . like I was once. She's about your age," she said to Jane. "Very attractive. Young. And serious

402

looking, like you are. Oh, so serious, she is! Do you know what she told me? She told me people could *control* their lives. . . . Can you imagine?"

"Eleanor, what are you talking about," interrupted Gerda. "You never met her. How could she have told you this?"

"Oh, yes, I met her," replied Eleanor mischievously. "I just didn't tell you about it!"

"I don't understand," Gerda said. Slowly and coldly.

"I didn't tell you because I knew you'd find it too interesting and then you'd force me to give you my story. You would have found it irresistible, and you would have talked me into it, and I didn't want to be talked into it. I wanted to mull over it myself."

"Then why bring it up now?"

"Because I *feel* like bringing it up, that's why!" Eleanor's eyes shone like a naughty child's, but her defiance was shadowed by uncertainty. She looked as if she expected to be punished by Gerda, yet still must have her defiant moment. "And I want to see if Jane here would do and say the things Nan Frampton did and said to me. I want to know whether my husband married a cold little bitch or whether I have simply been a fool."

"Well," said Gerda, curling her lip, "do go on. Don't let me stop you. I have my own problems to worry about." But she was waiting to hear.

There is going to be trouble in this kitchen yet, thought Jane. And in some way I am causing it. And yet she could not leave now. Leave? When, finally, she could hear a story in which a wife and a mistress actually met and talked?

"After Francis had 'declared himself' to her, or whatever he did," said Eleanor, "Nan Frampton asked if she could meet me. Francis conveyed the message, rather sheepishly, but he was also secretly pleased at the prospect, I could tell. At first I refused, 'What does she want?' I said. 'First to steal my husband and then for me to meet her and hand over the keys?' But of course I went. I gave in and went. She telephoned me the very next day after Francis had spoken about it, and she was very polite, almost as if she needed my *permission* or some-

403

thing, and she insisted that I be the one to pick our meeting place. It was late spring—a year ago this coming spring—and at first I thought the park, Lincoln Park. Francis and the children and I often used to ride bicycles there. But I decided on the Art Institute instead. I didn't want her to see me in all that spring light and pity me for being old and worn out. We met in that large room where all the famous Impressionists are. I arrived ten minutes before the hour, but she had come even earlier: determined to outdo me, even in courtesy. We sat together on one of those long leather things, and I'm sure everyone passing thought we were friends. We spoke very softly, as though we were in church, and I think I have memorized every detail in that Toulouse-Lautree painting, the one with all the green in it. She explained that she had wanted to meet me because she knew I was a whole side of Francis that she did not know, like the dark side of the moon, and she wanted to know that side of him, too. She apologized for being so much in love with him, but since it had been 'inevitable,' she said, she wanted very much to know what my 'life plans' were. My life plans! I told her Francis and the children had been my life, and she looked embarrassed, as if I'd come right out in this room full of lovely paintings and announced I had cancer. Then she started explaining to me —this girl who could be my daughter—how it was every persons's duty to develop a self, to fulfill that self. I said that when I was her age I, too, had grand plans for my 'self,' but that a husband who was an ambitious young doctor and four babies had a way of interfering with those plans. She said she was sorry that had happened— she kept treating me—oh, I wish I could explain it. . . . She took this attitude to me, as we talked, as though I were already in the terminal ward, and yet she asked about my 'life plans,' like those cheery doctors who lie to dying patients, tell them 'Oh, you'll be fit as a fiddle in no time!' . . . She said it was too bad that I had had to give up my career, but that just because I had felt it necessary, she didn't think it had to be so for everyone else. She said she planned to have babies, too. 'You don't just have them, and shut them neatly away in a nice frilly room labeled babies,' I said, because there was something about the way she said it that indicated she was used to packaging everything off in neat little compartments. She said of course not; she had already talked things over with her father, who is a successful pediatrician in Chicago, and he had agreed to pay for nurses while the children were small. 'Well,' I said, 'you're all right, aren't you? You've got everything, it seems to me.' And you know what she said? She pulled a long, serious face—honestly, that girl hasn't a shred of humor—and said, 'No, I haven't. I can never have Francis's past, as you do.' Isn't that too much? But now that I think about it, she may do herself in by trying to collect all the prizes. Children take energy, I don't care what anyone says, or how many nurses your father can buy you; they demand their share of attention and love. She might even find herself getting *interested* in them, and Francis is very jealous of people's interest and affection; he was jealous even of his own sons. No, if dear Nan isn't careful, she may find herself answering the phone one night and it'll be Francis explaining why he has to spend the night at the hospital, or some other story, and then she'll have her hands full, meeting women in art museums, trying to keep up with all his 'dark sides.' What do you think of all this, Jane? You have to tell me. You and she are the same generation. Would you behave like that with your Gabriel's wife?"

Jane, who had been deeply affected by the story, listening to it as one listens to a sort of alternate fate, now came rather cruelly back to "reality." "It's hardly the same situation," she said. "Seeing that Gabriel did not 'declare himself' to me. I never had the opportunity to behave as Nan Frampton behaved to you. I don't know what I would have done. It's hard to say. I mean, I can say theoretically to you that I don't think she had to— well—gloat so much, flaunt her victory as she did. But maybe she saw it differently. Maybe she was really sad that a part of Francis—all those years with you—would always be denied her."

"I suppose you think I should have handed over the past to her, as well, if I could have," said Eleanor curtly. Jane understood that Eleanor was identifying her with the girl who had stolen her happiness, projecting the image of Nan on her, just as, on the afternoon when she and Kitty were packing up Edith's things, Kitty had worked herself up into an old rebellion against Edith and actually glared at Jane as if she had become Edith.

Certain chords in that conversation with Kitty now reverberated through Eleanor's story, and Jane saw how it was futile and unkind for the "daughters" of the world to announce to the "mothers" that, yes! everything was still possible, from outrageous happiness to fulfilled and unbroken selves. It was cruel to shine these too bright might-have-beens upon the tired countenances of older women who had lived by other lights. She had been just on the verge of telling Eleanor about her friend Sonia Marks, who was not a cold bitch and yet had got away with it all: another woman's husband and the profession she wanted and the children, too. But Eleanor did not want to hear such a story. It was Jane who wanted to add such stories to her stockpile of hopes.

"It's hard to say," she began lamely, "what I would have done if—circumstances had been different. . . ."

"That shouldn't be any problem for you with your imagination," said Gerda sarcastically. "Go on and try. Can't you see Eleanor needs help, which I obviously have been unable to give her, though God knows what generation she thinks *I* belong to. . . ."

"Oh, Gerda, I didn't mean . . ." stammered Eleanor. "Oh, dear—now I've hurt your feelings. It was just that Jane has a married man that could have been Francis, and I wanted to now if she would have behaved to me as Nan Frampton did, at the Art Institute."

"But I *don't* have him," protested Jane. She was exasperated and exhausted. "I don't have anything at the moment, except confusion. I can't help anybody now. I can't write other people's articles or tell them how I would have behaved if I'd been somebody else."

"No one's asking you to write anyone's article, you silly cunt," said Gerda. "Go to bed, then, why don't you? Nobody's asking you for help, because you can't even help yourself. You can't do anything except wander around inside your own head, like an old maid in her attic.

Do you know what, Eleanor? Jane once broke off an engagement because she had a fight with her future mother-in-law about the passports of her unborn children."

"Why are you attacking me, Gerda? And please save your contemporary language for your newspaper. Why are you both so angry with me? What have I done? Is it because I haven't come here with Gabriel's ear in a box? Because I haven't given up love like you, Gerda?"

"You are so goddamn self-righteous," said Gerda. "I'll call things by their names even if you won't. The thing between your legs is a cunt. The thing you won't do around Gabriel is let him hear you shit. The thing you mean to him is a good fuck with a Ph.D. And the thing I've given up is all the *crap* we've been taught to call love."

"I don't have to listen to your vile language or your stupid definitions," said Jane, getting up from the table.

"YOU'RE GOING TO LISTEN!" cried Gerda, slamming her hand down so violently that the lighted tip of her cigarette flew across the kitchen. Eleanor got up at once to stamp it out. "God, you're such a fence-sitting Southern bitch! I'm so sick of your avoidances and evasions and illusions and your cringing little refusals to see the *truth,* to see things as they *are!* You just can't face the fact that you have to cut through all the crap and the shit if you want to live. That's what I'm trying to do, and you hate me for it because you can't stand to do it yourself. You can't bear the smell of reality. You spend all your time making up lovely old nineteenth-century lies to cover up what is just one big crock of shit! Your so-called 'beautiful love affair' with Gabriel Weeks—you want me to tell you what it is, or was, or whatever the hell you're kidding yourself about its present status? Fourteen furtive fucks over a period of two years. How's *that* for alliteration? That's Jane's alliterative love affair for you—"

"Please girls," interrupted Eleanor. Her voice was trembling, but it was sensible, mature, like a mother trying to separate two fighting daughters. "What we all need is some sleep."

"WHAT WE ALL NEED IS SOME TRUTH!" shrieked Gerda.

Her eyes were glazed, like a madwoman's. "Shut up, Eleanor. If you'd caused a few more scenes in your time, you wouldn't be in the mess you're in today!"

"Ah, how could you—" began Eleanor. She went very pale. She bowed her head and clasped her strong hands together as though she wanted to break them.

"Truth for you seems to be as many four-letter words as you can cram into a sentence," said Jane. "And living, as far as you're concerned, is blowing in a circle like a tornado. You have run around in circles ever since I have known you, telling yourself you were moving through life. But what have you to show for it? You've destroyed everything you've touched. But you can never touch what Gabriel and I have had. You can't defile it with your cheap words. You can't even *understand* it."

"You liar, get out of here!"

"I'm leaving right this minute." Jane turned and walked out of the kitchen.

Eleanor began to sob.

As Jane hurried through the flat, wondering where on earth she would go at this hour, she heard Gerda say, "Oh, God, I'm so sorry, Eleanor. Please. I'm in a panic over this deadline and then she comes in here with nothing to offer and *moralizes.* . . ."

"How could you say what you said?" moaned the other. "That's what I get for confiding in you. You turn it around and twist it like a knife in me. *Now* you see why I kept some things to myself!"

"Oh, Christ, not you, too, Eleanor. Don't you start on me at this time of night—I mean morning. Keep your precious story. A lot of good it's done you. I'll make out. I always have."

"I thought of you as a daughter."

"I am your *sister,* Eleanor."

The two women pasting up the newspaper suddenly busied themselves and would not look at Jane as she passed their worktable.

She shut herself in the bedroom and fell on the bed. Tears of anger and self-pity spilled upon Eleanor's fresh pillowcases. She could be asleep in Gabriel's arms now tucked away with him in the present moment, far away from strident insults and the basement crises of weeping, screaming women. Had she buried her grandmother and sadly told her lover it was not enough and flown through the freezing winter night to a friend in order to be told she was useless, futile, a "silly cunt" who couldn't even help herself, a "good fuck with a Ph.D." Who had deluded herself into believing "fourteen furtive fucks" constituted an idyllic love?

Yes, she must leave. This was not the place for her. How she wanted to be gone from the peevish basement filled with so much hatred and disappointment! She would rather catch pneumonia in the bitter cold night, trying to find a taxi. She would rather get stiff joints at the airport sleeping in a chair. She shouldn't have told Gerda she had nothing to show for her life; that was cruel. And yet she had been dying to say all those things for years, and Gerda had been dying to say what she had said, and now they were said. And what did it amount to, other than that each, in her own style of rhetoric, had accused the other of doing nothing with her life?

She must get up and leave. But she continued to lie exhausted on the bed. She must prove that when she said "I decided to leave . . . I'm leaving . . ." she meant it. When had an action of hers been real, when? Her life *did* seem one long string of "avoidances and evasions and illusions" at this moment.

Fighting with Nancy Bruton over those poor little unborn babies.

Borrowing five hundred dollars from Ray to have an imaginary abortion.

Buying a dress she had not tried on to please a saleslady.

Looking up a name in a college catalogue, dreaming a person, dreaming what this person was going to mean to her.

Tracking down the Villain who had been the main figure in the staple cautionary tale of her childhood, then failing to confront him with his crime.

Defending Nan Frampton, whom she had never met, who probably *was* a cold bitch, because, for a moment, she had become so envious of Nan's dénouement that she imagined it as her own, imagined how she herself might say to Ann Weeks, "Ah, but I can never have his past; that will always belong to you."

Beyond the closed door came the voices of Eleanor and Gerda. Without Jane, they were reestablishing their dialogue. Their words flowed slowly, experimentally; there were no longer the strident rhythms of accusation or recrimination. They are attached to each other, she thought. Each is filling a needed place in the other's life. I was the explosive factor. Gerda feels lonely and brave in her basement and needs Eleanor's support, her gentle washings-up and wifely ministrations. And Eleanor needs to have the spark of life kept alive in her. She needs the example of Gerda's energy and anger and explicitness. I came here and made Gerda jealous when Eleanor gave *me* the Nan Frampton scoop. And I became a Nan-surrogate to Eleanor. The old adage has been proved one more time. Three's a crowd, and I was number three.

Then she heard the scrape of a kitchen chair and someone was coming toward the bedroom.

Ashamed of her third-class playacting, she bolted from the bed, and, by the time Gerda called her name through the door, Jane had accomplished the gesture of having slipped into her coat. To show she was a woman of her word and was "leaving."

"Come in," she called.

Gerda entered, looking calm and detached. Her eyes still smoldered, but she had otherwise managed to get herself in hand. "Hi. Can we talk a minute?"

"It seems to me we've said just about everything," replied Jane.

"Yes, well . . ." Gerda sighed. "It's been brewing for a long time, I guess. Listen, take your coat off. It's almost three in the morning. You might as well stay a few more hours till time for your plane. You won't be defiled or anything."

"I'm sorry I said some of those things, Gerda. I went too far. They just came out before I could stop them. But you said some pretty terrible things yourself."

Gerda gave a harsh little laugh. "Yes, we both said a few unforgivable things. I don't forgive you and I don't expect you to forgive me. They would have come out sooner or later, anyway, you know. It's just tonight everybody was tired or upset about something and that sparked it off. Anyway, take off your coat and go to bed. Eleanor now insists I take her story to fill up my space; otherwise she 'can't stay under my roof another day.' So we'll write it up tonight and I'll make my deadline, Eleanor will feel like a martyred heroine, and you'll get a few hours' sleep and go back to your school and do whatever you have to do."

"Do nothing," Jane reminded her. "Live in my head. I feel I'm to blame for Eleanor's capitulation. I've probably set her back months in her recovery."

"Oh, don't be silly. What capitulation? It'll do her good to name names. All she was doing before was trying to protect Francis, so he could have his new wife and everything and not have to suffer any guilt. It'll do him good to feel guilty. That is, if he even reads it. I know—I'll send him a copy. I'll mail it to his hospital."

"Won't he sue?"

"Oh, sue! Let him. I'd enjoy that. I really would."

And Jane could see from Gerda's face that she would enjoy it.

Gerda sat down on the bed and found a match in her pocket and relit her current cigarette, which had gone out. "Poor Eleanor. She is a martyr. Her husband had a horrible temper and she can't stand to hear a voice raised. She'll do anything to keep the peace. She ought to have clobbered him more often. Nan Frampton probably does and he adores it."

"Oh, I think most people are terrible," said Jane vaguely, taking off her coat. She sat down on the bed, too.

Gerda leaned forward suddenly and kissed Jane. She tasted of years and years of cigarettes.

"We are terrible, you and I," she said, her eyes wickedly bright. "We say things aloud that most people don't even let themselves think. That's why we'll survive. You have to be terrible to survive."

"I wonder how terrible . . ." Jane murmured. She was thinking: For twelve years, during the most intimate

411

moments of our friendship, Gerda and I have never, not once, touched. We never felt the need to exchange those insincere little kisses and hugs Southern women who detest each other lavish on each other in public. And now, at last, Gerda has kissed me. "I want to explain something about the letter I wrote to Gabriel."

"Why? Forget it! Why should you have to explain to me?"

Jane laughed now. "I *don't* have to. I just feel like giving myself credit for accomplishing an action. It may have seemed wishy-washy to you, but I was serving him notice, in my own understated way, that my patience was running out. In fact, I am beginning to think I've used up my lifetime supply of patience on him already. His *image* of me is too patient. I want more."

"Well," said Gerda wryly, "I just hope you don't end up exchanging his image of you for another man's image, that's all."

"I don't know," said Jane, inspired with a sort of insurrectionary heterosexuality in this basement. "If I ever found one who saw me as large as I'd like to be, I might ask him to stick around."

On this note, the two of them said good night.

Jane slept badly in Gerda's bed made over to her by Eleanor. She dreamed pieces of dreams, then woke, again and again, to the drone of Eleanor's sad story being echoed by the typewriter keys. The older woman told all, often stopping to cry a little, and Gerda rapped it out on her electric machine.

Jane dreamed Nancy Bruton was the saleslady at Saks. Jane was explaining to her how she had left her dress in the taxi. Nancy took her by the shoulders and shook her till her teeth rattled, and cried, "You'll never be happy!"

Then she woke and heard Eleanor. ". . . for years he had affairs, but I pretended not to know . . . I wanted to hold on to what I had . . . he was so much nicer to me when he was in love with someone . . ."

Sometimes Ann Weeks took over the story. ". . . it went on for months, years . . . I knew it was serious and I said nothing. The others had passed. One night I heard him

412

crying in the bathroom. I went in and he was sitting on the toilet, his face in his hands. 'I can't live without her,' he said. 'I can't endure this life of lies.' I told him there were no lies, as I already knew. I said as long as I could still be his wife, I could manage somehow or other. I could not endure a divorce I said. He said he would try and work things out, but he didn't, and I endured. . . ."

Jane woke, her heart pounding. So I got him, she thought. Gabriel has left Ann. The other was a dream.

Then she really woke and realized that "the other" was the reality.

Toward daylight there were rustlings of paper, groans, the whistle of a kettle, hurried footsteps. "I'll take this to the printer's," one of the women said. "Go to bed, Gerda, you look dead." "I'm going home," said another. "What time does Jane have to make her plane? Should we stay up and wake her?" (Eleanor) "No, she has this little clock. She can make it herself." (Gerda)

Then there were sound of boots being put on, laughs as someone wrestled with the stuck door, then sudden girlish cries: "Snow! Look at it come down!"

Jane burrowed into the warm covers, wanting to sleep forever, terrified of being snowed in in a place where she was not wanted. She gave up, pressed in the alarm button of "old T.F.," and dressed.

She got her things together, including Von Vorst's inconvenient little plant, and tiptoed past the sofa where Eleanor slept covered in a crocheted afghan. She looked purified, younger, and yes, rather like a martyred saint.

Gerda was curled up on the floor, inside a sleeping bag, beneath the nude painting of one of her former selves. The spotlight above it had been turned off.

As Jane let herself out, into the falling snow, she was pretty sure Gerda had only pretended to be asleep.

XVIII

Snow was falling upon the Midwest, and would continue to fall, said the weather forecaster, through the remainder of the night and into the morning. Approximately twelve to fourteen inches was expected by Thursday morning. His name was Dallas Yoder and he always wore a bow tie and used the same placid monotone for sunny skies and tornado warnings. He was tall and skinny and his profile looked like a picture of Jack Frost Jane remembered from a coloring book she had as a child. Dallas Yoder explained to her that she was in for a long spell of bad weather and why this must be so. A rapidly falling barometer. Increasing winds. Low pressure. Occlusion. Storm centers stretching like a string of black pearls from Calgary down to Great Falls, from Bismarck over to Des Moines and up again to Chicago, Detroit, and Buffalo. No, she was in the middle of it, all right, and he rapped his pointer twice at her city to impress this fact upon her. There was no such thing as good weather for her in the coming days, only different varieties of bad. And yet his monotone, almost comically secure, was incapable of convincing anyone of disaster. It belied his sharp, frosty features, the long, thin nose like an icicle. Perhaps it was this combination that made him the perfect forecaster. She believed in Dallas Yoder, somehow.

It was 11 P.M. Wednesday. Exactly one week since Edith's last night on earth. No classes till Tuesday. In the space between: silence, solitude, snow.

The man who lived in the concrete-block house behind, who kept bird-feeders, and played Mozart, was shoveling snow in the dark. Just before switching on the eleven o'clock news, Jane had watched him for a while. She had stood in the bathtub, in the dark bathroom, in order to observe him from an unlighted window. A lonely figure bundled up to the ears, doggedly clearing a path from his door to the sidewalk. New snow fell on his head as he worked, on his stooped shoulders, and on his newly shoveled walk. Now why did people do that? Why didn't he wait till morning, till it had finished falling? Perhaps he was afraid. Afraid to take on all that snow at once.

Nothing new on national news. A few shots of a war, in a place where snow never fell, a war she had been watching, in its perfunctory snippets and shots of continual coverage, for years. A politician's angry face appeared briefly, denouncing an opponent. Nothing new.

A clever ad for a painkiller more effective in less time than all competitive painkillers, and on to local news.

"The man who may be the Enema Bandit was almost apprehended early this evening in a local Laundromat, when a former victim spotted a young man whose shoes she recognized putting a woman's nylon stocking into a machine with the rest of his clothes. Thinking she ought to warn him that the delicate garment might not survive the ordeal, and meanwhile to get a closer look at his shoes, she approached him. The man apparently recognized her and fled into the snowy night. The young woman, a student at the university, whose name is being withheld, told police the suspect wore 'a pair of black Keds with a spot of white paint on the toe of the left shoe.' She described him as being 'about twenty-five or so,' with short brown hair and wearing the metal-rimmed 'granny glasses' currently popular with students. Of medium height, thin, and wearing a windbreaker of a light beige or tan color. 'He was not wearing the glasses the last time I saw him, because he had the stocking over his face,' she said. 'But it will be a long time before I forget those black Keds with the spot.'"

The camera faded out on the newscaster's barely suppressed smile and faded in on the face of the state attorney general.

"We have every reason to believe that at this time the Enema Bandit is hurrying away from this state as fast as his Keds can carry him in a snowstorm," he said. He assured viewers that although the state troopers had their hands full with hazardous highway conditions, pileups on the thruways, etc, they had in no way relinquished the possibility of apprehending the suspect. He urged drivers on Interstate 74 not to pick up any male hitch-hiker ("He may be armed"), and suggested that women recheck the locks on their doors and not go out unless absolutely necessary, "though, again, I have every reason to believe that this pervert has finally had the"— and the watchful viewer could see that elected official regretfully, with a momentary smirk, sacrifice the best *bon mot* of the case to the code of public decency he had sworn to uphold—"living daylights scared out of him."

The Laundromat attendant, a camera-shy black woman in middle age, was shown briefly going through the Enema Bandit's abandoned washload. Without looking up, she murmured the inventory: "Four pair of socks, six undershirts, six pair of Jockey shorts, two white shirts, a blue shirt, and one lady's nylon stocking . . ."

"And so," commented the local newscaster, "we may have seen the last of the famous Enema Bandit. Looks like he'll have to buy himself a new pair of shoes and some underwear, however!" He said the state had slaughtered 1,967 beef cattle and 1,446 hogs today, under federal inspection, and wished his viewers a pleasant good night.

Jane pressed a button and his cheerful face shrank to a square and then disappeared into blackness.

A postcard, a letter, and a note had been waiting in her mailbox when she arrived home from the airport.

The card was of a slightly frowning angel with blue wings and a rich red cloak. In his left hand he held a golden scepter; with his right, he was signaling to some-one.

Gerard David, Flemish, active by about 1484, died 1523
"The Archangel Gabriel" The Metropolitan Museum of Art

The message was dated Tuesday morning, 10:15 A.M. That was one of the things she loved most about him, the way he remembered to put times on letters, as if he knew how important it was for her always to know.

I do, you know, was the cryptic message, but she understood. She had already read it three times before she unlocked her door. "Ah," she had said, shaking her head at the card, "but you love oranges, too."

But her eyes filled with tears, because she could see him buying that card. Why, he must have gone straight to the rack, before ever entering the galleries, to get that card and write on it what he could not bring himself to say in two years, not even on the previous night when she had cried him to sleep—not even now, in so many words. He had sent it air mail. He had wanted it to be there if at all possible when she returned, and it had been.

The note was on a piece of yellow paper, folded double. It was from Sonia Marks. *Call me as soon as you get back. I have some interesting news for you.*

The letter was, of course, from Kitty, written on the evening of Jane's departure—with fewer typos than usual.

Dearest Jane,

I miss my little girl very, very much, more than ever now. I lit your candles and prayed for your happiness and that you would have a job next year. I feel sure they will ask you to stay on, they know a good think [*sic*] when they've got it. Emily's candle, unfortunately, went slightly awry. She got the B in torts I was supposed to ask for, but John just called, very upset, about an hour ago. Emily found out from the law professor she *hates* that he had flunked her in a course she expected to get an A in, and now she's on probation. John said she had locked herself in the

417

bedroom and wouldn't let him in "even for his pajamas." Wanted to know what he should do. I said leave her alone, that's her way of liking [*sic*] her wounds, she would come out when she was ready, more determined than ever, and pass everything with flying colors. Nothing will hold that child back, I am sure of it.

Found the little theatre program you wanted. It was, of all places, in the box which had all your letters to her, so she must have thought of it as yours already. I'm enclosing it. I had a close call earlier this evening. Ray and I were going through her papers, bonds, securities, etc., and I found the 1900 census paper for the Dewar family, which gave her age. Managed to hide it from Ray, who has always been curious about it, and you know she would never have told him. Do let me know if you change your mind about the silver; I would be glad to send it on. You could be using it; it was part of her, after all. And anything else you want, but is too big to send, I'll keep for you here. We are all hoping to see you again soon; what about the Easter holidays? The dogwood will be out and everything so lovely. Remember I love you and God loves you, too. It was so good, the little talk we had Sunday. I cherish every moment of it. Hope NY was nice. Jack says to tell you he is "meditating on the trip," whatever that means. He said you'd know. I don't dare ask my boys what they mean by "trips" and such for fear they might tell me.

Love, Kitty

And there it was, hers to look at for as long as she liked, at last, without Edith's hand fluttering close by, ready to snatch it away again, rationing its appearances in order to preserve the efficacy of its message. *"Sister I am in grave trouble please can somebody come the villain has left me."* Jane Clifford, Custodian of Unwanted Family Secrets, could now ponder its message, uninterrupted, and draw all the conclusions she liked concerning the unpunctuated, quick-penciled alarm of maidenhood in distress in 1906, the cast of characters (one of whom

418

she now knew), and Louis Hirshowitz's solemn reminder about the relationship of wisdom to time.

Looking down the cast, she had saluted the gentle old villain:

ROBERT CURTIS, A MAN ABOUT TOWN—Hugo Von Vorst

and then sat for some time, gazing at this document which had held her imagination for so many years, and remembering the slightly quavering basso profundo as it declared mildly, with even a certain lack of interest, "Cleva Dewar. No, I don't think I recognize that name at all." And as she had tried to square his words with "the evidence," a strange thing had happened. She suddenly realized the evidence might not be what it had so simply seemed.

For Cleva's message was written in the margin, *above* Von Vorst's name. It was written exactly beside another name, the name of the wronged hero in *The Fatal Wedding*:

HOWARD WILSON, THE HAPPY HUSBAND—Edwin Merchant

Why had Cleva penciled her message beside this name when there was ample space for her to aim her accusation arrow-straight at the person who'd done her in? Or had it been *Edith* who had made the leap of faith—rather, the leap of accusation—herself pouncing on Von Vorst because, after all, she had seen the play and wasn't *he* the villain? Oh, one might argue that someone desperate enough to write such a note would not only neglect the niceties of capitalization and punctuation but also fail to keep a neat margin when annotating her seducer, but the doubt was now planted for all time in the Family Researcher's tireless mind: Was Edwin Merchant Cleva's villain? Was Von Vorst telling the truth? Was Cleva using the word "villain" the way she, Jane, used "son of a bitch" when she told Gerda over the telephone, "I have left the son of a bitch forever"? Did "villain" in 1906 simply mean the person you hated

419

because he had hurt you—as "son of a bitch," "prick," "bastard" meant today—regardless of what mild creature played Villain or Man About Town on the stage? If so, Jane had thought, again despairing of ever getting to the bottom of anything in her life, Edwin Merchant might well be Frances's father and all her own detective work of yesterday was simply one more "illusion" to add to her lengthy list.

How would she ever know whether Edith, in her own private and more prolonged perusals of this last message from her sister, had paused, briefly baffled, at this name directly opposite Cleva's scrawl, and then had shaken her head and gone on, casting her beliefs with face value, not irony? Or whether Edith had suspected Edwin Merchant and kept her suspicions to herself because it was too late to help Cleva, anyway, and decided to keep it simple for the good of her girls, reasoning that a villain playing a villain speaks plainly and hits doubly hard, whereas a villain in the guise of a wronged husband might confuse the young minds for whom one was weaving a cautionary tale? And besides, "Von Vorst" (as the old actor himself was the first to admit) *sounded* so nice and villainous.

Jane had felt relief in being able to suspend her own doubts about the veracity of the gentle Von Vorst, because of the lack of evidence implicit in the old program. She *wanted* to acquit him of his "forgetfulness" about his old love. That had bothered her most. But she was also sad to relinquish, by her acquittal, the "real" connection with him. She wanted all the real connections she could get, just now, and somehow it was as if she were losing another member of her family this week. It had been "Von Vorst the Villain," echoing with the regularity of the mention of a distant (diapproved-of) uncle, all through her childhood, her girlhood. Not "Edwin Merchant." *Merchant?* A villain? A lover of apt words was bound to have trouble with that one. It would take her a while.

Curious about Sonia's note, Jane had telephoned before she even unpacked. What news did Sonia think *she* would think "interesting"? Perhaps a new man come to town that Sonia had spotted and mentally appropriated for her friend Jane: the golden mean at last between Heathcliff and Mr. Knightley.

Sonia told Jane that Max, her husband, had just received "unofficial word" that a fellowship he had applied for had been renewed and he would be taking next year off to work on his book at home. "So that means one unexpected vacancy next year. I talked to the chairman yesterday; he said there were several others whose contracts are up and they'll be trying for another year, but Max and I were talking about it, and he does carry a little weight, and it *would* be his position that would fall vacant, and—well, frankly, Jane, my feelings are you could get it. You're a good teacher, word gets around, and, as I said, Max and I will do what we can. That is, if you want us to. I know the place is rather bleak for someone alone, but it has its compensations. Anyway, if you're interested, you should go in as soon as possible and tell the chairman."

"Was Max's renewal for a Guggenheim, by any chance?"

"Well, I'm not supposed to say. But yes. The announcements don't come out till April."

"Tell him congratulations from me."

"Well, okay. Except I shouldn't have told you. They always write you, in late January or early February, to ask you how much you'd need if you got one. And that means you've got it and have time to tell your chairman and everything, but everyone's afraid to say anything till it's really announced."

"I understand that. I think it would be sensible for me to try to stay one more year. Especially since"—she laughed dryly—"I haven't even applied for another job."

"Good. And listen, the other thing was, how about lunch next Tuesday, at noon, after our classes? We can compare notes. By the way, I checked our preregistration lists. Both sections are full. And you know what? At least half signed up are men."

"I don't care. I don't hate the idea of men and women in equal numbers."

Sonia laughed. "No, I know what you mean. I don't either! Listen, how did the funeral go?"

"Oh, fine. I'll miss her a lot. My mother and I had an interesting talk."

"*That's* always nice."

"Yes."

"Did you just get back?"

"I stopped over for a couple of days in New York and a night in Chicago. What did you and Max do?"

"Oh . . . nothing much, except grade papers and eat too much. Uneventful married life. You're the one who gets around."

As dusk fell and snow continued to pile up, Jane had experienced a bad hour. It was the hour when she knew Gabriel would arrive home. She did not question for a minute that his flight might be canceled or delayed when he was on his way home to Ann. No, today his plane would touch the runway right on time, even in a blizzard, and Ann would be there to meet him.

Would he kiss her? Of course he would! What man returning home from a "business trip" did not kiss his wife at the airport? Francis Tibalt had probably kissed Eleanor at airports till the end. And then the Weekses would drive carefully home, Gabriel taking the wheel. "Any mail?" he would ask. "Yes," she would say. "A letter from the Guggenheim Foundation. I was afraid to open it." "Was it thick or thin?" he might ask. "Pretty thick, I think," she would say. "But isn't it too early to hear? I thought you said April." "I don't know, I don't know," he would answer, concentrating on the snowy road, perhaps driving a little bit faster.

When Bobby Mulvaney had become the youngest member ever to be elected to his state House of Representatives, he had sent Gerda an announcement, clipped from the local paper. The envelope (containing no accompanying letter) was forwarded to her at the lowest point in her life. She had been teaching in the black high school at the time, worn down with debts, frazzled with overwork and despair. She had telephoned Jane, shrieking what a fool she had been; she had had the world in her lap, all that security, and thrown it over for a cheap lay! She had loved Bobby—yes, she saw that now: he was so generous, so unselfish, so manly. That devil of a father had plotted to break up the marriage because he could not have her himself. After she had shrieked for a while longer, she grew calmer. At the end, she had laughed and said, "Do you want to know what *really* kills me? I know it's stupid, but nevertheless it's true. I would have loved to be there with him, to celebrate. I would love to have gone to the banquet with him as Mrs. Robert Mulvaney. I know just the sort of thing I would have worn and everything."

Now, similarly, Jane was tormented as she imagined it, second by second. Gabriel would be opening his letter: "We are pleased to inform you that you have been nominated . . ."

And he would not share it with her.

At dark she had opened a can of lentil soup and unpacked. She replaced Tempus Fugit on her bedside shelf and then kept running into the bedroom every five minutes to check the time. She thought: If he did want to call me before his supper, he would just have time to drive down to the Art Building. . . . Now he's eating supper—*they* are eating supper . . . celebrating with a glass of wine? A bottle . . . drinking toasts to his good luck, then going upstairs to celebrate some more . . . perhaps —because of recent developments, which he would/would not confess to her—celebrate the renewal of their marriage . . . drink the second bottle in bed, among tumbled sheets. . . . "Here's to beginning again!" . . . Now it is after supper. . . . It would take him seven minutes or so to drive down to the Art Building and call and tell me the news. Perhaps there was no letter for him. Perhaps he'll call me anyway. How sad if he called just to say hello, and I said, "Did you have any interesting mail when you got back?" and he said, "No, not much of interest." "I'm not the sort of scholar who gets grants," he had often told her when she had been insisting and insisting he try again, open up the old disappointed hopes. Perhaps he had known, better than she.

And as the early evening had worn on, she went about her rooms weeping, pacing and weeping. Why was life so unfair! Was some malevolent God trying to strip her of everything, leave her with the bare prison walls of her subsistence (and maybe not even that, next year)?

She had fought down the urge to call Gabriel at home, hang up if "she" answered, and, if he answered, simply whisper "Say it's a wrong number, but call me when you can!" And he would have called, she knew that. If the woman in the Blake poem had invited the angel back, he would have come. Angels did what you let them. No more, no less.

But she had written Von Vorst, instead, to get through the worst moments of temptation.

Dear Mr. Von Vorst,

Just a note to tell you that I and the little *Crassula* plant are safely back, having both survived the snow-storm, which threatens to go on for several days. I have put the plant in the kitchen window (an east window) and, as I do not have to start teaching till Tuesday, think I will stay inside and avoid this weather.

I looked up the scene in *Oliver Twist* where Sikes does Nancy in ...

"No, that's a lie," she had said, putting down her pen and going to get her *Oliver Twist* (checking Tempus Fugit as she went. Oh, Gabriel, please call! No, don't!) and rereading the scene. Dickens's Sikes had used a pistol first and then clubbed her down when she struggled to her knees, blind with blood, to pray for him. God! How bloody it all was! She had not remembeed it being so bloody. Perhaps Von Vorst's dramatic telling of how he had acted it, the inside knowledge of the red ocher, the reported shrieks of all those consummated ids from the gallery had made her feel it more. It was possible.

and the power of that scene was fresher, more im-mediate for me, because of having listened to you describe the way you played it. I wish I could have seen you play it. I may write a paper on the villains in Dickens and, if so, may I quote you on your insights about melodrama and the naturalism of the dream life?

Do pat Ethel for me. I wonder if, by any chance, you remember an actor called Edwin Merchant? He played the happy husband in *The Fatal Wedding* when you did the Wilkes-Barre tour.

I am glad to have met you and hope to see you the next time I'm in the city.

Jane Clifford

She decided not to use the stamped self-addressed envelope he had given her, for fear he might think she was trying to discharge an unpleasant duty as quickly as possible. Perhaps she would write the Dickens article. Play the academic game and pose as a "professor" while secretly pursuing her real profession: researching her salvation. She could hear Gerda laughing at that last. Perhaps she would always be hearing Gerda, even in her nineties.

And now there was not even the eleven o'clock news between her and insomnia. And, beyond that, the five more days of exclusive company with herself.

When she had given up all hope of the telephone ringing, of course it rang. She let two rings go by. What a silly habit! How long had she been doing that? *Don't ever let them think you're too eager,* Kitty had instructed her early in her teens.

Will I go to England with him if he's got it? she thought. I must decide now, before I pick up the receiver. Otherwise I'll be lost. I'll be another *Love Short Stories* statistic, just like all those girls in Kitty's file, who needed only a word from the man to throw everything else out the window.

What a coward you are, Jane! Decide!

Two more rings.

I won't go, she vowed, if you'll let it be him. Just so we can have a compassionate ending. Just so I can hear his voice again. She answered.

The voice at the other end was inaudible.

"I'm sorry, can you talk louder? We have a bad connection."

"Dr. Clifford?" Faintly. It was not a man.

"Yes?"

"This is Portia."

Portia? "Oh! Portia Prentiss? How are you, Portia?" Jane struggled with her disappointment. "Are you by any chance calling about your grade?" For a minute she could not remember whether she'd given the girl a C or a D. She was relieved when she remembered. It got her off the hook for tonight. And she needed every grain of grace she could get.

"No'm. I picked it up today. I went to the English office to ask specially. My adviser told me I should. I flunked Earth Science and Math, and I would've been in bad trouble if I hadn't got your C." And the girl gave a funny little laugh that sounded like a whimper. "What I was calling about was, my adviser said I ought to make sure I could get in your next class, the one you're teaching next semester. I already went down and bought one of the books, so I could get started."

"Which one did you buy, Portia? We're going to start with *The Odd Women*." Jane knew exactly what had gone through Portia's adviser's head: "Aha! A softie. Better tell Portia to stick with her." Or perhaps: "Isn't she the Southern woman? The one who's overcompensating for what the Dutch started in 1619? Good luck for little Portia! I'll tell her to stick with Clifford."

"Just a minute, let me get it," said Portia. Something crashed loudly. "Oh, shit!" she heard Portia say. "I dropped the whole telephone," she came back and explained. "It's the one called *Daniel Deronda*."

"Oh. Well, that's the last book for the course. It's the longest and hardest. It poses some questions I can't even answer yet. We'll be doing that last."

"Oh-oh. Flubbed again," said Portia huskily.

"What you want is George Gissing's *Odd Women*," and Jane began telling Portia the plot, slowly, over the telephone, thinking: I should have known. I am not going to be allowed to get away with anything in this life. I shall have to live with the consequences of every action.

And it even crossed her mind that she had unconsciously given Portia the C to keep her, because she knew she had failed her first semester and wanted to redeem her failure. Already she envisioned afternoon tutorial sessions with the girl during which she would patiently tell her the plots of each novel, put thoughts in her head, as you force-fed young birds who had fallen from nests too quickly. And when term-paper time came, she would feel delicately around in Portia's head to see if anything had rooted, and seize on it for her topic if it had. Kitty would not approve. The girl is out of her element; she will never be able to survive; let her go back where she is comfortable again, Kitty would say. But who wanted to creep along in comfort when there was one chance in a thousand of flying? There was about one chance in a million that Portia would get through *Daniel Deronda*. Planning ahead, Jane was already wondering how she could keep the plot of that long novel straight for Portia.

Was it better to glimpse something you could never attain, or better not to have seen at all? She would have to think about that. And she had five days to sit and think.

After she said good night to Portia, she made herself the usual hot milk and rum, and drank it quickly, and went to bed. She fell into a fake, easy, shallow sleep and dreamed that Portia had come for her first tutoring session. It was springtime and the two of them sat on a grassy slope and she had her arm around the girl. Then she kept sniffing something familiar. It was Fleurs de Rocaille. Portia was wearing Edith's perfume. She looked up from the lesson to ask Portia how she had come to select such a subtle perfume, but it was Edith who sat beside her, a young Edith Jane had seen only in pictures. She wore a long dark skirt and button shoes and her hair in a pompadour. "I thought you were dead," said Jane. "No, I just want to understand this lesson," replied Edith in a weary voice.

And then she was in her bed again. *And someone was sliding down the low roof of her duplex, just outside the bedroom window, trying to keep his foothold in soft-soled shoes.*

Her heart began to beat frantically. Tempus Fugit said a quarter to midnight. She had not been asleep five minutes!

Now she was not asleep. No, this time it was real. This was no dream of being awake. The soft sliding continued outside her window. It was no imaginary sound. He was there this time, all right.

She calculated the distance between the bed and the telephone in the hall. She might just have time to get the operator, say, "He's just breaking in, my address is ——— ———," and give her address in case she was cut off before the operator connected her with the police. But she was frozen, a woman alone in frozen terror, bathed in the amber light of Panasonic's "NIGHT" intensity. He was perhaps looking in on her at this moment, desperate in his own fear, his gun trained on her slightest wrong move.

Perhaps she could reason with him.

Always she reasoned in her mind with the escaped inmates, the murderers, the drug addicts, and petty thieves who somehow managed to overcome her locks and bolts and break into her night worries. She told the escaped inmates that they were not really crazy, only misunderstood. She told them about R. D. Laing. She coaxed them, like slow students, into exemplary behavior. "Go ahead and kill me," she had once told a murderer, "I am sick of this life" (she had been unhappy about Gabriel), and he had turned his head away from her and fled, ashamed of her for her cowardice, her lack of will to live. "If you want the television, you'll find it in the kitchen; you can probably get a hundred for it," she told the addicts. "My purse is on the table" (to the petty thieves), and to both: "I am covering my eyes with my hands. I cannot see you. I won't be able to identify you to the police. Take what you need and go."

Though she knew "in real life" criminals were usually beyond words. That's what made them criminals. They could no longer listen, no longer hear, and that's why you were in for it.

But he might listen. He was not yet beyond words. She could not believe anyone who felt compelled to do his laundry had become completely antisocial. "You have made a few regrettable mistakes, but you've done nothing irrevocable.

"In a way I really feel for you. I understand you. But we don't have time for dalliance tonight. Take my advice and get out of here. Go in my closet and dress yourself in my warmest clothes; take my purse with what's left of Ray's cash and my credit cards, and identification, and put a scarf over your head and start walking. If anyone stops you—a campus policeman or somebody— tell him you're Jane Clifford, a professor in the English Department; show him your faculty card, and if he asks what you are doing out alone, tell him you're walking your insomnia to sleep. Then walk fast to the bus station and take the first bus out and don't get off till you've reached the place where the snow melts away and you think you can turn your oddities inside out like a sock and find your own best life by making them work for you instead of being driven by them. That's the best advice I have to offer."

The huge mound of snow fell crashing from the low roof outside her bedroom window.

All was silent, safe and still. Her heartbeat slowed from melodramatic terror to its usual insomniac tick. From the little concrete house behind came the barely audible tinkle of a soul at the piano, trying to organize the loneliness and the weather and the long night into something of abiding shape and beauty.

THE BEST OF
WARNER ROMANCES...

YOUR WARNER LIBRARY OF REGENCY ROMANCE...

THE FIVE-MINUTE MARRIAGE
by Joan Aiken
(84-682, $1.75)

When Delphie Carteret's cousin Garth asks her to marry him, it is in a make-believe ceremony so that Delphie might receive a small portion of her rightful inheritance. But an error has been made. The marriage is binding! Oh my! Fun and suspense abounds, and there's not a dull moment in this delightful Regency novel brimming with laughter, surprise and true love!

LADY BLUE
by Zabrina Faire
(94-056, $1.75)

LADY BLUE is the story of Meriel, the beautiful governess to an impossible little boy who pours blue ink on her long blonde hair. When she punishes the boy, she is dismissed from her post. But all is not lost—the handsome young Lord Farr has another job in mind for her. Meriel's new position: Resident "ghost" in a castle owned by Farr's rival. Her new name: Lady Blue!

AGENT OF LOVE
by Jillian Kearny
(94-003, $1.75)

Was Alicia the innocent she seemed, delighting in her first London season? Was Rob the dashing young blade he appeared to be as he escorted her to routs and ridottos? They played the conventional games of love—but were hearts or empires at stake?

ACCESSORY TO LOVE
by Maureen Wakefield
(84-790, $1.75)

A love child must be very careful to be seen as fleetingly as possible—and never to be heard at all. For a love child is an embarrassment to her unwed mother, to her wealthy father and to a society that doesn't like to have its conscience troubled. But when the child becomes a woman as enchanting as Saranne, she can't be hidden forever! Saranne was surrounded by love—surely some of it someday could be hers....

THE MIDNIGHT MATCH
by Zabrina Faire
(94-057, $1.75)

He saved her honor. She saved his life. Was what they felt for each other love or gratitude? What had she done? Carola trembled at the thought—she was married to a perfect stranger . . . But she saw his chest move . . . he breathed. She was so happy!

MORE OUTSTANDING BOOKS
FROM WARNER BOOKS